ELENA FORBES

JIGSAW MAN

SPIDERLINE

First published in Great Britain in 2015 by Quercus Editions Ltd.

This edition published in 2015 by
House of Anansi Press Inc.
110 Spadina Avenue, Suite 801
Toronto, ON, M5V 2K4
Tel. 416-363-4343
Fax 416-363-1017
www.houseofanansi.com

Distributed in Canada by
HarperCollins Canada Ltd.
1995 Markham Road
Scarborough, ON, M1B 5M8
Toll free tel. 1-800-387-0117

Distributed in the United States by
Publishers Group West
1700 Fourth Street
Berkeley, CA 94710
Toll free tel. 1-800-788-3123

House of Anansi Press is committed to protecting our natural environment. As part of our efforts, the interior of this book is printed on paper that contains 100% post-consumer recycled fibres, is acid-free, and is processed chlorine-free.

19 18 17 16 15   1 2 3 4 5

Library and Archives Canada Cataloguing in Publication

Forbes, Elena, author
Jigsaw man : a Marko della Torre novel / Elena Forbes.

Issued in print and electronic formats.
ISBN: 978-1-4870-0023-3 (pbk.). ISBN: 978-1-4870-0024-0 (html.)

I. Title.

PR6106.O73J53 2015   823'.92   C2014-907723-8
C2014-907724-6

Library of Congress Control Number: 2014957207

Cover design: Alysia Shewchuk
Text design and typesetting: Hewer Text UK Ltd., Edinburgh

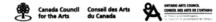

We acknowledge for their financial support of our publishing program the Canada Council for the Arts, the Ontario Arts Council, and the Government of Canada through the Canada Book Fund.

Printed and bound in Canada

JIGSAW
MAN

Also by Elena Forbes

Die with Me
Our Lady of Pain
Evil in Return

For Tracy Alexander

One

Her eyes were open but she was in La La Land. She lay on the bed in her underwear like a disgusting blow-up doll, the faint rise and fall of her breasts the only sign that she was still alive. He had kept physical contact to the absolute minimum, but he knew all about forensic wizardry and removing her dress had been a necessary precaution. Hopefully, the hotel room would be awash with all manner of fibres and human DNA and any trace that he might accidentally have left would be lost amongst it all.

He put on disposable gloves and went into the bathroom where he poured the rest of the champagne down the sink. He put the cork, wire casing and empty bottle in his rucksack, which was standing ready by the door. He washed the glasses quickly, paying particular attention to remove the foul smear of lipstick she had left on hers, then dried them on the tea towel he had brought with him. He checked the photo he had taken earlier on his phone and replaced them on the tray on top of the mini-bar, exactly as he had found them. His clothes were ready by the door, along with the rucksack, which he had stuffed with as many of her things as he could fit into it. There wasn't room for her coat, but he hadn't touched it at any point and he decided to leave it in the wardrobe where she had hung it.

Excitement welling, he paced backwards and forwards around the room, giving it a final once-over. He would check it again before he left, but it all looked perfect, nothing out of place. He zipped up his wetsuit, pulled on the rubber mask and went over to the bed. Just to make sure he wasn't going to have any trouble, he waved his hand in front of her face and pinched her arm hard, but there was no reaction. He turned on the TV, the volume up high enough to cover any unwanted sounds, then carefully got onto the bed and straddled her. The wetsuit was a little on the tight side and restrictive, but he couldn't risk taking it off. Nor did he want his skin to touch hers. He flexed his arms and shoulders, trying to create some give, clicked his knuckles one by one, then took some deep breaths as he steadied himself. He needed to clear his mind of his surroundings, and focus. When he felt ready, he put his hands around her neck, locked his thumbs tightly together, took some more slow breaths and closed his eyes. As he started to press down, he tried to picture another time not so long ago, another room, small and dimly lit, furnished with old-fashioned musty things, and another woman lying beside him on the sofa. But the image was half-formed and unstable, like a reflection in rippling water, fading into nothing around the edges. He wanted to shout out in frustration; all he needed was to see her face. He took another few deep breaths, but it was no good. He couldn't get into it, the sweet spot, or the zone, as he liked to call it. The musky perfume the slag was wearing was overpowering, putting him off his stride. Grasping her tighter, breathing only through his mouth, he tried again.

Now he saw a man's face, soft-featured and tanned, his lips mouthing something as his watery eyes opened in a pathetic look of surprise, followed by sudden realisation. He felt the heat of the sun on his back, the rocking of the little boat, smelt his own stale sweat and the salt of the sea. It wasn't where he wanted to be. He shouted at the man, told him to fuck off, and squeezed harder, eyes screwed tight shut, as he tried to re-focus. The man's image dissolved. From the darkness other faces drifted ghost-like into view, a washed-out collage of pale, insipid, interchangeable girls and a devilish old woman out to spoil his fun, laughing at him, mocking his ineptitude. *Lost your touch? Lost your mojo? Not up to it, are you? Never been up to it, you nasty little bastard spawn, nasty little impotent piece of shit . . .* He punched her wicked face, hit it again with all his force, again and again until finally he silenced her. With a knowing look she held a bony finger to her lips, winked at him and disappeared, back down into hell where she belonged.

But nothing appeared in her place. Fucking nothing. Breathless now, and hot with rage, he rocked backwards and forwards, squeezing harder and harder, shaking the limp neck until it felt like a wet rag in his hands, until he was sure there must be no life left. Still it wasn't enough. The magic wasn't working. It was fucking useless. He couldn't conjure up the one he wanted. As he threw the body down on the bed, tears filled his eyes. He was cursed. She wouldn't come to him.

Two

Banging. More banging. Louder. Someone shouting his name. Mark Tartaglia opened his eyes. He was lying on a bed, in the dark. Unsure where he was, he stretched out his arm and felt the cool, smooth space beside him. He reached out further. Nobody there. Light filtered through the open crack under a door and, as his eyes gradually adjusted, he made out familiar shapes. He was at home. He peered at the luminous face of his watch. Just before six o'clock. About half an hour before he needed to get up. The room was cold, yet he was sweating. His head throbbed and he took several long, deep breaths, trying to fix in his mind the sequence of events the night before, images unravelling like jerky little clips of film. The bar-crawl with his cousin Gianni to celebrate Gianni's decree absolute; beer and vodka chasers, and ending up in some fancy new boutique hotel in the West End. Dim lighting, loud music, lots of people. More of a nightclub than a hotel bar. More drinks. Something unmemorable to eat. A foursome of giggling, very young women, stragglers from an office Halloween party, who had joined them without much persuasion. More to drink; champagne this time. Later, a woman with long, dark hair, on her own, who had met his gaze several times from across the bar. Early forties, tanned and slim. Not a pro; he clocked that immediately from her body language. He'd seen her again in the courtyard at the back when he'd gone out for a smoke and they'd exchanged a few words over a cigarette until her phone rang. Then the slip of paper with her room number that she

4

had discreetly dropped in his lap on her way out of the bar. *If you're looking for something different . . .* The accompanying smile that spoke more than words. He'd been drunk, but not so drunk as to not know what he was doing when he'd made his excuses to Gianni, saying he was tired, and knocked on her door fifteen minutes or so later.

He stretched out into a star shape, enjoying the chill of the sheets in the furthest corners, and closed his eyes as he ran through the sequence of events again in his mind. He barely remembered the taxi ride home, or letting himself into his flat. Her name was Annika, no, Jannicke. From Oslo. Over in London for a few days on business. The pale circle on her ring finger said she was married.

The banging started again. He wasn't dreaming. A man was shouting his name and he opened his eyes. The noise seemed to be coming from the front of his flat. As he eased himself into a sitting position in bed and reached for the light switch, he caught a fleeting scent of a woman's perfume. Slowly he got to his feet, head aching, mouth sour and dry as dust. He had no idea what he had done with his clothes. Unsteadily, he grabbed a towel he found lying over a chair, wrapped it around himself, and stumbled into the sitting room. The lights were on, the shutters gaping open. A man was standing in the front garden, peering through the window. The man waved at him. Silhouetted against the acid-orange glare from the street lamp, it was difficult to see his face clearly and it took Tartaglia a few moments before he recognised Nick Minderedes, a detective constable in his team. They'd been on call for the past five days, the next murder investigation team in line for any case of suspicious death that came into the Homicide West jurisdiction. A diet of early nights was the prescription, just in case, and a clear,

5

sober head. Sod's law that something had happened on the one night he had been out getting lashed.

Tartaglia let himself out of his flat and opened the front door.

Minderedes stood on the doorstep, dressed even at that hour in a sharply-cut suit and tie, his face shaved, his short black hair still wet and spiky from the shower. He looked alert, as though he had been awake for hours. It was ironic that he was usually the one burning the candle at both ends.

'Sorry for the noise, boss. Didn't want to rouse the whole street but you weren't answering.' As he spoke, a window was slammed shut immediately above them.

'What's up?'

'Suspicious death in the West End. I need to take you over there now.'

'Couldn't you have phoned first?'

Minderedes's brown eyes narrowed. 'I tried. Many times. Some cabbie with an attitude finally picked up. Said you'd left it on the back seat of his cab a few hours ago. Said it'd been ringing non-stop ever since.' His eyebrows raised a fraction as he spoke.

Tartaglia gave him a blank stare. *Fuck.* The phone must have fallen out of his jacket pocket on the way home, but it was none of Minderedes's business where he had been or what he had been doing.

'I told him to drop it over to the office later,' Minderedes continued, still looking at him inquiringly. 'Meantime, we need to get going.'

Tartaglia stifled a yawn. 'OK, give me ten. You want to come in and wait?'

Minderedes shook his head. 'I'll be outside in the car. I'll call the DI from the local station and let him know we're on our way.'

Tartaglia closed the front door and retreated back inside. The heating was just kicking in, taking the chill off the air, the pipes were making a distant tapping sound as they warmed up. He went into the kitchen, put a pot of strong coffee on the stove and poured out a large glass of water, which he knocked back in one, along with a couple of Hedex. In the bathroom, he turned on the shower. Waiting while the water warmed up, he stood at the basin and splashed some cold water on his face, then ran his fingers through his hair and over the thick black stubble on his chin, studying himself in the mirror. Not good. Not good at all. He stuck out his tongue and grimaced in disgust. Dark circles shadowed his eyes like bruises and his skin looked sallow in the bathroom light, his summer tan having all but faded. Not much he could do about that, but if nothing else, even if it cost him an extra few minutes, he would have to shave. There'd be no chance to do so later on and it made all the difference. Somehow he had to minimise the obvious signs of a night of next to no sleep. At least he generally kept himself in good physical shape, even to his critical eye. Give or take a couple of pounds, he weighed the same as he had done ten years before and outwardly looked much the same. But some things were deceptive. Ten years on, he knew he was a different man, although he had no desire to examine or define what had changed. He put his hand under the shower, checked the temperature and stepped in, closing his eyes again and letting the water run over him.

Fifteen minutes later he was dressed and ready to go. It was still dark outside, the pavement slick from overnight rain and the air sharp with cold. Apart from the odd light on here and there, there was little sign of anyone stirring. Minderedes was waiting for him a few doors down, the shiny black BMW pulled up across someone's drive. Tartaglia slid into the passenger seat and slammed the door shut. Capital Breakfast burbled through the speakers. Minderedes helped himself to a stick of gum and put the car into gear.

'Where are we going?' Tartaglia asked, stretching out his legs as they sped off down the narrow street towards Shepherd's Bush Road.

'Some posh new hotel called the Dillon. That's all I know.'

Tartaglia frowned, wondering if he had heard correctly and glanced over at Minderedes. 'The Dillon, you say.'

'That's right. It's in the West End. Just off Marylebone High Street. We should be there in fifteen, if we're lucky.'

Tartaglia said nothing. The Dillon was where he had been only a few hours before. Thinking it must be some sort of a joke, he glanced again at Minderedes, but his expression was deadpan as he concentrated on the road in front, driving at his usual breakneck speed. Minderedes was generally a bad poker player, so maybe it was for real after all.

'What's happened?' he asked flatly after a moment, having watched the DC carefully out of the corner of his eye.

'Woman found dead in one of the rooms in the early hours.'

'What, a guest?'

'I don't know. Steele's been trying to get hold of you. Do you want to use my phone?'

'In a minute.' Tartaglia slid down a little in his seat, folded his arms and studied the empty road ahead as they accelerated past Olympia. Before he spoke to his boss, DCI Carolyn Steele, he needed to get things clearer in his mind. He believed in coincidence about as much as he believed in the tooth fairy. Things happened for a reason, particularly in his line of work. Like a conjuror's trick, the apparently inexplicable usually had a simple explanation, if only you knew where to look. But he found it strange that he should be going back to the same hotel only a few hours later to investigate a murder. Still not quite believing it, refusing to give in to alcohol-fuelled paranoia, he told himself that it couldn't be anything to do with Jannicke. What were the chances? She wasn't the only woman in the hotel, by any stretch. There must be a good forty or so rooms and at least as many guests, plus staff. No point jumping to conclusions.

A wave of nausea hit him and he closed his eyes for a moment, massaging his temples and the bridge of his nose, as he tried to work out what to do. No doubt he had been captured on camera somewhere in the hotel. He hated having to explain himself to anybody, but there was no way around it. He would have to come clean, and as soon as possible. He pictured the inevitable awkward conversation with Steele, a woman whose private life, if she had one, never impinged on her work. Hopefully, she would accept a basic explanation of what he had been doing there and that's as far as it would go, from the work point of view. Other than being in the wrong place at the wrong time, he had done nothing against the rules. Why, then, did he feel as though he had?

From nowhere, a conversation from the previous afternoon with his sister, Nicoletta, bubbled to the surface. He had been sitting at his desk in the office going through some paperwork when she called. He could still hear the sound of her voice, heavy with recrimination, reminding him that he was supposed to be going over to her house for dinner that evening. He had no recollection of it but she insisted that a definite arrangement had been made. His niece and nephew were dying to see him. She had asked some other friends too. Done all the shopping and cooking. He had to admit that she sounded convincing. Maybe he *had* forgotten. It wouldn't have been the first time. He had been in court for most of the past week, giving evidence in a murder trial. It hadn't been going well and it was preoccupying him. He had tried to tell her that he had made other arrangements, but she wouldn't listen. Finally, when forced, he had explained that he was seeing their cousin Gianni and couldn't let him down, and she had let rip. His being at work had made no difference.

'You're going out to *celebrate*?... Celebrate failure, more like, he's hopeless... you're no better... bad influence... both need to grow up, get a life... selfish... midlife crisis...'

Blah, blah, blah. Midlife crisis? Jesus! He and Gianni weren't even forty yet. It was as if he were still fifteen, under the thumb of his older sister, the woman of the world who thought she had all the answers. He had held the phone away from his ear – he had heard it all before – but even from a foot away, the gist was clear. He caught the word 'commitment' several times. Or maybe it was 'commitment-phobe'. What could he say? 'Marco? Marco? *Are you there*? Listen to me, will you?' He had been on the point of replying, telling her to get lost, when he had heard a movement behind him. Someone was in his office. Swinging around, he had found Nick Minderedes standing right behind him, mouth puckered as he fought back a grin. It wasn't clear how long he had been standing there, but he must have heard enough.

Tartaglia looked at Minderedes, whose eyes were still focussed ahead on the road. He could have no idea what was going through Tartaglia's mind. Nicoletta's words echoed again: 'You're not thirty any more...' He felt a stab of unaccustomed guilt then felt like slapping her. What was he supposed to do? Live like a monk? He didn't need to justify himself to anyone but he had the feeling he was still going to pay for it.

Three

The Dillon Hotel occupied a stretch of large early Victorian terraced houses set back behind railings, close to Manchester Square, not far from Marylebone High Street. The area immediately outside had been cordoned off and Tartaglia and Minderedes were forced to park a little further down the street and walk back. As they checked in with a uniformed officer, a short, heavy-set man with thinning salt and pepper hair detached himself from a group standing by the main entrance. He was wearing a baggy grey suit that had seen better days and had the tired, puffy eyes of somebody who had been up all night. He greeted them, introducing himself as DI Johnson from Marylebone CID.

'I hear it's one of the guests, a woman. Is that right?' Tartaglia asked, as they walked with Johnson up the wide stone steps and in through the open front door. He hoped there was no trace in his voice of the irrational anxiety he felt, again telling himself that it couldn't be Jannicke.

'Yes, the victim's female,' Johnson replied, leading them past the white, panelled reception area and down the main corridor, 'but we're not sure who she is, or if she was staying in the hotel. She was strangled up in one of the rooms on the second floor.'

'What time was this?'

'Let's go in here and I'll fill you in,' Johnson said, looking around as though worried somebody might overhear, even though there was nobody within earshot. They followed him into a book-lined snug, with a small bar in one corner. Tartaglia hadn't noticed it the previous evening, although the leafy courtyard where he had met Jannicke while having a smoke the night before was just beyond the tall pair of French doors. Johnson appeared to be using the room as a makeshift office. Two small tables had been pushed together, with a cordless phone, papers, and several half-drunk cups of black coffee spread out on the surface.

'So what exactly happened?' Tartaglia said, growing increasingly impatient.

Johnson shrugged. 'Some sort of romantic tryst gone wrong, possibly, although she could easily be a pro. The room's booked in a man's name, Robert Herring. She was lying on the bed, not wearing much. The man called room service from the room and ordered a bottle of champagne and some food. When it was brought up, they found her.'

'Yes, but what time?'

Johnson picked up a piece of paper and peered at some notes. 'The call came from the room and was logged on the in-house dining system, as they call it, at twelve-fifty-one a.m. About half an hour later a waiter goes up to the room and knocks on the door.'

'So, around one-twenty-five?'

'Thereabouts.'

Tartaglia stared at him for a moment, hoping his relief was well hidden. At one-twenty-five he had still been in Jannicke's room and she had certainly been alive, so it couldn't be her. He had left Jannicke's room a few minutes after two. He remembered looking at his watch.

'There's no answer so he lets himself in with a passkey,' Johnson continued. 'He sees her on the bed, but there's no sign of the man. It's clear something's wrong so he calls the duty manager who comes up and takes a look and decides she's dead. He then dials 999. The call came in at one-thirty-nine and we got here just after two.'

As Johnson spoke, it struck Tartaglia that he had actually been there, in the hotel, at the time of the murder. It was something that had never happened to him before in connection with his work and he felt a little shaken by it. Had the killer stayed around afterwards to watch the action, maybe waiting downstairs in the bar until the police came? It wouldn't be the first time.

He thought back, picturing himself leaving Jannicke's room – nobody in the corridor outside – then coming down the main stairs and turning into the hall. A few people were still milling around in the lobby and in the large sitting room beyond. Nothing particularly noteworthy about that and he didn't remember seeing anybody on their own, let alone acting oddly. The bar had still been open and an Alex Clare song he particularly liked had been playing. He was half tempted to stay and listen, but had felt suddenly very tired. Leaving the building, he hadn't been aware of anything out of the ordinary. Nobody hanging around outside or behaving suspiciously, no commotion, no sirens, no blue lights or obvious unmarked cars pulled up outside in the street. He must have left just before CID got there. It had been raining earlier and he recalled how pleasantly fresh the air had felt. He had paused to light a cigarette then walked on, eventually hailing a cab along George Street. As far as he was aware, he had witnessed nothing relevant to the investigation.

'How long had Robert Herring been staying?' he asked Johnson.

'He arrived yesterday evening, just after seven p.m., and appeared to be on his own. He was given a large double on the

13

second floor, but he only asked for one key. He gave a home address in Manchester, which we're checking along with his other details. There's also a mobile number, but the phone's switched off. The credit card that was used to secure the room is in a different name. Nobody at reception remembers seeing the woman or anybody asking for Herring and according to the switchboard no calls were put through to that room all evening. As I said, she could be a pro, or a girlfriend – or a guest staying in one of the other rooms, but until we speak to everybody, we won't know. A lot of the guests are still asleep.'

'What about the hotel staff?'

'We're taking statements from anyone still here who was on duty last night. I can give you the full list of names.'

Tartaglia looked at Minderedes. 'You'd better start waking up the guests as soon as the rest of the team gets here.'

'A few are already up,' Johnson said, 'but we told them to go back to their rooms. We've closed off the second floor entirely, so nobody can go in or out. We've left the main stairs open but we've stopped access to the lifts and the back stairs unless authorised. Do you want to take it any further than that?'

Tartaglia shook his head. 'That's fine for now. Just make sure nobody leaves the hotel until they've been spoken to and their IDs have been checked.' Theoretically, he would have liked to lock down the entire hotel, but it wouldn't be practical.

'Have you got a map of this place?' he asked.

Johnson handed him a sheet of paper. 'This is the ground floor.'

'What about cameras?'

'There are a few dotted around, here and here,' he said, marking the paper for Tartaglia. 'It's pretty minimal coverage, though. The manager gave me some spiel about guests needing their privacy. I suppose they get their fair share of celebs here, but luckily there's a camera at reception, so we should be able to get a visual of Herring.'

'Where's Security?' Minderedes asked.

'In the basement, next to the gym,' Johnson replied.

'Start with that,' Tartaglia said to Minderedes. 'I'll come and find you when I'm done with the crime scene.'

'The CSM was looking for you,' Johnson said to Tartaglia, as Minderedes disappeared out of the door. 'She's still up in the room. I can take you there now, if you're ready. This place is like a rabbit warren.'

'Carry on with what you were doing. I'll find it myself.' He wanted to be on his own for a minute. Try and clear his thoughts. The room where he had been with Jannicke had been on the first floor at the front of the building, not that he'd paid much attention to the location at the time. He remembered using the main stairs by reception and that was about it. He wondered whether she was already up and getting dressed, and if he would bump into her at some point. It would be a little awkward, but he felt no real embarrassment.

'It's number 212, at the back of the building,' Johnson said, following him out of the snug. 'There's a lift that gets you out right by the room. Go through the bar, and you'll come to it.'

Tartaglia glanced at the map. The hotel was a rectangle, with four wings built around a long central courtyard. He remembered reading in some blurb the previous night that the rear wing had once been a small theatre or cinema. The bar was empty and silent, apart from the distant sound of a hoover, and the strong smell of cleaning products hung in the air. Grey early-morning light filtered in through the row of tall windows and the room looked more austere and less welcoming than he remembered it. As he passed the table where he and Gianni had been sitting only a few hours before, he wondered what

15

time Gianni had left and whether he had gone home on his own.

The lift was outside the entrance to the restaurant. He heard the clatter of plates and cutlery and saw staff through the glass panel of the door preparing for breakfast. He showed his ID to the uniformed PC guarding the lift, then took it up to the second floor. Breakfast TV blasted from one of the rooms nearby. It wouldn't be long before people would be up and about and the usual complaints would start about being delayed and having to account for themselves, along with the inevitable, probing, ghoulish curiosity.

The section of corridor between the lift and room 212 had been taped off and a pathway marked out on the carpet leading to the door. Tartaglia helped himself to protective clothing from a box on the floor and was about to head towards the room when he saw Tracy Jamieson, the crime scene manager, emerging from the lift behind him.

'There you are,' she said cheerily. 'I was wondering when you'd get here.'

'Why are you so perky this morning?'

'No reason. I tried calling you but some funny bloke answered your phone.' Tall and athletic, she was fully suited and masked, but he could tell from her brown eyes that she was smiling.

'I left it in a taxi last night.'

'Ah . . . These things happen. I'm afraid I had to make a start without you.'

'So where are we?' he asked, grateful that she wasn't going to make a song and dance about it.

'As you can see, we've cleared a path so you can go into the room. It looked sexual, so I asked for a pathologist.'

'Who's on call?'

'Arabella. She's already been and gone. She's pretty certain, from a quick visual, that cause of death is manual strangulation. There's clear bruising to the neck and very obvious petechial haemorrhaging. She took some intimate swabs so we don't lose anything, but said the rest could wait until later.'

'Was the woman killed in the room?'

'We think so. On the bed. Someone's pummelled the right side of her face. She was still alive, judging by the swelling and bruising and the amount of blood on the sheets. I've examined the areas of exposed skin and she's now ready to go. I want to get her out of here before the world wakes up, so they'll be bringing a stretcher up any minute now.'

'Do we have an ID?'

Jamieson shook her head. 'She's in her underwear but her clothes and personal things are gone, apart from an overcoat and a pair of heels in the cupboard.'

He wasn't thinking clearly, but the most obvious solution was that the killer had taken her clothes and personal things for some reason. Why he had left the shoes and coat behind was another matter.

'How far have you got with the room?' he asked.

'Nothing interesting so far. The photos and video are done. I can walk you through it all later, if you want. We'll do light-sourcing and fingerprints but, given it's a hotel, how far do you want to take it?'

'That's fine for now. I'll just take a quick look at the room, then I'll get back downstairs.'

Jamieson led the way to the door and clicked it open with a passkey, saying, 'I'll be back in a minute.'

Inside, a room-service trolley was parked up against a wall of the small internal lobby. An unopened bottle of champagne stood in a watery ice bucket beside two unused flutes. He

17

pulled it out and looked at the label. Krug. No ordinary champagne, he noted, wondering how much a bottle would set you back in such a place. He lifted the metal covers off two plates. Half a dozen oysters beneath one; some sort of white fish under the other, with a gravy boat of what looked like congealed Hollandaise under a napkin on the side. So, the killer rings down to room service and orders food. Things must have been going well up to that point. Then something goes wrong and half an hour later, the woman's dead. Was that what had happened? It didn't quite stack up.

There was a small marble-clad bathroom to one side. The lights were on and he gave it a cursory look before pushing open the bedroom door. As he went in, he was hit by a blast of chill air. Someone had been sick on the floor just inside the room. The waiter, he assumed, or someone else from the hotel. The room was spacious and almost identical to Jannicke's, with a modern black four-poster bed pushed up against one wall, a desk in one corner and a couple of armchairs grouped around a coffee table. The heavy red-striped curtains were still drawn, as they had been the previous night, and the lighting was very dim. Even so, he could see that the bed looked as though it had been hit by a typhoon, sheets and duvet half on the floor, pillows and cushions scattered around. The victim lay across the bed on her side, dark hair covering her face, her body partially hidden under a tangle of blood-stained sheets. He had never had a problem being alone with a body before, but he found it all suddenly oppressive and, in the shadowy light, felt strangely disorientated, almost intoxicated again. His vision blurred and for a moment he saw another woman lying before him, looking up at him, mouth slightly open, as if about to say something. It was as though no time had passed, he was in a room on the opposite side of the courtyard, it was still night outside, and he had never left the hotel. He blinked and shook his head. Maybe he was still drunk. He would get some strong black coffee as soon as he was done. He heard a noise and turned to find Jamieson in the doorway, holding a large, folded plastic sheet.

'Was this how you found her?' he asked a little abruptly, trying to recover himself.

'More or less. Arabella didn't need to shift her much to get what she wanted.'

He looked again at the scene in front of him, the chaos of the bed, the blood, the body lying untidily in the midst as though it had been violently discarded. He would study the photographs and video that had been taken but it looked as though there had been quite a struggle. Frenzy was the word that came to mind.

'Were there any defence wounds?'

'Doesn't look like it.'

'What about restraint marks?'

'Again, nothing Arabella commented on.'

He frowned, surprised. He would call Arabella Browne later for more of an insight. Also, if the victim was drunk or had been drugged, it would show up on the toxicology report. Hopefully, the post mortem and forensic analysis would reveal more clues. He gazed around the room again. Apart from the area immediately around the bed, he was struck by how tidy it all was, nothing out of place. The air conditioning was making a racket above him and he suddenly felt very cold. He checked the thermostat on the wall. It was on the 'Low' setting, reading sixteen degrees, with the fan turned up to the maximum.

'Did anybody change the thermostat?'

'No. It's been like this since I got here. Wish I'd put on my thermals.'

19

He frowned again, wondering why somebody might have deliberately turned down the thermostat when it was only a few degrees above zero outside. It was hardly conducive to a romantic atmosphere.

'You say her clothes are gone. Did you find anything belonging to the man who booked the room?'

'No.'

He made a mental note to ask if Herring had checked in with luggage and if anybody had taken it up to the room. Unless the victim had left her things in another room in the hotel, Herring would have needed something to carry them in, something that wouldn't draw attention to him when he left the hotel in the early hours of the morning.

Jamieson unfolded the plastic sheeting and spread it out on the bed beside the body.

'Can you give me a hand?'

Together they rolled the woman over onto her face and Jamieson started to untangle the bed sheet from the body's legs. 'Hang on. Take a look at this,' she said, indicating the back of the woman's thighs.

He peered over her shoulder. Faint, uneven red lines crisscrossed the woman's skin in places.

'We need some light,' Jamieson said, unzipping the front of her suit. She pulled out a small torch, which was hanging on a cord around her neck, and shone it on the woman's legs. The white beam illuminated what looked like a series of crudely formed capital letters. At first Tartaglia thought they had been tattooed on the victim's skin, but looking closer he realised that they had been scored by something sharp, deep into her flesh. There was no bleeding, so the cuts had been made post-mortem.

'Did you find a knife or anything with a blade?' he asked.

She shook her head, peering at the marks. 'Whatever it is, the blade's really fine and sharp. Like a Stanley knife.'

'He may have taken it with him, but we should be looking at corridors, bins, stairwells, drains, anywhere close where he might have ditched it. I'll get a search team onto it right away. Can you read what it says?'

' "E" something, then "O" something, then "S" something. The last bit looks like "Som". She crouched down until her eyes were almost level with the top of the woman's legs. 'That's better. I can read it now. *"ERIS QUOD SUM."*'

He squinted, but still couldn't see clearly. 'Are you sure?'

'Yes. I'm pretty sure.'

She passed him the torch and he crouched down beside her, angling the beam until he could make out the letters clearly. Eris Quod Sum. She was right. It was part of a familiar quote, although he couldn't remember what it was from. *Eram quod es. Eris quod sum.* He looked up and met her gaze. 'It's Latin,' he said. 'You find it on gravestones. It's the dead speaking to the living. "I once was what you are now. What I am, you will be." Basically, we're all going to die.'

'How very ominous. I didn't know you spoke ancient Italian.'

'Benefits of a good Catholic education,' he said, getting to his feet. 'Did Arabella see this?'

'No. She was in and out of here like greased lightning. Sounded like she had the flu.'

'I'll catch up with her later, then.' It would have been useful to have Arabella Browne's initial input right away, but it could wait.

'Who's the message for, do you think? It's pretty ominous.'

He grimaced. His head ached and he had seen enough for now. 'It's probably a wind-up. *CSI* gives them all sorts of creative ideas. Let's get her out of here ASAP. I need to get back downstairs.'

They rolled the woman onto her back and as Jamieson moved to bag up her feet and hands, Tartaglia glanced automatically towards the woman's face. His mind was already sorting through a quick priority list of things to be done next, but something caught his attention, some sort of fleeting impression of familiarity that made him pause. He looked at the woman again, hoping that it was a trick of the dim, shadowy light or his own tiredness and state of mind. Her face was bloodied and disfigured on one side by the beating she had received. Death also had a way of robbing a person of their humanity and turning loved ones into strangers. Still unsure, he moved over to the other side of the bed and as he brushed back the remaining hair from her face, the breath caught in his throat. Unable to speak, he blinked, studying every detail and contour, hoping that somehow he was mistaken.

'What's up?' Jamieson asked somewhere in the background.

He inhaled deeply, then exhaled, staring blindly down at the body before him, automatically noting the cuts to her face, the bruising and swelling and obvious signs of strangulation, wishing that she were someone else. But there was no doubt about it and it was pointless wasting any more time. The hideous consequences started to unfurl in his mind. What should be done, how to handle it, who to call first . . .

He pulled off his mask and rubbed his face with his hands. Even though the room was like a fridge, he was sweating. He felt suddenly feverish and claustrophobic.

'Mark? Are you OK?'

He looked up at Jamieson and shook his head. 'No. I'm not OK. I know her.'

Four

The car braked, then swerved to the right, rousing Tartaglia out of sleep. Minderedes leaned on the horn and muttered something unintelligible as he overtook a cyclist who had stopped in the middle of the road. Tartaglia stretched his shoulders, yawned and checked his watch. It was just after five in the afternoon but already dark. The day had gone quickly enough and the events of the morning seemed a distant memory. Gazing vaguely at the lit-up shop windows and passers-by as they sped past, he thought again of the woman whose corpse he had helped to zip inside a body bag that morning. Her name was Claire Donovan and her sister, Sam, had once been a detective sergeant on his team. Working closely together for almost two years, he and Sam had become good friends, although she had left the police a few months before to go back to university to study for a post-graduate degree. He hadn't seen either her or Claire since. He still felt shaken by the discovery of Claire's body in the hotel room early that morning and had spent the intervening hours trying to block out the memories, forget the Claire he had known, and do his job as best he could. But disturbing images from the darkened room kept crowding into his mind and he worried about his ability to see things objectively. Sam Donovan was also at the front of his thoughts and he wondered how she was coping with the news.

Other than the identification of the victim, little progress had been made with the case so far. The name Robert Herring had turned out to be an alias and the Manchester address entered into the reception log was equally fake. The mobile number 'Herring' had given was still switched off and untraceable and the credit card used to secure the booking had been Claire Donovan's own. He had checked in just after seven o'clock the previous evening and the video footage taken of him at reception showed a youngish man of medium height and build. He was dressed in bulky winter clothing, with a thick scarf wound around his neck and a beanie pulled down low over his brow. The little that was visible of his face was disguised by dark-lensed aviators and a good few days' worth of beard. He looked like a wannabe in the music or film business, not at all out of place in a hotel like the Dillon. He wore gloves and was carrying a large, black rucksack. CCTV footage showed him taking the back stairs up to the room and later, just before eight-thirty, Claire Donovan entering the building and going up to the second floor. The handbag she'd been carrying was still missing, but her coat and the shoes she was wearing looked to be the same as those left in the hotel room's cupboard.

Just before one in the morning, five minutes after making the call down to room service, Herring was filmed leaving the building via the front entrance, walking down the street in the direction of Marylebone High Street and melting into the night. By that time, Claire Donovan was already dead. He was dressed the same as when he had arrived at the hotel earlier, the rucksack – which must have contained Claire's things – slung over his shoulder. The search for the knife or blade used to cut Claire's legs had proved fruitless and it looked as though he'd taken that with him too. Tartaglia had watched the footage over and over again, studying the man's body language and familiarising himself with what little there was to be seen. Herring moved quickly and purposefully, head down, as

24

though he knew he was being observed. He was calm, even-paced, not a man in any hurry or panic, and Tartaglia was struck by how confident he seemed for a man who had just committed murder. It was extraordinary. Why had he made the call to room service? Why not leave it for housekeeping to find the body the following day? Why had Claire booked the hotel room for Herring and what was her connection to him? These, and myriad other mushrooming questions, remained unanswered. Neither her sister, Sam, nor any of her work colleagues that they had so far spoken to, knew anything about this man. Claire's phone was missing and switched off, but hopefully her laptop might reveal some important clues.

Tartaglia had just started to doze again when the car took a sharp left and a moment later pulled up abruptly.

'We're here, boss,' Minderedes said as Tartaglia opened his eyes. They were outside the small terraced house where Sam and Claire Donovan had lived, which was located in a quiet maze of narrow streets in Hammersmith, close to the river.

'I'm just nipping over to the office for some things, then I'll be back. They called to say they need more evidence bags. How long will you be?'

Tartaglia rubbed his eyes vigorously and reached for the door. 'I dunno. Maybe five minutes, maybe five hours. Just hurry up.' Their office in Barnes was just over Hammersmith Bridge, on the other side of the Thames, but at that hour the traffic around Hammersmith Broadway was particularly heavy. What should be no more than a ten-minute journey, door-to-door, could easily turn into half an hour and Tartaglia didn't want to find himself stranded. He was expecting a call any minute from the pathologist's office to let him know what time Claire's autopsy was scheduled that evening and he needed to be ready to go over there at short notice. Normally, he didn't need ferrying around. He had his motorbike, a Ducati 998, which in his view was infinitely better than a car. But he had dropped it off the previous day at the garage for a service and he would have to rely on Minderedes for the next few days.

He climbed out of the warm cocoon of the car, acknowledging Minderedes's murmured 'give Sam my condolences and best wishes' with a nod. Minderedes and Donovan had rarely seen eye to eye in the past, but it didn't matter any more. Wrapping his jacket tightly around him, Tartaglia looked at the house. The curtains were roughly drawn but he could see light through the gaps and the shadows of people moving around. Donovan was inside, being looked after by Sharon Fuller, the family liaison officer, as well as his boss, DCI Carolyn Steele. Two other detectives from his team, Dave Wightman and Hannah Bird, had already started searching the house and going through Claire Donovan's possessions, bagging up anything that looked interesting or might possibly give a clue to the identity of the man who had killed her. Tartaglia wondered how Donovan felt about having her home invaded at such a time, even though she knew it had to be done.

As the tail-lights of the BMW disappeared around the corner, he pulled out his phone and texted Steele to say that he had arrived. He crossed the road, sat down on a low garden wall opposite the house and lit a cigarette. When he had spoken to her half an hour earlier to tell her that he was on his way over, she had told him to wait outside. He had spent many a happy hour at the Donovans' house and it felt odd to be forced to loiter outside like a stranger. He had explained to Steele earlier that day about losing his phone and about having been in the Dillon Hotel at the time of the murder. She had made a couple of sharp comments about needing to have an early night when on call, but otherwise seemed to have taken what he had said at face value. His alibi would have to be checked like anybody else's, but otherwise it seemed there would be no repercussions. Something else must have happened, but he was at a loss to know what it was about.

A minute or so later the front door opened and Steele came out, bundled up in a long, belted, beige-coloured coat over her usual dark trouser suit. She must have a wardrobe full of them, he often thought. He tossed away the remains of his cigarette and crossed the road to meet her.

'Let's go somewhere,' she said, pulling on leather gloves and knotting a silk scarf tightly around her neck, her voice hoarse from the tail-end of a cold. 'We need to talk. Did you come by car?'

'Nick dropped me off. He's gone back to the office to get some stuff.'

'Let's sit in mine, then.' She walked over to a silver Audi parked on the opposite side of the street and clicked open the locks.

'What's up?' he asked, sliding into the passenger seat.

'I need to speak to you before you see Sam.'

'How is she?'

Steele switched on the ignition and turned the heater up to maximum. 'As you'd expect. I did my best to talk to her and ask if she knew anything that might help us, but she's in a pretty bad way. The doctor's given her a sedative to calm her down, plus pills to help her sleep tonight. She and Claire were close, weren't they?'

'Up to a point. They got on OK, but they are . . . I mean they *were* . . . very different.' Like chalk and cheese, both phys-ically and in terms of character, he'd always thought, marvelling at the vagaries of genetics. Claire, the elder, had been striking, on the tall side, with dark, wavy hair; Sam was small, prettier, with light brown hair. While Claire had been more outwardly confident and gregarious, he had always felt she lacked her sister's inner core and complexity.

'Still, they shared a house together,' Steele said. 'That must count for something. Unfortunately, she doesn't seem to know much about what her sister was up to, or what she was doing in that hotel.'

'You know Sam's been living in Bristol for the last couple of months.'

'There's the phone, Facebook, email. Surely they kept in touch? You know her better than I do. Do you think she's telling the truth?'

He looked at her, surprised. Although Steele never socialised outside work, she had a good enough feel for Sam's character. 'Sam? Why wouldn't she?'

'I have to ask.'

He nodded. 'I wasn't that close to Claire, but I'd say it's perfectly possible she kept things to herself, particularly if the relationship, or whatever it was, was something new. From what I gather, she didn't have a great track record with men and it was a bit of a sore spot.'

'Sam said she was bad at picking them. Maybe it runs in the family.'

Her tone made him look over at her again. 'What's that supposed to mean?'

She gave him one of her tight little smiles, her pale, cat-like eyes also giving nothing away. She would have done well in politics, he always thought. According to the rumour mill, she was destined for higher places than running the Barnes Murder Squads. 'I'll come onto that in a minute,' she said. 'Thinking about practical things first, it will be very strange for Sam to be on the outside of the investigation, and probably very frustrating.'

'Yes, I'm sure. But I shall, of course, keep her on the outside.' He wondered if this was the purpose of the conversation. Did Steele really think that he couldn't be trusted where Donovan was concerned?

'There's something else.' She paused, as though choosing her words carefully. 'You two had some sort of a falling out, didn't you?'

'Not exactly.'

'Lovers' tiff?'

'We were never lovers. You know that.'

'When did you last see Sam?'

'A few months ago. What's this all about?'

She folded her arms and tilted her head to one side. 'I need to know exactly what went on between the two of you.' When he didn't answer, she added: 'If you were *just good friends*,' she emphasised the words, 'why haven't you seen her since she left the Met? What exactly happened?'

Wondering who she had been listening to and where this was going, he said: 'I don't really know. We just haven't seen one another for a while. There was no row, no falling-out, nothing at all like that.'

'So?'

'Look, I just got the feeling that she didn't want to see me.'

'And you just let it go?'

'Why is this important?'

'I need to understand. For *professional* reasons, of course.'

He looked away but could feel her eyes still on him. He didn't like discussing such things with anybody, but he knew Steele wouldn't let it go. 'I don't know. I had the feeling that I'd done something wrong, let her down in some way, although she never actually said so. I haven't got a clue what it was all about.' Even as he spoke, he knew it sounded odd, but he had never really tried to put it into words before. Besides, it was only half the story.

'You didn't try and find out?'

He shrugged. 'I thought it would all blow over, but it didn't, then she went off to Bristol and life went on. Does it matter?'

'Yes. She can't stay here. We need to search the house thoroughly and it would be much easier if she weren't there.'

He nodded. 'I'm sure she, of all people, understands that.'

'You'd think so, but she's not rational at the moment. When I told her she'd have to move out temporarily, she was quite resistant and got quite upset. When I insisted that there was no choice, she asked if she could stay with you.'

He looked at her aghast. 'With me? What about her parents? They don't live that far away.'

'It's not that simple. They're in Australia, visiting relatives, and her dad had some sort of a heart attack when he heard the news about Claire. Understandably, Sam doesn't want to stay in their house on her own.'

'Jesus. Poor Colin. Is he going to be OK?'

She shrugged. 'He's still alive, but he's in intensive care.'

He sighed heavily. He had seen it so many times before. The fallout of a murder was far-reaching, affecting families and loved ones in unimaginable ways.

'I asked her if there wasn't some other family member, or friend, she could stay with,' Steele continued. 'But she said no. I offered to have her, as did Sharon, but she refused. She was quite definite about it. If she was going to be made to move out of her home, in these "horrible circumstances" as she put it, she wanted to stay with you. Obviously, I said I would have to speak to you first. So – *can* she stay with you, just for a few days? It would make everything so much easier.'

He gazed out of the window, not sure what to say. He felt deeply for Donovan and had some inkling of what she must be going through, even though he had never experienced such a thing himself. If it had been three months before, he wouldn't have hesitated to offer her a room, or his whole flat if need be. But things had changed between them. Something had happened and he had barely spoken to her since. It was odd that she wanted to stay with him.

'Do you have a spare room?' Steele asked.

'I have a box room. It's full of stuff at the moment.'

'Surely it won't be too difficult to make some space? After all, it's only for a few days. Sam can move back into the house as soon as we're done, if that's what she wants.'

'What about Justin?' he asked, referring to Justin Chang, one of the DCs on his team. 'They had something going on together at one point, I thought.'

'Nothing meaningful, at least not on her side. Anyway, it's not Justin she wants to stay with.'

He met her gaze. She was only a few years older than he was, but sometimes the gap felt like a generation. 'You really think this is a good idea?'

She frowned. 'No, I don't actually. You know what I think, Mark. I've said to you before I thought she was . . . well, that Sam was in love with you, or something along those lines. Why she felt that way, well . . .' She shrugged. 'Maybe that's why she chucked in her job.'

'You're blaming me?'

'No. It's her own stupid fault. She should have known better, but I'm pretty sure it's why she hasn't spoken to you in months. She probably finally saw sense and wanted to get some distance from you.'

He shook his head. There might be an element of truth in

what Steele said, but it wasn't the whole story. Something else had soured things between him and Donovan. Back in the summer, they had been working on a case involving a series of killings that proved to be linked to the unsolved murder of a young girl. Towards the end of the case, desperate for a resolution and in order to prevent any further deaths, he had taken a risk to flush out the killer. It had involved putting another man's life in jeopardy, although if the cards played out as he expected, he hadn't viewed the risk as being that great. He knew that he had crossed the line, both morally and professionally, but in his view it had been a gamble worth taking.

He had never discussed what had happened with anyone other than Donovan, and he was sure Steele knew nothing about it. But it had been a step too far for Donovan and she had said so. He reminded himself that she had seemed generally dissatisfied with life for a while even before those events, but maybe it had been the tipping point, providing the excuse she had been looking for to throw in the towel, both with him and her job. Since then, she had ignored all his attempts to patch things up and for the last couple of months hadn't returned his calls. Still more hurt than he cared to admit, he didn't understand why she was now so keen to stay with him; not that he had any intention of explaining that to Steele.

'Well, if it's distance she wants, staying with me isn't going to achieve it,' he said, after a moment.

Steele nodded. 'As I said, I think it's a crap idea. But she's over twenty-one and I'm not her minder. We need to get her out of there now, preferably with her cooperation. That's the priority.'

He sensed he was losing the argument. 'It's going to be bloody awkward having her around. She's going to want to know what's going on. How am I supposed to—'

Steele held up her hand. 'I agree, it's a tricky situation. Impossible, really. That's why I've decided to take you off the case.' She spoke matter-of-factly, as though it was just a routine matter. She wasn't known for her emotional intelligence, but he was dumbstruck at her lack of finesse.

He stared at her. 'You're kidding.' But he could see she wasn't. 'That's ridiculous.'

'Mark, you're too close to things. You knew Claire, you know Sam.'

'You think I can't handle it?'

'No. That's not what I mean, I—'

'I will do everything I can to find Claire's killer, and not just because she's Sam's sister.'

'I know you would, but so can one of the other teams. Equally well.'

'Is this because I was at the Dillon last night? I told you all about that. I've done nothing wrong.'

'But it makes things awkward. You must see that. You were there when this happened. If we catch whoever did this and it comes to trial and you have to give evidence, it might muddy the waters. Imagine how the press might spin it if they ever got hold of it. There's also something else.'

He shook his head, not believing what he was hearing.

'It's important.' She waited until she had his attention. 'You know the Sainsbury's car park body?' she continued, referring to a current case he had been investigating.

'The dead tramp in the car? What about it?'

'You had a message from Dr Moran at the mortuary. They've done the post-mortem and things are not as straightforward as they looked. He says it's not one body, but four.'

'Four? How can that be? There was just one body in the car, or what was left of it after the fire. I saw the photos.'

'It seems that the body parts come from four different people, three men and a woman. They were assembled to look like one.'

'Jesus.' He threw his head back and sighed, exhausted by it all.

'So you see, you're going to have your hands full enough with this one. You can't handle both.'

He closed his eyes for a few moments, picturing the burnt-out wreck of a stolen Fiat Panda, with the charred remains of what they had thought was a man lying curled up asleep in the back. They had assumed he was sleeping rough and had climbed into the car for warmth. When the local CID arrived on the scene, the first theory had been that he'd set himself alight by accident. Then traces of accelerant were discovered in and around the car and the murder squad had been called in. Even so, it had barely merited more than a couple of lines in the local press. Dead vagrants made poor copy. But four people, made to look like one... Without knowing any further details, he could already imagine what the media reaction would be.

'We must keep it under wraps for as long as possible,' Steele said. 'As soon as you've got Sam settled at your place, you'd better get over to Westminster and see Dr Moran. He said he had an autopsy to do but that he'd be finished around nine.'

They walked across the street together in silence, Tartaglia's head spinning. He didn't know what to focus on, the Dillon case he was being forced to leave behind, Sam Donovan coming to stay for an indeterminate period, or the car park body or bodies. He could do with a stiff drink and a cigarette, but there was no chance of either with Steele around.

Steele unlocked the front door and he followed her into the narrow hall. He heard noises and footsteps coming from the first floor.

'Sam's in the kitchen,' Steele said, unbuttoning her coat. 'Sharon's with her. I'll just check on Dave and Hannah upstairs and I'll come and find you.'

Feeling suddenly nervous about seeing Sam Donovan again, he walked along the passage to the rear of the house. The kitchen was down a couple of steps, in an extension that took up a large part of the small garden. DS Sharon Fuller stood at the sink in front of the window, washing some dishes, the radio was playing quietly in the background. Short and plump, with a tidy bob of pale blonde hair, Fuller glanced over her shoulder at him as he came into the room and arched her eyebrows meaningfully in greeting. Sam Donovan was hunched over the kitchen table in the centre of the room, a mug of something in front of her. She barely seemed to register that he was there. His first impulse was to go to her, put his arms around her and gather her to him. Three months ago he wouldn't have thought twice about it. Instead, he stood awkwardly just inside the doorway, not sure what to do. From what he could tell, she had lost weight since he had last seen her. She looked too thin, he thought. She had also dyed her short, naturally light-brown hair platinum blonde. For a moment she reminded him of a photo he had seen of Edie Sedgwick, or maybe it was Sienna Miller playing Edie Sedgwick. He was also struck by how small she looked, how fragile. He had never thought of her as fragile before, or vulnerable, and his heart went out to her.

'I'm so sorry, Sam,' he said, still hovering by the door.

Her eyes met his and silently she mouthed 'thank you'. She had a bleary, unfocussed look, which he assumed was down to the medication she had been given.

'Mark says he can have you to stay,' Steele said, coming into the room behind him. 'If that's what you want,' she added.

'Yes,' Tartaglia murmured. 'Of course.'

Donovan nodded slowly and went back to staring into space.

'Have you got her things together?' he asked Fuller.

'That's all she packed,' Fuller replied, pointing a soapy finger towards a small overnight bag sitting by the door. 'She wouldn't let me do it and I doubt it will be enough, but I can always bring over more if she needs it.'

'We'll be done here relatively quickly,' Steele said, looking at Donovan, although she didn't seem to hear. 'Hopefully, it should only be for a day or so.'

Tartaglia said nothing, but he wasn't so sure that Donovan would want to move straight back into her house. Even though Claire hadn't been murdered there, it would hold so many memories. He would give it a couple of days, see how things panned out, and then maybe another solution would have to be found. At least if he was working on a totally different case, it would make things a little easier. Maybe Steele was right after all.

'How long will Nick be?' Steele asked Tartaglia.

'Should be back any minute. Shall we wait here for him?'

Steele glanced at her watch. 'No. We need to get on. I'll give you a lift. Call him and tell him to meet you at your flat. He can take you over to the mortuary.'

'Are you sure there's nothing else you need?' Tartaglia asked Donovan, picking up the small suitcase and finding it surprisingly heavy.

'Just my work,' Donovan said faintly, slowly getting to her feet. 'My bag's in the hall.'

Five

'When will we get the DNA results back?' Tartaglia asked Dr James Moran.

'Should be sometime tomorrow, if we're lucky.' The last word was distorted by an explosive sneeze. Moran took a crumpled handkerchief out of his pocket and blew his nose loudly a couple of times. 'Sorry. There's something doing the rounds here. I hope I'm not going down with it.'

They were standing in one of the recently refurbished suites of rooms in Westminster mortuary. Moran's pudgy face was pale and sweaty and Tartaglia didn't hold out much hope of his resisting whatever bug was threatening to lay him low. Maybe he had caught Arabella Browne's flu. Moran was roughly his own age and had recently transferred to the Westminster-based team of pathologists, from another location somewhere out of London. He was short and a little overweight, with a receding hairline and old-fashioned steel-rimmed spectacles, which gave him an earnest look. From what Tartaglia had heard, he was struggling with the increased hours that working in the capital involved, on top of the daily commute home. Wondering if Moran would last the pace, or whether Moran's wife would put up with the strain on their family life, Tartaglia stared down at the blackened skeletal frame laid out on the gurney in front of him.

The smell coming from the remains was powerful and made him want to retch. The flesh on some of the body parts had clearly been decomposing before the parts had been set on fire.

The logistics of assembling a body the way the killer had done, suggested he must be storing the parts somewhere, most likely a freezer. He recalled the area of waste ground where the green Fiat Panda had been found, next to the Sainsbury's car park in Lambeth, and ran through in his mind the video footage from the crime scene, taken just after the car had been found. Although the entrance to the waste ground from the road had been boarded up, part of the fencing between it and the car park had been vandalised and it was being used as an overspill when the Sainsbury's car park was full. The Panda had been reported stolen from outside a house in Tooting five days before the fire was discovered. They didn't yet know whether the killer had transported the body parts in the boot of the car, or covered up on the back seat, or even separately in bags or a suitcase. An appeal for witnesses who might have noticed when the car had been left there had so far drawn a blank. CCTV footage, which barely extended to the outer limits of the car park, let alone the area beyond, was inconclusive. The best estimate was that the car could have been sitting there for anything up to twenty-four hours before the fire was spotted and the fire brigade was called out. It was also unclear if the car had been dumped by joy riders, and the killer had used it opportunistically, or whether the killer had stolen the vehicle as part of his plan.

There had been two possible identities put forward for what they had believed was a single body in the burnt-out car. The first was a vagrant who went by the name of Dodger. Described by those who came across him as being anything between the ages of fifty and seventy, rumour had it that he was an ex-soldier who had seen action in the first Gulf war. He had been a regular in the area for a while and had often been seen at the back of Sainsbury's at night, sitting by the warm air vent from the bakery. He hadn't been seen since the fire and the first assumption had been that it was his body in the back of the car. However, they didn't have much to go on; just an artist's impression of him, which revealed little more than a heavily bearded face. They needed to find out Dodger's real identity and try to trace any living relatives to see if they could get a familial DNA match. If he wasn't one of the four victims, they needed to find him urgently to ascertain if he had seen anything suspicious on the night the car was set on fire.

The second possible murder victim was a businessman named Richard English, whose wallet containing driving licence and credit cards had been found on the ground beside the burnt-out wreck, still just about intact enough to be identifiable. A set of keys had also been recovered close by, the fob bearing the initial 'R'. English had been reported missing two years previously and none of the cards had been used since that time. English's wife, Lisa, had been briefly interviewed and had given permission for their young daughter to be swabbed to see if there was a familial link.

'Can you check to see if any of the body parts have been frozen?' Tartaglia asked Moran.

'No problem. I'll get back to you tomorrow, if that's OK.'

'And we'll need to establish how old the bones are, although something smells pretty recent.'

'I'll call in an anthropologist, if you're OK with the cost?'

Tartaglia nodded. 'Were the bones all cut up in the same way?'

'Yes. As you'll see when you get the images, they were dismembered quite cleanly at the joints, using some sort of a serrated blade, probably a hacksaw. There are also a few traces on some of the bones of a sharp-bladed knife having being used.'

'A professional job?'

Moran sniffed loudly. 'Hard to tell. Could just be somebody with basic butchery skills, or access to the Internet.'

'And you're saying the arms and legs are female?'

'That's right. And the hands. I might have picked up the mismatch sooner if it had been the pelvis or skull. Much easier to spot. The skull and torso belong to two different males.'

Tartaglia stared at the pieces. Why bother to get hold of four bodies, cut them up and fit them together somehow to make one. A number of people had access to body parts or whole bodies: medical students, or mortuary or hospital attendants, for starters. But without having an idea of the age of the various parts, let alone some sort of ID for the bodies, it was impossible to know where to start. In the meantime, how the hell was he going to keep it all quiet?

'What samples were taken at the post mortem?' he asked. It had been carried out earlier that day, while he had been busy at the Dillon Hotel.

'We managed to get a few soft-tissue samples here and there, particularly from around the tops of the legs and the thighs, but I've also taken samples of bone and some teeth.'

'Any news on the DNA sample we sent to the lab from Richard English's daughter?'

'I've been chasing it. We should hear back by tomorrow.'

'What about the age profile of the victims, or any other identifying characteristics?'

'As you know, these things aren't precise, but I'd put victims B and D, the owners of the torso and legs, in the mid-twenties to mid-forties range, although D is at the younger end of the spectrum. No sign of cause of death for either. As for victim A, the owner of the skull, he's older. Looking at the cranial sutures, they're getting really smooth, so he's got to be post-middle age.

There's a depressed fracture to the top right-hand side of the skull, indicating a blunt-force injury of some type. Although it's difficult to say categorically without seeing the rest of the body, the blow would have been sufficient to cause death on its own. Based on bone density, victim C, the female, is elderly. As with victims B and D, no sign of cause of death. I'll send you a full analysis some time tomorrow.'

Tartaglia felt suddenly woozy, questions multiplying like flies, answers nowhere to be seen. Where did Richard English fit in? Was it sheer coincidence that his wallet had been found at the scene, or was he one of the victims? According to the file, he was in his late fifties, so not an instant match for either victim A or B, although as Moran had said, such things weren't precise. Not for the first time that day, Tartaglia had the uncomfortable feeling of being out of control, nothing making sense. The charred remains in front of him swam in and out of focus, the stench unbearable. He needed to get out of there. He looked up at Moran, tried to stifle a yawn and failed.

'Anything else I should know?'

Moran shook his head, giving him an appraising look. 'That's about it for now. I'd go and get some sleep, Mark. I think you're going to need it.'

Minderedes pulled up outside Tartaglia's house and Tartaglia got out of the car. As he turned in through the gate and walked up the path, he heard music coming from inside. He unlocked the front door and let himself into his flat. Music filled the room from his new Bang & Olufsen system and he recognised the song. 'Down' by Jay Sean. Donovan had always liked it but it brought back less than pleasant memories for him. The last time he had heard it, he'd been with her, in a bar off Shepherd's Bush, when she had told him she was leaving the Met. 'I've had enough. I've just come to the end of the line. Nothing personal,' she'd said. He could still hear her words, the song linked to that memory. He wondered if she remembered as well.

She sat curled up on the sofa, legs tucked under her, staring vacantly ahead. Her bags were still by the front door of the flat, where he had left them a couple of hours before. Apart from plugging her iPhone into the sound system dock, it didn't look as though she had moved.

'Are you hungry?' he asked, taking off his jacket and boots, which were wet from the rain. He had to repeat himself before he got her attention. She shook her head. 'Glass of wine?' She looked blearily over at him and he mimed raising a glass to his lips, then mouthed the word 'wine'. After a moment, she nodded.

He went into the kitchen and opened a bottle of Barolo from a case his father had sent him. It was just as well she wasn't hungry as he'd had no time to shop. He had a quick check in the cupboards and the fridge. Sardines on toast was about as much as he could cobble together, but that didn't really appeal. Perhaps he should get a takeaway, maybe Indian, or Thai, or maybe Sushi . . . He ran through the list of local options in his head, but nothing really grabbed him, and he felt too tired to wait. Still mulling it over, he took the two glasses of wine back into the sitting room and handed one to Donovan. She took it from him automatically, barely glancing up.

He sat down in a chair opposite, put his feet up on the coffee table and lit a cigarette. She gazed away into a far corner of the room. It was as if he wasn't there. He still couldn't fathom why she had decided to stay with him. The song that was playing, something catchy by Taio Cruz, segued into Plan B's 'She Said', which was more to his liking. He had decided to let her have his bedroom and he would sleep on the sofa. Even if he had had the energy to clear out the box room and blow up the air mattress somebody had lent him, it was cold and uncomfortable. He needed a decent night of sleep if he was to survive the next day. He had half-hoped to find her already tucked up in bed by the time he came back from the mortuary. He wanted to be by himself and let the events of the day gradually fall into place in the peace of his own home. But that wasn't to be. How was he going to be able to move her into the bedroom so that he could go to bed? He finished his cigarette and decided that if he was going to sit there listening to music for a while, he must have something to eat. After a moment's thought, he took his phone from his jacket pocket, went back into the kitchen, where it was quieter, and ordered a selection of meze from a Lebanese restaurant around the corner, plus a couple of beers. Maybe if she saw him eating she would feel like having something too. They told him they would deliver it to his flat in fifteen minutes and he loaded a tray with plates and cutlery and went back into the sitting room.

Donovan still hadn't moved, although she seemed to have drunk some wine, which was a good sign. He sat down again, leant back heavily into the cushion of the chair and put his feet back up on the table, his thoughts turning automatically to the next day's work. There was the team briefing in the office at seven, after which he and Minderedes were due to drive over to the car park in Lambeth where the burnt-out Panda had been found. The priority was to find the homeless man known as Dodger, who might have witnessed what had happened. After that, they were due to interview Richard English's wife, Lisa. As the music changed to Adele's 'Someone Like You', he glanced over at Donovan. Her expression had changed and he saw tears flood her eyes and stream down her cheeks. She put her glass on the coffee table and covered her head with her arms, her body shaking.

He waited a moment, then, wondering what was the best thing to do, got up, crossed the room and sat down beside her. Without thinking, he put an arm around her and pulled her to him. She felt as rigid as a block of stone, but he continued to hold her, stroking her, trying to soothe her, until he felt a gradual, almost grudging release of tension. After a few minutes, her shoulders stopped shaking and she pulled back and looked up at him.

'Sorry. This song . . . Makes me think of Claire.'

'It's fine. Don't worry. Shall I put something else on?'

She nodded and he got up and took her iPhone off the dock. He went and got his phone and sat down again beside her, tabbing through until he found a playlist of old stuff he'd put together to help him wind down late at night. He quickly checked the songs. It probably wasn't her cup of tea, knowing her and Claire's taste in music, but at least it wouldn't have any painful associations. His phone synched with the speakers, he pressed play and Moby's '18' filled the room.

'I keep thinking . . .' she said, after a few moments. 'I keep thinking "why". I mean, why Claire?' She spoke quietly, her words a little slurred, and he could only just make out what she said over the music.

He didn't know what to reply. It was the question that everybody asked who had lost someone. There was usually no good answer.

'I need to know why,' she continued. 'Everything I did before . . . with work . . .'

'I know how difficult this is for you. But we don't know why yet.'

'What happened? What was she doing in that hotel? Did you see her? Please . . .'

Again he tried to blot out the images of Claire from that morning, as though somehow there was a risk that Donovan

44

could telepathically see them too. He held his fingers to her mouth. 'No, Sam. You know I can't tell you.'

'Why?'

'Because I can't. And it's best you don't know.'

She shook her head. 'Steele said . . .' Tears welled again in her eyes as she stared at him. 'She said Claire'd been strangled.'

He nodded.

'In a hotel room.'

He nodded again, wondering how much she had been told, although he was sure Steele had kept it to the bare minimum. Even though Donovan was a former colleague and friend, in her current state there was little point revealing more than was absolutely necessary.

'She asked why Claire was there, like she was . . . she sort of implied she was . . .'

'An escort?'

She nodded.

'It's an obvious question, as you know. It has to be asked.' Steele had put the same question to him: was there was any chance that, either for kicks or money, Claire Donovan had visited a stranger in his hotel room. He had told her that, based on what he knew of Claire, plus the fact that she had booked the room with her own credit card, made it seem highly unlikely. 'She knows Claire was a successful lawyer,' he continued. 'She didn't need the money and I made it clear that it couldn't possibly be that, so don't worry on that score.'

She frowned. 'But why was Claire there, in a man's room? Who *is* he? I mean she must've . . .' The words tumbled out haphazardly, as though she was talking to herself and didn't expect an answer.

'We don't know who he is or why she was there.'

'She must've known him, trusted him. She . . . Was she—' She stopped and looked up at him again. *Raped*. That was what she wanted to ask, but he wasn't going to fill in the gaps for her and raise further questions, nor would he lie. He needed to stop the flow.

'We need to wait for the post-mortem.'

'You saw her. What did she look like? Did she suffer?'

'Please, Sam. Don't.'

She shook her head. 'Don't ask. I know. Sorry. It's got to be someone she knew.'

'It looks that way.'

'Not a stranger.' She turned to him. 'Tell me what *you* think? Please.'

He sighed, not knowing what to say and wondering how to stop the questions. 'She wasn't abducted. From what we can tell, she went up to his room of her own accord. Knowing Claire, I don't think he was a stranger.'

It was as though she hadn't heard him. 'His name's Robert Herring. Herring, like red herring. Like Mr Kipper. Do you think—'

'I can't tell you anything more about Claire,' he cut in, although he had had the same thoughts initially. *Mr Kipper*, the man who had abducted and presumably murdered the estate agent Suzy Lamplugh nearly thirty years before, the crime still unsolved. But the MO had been totally different. Whether or not the name was some sort of allusion to a red herring was not something worth wasting time over for the moment. 'However hard it is, you need to try and stop thinking about it and let us get on with the investigation. Anyway, as of this evening I'm off the case.'

She stared at him. 'Off the case? Why? Because of me?'

'No, something else. Another case I was working on just

before has blown up big-time and I have to focus on that. There won't be time to follow both.' He had no intention of mentioning his own connection with the Dillon Hotel, of telling her that he had been there at the time of Claire's murder, and that he had seen nothing. However irrational, the thought made him feel worse than useless.

She looked at him for a moment, as though struggling to take in what he said, then closed her eyes and leaned back against him with a sigh, her head heavy on his shoulder. He was surprised she had let it go so quickly, but maybe her state of mind, as well as the medication she had been given, had dulled her usual persistence. He sat with her, unmoving, for a while, until he realised she must have fallen asleep. Not wanting to wake her, he gathered her up in his arms and carried her into the bedroom, where he laid her down on the bed. He pulled off her boots, eased the duvet over her, and turned off the overhead lights, leaving a bedside lamp on in case she woke up and forgot where she was. He closed the wooden shutters and watched her for a moment, listening to her soft, rhythmical breathing, until he was sure she wasn't going to wake. Seeing her there, in his bed, he felt a sudden pang of regret that he had ever lost touch with her and, for a moment, he reflected on what might have been.

Then he shut the door and went back into the sitting room. Alex Clare was singing 'Too Close', and as he sat down with his glass of wine to wait for his takeaway to be delivered he listened to the lyrics and his thoughts turned again to Sam Donovan. Their brief physical closeness had reawakened a complexity of feelings, not least of basic physical attraction, which he usually tried to ignore. It had no place in their friendship. Sex was easy, commitment a lot more difficult. As his sister's words rang in his head again, he pictured Jannicke and the brief but pleasurable episode at the Dillon. He felt no guilt, but briefly wondered if his life would always be that way. Perhaps he wasn't ready yet for anything much more, or maybe the cliché was true: maybe he just hadn't met the right person. As for Donovan, something always held him back from making a rash move in the heat of the moment. With expectations so high on both sides, any relationship was doomed to failure, he was sure. What was the point of risking a good friendship? As with the song, they were *too close*. Not for the first time, he told himself to put it to the back of his mind, that it was one of those things best left.

His eyes drifted to the files and footage from the car park body case spread out on the coffee table in front of him and his thoughts turned again to the next day. Until the DNA results came back, the focus had to be on Richard English. For the moment, he was the only lead they had.

Six

The sky was grey and heavy with cloud, a cold drizzle just setting in again as Tartaglia climbed out of Minderedes's BMW. It was nearly eleven in the morning and they were in Markham Square in Chelsea, where Richard English had lived. Tartaglia's head felt thick but he didn't mind a bit of rain and it was good to have some fresh air and get out of the office for a while. The briefing meeting earlier had not gone well. His team had greeted the news that they had been taken off the Dillon Hotel case with unanimous and loud objections. Sam Donovan had been universally liked and everybody wanted to help find her sister's killer, but Steele had been immovable. He was glad that it was she, with her calm, unemotional manner, who had had the job of explaining that the case had already been reassigned to the other team under her command. In the end they had been forced to accept it, but it was going to be difficult to keep everybody focussed on the car park case, when their hearts and minds were elsewhere.

A quick visit to the Sainsbury's car park had yielded nothing. They had been over the ground again and looked at the logistics of what might have happened, but nothing new had emerged and the homeless man known as Dodger was still nowhere to be seen. Things had not improved as the morning wore on; the lab result had shown that the DNA sample provided by Richard English's daughter had no familial connection with any of the body parts. However, the wallet was still considered significant – it had to have been placed at the scene deliberately – but if none of the body parts belonged to English, what was his connection to the others? Could he possibly be a suspect?

English's house was almost at the end of the terrace, with a shiny dark-green door and a knocker in the shape of a dolphin. Halloween had been and gone a few days before but a huge pumpkin still stood grinning on the doorstep and the window overlooking the road was festooned with garlands of fake cobwebs and spiders. Tartaglia pressed the bell and the front door opened soon after.

'Are you the police?' A young, blonde-haired woman peered short-sightedly up at him.

'DI Mark Tartaglia.' He held up his warrant card.

'I'm Lisa English. I was expecting you. Come inside.'

She was of medium height and very thin, dressed in tight, light-blue tracksuit bottoms and a T-shirt with some sort of logo on the front mapped out in tiny crystals. He followed her into the sitting room, where she motioned him towards a beige-coloured leather sofa.

'Do sit down. Would you like tea or coffee?' Her voice had a brittle tone, with a trace of a South London accent.

'I'm fine. Thanks,' he said, making himself comfortable. 'We've got the results back from the lab of the DNA sample taken from your daughter, Mrs English. There's no familial link with the body we found in the car, which means your husband may still be alive.'

He had expected a look of relief, or surprise, but her face showed no emotion. 'I thought you found his wallet,' she said flatly, sitting down opposite him in a large armchair and crossing her legs. 'His credit cards haven't been used since he disappeared. You can check with the bank.' She sounded almost irritated.

'Yes, they are still in his wallet, but whatever the explanation, he isn't the man in the car.' He was careful to use the singular. 'We also found a set of keys close to the wallet, which we assume belong to him. Could they be for here?' He held up the plastic evidence bag containing the keys, showing her the fob with the initial 'R'.

She studied them closely for a moment, then shook her head. 'Our front door's got a Banham lock. If they're his, they'll be for his office, or maybe his flat.'

'His flat?' The only address listed in the report was the Markham Square house.

'He'd moved out. We were getting divorced.'

At least that explained her strange reaction. 'I'm sorry. I didn't know.'

'It was for the best.' Her mouth tightened. 'There's something... I don't want it to go further than this room. It's possible Charlotte isn't Rich's daughter.'

He looked at her surprised. 'Why didn't you tell us this before?'

She shrugged, a gesture of what he hoped was embarrassment, although he doubted it. She didn't look the type. 'I didn't know for certain, until now.'

'Does he have any close relatives? Parents, or siblings? We really do need to try and get a DNA sample, if only to eliminate him.'

'Rich was an only child and both his parents are dead, but he has two sons from his first marriage. Last I heard, the eldest is off travelling somewhere on his gap year, but you can try the younger one. He's at some posh boarding school out of London. He's an absolute dead ringer for his dad. He's definitely Rich's son.'

'We'll contact him immediately, if you can give me the mother's details?'

'Sure.'

She still seemed oddly detached, even for a woman who clearly didn't like her missing husband. 'Are you alright, Mrs English?'

'Of course I am. Why do you ask?'

'Talking about what may have happened to your husband doesn't upset you, then?'

Her brown eyes widened. 'Why should it? I just hoped you'd be telling me it was him in that car.'

Taken aback, he studied Lisa English closely. In his experience, divorce was rarely something cut and dried. Emotions ran high, and in all sorts of directions. Complete calm and such coldness were unusual, even after a gap of two years, and he decided that her blasé attitude must be an act. He suspected that, underneath, she felt the bitterness of somebody badly hurt, and he guessed that Richard English had left her, not the other way around. She wasn't wearing any make-up, not that she needed it; she was pretty enough. She was older than he had initially thought, maybe late thirties, heading towards forty, a tricky age for some women. He noted the light sprinkling of freckles on her cheeks and small nose, the way her mouth turned down at the corners, and the fine laughter lines around her eyes. He couldn't imagine her laughing or having a sense of fun, but maybe he wasn't seeing her on a good day. The photos of English in the missing persons report showed a middle-aged man with the bulky build of an ex-rugby player gone to seed and a taste for loud, striped shirts and shapeless leather jackets. He struggled to picture the two of them together.

'So there was no love lost between you?'

'That's one way of putting it. I'd just like to know if he's dead. We've been in limbo too long.' She looked at him, as if daring him to make some sort of judgemental comment.

He decided to change the subject. 'Mr English was clearly a wealthy man,' he said, more as a statement than a question, appraising the expensive furnishings and wondering if money was behind Richard English's disappearance and possible murder.

'Making money's all he cares about.'

'What sort of work was he involved in?'

'Hotels and restaurants and stuff. You'd better ask Ian, if you want the full gen. I didn't get involved.'

'Ian?'

'Rich's business partner.'

'He's the one who reported Mr English as missing?'

'Yes. He can fill you in better than I can. Rich is the man with the Midas touch, the creative one. Ian's the numbers guy, Mister Nuts and Bolts, or at least that's what Rich always calls him. It's the perfect marriage.'

'You keep referring to Mr English in the present tense. You think he's still alive?'

She shrugged. 'I don't know what to think, really. I've been through it all in my head over and over again. If he'd had an accident, we'd know about it. He carries ID. He certainly likes a drink, particularly if it's some special, fancy vintage, but he doesn't do benders, he doesn't go AWOL and he's not the sort to top himself. He loves himself far too much. So something must've happened. Sometimes I wonder if he's done a runner.'

'A runner?'

'It's possible. If something's up, it'll be to do with work, I'll put money on it.'

'So you think he disappeared deliberately?'

'I don't know, but if he's in some sort of trouble and he's taken off, Ian would look after everything for him. That's the only thing I can think of.'

He looked at her, intrigued. She seemed to be telling the truth, and assuming her description of her husband was accurate, she was right: people like Richard English didn't just disappear into thin air. 'Did he have any enemies?' he asked.

'Again, you'd better ask Ian.'

'Tell me more about Ian,' he said, curious, deciding that he should be the next priority.

'He's like Rich's brother. They've known each other since school. I often felt like Ian was the other woman in our relationship.'

'If your husband *is* dead, are you the main beneficiary?'

She shifted in her chair and re-crossed her legs. 'I get half his estate, according to the solicitor. Luckily for me, he hadn't gotten around to changing his will before he disappeared.' She didn't bother to mask the satisfaction in her tone.

'What happens to the rest of it?' he asked, thinking that if English had deliberately decided to disappear, it didn't sound very carefully planned.

'Ian gets some shares in the business and the rest is put in trust for Charlotte and his two kids from his first marriage. Once he's officially declared dead, that is.'

'Do you know what your husband was worth?'

She smiled openly. 'Tens of millions, from what the solicitor says. Rich was a right sod as a husband, but he knew how to make money.'

Struck again by her directness, which against his better judgement he found disarming, he was silent for a moment. Money was always one hell of a motive for murder, but he reminded himself that it was none of his concern, unless English was one of the victims in the car.

'One last thing, when did you learn that Mr English was missing?'

'Ian called me right away when he didn't show up at work. He wanted to know if I had any idea where Rich was. I told him I hadn't seen Rich in weeks but I was sure he'd turn up. Bad pennies always do, don't they?'

'Thanks, Mrs English,' Tartaglia said, getting to his feet. 'I think that covers everything for now.'

Seven

Adam Zaleski paused outside the terraced house in Bedford Gardens and looked up. It was a pretty doll's house, with Georgian-style windows and an ornate little iron balcony across the front, on the first floor. To give Kit his due, he had taken good care of the place, which was surprising for somebody with such slovenly personal habits. The paint was peeling here and there and the brickwork could do with cleaning, but it required no major work and wouldn't be too difficult to fix. Kit had chosen a nice shade of off-white for the windows and a lovely blackish green for the front door and the lantern beside it. The interior was a restrained homage to the eighteenth century; subdued colours, scrubbed oak boards and an abundance of marble fireplaces. It was all as impractical and pointless as Kit himself. Luckily lots of people liked that sort of thing and it should show well when the time came to sell. Must be worth several million, he thought. The pictures and furnishings would also fetch a tidy sum at auction. It was quite a contrast to the modest, threadbare little house in Ealing where Adam had grown up with his grandparents. Pathetic, hopeless Kit, just a member of the lucky sperm club. He had done nothing to deserve it. But then neither life, nor death, was fair.

The phone in Adam's pocket chimed. He took it out and looked at the text on the screen.

Hi Tom SO SO sorry but can't make tonight. new case come in and we are all on overtime :(maybe in a couple of days? Sxx

56

He smiled. There was no rush, at least as far as he was concerned. He texted her back, telling her to let him know when she was next free, then pushed open the wrought-iron gate and walked into the small front garden. The low hedges still looked relatively neat, but the rest needed a proper tidy up. The ancient wisteria and magnolia had shed their leaves, making a soggy, thick carpet of brown on the paved path, which was slippery to walk on, particularly after the rain. He would need to go and buy a shovel and a broom to clear it all. Whoever was supposed to be looking after the garden while Kit was away had clearly done a bunk, no doubt pocketing the money and hoping Kit wouldn't be back until the Spring.

He went up the couple of steps to the front door, put down his shopping and fumbled in his coat pocket for the key. There was a hole in the pocket but no key. He rummaged around the hem until he found it, turning up some loose change and an old roll-up in the process that must have been there since Kit had last worn the coat. As he put the key in the lock, he heard the phone ringing inside. Leaving his shopping on the front step, he opened the door and rushed into the sitting room. He heard the answer machine kick in and Kit's whiney, nasal tones:

Hi, this is Kit. No point leaving a message as I'm not here and probably won't be back until God knows when. Call back later, or never. Whatever takes your fancy.

Such a stupid message. It also sounded as though it was playing at slightly the wrong speed. He picked up the receiver, but there was nobody at the other end. He dialled 1471 but the number was withheld. Trying to put it out of his mind, he collected the bags of shopping and took them downstairs to the basement kitchen. It was small and located at the back of the

57

house, going out onto the garden. The layout of the house was very odd, with a dining area up a few stairs off the kitchen extension and a library-cum-TV room at the front, although the TV was so old and small it was hardly worth watching. If he had been intending to stay longer, he would have had to replace it. The ground and first floors were used as sitting rooms, the furnishings stiff, formal and uninviting. He couldn't imagine why Kit needed them all. From what he had gathered, Kit had never been a great one for entertaining; far too bloody lazy. There was only one decent-sized bedroom in the whole house, which was located all the way up the rather narrow stairs, on the top floor. The only other bedroom was tiny and on the ground floor, clearly designed to put anybody off from staying long. Typically, Kit had arranged it all just to suit himself.

He put on the kettle to make a cup of tea. He had just started to unpack the bags into the fridge – deciding that he would have tomato soup and salad for lunch and the shepherd's pie for dinner that night – when the phone started to ring again. He hesitated for a moment, wondering whether or not to answer it, then grabbed the receiver off the wall.

'Kit's phone.' There was no response. 'Hello?' He thought he could hear somebody breathing at the other end. 'Is there anyone there?' The caller hung up. Again he tried 1471 but again the number was withheld. It was probably the same person. Hearing a strange voice, the caller had decided to hang up. That was all there was to it. Or maybe it was just a wrong number . . . A woman had called a couple of days before, asking to be put through to accounts and had been very apologetic when he had explained that the number was for a private house, not a company. But the phone had rung quite a lot over the past couple of weeks since he'd been staying here. Sometimes the caller put the phone down immediately he answered; other

times there was the same pause before the call was discon-
nected. Once he thought he heard the faint sound of voices in
the background, but it could have been the TV or a radio. A
couple of times a man had asked for Kit, and had sounded
annoyed when he said Kit was still away. Maybe he should just
unplug the phone. That way, he wouldn't have to answer any
questions about Kit's whereabouts.

Eight

The offices of English, Armstrong & Partners were in an eighteenth-century terraced house just off St. James's Square in the West End. It was an area teeming with gentlemen's clubs, fine-art dealers and hedge fund managers, where rental costs commanded a small fortune. Based on location alone, the business appeared to be successful. Minderedes had called ahead and when he and Tartaglia arrived, they were told that Ian Armstrong was finishing up a conference call and would be down shortly. They were shown into a large, thickly carpeted meeting room at the front of the building on the ground floor that reminded Tartaglia of an expensive dentist's waiting room.

'Black or white?' Minderedes asked, helping himself to coffee from the selection of hot and cold drinks on the side table.

'Black,' Tartaglia said, picking up a glossy brochure from a display rack by the door. The name 'Stoneleigh Park Hotel' was printed across a picture of a neo-classical Georgian mansion. Inside was a series of interior shots and a blurb about the place's history, its Michelin-starred restaurant and its spa. He had read about Stoneleigh Park somewhere, he thought, not that he had the time or reason to go to a place like that. Or maybe his sister, Nicoletta, had told him about it.

Minderedes brought two cups of coffee over to the table. 'You really think Lisa English is somehow involved in her husband's disappearance?' he asked.

'Anything's possible.' They had been through the various scenarios in the car together but nothing stood out. 'On paper, she has the most to gain financially.'

As Minderedes sat down, his phone started to ring. 'It's English's first wife,' he said, looking at the screen. 'I left a message for her. Shall I take it here?'

'No. You'd better go outside. Armstrong should be down any minute and I don't want him knowing what's going on. Tell her we need a DNA swab asap from her son. And while you're at it, call the office and see if we've had any more luck with the DNA samples from the mortuary. I'll come and find you when I'm done.'

A moment later, he heard the front door slam and saw Minderedes streak past the window, one hand futilely attempting to shield his hair from the rain, his mobile phone cradled in the other, as he ran in the direction of the car. Tartaglia looked around the high-ceilinged room, then got up from the table and went over to study the numerous framed business awards hanging on one of the walls. Some related to hotels, others to various property funds.

He had just finished his coffee and was debating whether to help himself to a refill when the door opened and a small, slim, grey-haired man walked in. He was conventionally dressed in a dark suit and white shirt, with a plain blue silk tie, and wore polished black lace-up shoes. Mr Nuts and Bolts was how Lisa English had described him; to Tartaglia he looked like an accountant, albeit a well-heeled one.

He held out his hand, with a flash of gold cufflink at the sleeve. 'I'm Ian Armstrong. I hear you've found Richard's wallet – and that there's a body. Can you tell me what happened?'

They sat down at the table and Tartaglia outlined the basic details of the car park fire.

'Are these his keys?' He passed Armstrong the clear plastic bag.

Armstrong peered at them, before passing them back. 'Those are definitely Richard's, I recognise the fob. So it looks like it's him in this car?' He spoke quietly, with an indeterminate northern twang.

'We're waiting for DNA confirmation.'

'But you're from a murder squad, so we're talking foul play?'

'It looks that way.'

Armstrong examined his well-manicured nails, and nodded thoughtfully. 'I suppose it's inevitable. I mean, I knew something must've happened to him, but where's he been all this time? That's what I'd like to know.'

'So would we, Mr Armstrong,' Tartaglia replied, studying Armstrong closely. His face gave little away but his reaction seemed genuine enough. 'Could you tell me a bit more about your business and Mr English's role in it?'

Armstrong leaned back in his chair and steepled his fingers in front of him. 'Richard and I have known each other for over forty years. We built this business up more or less from scratch and we have a number of interests. I deal mainly with the property side of things, while Richard was more involved with the hotels.'

'Stoneleigh Park's one of yours, then?' Tartaglia asked, gesturing towards the brochure.

'Yes. It's our flagship.'

'Is the business in good financial shape?'

Armstrong gave a faint smile, like a woman who'd been paid a compliment. 'I'd say so. We turned in a pre-tax profit last financial year of just under twenty million.'

'You and Richard English own the business?'

'We have some outside backers but we control the voting rights.'

'Is there any reason you can think of why Mr English might have wanted to disappear? Anything going on in his business he might have wanted to get away from?'

'No.' Armstrong's tone was emphatic. 'Naturally,' he continued, 'I went through all likely scenarios in my mind when he went missing, but there's no reason at all I can think of.'

'His wife seems to think it's a possible explanation.'

Armstrong rolled his eyes. 'I wouldn't go listening to Lisa, Inspector. She watches too much telly. Anyway, Richard's not the sort of man to run away from trouble.'

Tartaglia was surprised that Armstrong dismissed the idea so casually. If he had been secretly helping English in some way, either financially or in concealing his whereabouts, it would be traceable. But that didn't concern the murder investigation for now.

'Did Mr English have any enemies?' he asked.

Armstrong sighed. 'This is business, Inspector. You can't make an omelette without breaking eggs, as they say.'

'Enough for somebody to want to kill him?'

Armstrong shook his head. 'I don't see it. Everything we do is above board. We've never been on the wrong side of the law. We haven't had to.'

Again, this was something they would check more thoroughly in due course, if there was a stronger reason to do so. 'You reported Mr English as missing only a couple of hours after he failed to turn up to a meeting. You were pretty quick to raise the alarm.'

'It was a very important meeting with one of our major investors. Richard was supposed to lead it. When he didn't show and didn't call, I knew something was wrong.'

'It says in the report that he hadn't been in the office for a few days.'

'That's right. He'd been dealing with an issue at one of our hotels up in Scotland, but he was on the plane down to London that morning. His PA spoke to him just after he landed. He told her he was getting the Heathrow Express to Paddington and was going to stop by his flat to change his clothes before coming into the office. That's the last we heard of him. The missing person investigation was pretty unsatisfactory, so I hired a PI. He's an ex-copper and he went through everything, looked at all the angles, but he also drew a complete blank.'

'Who's the PI?' Tartaglia asked.

'A man called McCann. He came highly recommended.'

'Mike McCann?'

'I don't remember his Christian name but you can talk to him if you like.'

'Thank you. Is it possible Lisa helped Mr English to disappear?'

Armstrong frowned. 'Absolutely not.'

'Why is that such an odd idea?'

'Because it is. I knew everything that went on with Richard. *Everything*. We had no secrets. Besides, they weren't speaking.'

'OK,' Tartaglia said, surprised at his vehemence. 'Tell me a bit about their relationship, their marriage.'

'What's there to tell? Let's just say it had run its course and it was time to move on.'

'How did she feel about it?'

'How did she *feel*?' Armstrong looked puzzled, as though it was an odd question. 'Upset to start with, I guess. Nobody likes being yesterday's news.'

His tone was matter-of-fact, but genuine feelings, such as those Tartaglia sensed when talking to Lisa Armstrong, were not so easily dismissed. Maybe in Armstrong and English's

64

world feelings didn't matter, or didn't exist; maybe money was all that counted and people could be bought off.

'Could she have had a hand in his disappearance, do you think?' Tartaglia asked.

Armstrong looked at him thoughtfully. 'Bumped him off? I did wonder, what with his disappearing so soon after he filed for divorce. But if she was mixed up in it, she'd have needed help. I had McCann watch her – cost an arm and a leg – but according to McCann there was no evidence she was seeing someone else.'

'Was Richard English seeing anybody else?'

'A girlfriend, you mean?'

Tartaglia nodded.

'Nobody serious.'

'I'll need her name and details when we're done.'

Armstrong sighed. 'You're wasting your time. She knows nothing.' He leaned forward towards Tartaglia. 'Look, Inspector, neither of us was born with a silver spoon and we made it up the ladder the hard way. As far as Richard was concerned, the business was his family. He put everything into it and it was everything to him. Nothing else mattered.'

Tartaglia wondered if Armstrong was actually speaking for himself, although what he said tallied with Lisa English's account of what her husband had been like. But maybe Mike McCann would be able to reveal another angle.

'So, you'd describe Richard English as ruthless?'

'Single-minded, focussed, obsessive. Like all successful people, very driven.'

'If anything or anyone got in his way he'd remove them?'

'Yes. Though without breaking the law, obviously.'

'I hear you inherit some of Mr English's shares if he's declared dead. Is it a meaningful amount?'

'It gives me just enough for control of the business. That's the whole point of it.'

'How much are they worth?'

'The company's not quoted, but based on our last set of accounts and the valuation formula we use, they probably come to a few million pounds, that's all. But they're voting shares, as I said. The strategic value is worth a lot more than that to me. My will is made out in Richard's favour in exactly the same way.' He made it sound as though nothing could be more natural and fair.

Armstrong surely couldn't be so disingenuous, and it was Tartaglia's turn to smile. 'Yes, but you're sitting here, alive, Mr Armstrong, while he's missing.'

Armstrong's expression hardened. 'Before you go getting any silly ideas, I wouldn't have harmed a hair on Richard's head and I miss him more than anything. He was closer to me than anyone.'

Tartaglia returned his stare. 'Then what do *you* think happened to him? You must have a theory?'

Ian Armstrong leaned back in his chair and sighed. 'Honest to God, Inspector, I've absolutely no idea. I've thought about little else for the last two years, I can tell you, and I'd give a lot more than my right arm to find out.'

Even though he spoke forcefully, it didn't ring true. He must have formed some sort of an idea, however unlikely, about what had happened and why his business partner had disappeared without warning off the face of the earth. Given that he seemed to want to solve the mystery, it was odd that he didn't want to share his thoughts. They would need to look into English's finances, but assuming he wasn't in financial trouble, it gave Lisa English a strong motive to get rid of him. There was also the possibility that he was in some other kind of hot water and had needed to disappear. Maybe he had arranged it all to look as though he had been murdered, or possibly he and Lisa had arranged it together and the so-called split was just a cover story. But if so, who were the other victims in the burnt-out car?

Outside in the street, it had stopped raining. Tartaglia took a few deep breaths of the cold, damp air as he walked quickly along to where Minderedes was parked. He was struck again by the force of Armstrong's denial when he had suggested that English might have kept secrets from him, or might have planned to disappear without involving him. The reaction had seemed genuine, but maybe the man was a good actor.

The BMW idled in the parking bay, windscreen wipers flipping back and forth rhythmically. Tartaglia opened the door, slid into the warm passenger seat and stretched out his legs. Minderedes was still on his phone.

'He's here now,' he said to whoever was at the other end, glancing over quickly at Tartaglia. 'OK. I'll tell him.' He hung up. 'That was the Guv'nor. She wanted to know if we'd heard anything from Sam. I said we hadn't, so I think she's going to send Sharon over to see her.'

'Good idea,' Tartaglia replied. Donovan had been asleep when he left home early that morning, or at least the bedroom door had been closed, with no sign of a light on the other side. Things had been moving so fast since then that he'd had no time to call her to check how she was, let alone find out what was going on with the Dillon investigation. 'Any news on the DNA?'

'Not yet. They're still checking all the relevant databases. In the meantime, I've arranged to meet the first wife.'

'What about the son? When can we get a DNA sample?'

'She's ringing the school to sort it. Someone from the local station will be going out there to take the swab. Where to now?'

'I need to make a call. Did you ever come across a DI called Mike McCann when you were working up in Hendon?'

Nine

Tartaglia managed to get hold of Mike McCann almost immediately and had arranged to meet him in a coffee bar around the corner from the PI's office, just off Tottenham Court Road. Although the lunch hour was nearly over, the place was still full, with a queue stretching almost to the door. McCann sat hunched over a table at the back, reading a well-thumbed copy of the *Independent*.

'Didn't know you were a veggie,' Tartaglia remarked, sitting down after the initial pleasantries and scanning the short but interesting-sounding menu.

'I'm not,' McCann replied, his Northern Irish accent undiluted by more than twenty years of living in London. 'But it's the best place for miles. I could almost give up meat if my wife could learn to cook this sort of thing.'

Of medium height and build, with thinning brown hair and regular features, McCann had the sort of unremarkable looks that helped him blend into any crowd. He had worked undercover, both in his native Belfast during the Troubles and then for the Met for several years, before moving to a less frontline role. He had happily opted for early retirement and the last time Tartaglia had seen him was a few years back at his leaving do, in a pub near the Peel Centre in Hendon. McCann had subsequently set up in business as a private investigator with another ex-policeman, and word on the grapevine was that they were doing very well.

McCann ordered a plate of Moroccan-style meze, while Tartaglia decided on wild mushroom-stuffed pitta bread and a salad. The place wasn't licensed and both men chose coffees from a small but exotic list on the blackboard.

'So, you think you've found Richard English?' McCann said.

'We're not sure it's him yet, but there's a good chance. I need to find out more about what happened.' He didn't want to be evasive with McCann, but the less he said for the moment, the better.

McCann shifted in his seat, folded his hands on the table in front of him and gave him a look that said he understood the score. 'Well, Ian Armstrong brought me in after about a week, when there was no result from the missing person investigation. I can't fault what the team did, but you know what it's like.'

Tartaglia nodded. Missing Person investigations were a question of priorities and resources, and he was familiar with the statistics. Every year, in the UK, roughly two hundred thousand people went missing, usually of their own volition. Almost all turned up within a year of their disappearance and only a small number were never found.

'I got a look at the file,' McCann continued, 'and there was no indication that any crime had been committed. Armstrong insisted that English wasn't in any sort of financial trouble, so the general view was that he must have had some sort of mid life crisis or breakdown and had gone off somewhere, either on his own or possibly with a woman.'

'What's your view?'

McCann shrugged. 'He's not the type. No history of mental illness or issues with self-confidence; if anything, the opposite. He'd just initiated divorce proceedings and had moved out of the marital home. I interviewed a good cross-section of people who knew him – immediate family and friends of course – and people he worked with, as well as a couple of his clients. Nobody gave me the impression he was the sort of man who'd just wander off without telling anybody, or be led astray by the female sex.'

Tartaglia nodded. McCann's judgement was usually acute, and what he said tallied with the little he himself had already learned that day. 'Could there be some other reason why he wanted to make himself scarce, I wonder?'

'It's one of the first things I considered. But the man's the type who cares about how he puts his toothpaste on his toothbrush, and how the tube is squeezed.'

'I'm warming more and more to him by the minute.'

McCann's rubbery mask of a face cracked into a wide grin. 'If he'd decided to disappear, for whatever reason, he'd have planned it all very carefully. Instead, he leaves all sorts of unfinished business and loose ends, not least a highly important meeting to raise more cash for one of his new little pet ventures, as well as on going divorce proceedings. I quickly came to the conclusion that something must have happened to throw him off track.'

A teenage waitress came over with their coffees, which she plonked down unceremoniously in front of them, before moving on to the next table to take an order.

'Foul play, you mean?' Tartaglia said, once she was out of earshot, mopping his saucer with a couple of paper napkins.

McCann tipped the contents of his saucer back into the cup and took a gulp. 'Or something blew up in his face and he was forced to react on the spur of the moment. But I have to tell you, we found no hint of anything like that, so foul play seems the most likely. We know he arrived at Heathrow that morning from Edinburgh, and records for his mobile show he used it twice in and around the airport after he landed. One call was to the office, the other to a shop about a pair of shotguns he'd ordered. CCTV footage at Heathrow shows him going down into the tube for the Heathrow Express. He was carrying a small suitcase and that's the last we see of him. The suitcase was never found, by the way. A couple of the cameras at Paddington were on the blink so we have no visual, but the last location we have for his smartphone was in one of the side streets off Paddington station. We assume he went out to look for a taxi. He was living in a serviced apartment in Mayfair close to the office and, according to what he told his secretary, he was intending to go back there to drop off his things and change. We offered a substantial reward for information, but no taxi drivers came forward to say they picked him up near the station and there's no sign he ever made it back to his flat. The next thing we considered is that somewhere en route he'd had an accident or been mugged, and lost his ID. We checked with all the local hospitals and mortuaries, but nobody matching his description had been brought in either injured or dead. We monitored his bank accounts and credit cards but the last transaction was at Edinburgh Airport that morning, when he took out a thousand pounds in cash.'

'That's a lot.'

McCann shook his head. 'Not for him. He liked to pay for things in cash.'

'If he'd decided to disappear, he'd have needed help. Was the split with the wife genuine, in your view?'

'From what I can tell.'

'Then the obvious person to help him would be Ian Armstrong.'

McCann looked at him with watery eyes. 'I agree, but why bring me in, then? Why not just leave it to the police investigation? They were going nowhere with it fast. Instead, he spends a small fortune trying to find out what really happened.'

'Maybe it's a smokescreen. He can certainly afford it.'

McCann shook his head. 'I don't see the point; plus he seemed genuinely worried, almost panicked, I'd say.'

'He didn't seem like a man easily panicked when I saw him this morning.'

'This was two years ago. Maybe "panicked" is a bit strong. Let's say he was surprisingly emotional, even a little paranoid, for someone like him. Unless he's one of the best bloody actors I've ever seen, he wanted Richard English found, and preferably alive, PDQ.'

'Had either of them received any threats?'

'Armstrong said "no", quite categorically. I have to say I didn't come across anything to suggest it, although if they *had* been receiving threats from somewhere, it's not something they'd be happy to advertise.'

'But still, you'd think he'd say something about it to you, even if he didn't want the police involved.'

'I can't disagree with that.'

Tartaglia sipped his coffee. As thorough as McCann appeared to have been, had he missed something? Maybe the pair weren't as squeaky clean as they appeared. Maybe there was something Armstrong couldn't risk anybody knowing about, particularly an ex-cop like McCann. But if so, why hire him in the first place . . . He looked searchingly at McCann. 'If somebody was blackmailing English, who else would have known, apart from Armstrong?'

'I can't think of anyone. I got the impression they kept most things pretty tight between themselves.'

'OK. Leaving that to one side for the moment, what about

the wife, Lisa? Could she have either helped English disappear – or had him done away with?'

'I don't see her helping him, after the way he treated her. Nor do I think she's capable of acting on her own.'

'That's what Ian Armstrong said.'

'It was one of the first things he had me look into, but I found no trace at all of anyone else being involved, at least not during the time we had her under surveillance.'

'OK. So, if we rule out Armstrong and the wife, is there anyone else close to English who might want him dead?'

'His sons both seem pretty indifferent to him and his first wife hasn't got a kind word to say, although she's very happy to take his money. He had a few mates he kept in touch with, mainly people he'd worked with over the years, but other than the odd business dinner and such, he didn't have much of a personal life. Except for Ian Armstrong, he wasn't close to anybody.'

'From what you're saying, if something nasty happened to him it's more likely to be to do with the business?'

'That's the line of inquiry I'd have prioritised, but Armstrong didn't like it one bit when I suggested it. He insisted I was on the wrong track, and because he was paying for my time I couldn't push it. In the end he told me I'd done enough. He settled my bill and that was that. I've often wondered when it would all resurface. I was sure it was only a matter of time.'

Tartaglia finished his coffee and put the cup down. 'As I said, we're not sure it's English we've found, but his wallet and a set of keys belonging to him turned up at a crime scene a couple of weeks ago. There was no cash in the wallet, but it contained all the missing credit cards.'

'You're talking about a murder, obviously.'

'Yes. A car was doused in petrol and set on fire in a car park in South West London.' He chose his words carefully. He didn't want to lie, but for the moment he felt it necessary to conceal the full details of what had been found in the car. The fewer people that knew the truth, the better. 'What looks like the body of an adult male was lying curled up on the back seat, burnt to a crisp,' he went on. 'The only thing we have to go on at the moment are the wallet and keys, which were found on the ground near the car, presumably either dropped or planted there by the killer for some reason.'

'No DNA match, then?'

'The first sample came up negative, but it may not be relevant. We're now waiting for another sample for confirmation. In the meantime, is there anyone else you think I should talk to?'

McCann pursed his lips thoughtfully. 'There's a man called Colin Price. He's the former manager of one of the hotels and his name popped up several times when I talked to other people. He and English didn't see eye to eye and I think he was sacked, although there was some sort of threatened legal action and he was paid off before it got to court. I thought it sounded worth looking into, if only to get a different perspective, but I never got to talk to him. Armstrong put the brakes on, which I found interesting.'

'You think there was something dodgy?'

'I don't know, but he was quite insistent I was wasting my time going in that direction. I was still planning on going to see Price when Armstrong suddenly told me I'd gone far enough with the investigation and to send in my report. End of. I'll dig out Price's details when I get back to the office. Last I heard he was running some fancy hotel near Oxford, and . . .'

Just then, Tartaglia's phone started to ring and he saw DC Justin Chang's name on the screen. With an 'I must take this,' gesture to his companion, he answered it.

'We've got a DNA match for victim B, Sir,' Chang said. 'The torso belongs to an ex-con, name of Jake Finnigan. I'm pulling his CRO file now. When will you be back?'

Tartaglia looked at his watch. 'About four, if I'm lucky. I need to find out where Nick's got to.' He hung up and got to his feet. 'Sorry, Mike. Something's come up.'

McCann stood up. 'No problem. I'll email you a copy of the report I did for Ian Armstrong, plus Colin Price's details. If there's anything else that comes to mind, let me know.'

Ten

Sam Donovan opened her eyes and stared up at the ceiling. The fading light cast faint ripples of shadow across it. She had slept fitfully the previous night and most of that day, drifting in and out of sleep, the nightmares that flowed no worse than the nightmare of being awake. The drugs had helped temporarily, dulling the pain. But they couldn't make it go away entirely and she hated the unfocussed feeling they gave her, her mind like glue. Beneath it all, the pain was still there, every tiny thought and memory a trigger, but somehow, she had to get through it, put the horror of what had happened to one side so that she could help find Claire's killer. Nothing else mattered.

She put a couple of pillows behind her head and sat up in bed. She had opened the shutters earlier in the vain hope that the daylight might keep her awake; now she stared out at the dark grey sky, watched little bursts of rain spattering against the window like handfuls of fine gravel. Soon it would be dark. She reached across and turned on the bedside light. It was a nice room, with a high ceiling and a large window overlooking the back garden. It was painted white like the rest of the flat, with bare, scrubbed wooden boards and minimal furniture. As a bedroom, it was clean and functional and tidy, the way Tartaglia liked his things. But she found it impersonal. She missed her own room with its mixture of colours and all her bits and pieces, although she was glad to be away from her house for the moment.

77

She wondered if Tartaglia minded her staying with him and if he had thought it odd her asking. After everything that had happened between them or – more importantly – not happened, it did seem a bit strange, almost surreal, to be lying here now in his bed. Their relationship had never been straightforward: there was a closeness on both sides that went beyond friendship, or at least that was what she had always thought. But things that should have been said, had been left unsaid for too long and eventually it had felt as though an insurmountable gulf had opened up between them. It was just not meant to be, and she had decided that she needed to move on. Since she had last seen him a few months before, she had left the Met and moved part-time to Bristol. Her world had changed and she thought she had too. The change of routine and physical distance had been useful to mark the boundary between the old and the new; it had also been good to forget what Tartaglia looked like for a while. But deep down, whatever their differences, whatever awkwardness had crept between them, coupled with the few months of ensuing silence, she still trusted him more than anyone else. When put on the spot by Steele the previous night, told to move out of her home, his flat was the only place she had wanted to go to.

She glanced at the small digital clock on the bedside table. It was just after three in the afternoon. The day was slipping away and she must force herself to get up. The first forty-eight hours in a murder investigation were crucial and she was wasting precious time. There were things she could be doing, people she should see. She had decided to go and talk to Steele. She had nothing to lose and she needed to find out as much as she could about what had happened. Perhaps there was a role for her to play in the investigation . . . She stretched her arms up above her head, then swung her legs out of bed. As she got to her feet, she felt suddenly giddy and sank back down on the edge of the bed. She noticed that she was still dressed in the T-shirt and jeans from the night before. The combination of wine and pills had knocked her out quickly and she had no recollection of going to bed at all; her last memory was of sitting on the sofa with Tartaglia's arm around her, her head against his chest. The previous few months of distance between them had melted away and it had felt almost like old times. He must have carried her into the bedroom and taken off her boots, which she now spotted neatly placed in a corner, with her cardigan hung over the back of a chair. He had been caring in every detail and she was pleased again that she had insisted on coming to him. Yawning, she stood up again, took a few moments to steady herself, then went into the kitchen. She put on the kettle and rummaged around in the cupboards until she found an unopened pack of English Breakfast tea. Tartaglia was a habitual coffee drinker, and she wondered how it had got there. Maybe it was left over from someone else who had come to stay, although she couldn't imagine who. She certainly hadn't seen any signs of female occupation in the flat so far. Not that she cared about that any longer.

Once the tea had brewed, she added a little milk and went into the sitting room to find Claire's satchel. It had been sitting in the hall at their house, underneath the small table, and she had spotted the mini iPad she had given Claire for Christmas slotted between a newspaper and a couple of women's magazines. In all the commotion of their house being searched and of her leaving to go to Tartaglia's, she had managed to pick it up and bring it with her without it being noticed. They had Claire's phone and personal laptop to work on, after all, and at least she had Claire's iPad. The code was probably her sister's birthday, which she used for almost everything. The iPad was synched with Claire's laptop and phone and would have a copy of her calendar and contacts.

But before seeing Steele, there was somebody else she needed to talk to; somebody who knew a lot more than she did about the day-to-day minutiae of Claire's life.

On the drive back to their offices in Barnes, Minderedes gave Tartaglia the gist of his interview with Richard English's first wife. Although she had added nothing new to their knowledge of her former husband, she had at least confirmed the picture of him painted by Lisa English, as well as corroborating the fact that English was definitely intending to divorce Lisa and that they were not on speaking terms. The clocks had gone back just over a week before and it was already dark as they crossed the Thames at Hammersmith Bridge. Nestled in a sharp loop in the river, Barnes was an absurdly rural pocket of London, more village than city, populated by professionals and media types, and with a remarkably low crime rate compared to most other London boroughs. Their offices were located half way along Station Road, in between the Green and the Common. The long, low brick building belonging to the Met dated from the Seventies and was considered a bit of an eyesore amongst the traditional, late Victorian housing that surrounded it. The building was closed off to the public from the road, with the main entrance through a car park at the rear, protected from the street by solid and anonymous high wooden gates. Few of the locals even knew the police worked there. There had been talk of the building being sold for redevelopment and the squads being relocated to more modern premises, but that had been going on for as long as Tartaglia could remember. In the meantime, they had to put up with the cramped and basic working conditions, the temperamental heating system that left a pervasive smell of damp in the winter, and the lack of decent air conditioning in the summer to cool the dusty, dirty, oven-like conditions. He counted himself lucky to spend more time out of the office than in it.

Once inside the gates, he left Minderedes to worry about where to put his car – somebody having taken what he considered to be his parking space – and walked across the yard to the main entrance door. The air was damp and it was threatening to rain again, a few warning drops falling on his face as he headed for the entrance. He heard a series of explosions coming from somewhere close to the road and caught the sulphurous whiff of gunpowder, along with wood smoke, carried by the wind. It was Guy Fawkes Night, he suddenly remembered. Although only late afternoon, fireworks parties were already starting and he wondered for a moment what his young nephew and niece had planned.

He went inside and up the main stairs to the first floor where the two murder squads, part of Homicide West Command, were based. The small, open-plan office at the front of the building was half full and he found DC Justin Chang sitting at his desk, leafing through some papers. Chang, in his early thirties, was originally from Hong Kong but had gone to school and university in the UK and had travelled the world before joining the Met.

Chang looked up. 'This is the man,' he said, handing Tartaglia some printouts.

Tartaglia leafed through them quickly. The mug shots showed the acne-scarred face and shaved head of forty-two-year-old ex-con Jake Patrick Finnigan; the record outlined a career in burglary and theft. It was a familiar story of a man who had spent more time in jail than out of it since his late teenage years, and there was nothing remarkable about it apart from the contrast with Richard English. Both came from humble backgrounds, but that was where any similarity stopped. What could possibly be the connection between them – if, indeed, there was one?

'He was paroled just over six months ago and hasn't been seen or heard of since,' Chang continued.

'Who are the next of kin?'

'According to the file, there's a wife in White City. The local station is sending someone round to break the news, as we speak. Her address is on the back page.'

'Thanks. I'll go and see her now. Any news on the other body parts?'

'Dave is still chasing.' Chang jerked his head in the direction of Dave Wightman, phone cradled under his ear.

'I'll be back for the meeting later on. Any news on the Dillon case?'

'Haven't heard anything, they're all out.' Chang hesitated before adding, 'How's Sam?'

Tartaglia stared at Chang, knowing that it was a loaded question, but Chang's broad face gave nothing away. 'She's not good, as you can imagine. You should go and see her.'

Chang nodded vaguely. 'I'll leave it a few days, let her have some space. Send her my love.' He swung back to his computer.

It was well known that Chang and Sam Donovan had had some sort of relationship before she left the Met, and it had possibly continued for a while after, although he had also heard via the grapevine that she had broken it off and that Chang had been upset about it. He had no idea why Donovan hadn't stuck with Chang. He was tall, nice-looking and bright, and had the settled air of someone comfortable in his own skin with nothing to prove. From a male perspective, he came across as a decent sort and interesting to talk to, although Tartaglia had long since given up thinking he could anticipate what a woman, and particularly Sam Donovan, would find attractive in another man. As far as he could tell, Chang was a much better bet for a long-term relationship than most, himself included, but Donovan had never seen sense on that score. He remembered a time when she had been edging towards some sort of involvement with another policeman, Simon Turner, a dysfunctional, difficult man and a serial adulterer. He had been totally unable to fathom what had attracted Donovan to Turner. At least Turner was well out of the picture, but it was a shame that things hadn't worked out with Chang. He wondered how Chang felt about it, and if Chang minded Donovan staying in his flat. No doubt Chang wasn't happy with the idea; he himself wouldn't have been, in Chang's place.

'Call her,' he said firmly to Chang, before turning to go. 'She needs her friends around her.' He knew it was a disingenuous remark, but what else could he say? The more people who went to visit Sam the better, and he was sure Chang was man enough to cope.

Eleven

'I still can't believe it,' Nicola Dawson said, her swollen eyes focussed on Sam Donovan. 'It doesn't seem real. I mean, I only saw her two days ago and she . . .' Tears began again.

Sam Donovan nodded, biting her lip as she reached out to Nicola and clasped her hand across the table, squeezing it for a moment. The bare contact gave her more comfort than anything that anybody had said or done in the past twenty-four hours. But what could she say? Nothing could make it any better for either of them.

They were sitting by the window of a Starbucks near Baker Street tube. Large patches of condensation obscured the glass, providing a welcome screen from the people hurrying past in the dark street on their way home. Nobody would probably give a damn about two women crying together in a café, but Donovan was happy to have some privacy. Small and plump, with shoulder-length wavy brown hair, Nicola had been Claire's assistant for over ten years and knew her better than most. She was a single parent and Claire had been godmother to her six-year-old daughter. They lived in Neasden and Nicola had agreed to meet Donovan on her way home from the office in Chancery Lane. She had said she needed to be home by seven but, like Donovan herself, she didn't appear to be in a hurry, welcoming the opportunity to talk about Claire. Donovan wondered whether they would have been better to go to the pub and have a few drinks, but in her current state she knew coffee was a more sensible option, particularly as she was going to see Steele afterwards.

'Did they say anything this morning about what had happened?' she asked Nicola after a moment. Detectives – people she knew and had once worked with – had been into Claire's office to speak to everybody there who had worked directly with her sister. It felt odd referring to them so impersonally, to think of it all in motion while she was on the outside, out of the loop when it mattered more than ever before. But it was something she was going to have to get used to.

Nicola blew her nose loudly. 'They said very little. There was more in the *Evening Standard* than what they told us.'

'I haven't seen a paper but I know she went to meet a man in a hotel,' Donovan said, not caring if it was supposed to be generally known. She was still struggling to remember the few things Tartaglia had told her the night before, some of the details temporarily lost in the fog left over from sleep and pills. 'Do you have any idea who it might be? Last I remember, she was complaining about never meeting anyone she fancied, but that was back in the summer.'

Nicola shook her head. 'They asked that. I haven't a clue who he is, but I knew there was someone that she'd started seeing. I took a message from him a couple of times. His name was Robert.'

'It's a false name. Do you have any idea where she met him?'

Nicola looked down at her cold, un-drunk mug of coffee for a moment. 'It wasn't the Internet or speed-dating, or anything like that. He sent her flowers – a huge bunch of lilies and roses, with lots of shiny paper and red ribbon. I remember thinking he must've spent a fortune when I went to collect them from reception.'

'Do you remember the name of the company they came from?'

'The police asked me that, but I don't remember, just the colour of the ribbon. I gave them to her when she got back from a meeting and she looked so surprised. Really bowled over. I asked her what was the special occasion and at first she seemed a bit embarrassed. But then she told me she had met some bloke, and that it had been something really funny, like in the movies; he'd bumped into her in the street – walked straight into her while he was talking on his phone. He was carrying a takeaway cup of coffee and he spilled some on her sleeve. It burned her arm and made her drop what she was carrying.'

'Where was this?'

'Right in front of the office.'

'So he works nearby?'

Nicola stared at her blankly. 'Why do you say that?'

She had probably had more than enough for one day and Donovan was sorry to have to keep probing, but she needed to find out everything Nicola knew. 'If you're carrying a cup of coffee you can't be going far,' Donovan said. 'I mean, you wouldn't go on the tube or get into a taxi with a cup of coffee, would you? And it's double yellows for miles around there so he couldn't have been in a car or a van, unless he had a driver.'

'I suppose you're right, but she never said.'

Nicola still looked dazed and Donovan made a mental note to keep her thoughts to herself. 'Sorry, I didn't mean to interrupt. Please go on with what happened.'

Nicola took a deep breath. 'Well, as I said, when he knocked into her, she dropped some things and he helped her pick them up. He was really apologetic and asked her where she worked and then he sent her the flowers.'

'She must have told him her name?'

'I guess so. She said she knew it was all a bit of a cliché but it was actually really romantic. Cliché or not, who does that sort of thing these days?'

Who indeed, Donovan thought. It was all sounding like some cheesy rom-com starring Jennifer Aniston. Like most City lawyers, Claire's working day was a long one and she often used to take papers home at the weekend. There was little room for a personal life, something she had complained about, although she had loved her job too much to make a change. As Donovan knew all too well from her own experience, the lack of a personal life could drive even the sanest and most independent of women to take risks and do some very stupid things. If nothing else, it would have made Claire so much more susceptible to somebody peddling a bit of old-fashioned romance. Had the coffee incident been a set-up? If so, what was it about Claire that had made him target her? Or was she being too cynical; had it, in fact, just been a genuine accident, with a fatal conclusion? Whichever the case, he had to have had charm and, knowing Claire, to have been decent-looking, to have succeeded in developing things further.

'Did she say what he looked like?'

'No. But I could tell she found him very attractive, although she didn't really speak of him much after that.'

'Did you say all of this to the detective you saw this morning?'

Nicola nodded and dabbed at her eyes with a clean tissue. 'I'm sorry, but I'd best be going now,' she said after a moment. 'I'd love to stay and talk all night but Olivia's going to be wondering if I'm ever coming home. It's the last thing I want to do after what's happened, but I said I'd take her to this fireworks party. My mum's looking after her but she can't cope with all the bangs.'

*　　*　　*

Tartaglia walked along the Uxbridge Road until he came to The Dog 'n' Bone. He had just been to see Finnigan's ex-wife, Tasha, who seemed very pleased to learn of his death. Parallels with Lisa English sprang easily to mind. According to Tasha, the last time she had seen Finnigan was just after he got out of jail six months before. He had appeared on her doorstep out of the blue asking for money, but she had sent him away and threatened to call the police if he didn't leave her alone. She said she had no idea what had happened to him after that, but suggested Tartaglia talk to an old friend of Finnigan's, a man named Mick Chapman, who lived not far away. She said she thought her ex had been staying with him when he came out of prison, and that at that hour, Chapman was usually to be found in his local pub.

It was one of a dying breed of old-fashioned boozers, with patterned carpet, dark furniture and mirrors plastering the green walls. A large, middle-aged woman stood behind the counter, polishing glasses. Tartaglia asked for Chapman and she gestured towards a man in a far corner of the room, seated at a table beside a couple of slot machines. His eyes were fixed on a TV on the opposite wall, which was showing a Premier League match, and he didn't seem to notice Tartaglia approach.

'Are you Mick Chapman?' Tartaglia asked.

'Yes,' the man said flatly, eyes still on the screen. 'Who wants to know?' He was thin and wiry, with short mousy brown hair, and wore paint-stained jeans, a red polo-neck and an old denim jacket.

'I'm Detective Inspector Mark Tartaglia.' Chapman looked round and he held out his warrant card. 'I'm afraid I've got some bad news. Your friend Jake—'

Alarm filled his large blue eyes and he got to his feet, hands hovering at his sides. 'Have you found him?' He looked to be roughly the same age as Jake Finnigan, although based on what

Tartaglia had seen of Finnigan's file, he was a good ten inches shorter and half his weight.

'Please sit down, Mr. Chapman,' Tartaglia said, pulling up a chair. 'I'm afraid Jake Finnigan's dead.' He waited for the words to sink in, watching Chapman's reaction closely.

Chapman sank back down into his chair, but said nothing, glancing away again towards the TV. After a moment, his face turned red and his lips puckered as though he was about to cry, but no tears came. He gave a heavy, broken sigh and took a large gulp of beer. 'I knew it. I knew something were wrong,' he muttered, then looked up at Tartaglia. 'What happened?'

'He was murdered,' Tartaglia said, still watching him. Chapman seemed unaffected by the words, as though he had assumed from the start that it wasn't an accident. He had the greyish, papery skin of a heavy smoker and Tartaglia noticed his fingers were heavily stained and twitching with nervous energy. He recognised the signs. 'Would you like to go outside for a smoke?'

Chapman nodded. He picked up his glass and followed Tartaglia outside to the street.

'I'm sorry but I need to ask you some questions,' Tartaglia said, as Chapman took a tobacco tin out of his pocket and set about rolling a cigarette. 'When did you last see him?'

'Months ago. He were waiting for me when I come home. He were just out of the nick that day and needed a place to stay. Tasha wouldn't have him back home, so I said he could kip on my sofa 'til he got himself sorted.'

'You say you knew something must have happened. What do you mean?'

Chapman shrugged and lit the cigarette, taking a long, deep drag before answering. 'He went out one evening and he never come home.'

'Where was he going?'

'To meet some bird.'

'You mean his wife?'

'Tasha? No bloody way. No, it was someone new.'

'You're sure of that?'

Chapman scratched his head. 'Yeah, I think so. Anyways, he left his stuff in my flat and when he didn't come back, I knew something was up.'

'Did he mention the woman's name?'

He looked up at Tartaglia surprised, as though the thought had only just occurred to him. 'No. Don't think he did.'

'What else do you remember?'

'We was sat watching the telly and having a beer. Then he gets a text from this bird – now I think about it, I'm sure he said she's Russian – there's these texts going back and forwards for about half an hour, and he's laughing and stuff at whatever she's saying.'

'What was she saying?'

'Search me. Then he says he's off out.'

'He didn't tell you where he was going?'

'No. He just said not to wait up for him. He had a big grin all over his face.'

'He took his mobile with him?'

Chapman nodded. 'Must've done.'

'Can you give me the number, please?'

'His phone's been switched off all this time.'

'I still need the number.'

Chapman took out his phone and, squinting at it, reeled off the number.

'When he didn't come home, were you worried?'

Chapman frowned. 'No. I wasn't his effing keeper.'

Tartaglia stared at him for a moment, wondering if he was

telling the truth. Chapman struck him as very incurious. Had Finnigan really not said anything about the woman he was going out to meet? Had Chapman not asked him how he knew her and where he was going? If they'd been a pair of close female friends, he wouldn't have believed it for a second. But thinking of himself and his cousin Gianni, and what his sister described as their appalling communication skills, he supposed it was plausible. There were some things that didn't need to be said; they were simply understood. Maybe it had been like that between Chapman and Finnigan too.

'How long had he been staying with you when he disappeared?'

'About a week, maybe.'

'Did he use any of the social networking sites?'

Chapman shook his head. 'He wasn't into computers.'

'What about email?'

'No, far as I know.'

'What about when he was inside, how did he keep in touch with you?'

'I'd go and see him, leastways when he was in the Scrubs.'

Tartaglia made a mental note to check where Finnigan had been in prison over the previous few years and what visitors he had had during his last stretch. 'Did you report his being missing to the police?' he asked.

Chapman looked at him as though he were mad. 'You think they'd care about a bloke like Jake?' He cleared his throat and shook his head. 'They'd fucking laugh me out of town.'

It was a fair point. With resources scarcer than ever and nearly a thousand people reported missing in the UK every day, the majority in the London area, there had been a recent move to cut back on missing person investigations. Only the disappearance of people thought to be vulnerable or at risk, or where their disappearance was out of character, was fully checked out. Other than logging the call, someone with an itinerant and criminal background like Finnigan would have no doubt been treated as 'absent' rather than 'missing' and his disappearance would not have been looked into. 'OK. Do you still have his things?'

'Yeah. I hung onto them in case he comes back. They're at home in my room.'

'Right. Finish your pint, Mr Chapman, and let's go and get them.'

They walked together in silence for a few blocks, crossed the Uxbridge Road, then Chapman stopped outside a KFC on a corner.

'The flat's upstairs. You want to come up or wait out here?'

'I'll come up,' Tartaglia replied. He wanted to make sure Chapman didn't remove anything from Finnigan's bag.

The entrance was in the side street, just past the KFC window. Inside, the communal parts were shabby and piles of post lay uncollected on the dirty carpet. The place smelled as though someone had been cooking curry recently. He followed Chapman up the narrow stairs to the first floor and waited while he unlocked the door.

Chapman switched on the light and took Tartaglia along a passageway to the bedroom. There was little furniture, just a mattress on the floor and a wardrobe in one corner, but it was tidy. The bed was made, and a couple of pairs of trainers and a pair of heavy-duty work boots were lined up under the window. Chapman heaved a heavy-looking rucksack down from the top of the wardrobe, almost falling over in the process, and dropped it at Tartaglia's feet.

'That's everything he had with him. When he didn't come back I put all the things he'd left lying around the flat inside it.

Probably smells a bit by now, but it's all in there.' He sniffed, put his hands in his pockets and looked at Tartaglia anxiously. 'What do you think happened to him?'

'We're trying to find out. His body was found in the back of a burnt-out car. He was already dead when the car was set on fire.'

Chapman looked puzzled. 'What, you mean this has only just happened?'

'Yes. Just over a week ago.'

'So where's he been since May?'

Probably cut up in pieces in someone's freezer, Tartaglia wanted to say. Instead he replied, 'We're still trying to put it all together. Thank you for your time, Mr Chapman. You've been a great help. If you think of anything else, please give me a call.'

Twelve

Adam was in Kit's small basement kitchen, opening a bottle of wine from Kit's cellar, when he heard the front door above him slam shut, followed by heavy footsteps on the bare boards in the hall. He froze. He ran through in his mind everything Kit had told him about the house; there had been no mention of anybody else having a key. Instead of turning down the stairs to the kitchen, the footsteps grew fainter and it sounded as though the person was going upstairs. Adam put down the bottle, quickly wiped his hands on a tea towel, then picked up a large, sharp knife from the block by the cooker. He took off his shoes and slowly crept upstairs, wincing at every creak of the ancient boards. He was nearly on the first-floor landing when he heard the footsteps thundering back down towards him. With his back to the wall, he braced himself, knife behind his back.

A tall young man in grey tracksuit bottoms and a matching hoodie bounded around the turn in the stairs at the half-landing above him and stopped abruptly as he caught sight of Adam.

'Who the hell are you?'

'I'm a friend of Kit's,' Adam replied. 'Who are you?'

'Strange he never mentioned you,' the man said, staring down at him with the arrogance of somebody who had a right to be there. 'What are you doing here?'

'I'm staying for a few days, that's all. What about you? I wasn't expecting anybody.'

'Clearly not.' The man was eyeing him up and down in an unembarrassed fashion. He was barefoot and extremely muscular, with very short, fair hair and a deeply tanned face. Kit had never mentioned having any immediate family and he didn't look like he was related to Kit, who was not particularly tall and slightly built, and had thinning, brownish hair. Nor did the man fit the description of any of Kit's ex-lovers, from what Adam remembered of Kit's occasional drunken musings and the motley collection of old photographs Kit kept in an old shoe box in his study. He was far too young, for starters, and too good-looking, although maybe Kit had deliberately omitted to mention him. It wouldn't be the first time; the little shit had slyly kept so many important details from him, partially out of spite as well as a foolish and mistaken desire to fascinate and tantalise. But whoever the man was, if he knew Kit, Adam would have to be careful.

'Are those your things in Kit's room?' the man asked.

'Yes. What about it?'

'And your name is?'

Adam returned the man's stare. 'Tom.' It tripped easily off his tongue, the first of the handful of aliases he used that came to mind. It was also the one that Kit called him, which was useful in case Kit had talked about him to anybody. The man had the manner of someone used to giving orders and someone who would probably know a lie when he heard one. But it was too late to worry about that.

'Well, *Tom*,' the man said, as though the name was open to question, his eyes still locked with Adam's, 'I suggest you move your stuff down to the spare room. I always sleep in Kit's room when I'm here. I take it he's away, then?'

'Yes. He's still in Thailand. And who are you?'

'My name's Jonny.'

He studied the man's expression. He was expert at reading people and something told him the man was lying. But did it matter? He decided to let it pass for the moment. The man clearly had a key to Kit's house, so maybe he had Kit's permission to be there. There was no point in stirring up trouble unnecessarily.

'Kit never mentioned you,' Adam said.

'Well, he never mentioned you either. When's he due back?'

'Another month or so, I think.'

'And how do you know him?'

'We were in the same house together at school,' Adam said. 'Although he was a bit older. We ran into each other when I was out in Thailand.' He had rehearsed the story many times and it sounded fluent enough to his ears. 'What about you?'

'Kit and I go back a long way. Do you have his permission to be here?'

Controlling his anger, Adam smiled. Normally, he would never allow someone to interrogate him in this way, but he had to keep calm. He couldn't risk any form of confrontation, let alone further questions being asked. Maybe if he was polite the man would let it drop. 'Of course I do. He gave me his key and told me to make myself at home.'

'Yes, I saw it on the hall table. I recognised the fob. Now, if you don't mind, I'm bloody knackered. I'd be grateful if you'd clear your stuff out of Kit's room PDQ. I need a shower and then bed. And I'm famished. I hope there's some food in the fridge.' He spoke as though he was entitled to what was there.

He started down the stairs towards Adam. For a big man, he moved with the grace of a cat, at home in his own skin and physicality. He also appeared at home in Kit's house. He had to be one of Kit's ex-lovers, although he wasn't at all what Adam had imagined to be Kit's type, nor did it make sense that someone like him would be interested in a weak, vacillating, wreck of a man like Kit. Maybe he was after Kit's dwindling trust fund. Adam flattened himself against the wall to let him pass, the knife still concealed behind his back. He wanted to shove it hard between the man's broad shoulders as he pushed past, but he checked the urge. He needed to find out more information, see how long he intended to stay, and then he would make a plan.

Thirteen

Sam Donovan paused outside Detective Chief Inspector Carolyn Steele's door, her hand raised ready to knock. It felt odd being back at the office in Barnes. She had worked there for a couple of years before quitting. Now, only a few months on, stepping into the building and walking up the stairs to the first floor, it seemed like an alien world and she felt unexpectedly nervous. The official view when she had announced her departure was that she simply needed a change. Everybody had wished her well and appeared to understand. That it had had as much to do with Mark Tartaglia as anything else, was something she had refused to acknowledge to anybody, although she knew there had been talk. Sharon Fuller was sharper than most and had certainly guessed the truth. With the benefit of hindsight, what had happened between her and Tartaglia felt less relevant now, and certainly a lot less painful than before. Maybe she had acquired some immunity, or perhaps the official view was right: all she had needed was a change.

She heard voices along the corridor, a man and a woman coming her way. As she listened, she recognised the man's as Justin Chang's. It sounded as though they had stopped by the coffee machine. It had been a while since she had last spoken to him, when she had broken off their relationship. He had taken it badly, refusing to accept the simple explanation she had given about needing to be on her own. Deep down, she still had mixed feelings about it and wondered if she had made a mistake. At times, particularly late at night when she'd had a drink or two, she felt lonely and she missed him. But it wasn't enough to warrant getting back together. She certainly didn't want to see him now, not in her current state. She felt too raw to cope with his sympathy, let alone anything else he might say . . .

She knocked on Steele's door and heard the DCI say 'Come in.'

Again she hesitated, but Chang's voice was coming closer. Taking a deep breath, she pushed open the door and went inside. Steele was sitting behind her desk, back to the window, reading some papers. The room was small, and tidy to the point of emptiness – none of the personal clutter most people gathered around themselves at work. Steele had been in the Barnes office for just over a year, yet it was as though she had just moved in and all her things were still in boxes somewhere, waiting to be unpacked. It was already dark outside but she hadn't bothered to draw the blinds. Lights were on in the terrace of low-built houses opposite and Donovan heard a loud bang from somewhere close by that made her jump, followed by childish screeches of excitement. A rocket cut through the sky, sending a shower of red and gold across the horizon.

'Yes,' Steele said impatiently, eyes down, still reading.

'It's me. I hope you don't mind . . .'

Steele looked up. 'Oh, it's you, Sam. What are you doing here?' She got up from behind her desk and came over to Donovan. Broad-hipped and broad-shouldered, she was dressed in her normal combination of dark trouser suit and plain shirt. It was a uniform she rarely varied, as though she couldn't be bothered to think of a different outfit, or wasn't interested. 'Come and sit down, will you?' She motioned Donovan to the small sofa against the wall by the door, pulled up a chair and sat down opposite. Her short black hair gleamed under the overhead light. As usual, she was wearing a minimal amount of make-up but her brows and features were strong and she didn't need much help to look striking. Aware that her own appearance left a lot to be desired – hair soaked and flattened by the rain and no make-up to cover her swollen, red eyes – Donovan consoled herself with the thought that at least the coat she had helped herself to from Tartaglia's wardrobe was so large on her that it easily disguised the motley array of garments underneath.

Steele crossed one leg over the other and leaned back in her chair. 'So, Sam, what can I do for you?'

'I want to know what's going on. Is there any news?'

Steele shook her head slowly. 'Sam, I'm really not sure I—'

'Please. I'm feeling a lot more together now, and I need to know what's happened. I don't want to have to read about it in dribs and drabs in the papers.' She looked into Steele's strange yellowy-green eyes, willing her to give a little.

For a while Steele said nothing, looking at her equally intently, as though trying to read her thoughts. The only sound in the room was the machine-gun popping and whizzing of fireworks coming from outside. Eventually Steele sighed. 'I can understand where you're coming from, Sam, and I guess in your shoes I'd want the same thing. But if I fill you in, will you be able to leave it there? I don't think so. You'll want to be a part of what's going on and you can't be. I know it sounds harsh, particularly after what's happened, but you've left this world behind.'

'I know, but Claire's my sister. I promise not to get in the way. I just want to feel in touch. Not shut out. Do you understand? It's horrible being in the dark.'

Again Steele was silent, her eyes still on Donovan.

'Please,' Donovan said. She felt it was her last chance.

Still looking intently at Donovan, Steele put her head to one side and scratched her lip thoughtfully. 'If I give you some info, do you promise to leave it alone?'

'Of course.'

'You *must* stay out of things, you understand?'

'Yes.'

'You were a good detective and I wish you were still working for me now, but you will have to keep your detecting instincts under lock and key. You're not part of this investigation. Is that understood?'

'Yes. Yes, I will.'

'Alright. And this is not to go further than this room.' She waited until Donovan nodded her assent before continuing. 'From the little we've been able to piece together from Claire's emails and what her phone provider has given us, she was having some sort of an affair with this man – the man she went to meet in the hotel. It appears that they met by chance and it all started up quite recently, only a few months ago.'

'When exactly?'

'The first text from her is a thank-you for lunch. It was sent on the twenty-ninth of August.'

Donovan thought back. The date meant nothing, but she would look in her diary. She'd been in Bristol at that time, trying to sort out digs and other things in preparation for the academic year ahead. She had barely seen her sister, and when she had it had been pretty rushed. She noted that Steele had left out the details of exactly where and how Claire had met the man, and hadn't mentioned the flowers he had sent her. Did she think it was unimportant, or had she decided to give Donovan just the very bare bones? Probably the latter, but if she asked about it and let on that she had spoken to Nicola, the shutters would come down and Steele wouldn't tell her anything more.

'Can you trace him from the texts and emails?' she asked.

'I was coming to that. He told her he lived in Manchester, but the address he gave at the hotel is false, as, I'm sure, is the name Robert Herring. The phone chip he used is untraceable. However, both the emails he sent her and the calls he made to her, came from in and around the London area. West London, to be more precise.'

'So, he lied. There's a surprise.' She felt a surge of anger and tears flooded her eyes. She wiped them away quickly with her sleeve, but they kept coming.

Steele got up and went over to her desk. She opened one of the drawers, took out a bottle of Rémy Martin and a glass and poured a large measure.

'Here,' she said, coming back to where Donovan sat. 'This should help.' She passed her the glass, together with a box of tissues, then sat down again. 'Are you sure you want to hear this, Sam? We can save it for another time if you like.'

Donovan blew her nose forcefully and took a slug of brandy. It caught on the back of her throat, making her cough, but the instant warmth felt good. 'It's OK. I'll be fine. Please go on.'

'There's no identifiable geographic pattern, unfortunately.'

'As though he knew someone might look for it.'

'Maybe. That email address and phone chip were only used for contacting your sister, nobody else.'

'So you're suggesting he did this deliberately?'

'It's looking that way.'

'But why?'

'It could be a simple explanation. He's married, or lives with someone. Whether he meant to kill her, or just deceive her, is another matter. It's very possible things just got out of hand in the hotel room.'

'Do you believe that?'

There was a momentary pause before Steele replied. 'Difficult to tell at the moment. There are a number of conflicting possibilities. Say he's married, wants a bit of fun on the side, a bit of romance. He gets himself a throwaway phone and an email address and tells her he lives out of London to explain why he's not always available. According to the texts between them, they met several times and had had dinner twice before. Your sister books the room, thinking she's in for a lovely, romantic evening, then something goes wrong. There's an almighty fight. He ends up killing her and then he legs it, just before one in the morning.'

'But you must have found his DNA, surely?'

Steele shrugged. 'It's a hotel, and the room's been occupied more or less without a break ever since the hotel opened a few months ago. There's no sign of sexual contact, if that's what you're getting at . . .'

Donovan frowned, trying to think it all through. What had Claire been doing there?

'Maybe he's a client or a business contact . . .'

Even as she spoke she remembered what Nicola had told her and realised her error, unless of course Claire had lied to Nicola. But why would she? Claire could have explained away the flowers any number of ways. If only she could get rid of the fog in her brain, maybe things would become clearer. She took another large sip of the brandy, letting it warm in her mouth before swallowing. No sexual contact. What was the point of the hotel room then?

'That's very odd,' she said after a moment, as dispassionately as possible. Steele looked at her and said nothing. 'I mean,'

Donovan continued, 'what man would lure a woman up to a hotel room if he didn't want sex?'

'I agree. Maybe things got out of hand very quickly and there wasn't the chance.'

'There's another way of looking at it,' Donovan said, after a moment. 'Maybe from the outset he meant to kill her.'

'OK, but if that's what he wanted, why go to so much trouble? If he wanted her dead, there must be so many easier ways to do it. And, anyway, why would he want her dead? He's not some ex-lover gone berserk, she barely knew him. The texts from both of them make it all very clear. We've checked the system and there's no record of anything similar happening anywhere else in the country, which is why I feel that, for some reason, it all went pear-shaped up in the hotel room.'

Steele spoke in her usual quick, clipped manner. She seemed to be talking frankly, but Donovan was sure it was an edited version. The strange, little, quirky details were missing. They were what mattered, what made all the difference, but there was probably no way of prising them out of her. Donovan decided to crosscheck everything Steele was saying with Tartaglia later. Maybe she could also use what she had learned as a lever to persuade him to be more open.

A series of loud explosions shattered the quiet and the sky through the window was filled with another burst of multicoloured light. She folded her arms and sat watching the arching trails of green and red mingled with gold. Shimmering splashes of white stars, like giant sunflowers, took their place, accompanied by more explosions. She needed to go home, get some sleep and think it all through again in the morning. Hopefully, the mist would lift and she'd be able to see clearly once more.

* * *

Tartaglia pulled on a pair of nitrile gloves and started to unpack the contents of Chapman's rucksack, which he'd laid out on a plastic sheet on the floor of his office. Chang sat beside him making an inventory.

'One pair blue denim GAP jeans size forty, one pair Primark navy tracksuit bottoms size XXL, one pair black Adidas shorts XXL, one pair Nike trainers size forty-eight and a half—'

'Forty-eight and a *half*?' Chang exclaimed. 'Bloody hell! Didn't know they made them that big.'

'Goes with the rest of him,' Tartaglia replied. 'You've seen the photos. He could have given Shrek a run for his money. One wash bag containing toothbrush, razor, Lynx Africa body spray . . .'

The list went on, a collection of unremarkable personal items and clothes, most well-worn and in need of a good wash, no items of any value other than a very scratched iPod. The side pockets yielded little of interest until he found a pocket inside another pocket, which was zipped shut and held together with a small combination padlock. They broke it open and found Finnigan's passport (expired) inside, along with just over two thousand pounds in cash, a very sharp knife with a retractable blade and a bundle of letters rolled up and held together with a rubber band. Tartaglia unfurled them and began quickly skimming through the contents of the various envelopes. A couple of letters and postcards were signed by Chapman, with a few from one of Finnigan's children, as well as a birthday card and a bunch of letters from his mother, sent from an address in Nottingham. Reading the letters, a mother's blind, unwavering love came through loud and clear: in spite of everything, Finnigan had been her blue-eyed boy. They would have to organise someone from the local force to go and see her as soon as possible in order to break the news of her son's death.

In amongst the pile, he found a letter from a woman called Tatyana. Written on cheap lined paper, the sort found in any local newsagent, the English was poor and the handwriting childlike. It revealed nothing about how they had met, but she talked about having been to see Finnigan in prison and 'liking very much' what she saw. The gist of it was that she couldn't wait for him to get out and that she was going to send him some 'very special pictures' of herself. He hadn't come across any photos in the bag, so either Finnigan had got rid of them or carried them with him, possibly in his wallet. It seemed very likely that she was the woman he had gone to meet. There was no address on the letterhead, just a date a few weeks before Finnigan was released from jail. The date corresponded to the postmark on the envelope, which showed that the letter had been posted in South West London.

'Call the prison. She will have had to produce ID and a proof of address to see him. I'll carry on here until you're done.'

While Chang went off to make the call in the next-door office, Tartaglia finished unpacking the rest of Finnigan's possessions. When he was sure there was nothing else of any interest, he began folding up the clothes and putting them back carefully in the bag with the other items. Finnigan's mother would probably want her son's things. He was just finishing the last few entries on the inventory when Steele poked her head around the door.

'Busy?'

'Yes. Justin's gone to make a call. With any luck, we may have found one of the last people to see Jake Finnigan alive.'

'OK. I'll get someone else to run Sam back to your flat, then.'

'Sam?'

'Yes, she's in my office. She wanted to know a bit more about what happened to Claire. I could see she wasn't going to give up on it so I gave her the basics. I just left out the material details. In case she asks you when you see her later, I'll fill you in before you leave.'

As she disappeared from view, Chang came back into the room. 'She's called Tatyana Kuznetsova and she lives in Kilburn. I've got the address. Do you want to go over there now?'

'No. I've got things to do. Call the local station, see if you can get an interview room, then you and Nick bring her in. I want to make this formal. When you're there with her, call me.'

Fourteen

Katy Perry's 'Firework' blared from loudspeakers as the last straggling tail of the procession pushed through the gateway at the top of the sports fields. Dressed for the cold, most still carried lighted torches and sparklers from the walk down the high street. They mingled with the rest of the crowd, already collected in huddled groups around the various food vans. Josh scanned their faces for Alfie and Ben, but there was no sign of them. Their mum was always running late. He just hoped they'd get there in time for the fireworks.

The voice of the announcer cut through the music.

'We'll be lighting the bonfire any minute now. Make sure you stand well back behind the tape. Fireworks start in half an hour.'

The crowd swarmed across the pitch and down the adjoining field towards the dark row of trees. Josh ran forwards, trainers slipping in the mud as he threaded his way as quickly as he could to where the giant tepee of wood stood at the bottom of the slope, near the stream. He eventually managed to push his way through to a place at the front by the rope, next to a group of teenage girls eating hotdogs. The smell of fried onions and ketchup made him feel hungry and he wondered what he'd be having for his tea. His breath made a cloud on the icy air and he hugged himself, tucking his hands under his armpits as he stamped his feet, trying to get some warmth into his toes. He gazed up at the bonfire. It was way bigger than last year's, made up of all sorts of things, from what he could see in the dim torchlight: planks, branches, pieces of furniture, and the gaps at the base stuffed with twigs and scrunched up newspaper. Looking up, he could just make out the bulky shape of the Guy, sitting like a king on top of it all, in an old red armchair.

'Here we go,' the announcer said cheerily. 'Light him up, boys. Let him *burn*.'

A couple of sixth-formers from school stooped down in unison, holding their lit torches briefly to the edges of the bonfire before scuttling back behind the rope. For a moment nothing happened; the twigs seemed to catch alight before being blown out by the wind with little puffs of smoke. He caught the smell of damp, smouldering leaves as well as a strong whiff of petrol. It had been raining heavily the night before and he was just beginning to wonder how long it would take to get going when flames jetted up in several places from the base of the bonfire, as though someone had turned on a gas fire.

In the flickering light he could see the Guy more clearly. He'd been dressed in an old pinstriped suit, with a shirt and tie, and a pair of work boots on his dangling feet. A cowboy hat was jammed down on his head, above a leering mask for a face that made him look like The Joker. The flames took hold quickly. Before long, they were licking the Guy's feet, catching the bottom of his trousers, then creeping like fingers up his bent legs. Josh could feel the heat on his cheeks and held out his hands, trying to blot out the music and the buzz of voices around him, until all he could see was the burning figure in the midst of the flames. A gust of wind sent a cloud of smoke and a shower of sparks over the onlookers but he stayed where he was, listening to the cracking and spitting of the wood as the flames leapt higher. The Guy's hat was on fire now, the mask blistering away until it had all but disappeared, leaving just a black, featureless blob of a head.

The flames reached high into the sky, the Guy caught in the middle of the blaze. Josh stared deep into the heart of the fire, imagining shapes and faces from long ago, instruments of torture, the masked executioner and the screams of a man being burned alive. *Remember, remember the fifth of November, gunpowder, treason and plot* . . . As the words flowed rhythmically through his mind, the Guy's head tipped forwards, lolling onto his chest. For a moment it looked as though he had gone to sleep. Then the head dropped into the fire. It bounced against something and rolled out onto the grass, coming to rest right by where Josh was standing. It lay there charred and smoking. Looking closer, it was amazingly lifelike, with a nose, dark sockets where the eyes should be, and a mouth. He even thought he could see teeth between the parted lips. Wondering if anyone else had noticed it, or if it was perhaps some sort of a joke left over from Halloween, he glanced around. Most people seemed to be busy talking amongst themselves, sipping their drinks, or watching the fire. He caught sight of a man standing on his own by the rope just a few feet away. He was looking right at Josh as though he had been watching him.

Then a woman screamed.

Fifteen

'I don't give a flying fuck that your visa's expired and that you're here illegally, Miss Kuznetsova,' Tartaglia said. 'But if you don't cooperate, the immigration services will be the least of your worries. Do you understand?' He smacked his hand hard on the table in front of her, making her start. She had the sullen, defiant stare of somebody used to being interrogated and he had decided that subtlety or charm would be wasted on her.

She pressed her thin red lips together and nodded.

They were sitting in an airless meeting room in Kilburn police station, he and Minderedes together on one side of the small, coffee-stained table, Tatyana Kuznetsova opposite. It had taken a while to track her down but they eventually found her waitressing in a Turkish restaurant in Salusbury Road, Queens Park – conveniently just a stone's throw away from the police station. She had refused the services of an interpreter, saying that she spoke English, although she seemed to understand a lot more than she was capable of expressing. She was younger than he had expected, in her mid-twenties, with short, chin-length black hair and a round, not unattractive face, spoiled by too much make-up. She was still in her work clothes: a grubby apron tied around her waist over a short black skirt, white shirt struggling to stretch across her show-stoppingly large and artificial-looking breasts. They seemed all the more extraordinary perched on her scrawny, bandy-legged little frame. Nonetheless, Finnigan must have thought ten

Christmases had been rolled into one when she visited him in jail, particularly after his long stretch inside.

'Do you recognise this man?' Minderedes asked, holding up a photograph of Jake Finnigan.

She gave an almost imperceptible shake of her head.

He leaned across the table and waved the photo in front of her face but she avoided eye contact, looking straight ahead like a sulky child pretending she was somewhere else. He slapped the photo down hard on the table in front of her. 'Look again. I think you do. You went to see him in Wormwood Scrubs Prison last March.'

She made no reply.

'There's a record of it. We've got scanned copies of the IDs you showed.' He held them up in front of her nose. 'Crystal?'

'Do you understand?' Tartaglia asked.

She shrugged, shifting her gaze momentarily to Tartaglia. 'OK. Maybe I go see him. What's the problem?'

'Jake Finnigan's dead. He was murdered. Do you understand what I'm saying?' He spoke slowly and deliberately. He wanted her to be in no doubt.

She nodded.

'This happened shortly after you went to see him, when he came out of prison.'

A flicker of something crossed her face and she narrowed her black eyes, as though quickly calculating something in her mind. Then her expression shut down again. 'This is very serious, Miss Kuznetsova,' Tartaglia continued. 'We have a letter you wrote to him after you went to see him. You sent him some photographs. "Very special pictures" you called them.'

'Dirty pictures,' Minderedes said, with an unpleasant tone.

She looked blank.

'Pornographic,' Tartaglia added. He was only guessing. They

hadn't seen the photos she had sent to Finnigan, but the odds were well in his favour.

'Do you like to take photographs of yourself naked and send them to older men?' Minderedes asked.

Her cheeks turned pink as though she had been slapped, the first sign of any emotion, but she made no reply.

'Did you like him looking at you? Did it excite you?' Minderedes said, emphasising each word.

'No.'

'What else did you do for him?'

'Do for him?' Again she looked at Tartaglia, as though he might help her but he decided to let Minderedes go with the flow. Sometimes it was better to observe and he was still undecided about her.

'Yes,' Minderedes said. 'Extras. You know what I mean.' He made a rude gesture with his fingers.

'Stop this,' she shouted.

'Stop? But we've only just started, Tatyana. Poor old Finnigan. He must have had the wettest dreams about you, looking at those special little pictures you sent him. All that time inside, with only blokes to suck him off. Must've really got him going, fantasising about you, don't you think? Was that what you wanted? Did you want him panting for you? Bet the poor old bugger couldn't wait to get out.'

She coloured again as he spoke and shifted in her seat, but made no reply.

'You talked about getting together when he came out,' Minderedes continued. 'Showing him some more of you "in the flesh", you said. Are you on the game?'

'What game? What is this?'

'Are you a prostitute?' Tartaglia asked. 'Do you take money in return for sex?'

113

Her eyes widened a fraction. 'No.' She glared at him, folding her pale, thin arms tightly around herself, but he wasn't convinced. Hard-up amateur or seasoned pro, it didn't matter what she was. He was sure she hadn't visited Finnigan or written to him out of love, or any other selfless motive. But what *was* her motive? He certainly didn't see her being responsible for the body parts in the Fiat Panda. Somebody else had to have been pulling her strings.

'When he came out of jail, you texted him,' Minderedes said.

'No.'

He looked at her disbelievingly. 'You saying you *did not* text him?'

'No. I do not text him.'

'You're a liar, Tatyana. You texted him and you asked him to meet you. We have transcripts of those texts.'

That was also a lie – they were still waiting for the downloads from Finnigan's phone service provider – but it was another low-risk gamble they had decided to take.

'He gets all hot and bothered with excitement,' Minderedes continued, 'gets himself all dolled up no doubt, and goes out to meet you. Poor bugger's never seen again. That is, until he turns up dead as a friggin' dodo in a car park in South West London. *Dead.* Capisce?'

'You're in big trouble, Tatyana,' Tartaglia said, deciding he would also switch to her Christian name. 'Big trouble. And you're wasting our time. If you don't start talking, I'm leaving you with Detective Constable Minderedes here, and he'll make sure that you're charged with as many things as we can think of. You may not give a stuff about Jake Finnigan, but if you care about what happens to you, you'll tell us the truth.' He stared at her until she looked away.

She chewed her lip for a moment, picking at a long red nail with her finger, then said, 'OK, maybe I text him once. But I no kill him.'

'First you say you didn't text him, then you say you did,' Minderedes said. 'Now you say you didn't kill him. Why should we believe a bloody word you say?'

She gripped the table with her hands. 'I know nothing about this. Nothing.' She started to get to her feet.

'Sit down,' Tartaglia shouted, staring at her until she sank back down in the chair. 'Things are looking pretty serious for you. Bad. Did you kill him?'

She looked genuinely shocked, as though it was only just dawning on her what was happening. Her tone softened. 'You make joke, right?'

'This is no joke. Certainly not for Jake Finnigan, and not for you either. Did you kill him?'

'This man . . .'

'Jake Finnigan.'

'You say he is dead?'

'Yes. Murdered. Do you understand that word?'

She nodded.

Palms face down on the table, he leaned towards her. 'This is not a joke, or a trick, Tatyana. I don't care what you did, or why you did it, who you fucked or how much money you were paid. I just need to know the truth. All that matters is finding the person who killed Finnigan. Again, do you understand?' He spoke slowly and deliberately making sure she got every word.

She lowered her gaze. 'Yes.'

'Right. Now you'd better tell me exactly what happened.'

At first there was silence, and Tartaglia was wondering what to do next when she gave a little sigh, then slowly, in broken English, began to tell them about a man she had met. He had come into the restaurant where she was working one day back in February. He wasn't a regular and she had never seen him before. He was on his own, business was slow, and they got talking. He said his name was Chris and he was nice looking, she said. Nice eyes, although his teeth weren't good, she said disapprovingly, like someone who smokes too much. He bought her a couple of drinks and told her he was a freelance photographer. He asked her if she was unattached, which she was, and what she was doing in the UK. He asked her about her family back home, her brothers and sisters, and eventually she told him she was trying to make some money to pay off some debts back home. He smiled, and told her he knew a way.

She had thought he wanted to take pictures of her but instead he told her that he wanted her to help him do a favour for a friend – a very good friend, he said – who was in prison. He said that the man was very lonely and was crazy for Russian women and would do anything just to get to know one as pretty as her. He said that the man had had a hard time in jail, that he was innocent of the crime he was supposed to have committed, and was due to be released very soon. All she had to do was to write to the man – as her English was poor, he would tell her what to say – enclosing a picture that he would take and asking if he would like a visit. That's all she had to do. Jake had written back straight away, saying he wanted to see her. She had given the letter to Chris, she said. For this, she was paid five hundred pounds. He told her to make the appointment and that when she returned he would give her another five hundred pounds. When she went to see Jake she wasn't to mention Chris by name, just to say that a good friend of Jake's had asked her to go and see him. She went to the jail, met Jake and talked to him for as long as she was allowed. He asked her how old she was and if she was single. He seemed to like her, she said. He said he liked Russian women, that he had heard that they were very passionate.

'He wasn't at all suspicious about who sent you?' Tartaglia asked, amazed that a hardened criminal like Finnigan could be so naive.

'Maybe a little,' she said. 'When I first go there he question me. He think it is joke. But then he really like me.'

It was the age-old thing, Tartaglia thought to himself. Sex, or the promise of it, could frazzle even the most sensible of male brains. Finnigan could hardly be described as sensible or level headed. He had also been inside for a long stretch. Maybe he had chosen not to think too closely why a young woman like Tatyana would want to pay him attention, let alone who might have sent her. She was the proverbial gift horse. A Trojan horse, in fact. According to Finnigan's psychological report, although of a relatively low IQ, he was self-confident and egotistical. He probably felt more than capable of handling most situations, particularly where a woman was involved.

Tatyana described how Chris had come into the restaurant again two days later. She told him what had happened with Finnigan and he gave her the money.

'Didn't you think it was a lot of money for what you did?' Tartaglia asked, still sceptical. 'Weren't *you* suspicious?'

'No,' she replied with a shrug.

'What the hell did you think was going on?' he then asked.

Her black eyes glittered with anger. 'I need money. I don't ask questions.'

Chris then said he wanted to take some pictures of her. He told her they were for Jake and said he would pay her another five hundred pounds. They met up outside Kings Cross station and he took her to a hotel nearby – she didn't remember the name – and bought her some drinks. Then he took some pictures of her in the bar. She had quite a bit to drink, she said. Then he said he would give her another five hundred pounds if she would take off her clothes and pose for him, like in the magazines. He said it would be a professional photo shoot. It wasn't a big deal for her because she had done some glamour modelling as a student back in Russia, and anyway she needed the money. Chris booked a room upstairs and they were there for about an hour, she said. She then had to write another letter to Jake, which he dictated.

'Did you have sex with him?' Minderedes asked.

She said very insistently 'No', that he hadn't asked for it or seemed at all interested. She started to think he must be gay, like a lot of English men. This was said with a pointed look at both Tartaglia and Minderedes, their dark Mediterranean looks and un-British surnames clearly lost on her, which amused Tartaglia but made Minderedes visibly bridle.

Tatyana said that the last time she had seen Chris was about a month later. He had appeared at the restaurant again and told her that Jake had just come out of prison and that he wanted to plan something really special for him. She thought he meant some sort of a party or celebration. He said she would be invited and would meet lots of new people. He asked her to send Jake a text saying she had heard he was out and wanted to see him. Again, he told her exactly what to say. He then said he had a present for her and he gave her a new iPhone. He asked if he could have her old Nokia in return and she gave it to him.

'What, with the SIM?' Tartaglia asked.

She shrugged as if it was unimportant.

'Didn't you think that was odd? He wants your old phone. Why?' Again she shrugged, as though it wasn't worth thinking about. He was growing exasperated at her stubborn lack of interest. He couldn't believe she was that stupid. 'He wants the

SIM. He wants to use it,' he said, watching her closely. 'He wants to pretend to be *you*.' Again, there was no reaction.

Her only response was that the phone was a cheap one and that anything important was backed up on her laptop, as though that was all that mattered. Tartaglia didn't believe for a second that she was so gullible, but she was being paid enough not to ask questions. Chris had then told her he would call her to fix things up for the party but she never heard from him again. When she finished her account, she sat back in her chair, arms still tightly folded, and looked at both detectives defiantly, as though she had delivered the goods and it was over to them.

Tartaglia watched her closely while Minderedes noted down a few more details for the statement she would sign. He wondered if she was merely a willing pawn or whether she could be more deeply involved, although she had only been in the country a couple of months before she went to see Finnigan in jail. There was also no reason to think she had ever met Finnigan before then, so it seemed unlikely. However, in spite of her broken English, she appeared sharp and streetwise. She must have had her suspicions that she was involved in some sort of a con, or at least some sort of elaborate practical joke, but she had clearly decided to look the other way. After all, whatever was going on was very profitable for her and, Tartaglia reflected, a lot of people who, if their palms were sufficiently greased, would happily play their part in strange situations and not inquire further.

Tatyana's reaction on hearing that Finnigan had been murdered also seemed genuine enough, and so far there were no grounds to think she had been an accessory to the crime. He still found it odd though, that apart from his initial wariness, Finnigan seemed not to have had a clue that he was being played and had lapped it all up willingly. What seemed clear was that Chris, or whatever his real name was, had known how Finnigan would react. He had known the man's weakness, and known that in the end he wouldn't question the gift that had apparently landed out of the blue in his lap. He had planned everything down to the last detail, and he had also chosen Tatyana well for her role. Assuming he wasn't just a middle-man with somebody else behind him calling the shots, his interest in Finnigan was personal. He had used Tatyana to get close to Finnigan and to lure him to his death. Why Chris had needed her in the first place, why he couldn't just kill Finnigan on his own, was another question. It seemed a very elaborate and risky way to go about things and there had to have been a good reason for it.

'Have you ever seen this man?' he asked when Minderedes had finished, pulling out a photograph of Richard English.

'No.'

He studied her carefully but there was no sign of recognition. 'Are you absolutely sure?'

She nodded.

'What about Chris? You'd be able to recognise him if you saw him again?'

'Of course.'

'Can you describe him?'

She pursed her lips, looking from Minderedes to Tartaglia. 'Not old man. Not like Jake.'

Jake Finnigan had been in his late forties, but maybe to her he had looked older. 'So, twenty, thirty, forty? What are we talking about?'

'Maybe thirty. And tall like you.'

'Like me, are you sure?' he asked standing up. 'Or like DC Minderedes here. Nick, stand up, will you?' Minderedes was shorter, around five-foot eight, although he normally wore shoes with a slight heel in an effort to seem taller. But Tatyana was very short, so anything Minderedes's height or more might look tall. 'Stand up, Miss Kuznetsova. What do you think?'

She got to her feet, put her hand on her hip, and looked sullenly from one to the other. 'Like you maybe,' she said after a moment, pointing at Tartaglia. 'Maybe not so much, I think. But he is . . . thin. He has no . . .' she pinched her almost non-existent biceps. 'How you say?'

'Muscles?'

'Yes, like he don't eat good or do man's work.'

'Was he clean-shaven? Did he have a beard?' He gestured to his face.

She shook her head. 'No beard.'

'What about his eye colour and hair?'

'He have brown eyes, I think.'

'You're not sure?'

She shrugged. 'They are nice eyes. But his hair is not black,' she said, still looking at Tartaglia.

'So what colour is it? Brown? Dark brown? Light brown? Blond? Red?'

'Brown, maybe a little red. He look very English.'

'You mean he has pale skin?' He didn't want to lead her, but he was getting tired.

She nodded and sat back down, as though she had done enough. The description wasn't very clear but maybe it would translate better onto a computer.

'OK. We'll need you to help us draw up an E-FIT – that's a computer-generated picture – of Chris. Nick will organise that straight away. Then you're free to go, although if you change your address, I want to know. Just in case he turns up, we'll need you to identify him. OK?

She nodded.

'Did he say where he lives or where he works?'

'No.'

'So he never told you how you could get hold of him, if you needed to?'

'No. He find me.'

'And he only came into the restaurant those three times?'

'Yes.'

'If he gets in contact with you again, or you happen to see him in the street, I want you to call me right away. OK? Do you understand?' She nodded slowly and he handed her his card. 'Is there anything else you remember? Anything at all distinctive about him or his behaviour that stands out, however small? Any distinguishing marks, like tattoos? Something a bit different?'

She looked at him, head slightly to one side, lips parted as though about to say something.

'What is it?' he said impatiently.

'There is one thing.' She was still staring at him, maybe debating whether or not to say anything.

'Go on.'

She shrugged. 'Chris, he have a mark on his hand, here . . .' She held up her palm. 'How you say?'

'A tattoo? A scar?'

'Yes. A scar. Like with knife. Like this.' She drew the sign of the cross on her hand.

It was past midnight by the time Tartaglia let himself into his flat. The sitting room was dark, no lights on anywhere from what he could tell. He turned on a lamp and went into the hall. The door to his bedroom was closed and he hoped Donovan was asleep. She needed as much rest as possible. He would have a shower before making up his bed in the sitting room, but first he needed to unwind and get his thoughts straight. In the kitchen, he poured himself a good inch of Lagavulin, then unlocked the back door and went out into the garden. Surrounded by the gardens of the neighbouring houses, it was small but private. He loved sitting out there whatever the weather, having a smoke and a drink and, during the day, listening to the birds. He pulled up a chair, shook a puddle of rain from the seat, sat down and lit a cigarette. With relief, he saw that the shutters of his bedroom window were closed and there was no light coming through the cracks. Steele had briefed him about what she had told Donovan and specifically instructed him not to give her any more information. He understood Steele's reasons, and agreed. Even though he was sure Donovan could be trusted, he wanted to spare her knowledge that would only cause her more grief, particularly the horrific little details that could stick in the mind for ever.

In the stillness, he heard the rasping cry of a fox somewhere nearby. He took a gulp of the whisky, enjoying its smoky taste. He thought of the mysterious Chris – presumably the killer of Finnigan and the other three victims – and once more he was struck by how incurious Tatyana had been, how apparently accepting and unquestioning of everything that had happened to her. Whether she was blind, or had deliberately looked the other way, didn't really matter. He wondered how Chris had chosen her; he was sure she *had* been chosen. Maybe Chris had gone to the restaurant by accident and on speaking to her, had realised that she would be perfect for his purpose, but it seemed more likely that he had seen her out and about – on the street, in a shop, on a bus, or on the Tube – and had followed her back to her place of work. He could have come across her anywhere. Trying to track him down via the patterns of her daily routine would be impossible. Wherever it was, he must have heard her voice to know she was Russian. It would be worth talking to Chapman again to see if it were true that Finnigan had a thing for Russian women and, if so, who knew about it. Even though there was still so much they were missing, at least the shadowy figure of the person they were looking for was beginning to take shape. He was smart, he was organised and highly manipulative, and they had an E-FIT, which they could start showing around. More importantly, they had found somebody who could identify him.

Sixteen

Adam heard the chime of a text and reached over to the bedside table for his phone.

**May be able to get away for a quick drink later if you're free.
Sxx**

He smiled. She was desperate for him, and why not? Women were stupid. They liked to dream, and a bit of flattery and flirtation went a long way in blinding them to reality. He put the phone down and lay staring up at the cracked ceiling. He had set the alarm for eight a.m. but by seven he was already fully awake, his mind buzzing. Who was the man upstairs in Kit's room? Having failed to find out his real name, he had decided to call him 'Gunner', after the Dolph Lundgren character in *The Expendables*. It suited him better than Jonny, at any rate. Whoever he was, he seemed to know the layout of the house pretty well, all the funny little places Kit used to put things, even the drawer where he hid the key to his cellar in case the cleaning lady found it. Had he really been Kit's lover? Anything was possible with Kit, but it was difficult to imagine the two of them together. The thought was also disgusting.

Adam had seen Kit naked more times than he cared to remember and it wasn't a pleasant sight, even if he'd been into that sort of thing. Kit would walk around the house with nothing on, as though it was the most natural thing in the world.

Amused at Adam's discomfort, playfully flaunting himself as though it must be a turn-on, he called Adam an uptight prude for refusing to do the same. It had been extremely irritating. He wasn't a prude at all. He looked after himself and was one of the small minority of people who looked better naked than clothed. But by keeping his clothes on, or at least some of them, he kept hold of the power with Kit. There was then always the tantalising promise of more, if Kit behaved himself. It was a precarious dance of the seven veils and he knew he wouldn't be able to string things out for long. Luckily, all he needed was a couple of weeks to get things straight and Kit was rarely together enough to pose much of a physical threat. His memory wasn't that accurate either.

Adam flexed his shoulders and stretched out on the narrow divan. His hands hit the wall behind, his feet hanging over the end of the bed. He wasn't particularly tall, but there was barely space to swing a cat. The rest of the room was equally uncomfortable. Just a chair and a chest of drawers, a tiny shaving mirror on the wall and a moth-eaten Turkish rug partly covering the old floorboards. The only advantage was that the room was on the ground floor. If Gunner went out, he would hear. The door had no lock and he had put the chair up against it to secure it. Even so, he had been unable to relax into sleep for more than a few hours at a time, knowing that Gunner was upstairs in Kit's room, sleeping off a skinful of Bells, judging by the empty bottle left on the counter that Adam had found when he went down to the kitchen for a glass of water in the middle of the night.

He was still reeling from what had happened the previous night: Gunner's sudden appearance in the house, being forced to move his things out of Kit's room. He cursed himself for having been so compliant, but the last thing he needed was confrontation and questions being asked. Still, he hadn't been thinking straight, and in his fury he had left one of his bags behind in Kit's room. He made a quick mental list of the contents and reassured himself that the things in it weren't important, just some clothes and a couple of pairs of shoes. There was nothing that he need worry about, should Gunner choose to have a little rummage around. But he hated the idea of him doing it, of his possessions sitting up there all night, made somehow vulnerable, with this arrogant stranger. He had become so upset about it that eventually, at about midnight, he had gone upstairs to ask for the bag. He had heard the sound of some sort of foul heavy metal coming from inside, but when he knocked Gunner had bellowed at him through the door, telling him to bugger off.

He assumed that the door was locked, although he hadn't felt like trying it. Kit's bedroom was the only room in the whole house with a lock. Kit had always locked himself in at night in case burglars or unnamed others broke in while he was asleep. Kit suffered from night fears, often talking in his sleep, sometimes even calling out. He would wake up sweating and have a headache the whole of the next day. Adam had never quite understood what it was all about; nothing like what Kit described had ever actually happened, as far as he was aware. But like so much about Kit, it wasn't rational. However, it made no difference whether Gunner had locked the bedroom door or not – Adam had no intention of going in while he was inside. What stupid drug or alcohol-fuelled whim had caused Kit to allow such a man into his life? More importantly, his presence in the house threatened to ruin everything.

Seventeen

A greyish but sharp glare streamed through the window of the BMW as Tartaglia and Minderedes headed out of London on the M3 towards Winchester. Tartaglia flipped down the sun shield, but it made little difference. He sank deeper into the passenger seat and closed his eyes, letting the innocuous sound of Rihanna's 'Diamonds' wash over him. He was exhausted. The sofa he was sleeping on at home was comfortable to sit on, but it was far too narrow for him to spread out the way he liked to do in bed. It was also on the soft side and several inches too short. He couldn't work out where to put his feet. Around three in the morning he had given up and put the seat and back cushions on the floor as a makeshift bed. He had eventually rolled off them and woke up with a stiff neck and a headache.

He'd got up and left the flat early that morning, with only time to grab a quick cup of black coffee on the way. Donovan was still asleep. They had received a tip-off about a fire involving a human body. It had been dressed up as a Guy and placed on top of a bonfire at a fireworks party in a small town outside Winchester. A follow up call to Winchester CID had established that the body was not in one piece. The head had rolled off into the crowd at the party and the officer described how the legs and arms had also fallen off as the rest of the body was being removed from the fire 'as though they weren't properly attached'. The similarities were sufficient to warrant further investigation, particularly as two witnesses had seen a man acting suspiciously around the bonfire. Apart from the ID for

Jake Finnigan, there was still no word back from the lab on the DNA samples taken from the other body parts in the Sainsbury's car park fire. He hoped to get the results later that day.

As he dozed, head against the cold glass, a jumble of images spun through his mind: night-time and the dimly lit bedroom in the Dillon Hotel, Claire lying across the bed; the fire in the car park, the charred fragments of body in the car; snake-eyed Tatyana; Chris, the man with the cross on his hand who doesn't want sex, Jake Finnigan . . . Why wait six months after killing Finnigan to set fire to his body? Wealthy Richard English missing for two years, his wallet and keys on the ground by the car, the homeless man known as Dodger . . . Were they one and the same? Lisa English, Ian Armstrong, so much to gain financially. Spidery red letters carved into Claire's thighs. *What I am, you will be . . . What I am, you will be . . . What I am . . . Who am I? Death. The Dead.* The words spooled round and round. *Claire is dead. You will be too.* Who was 'you'? Who did the killer mean? Were the words there for a reason, or was it just a tease . . .

'We're here, Sir. *Sir?*'

Minderedes's voice jolted him awake. He opened his eyes and saw that they had pulled up in a parking lot beside a large brick building, signed Recreation Centre. He glanced at his watch. The journey had taken the best part of an hour. He stretched and watched as Minderedes got out of the car and went to greet a stocky middle-aged man who had emerged from a nearby car. The DI from Winchester CID, Tartaglia assumed. They exchanged a few words, then came towards the BMW. As Tartaglia got out, the man came over and introduced himself as DI John Ramsey, based at Winchester.

'I understand there was a fireworks party,' Tartaglia said, once the basic introductions were out of the way and they started walking towards the playing fields behind the building.

'Yes. Happens every year,' Ramsey said. 'They usually get about a thousand people, or so. Sometimes more. They start with a big procession down the high street with torches and candles, then they come down here. The bonfire's at the bottom of one of the fields over there.' He jerked his head in the direction. 'Anyway, they set light to it. It's soaked in kerosene so it doesn't take long to get going. They're all standing around watching it go up as usual, and then Guy Fawkes' head falls off. It lands on the ground and some little boy sees it and realises it's not a bloody dummy, then people start screaming blue murder, you get the picture.'

'Where does the Guy usually come from?' Minderedes asked.

'The local school. There's a competition each year.'

'And who puts the Guy on the bonfire?'

'There's a rota of volunteers from the school, plus locals, but again, because it's a weekday, they had to use whoever offered. Somebody went to the school yesterday to get Mr Fawkes but was told he'd already been collected, although nobody can remember who by. Next thing he's sitting on top of the bonfire. Nobody asked any questions about how he got there and nobody's seen anything suspicious.'

'Any witnesses?' Tartaglia asked.

'The boy I told you about saw a man in the crowd acting suspiciously. Somebody else – a woman on one of the catering stands – said she saw a man hanging around earlier in the day who seemed a bit odd. That's about it, I'm afraid.'

'What about the rest of the body?'

'Gone off with the head to the mortuary.'

'OK. I'll need to speak to them when we're done. In the meantime, you'd better show me where all this happened.'

The area beyond the car park had been cordoned off and they signed in with a uniformed PC. Ramsey led the way, Minderedes following, picking his way gingerly through the muddy ground in what looked like a new pair of shoes. Fields and rolling hills stretched into the distance, with woods beyond. The grass was dotted with abandoned stalls and marquees, left where they stood the previous night. They followed a line of trees down a gradual incline towards an open space at the bottom where the charred remains of a huge bonfire sat in the middle.

'We had to get the fire brigade to put it out,' Ramsey said.

'How did they get access down here?' Tartaglia asked, looking around. As far as he could see, there was nothing but a narrow, well-trodden, muddy track.

'There's a lane just over there behind the hedge. It runs between the two fields. They use it to bring in the wood and stuff for the bonfire. It was all stacked under those tarpaulins over there to keep it dry until the actual day. Whoever brought the Guy must have come in the same way. You wouldn't want to be carting something heavy, let alone dodgy, all the way from the car park.'

Tartaglia nodded. 'And nobody saw the Guy brought in?'

'Nobody's come forward so far.'

'Who uses these sports fields?' Minderedes asked.

'People from the town and the local school. Whoever did this had local knowledge.'

Tartaglia nodded in agreement. 'I've seen enough for now,' he said. 'I'd like to talk to the witnesses as soon as possible. We have an E-FIT of a suspect we'd like to show them.'

'Right. I suggest we start with Liz Hallion. She runs a sandwich shop in the high street. I told her we'd be along. The boy – Josh – may be at school. I'll get one of my colleagues to check and if so, tell him to go home. We can go and see him after.'

'Do you celebrate Guy Fawkes night in Scotland?' Minderedes asked Tartaglia, as they started to walk back up the hill towards the car park.

'We have Bonfire Night, with lots of fireworks. It's really an excuse for a mini Hogmanay. Nobody cares that someone once tried to blow up your king . . .'

'*Your* king, you mean. Wasn't he Scottish?'

Tartaglia laughed. Although third generation Italian, he had been born and brought up in Edinburgh and counted himself as much a Scot as an Italian. 'OK, then. *Your* Houses of Parliament.'

'And you a Catholic, Sir. You should be on the side of Guido Fawkes.'

'Yes. I was forgetting that that was what it was all about. Religion has a lot to answer for.'

Donovan heard the sound of the front door banging shut and a moment later, Sharon Fuller bustled into Tartaglia's sitting room, carrying a large shopping bag and an umbrella. 'I've brought you some groceries,' she said. 'I'll just go and put them away.'

'Thank you,' Donovan replied from the sofa, wondering why Tartaglia had given Fuller a key. 'But I don't need anything.'

Fuller appeared not to have heard her and was already heading towards the kitchen. Reluctantly, she got up, turned off the television and followed behind.

'It's just a few bits and pieces,' Fuller said, starting to unpack the contents of the bag onto the counter. 'I noticed the fridge was empty yesterday. Mark's too busy to worry himself about such things at the moment.'

Irritated at the intrusion, along with the assumption that she couldn't deal with "such things" herself, Donovan watched from the door as Fuller put the various items away in the fridge and nearby cupboards. When she was done, she went over to the sink, washed her hands quickly, then turned to face Donovan. 'Cup of tea?'

'No thanks.'

'Been out somewhere?'

'No.'

'Your cheeks are pink and you've got a leaf in your hair.' She pointed.

As usual, she missed nothing. Donovan ran her fingers through her hair and found the dead leaf, which she scrunched up in her fingers. 'I just went out for a quick walk around the block, that's all. Needed some fresh air.'

'Let me make you a cup of tea? I could do with one myself.'

'OK,' Donovan said grudgingly. She hadn't the energy to argue. Simpler just to let Fuller go through the motions, then she would be gone sooner. She sat down at the table.

Fuller switched on the kettle and took out two mugs from the cupboard. 'Are you managing to sleep OK?' she asked, dropping a teabag into each of them.

'Yes.' It wasn't true but there was no point explaining. The pills seemed to take for ever to kick in and, when they did, they only knocked her out for a few hours. It wasn't enough. She had been back to see her GP, but he had refused to give her anything stronger. Whether it was the pills or the lack of sleep or both, she felt disorientated and could barely string two thoughts together, let alone a sentence. How was she going to be of any use in her current state?

Sharon was looking at her with concern. 'Are you alright, Sam?'

'Yes, I'm fine. I'm just a bit tired.'

'Are you hungry? Can I make you anything to eat?'

Donovan shook her head. 'I don't feel hungry.'

'What about some cereal, or I could make you a sandwich?'

'No.'

'OK. You just let me know when you need something.'

'I just need time on my own,' Donovan said, but Sharon had already turned away, busy pouring water into the mugs. She prodded them vigorously with a spoon, muttering something under her breath as she dropped the teabags in the bin and added a drop of milk to each mug.

'Here you go,' she said after a moment, coming over with the mugs to where Donovan was sitting and plonking herself down opposite. 'Have you thought any more about seeing a counsellor?'

'I've told you, I don't see the point.'

'I know, but it really helps a lot of people.'

'I'm not a lot of people. I don't want to talk to anybody about what's happened. It won't do any good.'

'I understand. I just thought maybe—'

'And I don't need looking after.'

Sharon peered at her over the rim of her spectacles. 'Yes, you do, Sam. I know you better than most and you're not looking after yourself. You look dreadful, if you don't mind my saying. Even if you've lost your appetite, you need to force yourself to eat, and you need to drink or you'll get dehydrated. However terrible you feel, you've got to try and make a bit of an effort.'

Donovan bit her lip and glanced away into a far corner of the room. Sharon was right, of course, and was just trying to be kind, but she felt sick, her stomach a tight knot. There was so much she ought to be doing, people she should be talking to about Claire. Looking through Claire's iPad, she was struck by what different lives they had led. Different friends, different taste in music, in books, in their choice of work, and in men. What was it about Claire that had attracted the killer?

'I know you probably don't feel like cooking,' Sharon was saying. 'Would you like me to drop some more food over for you later? I made a great casserole last night and there's some left over. I could stay and heat it up.'

'Thank you, Sharon, but I'm just *not* hungry. Really.'

'As I said, you've got to force yourself.'

'I'll pick something up from the shops when I go out. Or I can get a takeaway.' It was clear from Sharon's expression that she didn't believe her, but Donovan didn't care.

'Is there any news about your dad?' Sharon asked, after a moment.

Donovan shook her head. Hopefully her mother would call again later. She, too, was up all hours of the night, getting what sleep she could on a bench outside her husband's room, unwilling to leave the hospital even for a minute in case he took a turn for the worse.

She took a sip of tea. It was good and strong, but Sharon had put sugar in it. She put the mug down and stared at Sharon. 'You said you'd tell me what's going on with the investigation,' she said. 'You said you'd find out. Is there any news?'

'Not at the moment.'

'*Something* must be happening. There must be *some* progress.'

'I can ask again, but they won't give me the sort of details you want. You know that.'

Donovan shook her head. It wasn't true. If Sharon wanted to find out, she could. They would tell her. It wasn't just Sharon either. They were all keeping things from her, important things, the details that mattered, the details that would help her find out who had killed Claire. They thought they were doing their best for her, protecting her from the truth, but they were treating her like a child. There must be another way to get the information she needed . . .

Eighteen

Tartaglia and Minderedes followed Ramsey's car along the main road for a short distance to the small town of Aldford. It was nearly the lunch hour and the high street was busy with pedestrians and cars. The road was lined on both sides with fancy-looking teashops, antique shops and boutiques, and there was an ancient half-timbered building half way along on one side. It was raised off the ground on tall stone pillars, and a collection of market stalls stood in the space beneath, spilling out on either side along the road in front. Groups of shoppers gathered around. A car pulled out just in front of them and Ramsey motioned Minderedes to take the parking space while he carried on driving up the street. A few minutes later they saw him walking towards them on the opposite side of the road and they got out and crossed over to join him.

'I'd forgotten it's market day,' he said, stopping in front of a large café that occupied the width of two shops. They followed him inside. The room was full, buzzing with conversation, punctuated with the cries and laughter of small children. A queue of people stood waiting to be served in front of the counter, which was laden with cakes, salads and sandwiches. A short, dark-haired woman stood at the end, making coffee behind a huge espresso machine. Seeing Ramsey, she came out from behind the counter, quickly wiping her hands on her apron, and greeted them.

Ramsey introduced Tartaglia and Minderedes.

'I'm afraid there's nowhere to sit,' Liz Hallion said with an apologetic look. 'We'd better go into my office. It's a bit of a mess, but it's definitely quieter than in here.'

They followed Liz into a small room at the back of the kitchen and she explained how she ran a cake and coffee stand at the fireworks event every year. She had been busy setting up when she noticed a man hanging around. She thought there was something odd about him.

'What sort of time was this?' Tartaglia asked.

'About four-thirty.'

'So, it was getting dark.'

She nodded. 'We'd just started to put up the lights for our stand, when he sort of appeared from nowhere.'

'This was up by the top of the football pitch, near the recreation centre,' Ramsey explained. 'Not down by where the bonfire was.'

'Our stand is the first one you come to when you go through the main gate,' Liz continued. 'Anyway, this chap just seemed to be wandering around for no reason, watching what people were doing. Members of the public aren't allowed onto the ground until six o'clock, so I asked him if he was looking for somebody but he didn't answer and just walked off. I was a bit worried, as lots of young children come to the party.'

'The Guy was already on the bonfire by this time?' Tartaglia asked Ramsey, who nodded. Assuming it was the same man who had put the body on the bonfire, it was classic behaviour to hang around watching and be involved in what was going on.

'Can you describe him?' Tartaglia asked.

'He had a beard, with a woollen hat pulled down over his head.'

'What colour was the hat?'

'Navy, I think, or black. He was tallish, quite a bit taller than me, at any rate. I particularly remember his coat. It was long and a bit old-fashioned, made of dark grey tweed. Quite an expensive one, I think, which was odd, as he was pretty dirty-looking, like he slept rough or didn't wash very often. I thought maybe he'd picked up the coat at a charity shop.'

'By beard, do you mean stubble or something more than that?'

'A good weeks' growth, I'd say.'

'What sort of age are we talking about?'

She grimaced. 'Difficult to say. He was so covered up and his face was grimy, but somewhere in his late twenties or early thirties, I'd guess.'

'You didn't hear his voice?'

She shook her head. 'As I said, when I asked him what he was doing, he didn't answer me. He gave me a look, as if telling me to mind my own business, then just wandered off with his hands in his pockets.'

'Is this the man you saw?' Minderedes asked, producing from his bag a copy of the E-FIT that Tatyana had helped put together.

Liz took the sheet and studied it for a moment, head to one side. 'I'm trying to picture what he'd look like clean-shaven, but I just don't know. Sorry.' She handed the sheet back to Minderedes.

They took their leave and walked up the high street, Ramsey and Minderedes in front, discussing football, Tartaglia lagging a little behind. He was thinking about travellers and homeless people and beards and men possibly disguising themselves. Richard English was far too old to be the man Liz Hallion had seen, but had he disappeared by joining the ranks of the homeless? If so, why? It would have been a desperate measure and it didn't fit with the little he knew of his character, although it wasn't impossible.

At the far end, they turned right into another wide street lined on both sides with shops. Half way along, the shops petered out and a row of small, multi-coloured Georgian houses took their place. Ramsey stopped in front of one of them – the words The Old Bakery written in italics above the fanlight – and knocked. A moment later the front door opened and a woman stood on the doorstep. She greeted Ramsey and introduced herself as Annie Nichols to Tartaglia and Minderedes.

'Is Josh here?' Ramsey asked.

'I sent him to school this morning but when your office rang, I called them. It's only up the road. He'll be back any minute now. You can wait in here if you like,' she said, ushering them into a small, comfortably furnished sitting room at the front of the house. 'If you need anything, I'll be in the kitchen.'

There was practically no mobile signal in the house and Minderedes and Ramsey went out to the street to use their phones. Tartaglia sat down in a chair by the fireplace, where a large wood-burning stove was giving off a considerable amount of heat. He stretched out his legs, enjoying the warmth, and picked up a copy of the *Hampshire Chronicle,* which was lying on the floor by the fire. It was dated that day and he leafed through it quickly but there was no mention of what had happened the previous night. No doubt the next edition would be full of it.

The front door slammed shut, he heard voices, and a moment later a scruffy, freckle-faced boy with spiky brown hair burst into the room, followed by Ramsey and Minderedes. He looked to be about ten or eleven and was dressed in school uniform.

'Come and sit down, Josh,' Ramsey said. 'This is DI Mark Tartaglia and DC Nick Minderedes. They'd like to ask you some questions about what you saw yesterday, if that's OK.'

Josh sat down on a small stool by the stove, while Ramsey and Minderedes took the sofa. He leaned forwards, looking at Tartaglia, then Minderedes. 'It's a real head, isn't it?' he said.

'It's possible,' Ramsey answered.

'But you think it is?' Josh asked. 'I mean, you wouldn't stop the fireworks if it's just a dummy?'

'We can't take any risks,' Ramsey said. 'We have to do things by the book, just in case.'

'Well, it smelt pretty funny,' Josh said. 'And it looked like a real head. It had teeth.'

'Tell us about the man you saw,' Tartaglia said. 'I hear you thought he was watching you.'

Josh shrugged. 'The head was right at my feet, sort of smoking, like. It looked pretty weird but nobody else spotted it for a bit.'

'Apart from the man,' Ramsey prompted.

'Yeah.'

'Tell me about him,' Tartaglia said.

'He was looking at the head and then at me, like he knew what I was thinking, like he wanted to see what I'd do. I thought he was pranking me.'

Was the boy reading too much into things, Tartaglia wondered. But boys of that age were generally pretty sharp. 'Is there anything else you remember?'

Josh shook his head.

'How far away was this man from where you were standing?'

Josh looked across the room towards the open door. 'About over there, where Mum's bag is.'

Tartaglia followed his gaze out into the small hall. 'So, quite close?'

'Yeah.'

'But it was dark?'

'Not with the bonfire. I saw him, no problem.'

'OK. What happened next?'

'I was looking at the head, then this woman screams. Real loud it was, and she's pointing at it and screaming, then these stupid girls start screaming, then people start running back up the hill to the car park.'

'What did you do?'

Josh shrugged. 'Nothing. It didn't bother me.'

'So you stayed put?'

'Until the police come along and told us all to go.'

'What about the man? What happened to him?'

'I dunno. He wasn't there when the police come. They made us all wait and took everyone's name and address and asked us if we'd seen something. You were there,' he said to Ramsey, as though Ramsey knew it all and it was pointless asking him anything else.

'If you saw the man again, would you recognise him?' Tartaglia asked.

'Sure.'

'What was he wearing?'

'A coat and a beanie.'

'What sort of coat? What colour?'

Josh looked at him blankly. 'It was a coat. It was grey, I think.'

'Not a jacket, or anorak?'

'No.'

'What about the beanie?'

'Black, maybe.'

'What did he look like?'

'He had a beard . . .'

'A proper beard, or stubble?'

'Stubble. Don't remember his face.'

'What sort of age was the man?'

'I dunno.'

'Have a guess.'

Josh scrunched up his mouth. 'Well, he looked a bit like my friend Steve's dad. He's nearly forty but he tells everyone he's thirty-two.'

Tartaglia smiled. Children were usually very bad at estimating adult age, as though anything over twenty was a stretch too far to think about. However, his description of the man he had seen tallied almost exactly with what Liz Hallion had said. 'OK. Take a look at this computer-generated image and tell me if the face you see looks at all familiar.'

Minderedes pulled out the sheet and passed it to Tartaglia. As he held it up for Josh to look at, Tartaglia watched the boy closely but there was no immediate reaction.

Josh frowned. 'I don't think so.'

'If he had a beard, might that make a difference?'

Josh studied the image thoughtfully. 'Maybe. Maybe it's the man I saw.' He clearly wanted it to be so, but his tone was uncertain.

'Thank you,' Tartaglia said, giving Minderedes back the paper. There was no point pushing it. He could see that Josh was disappointed.

'The head *is* real, isn't it?' Josh asked again, as Annie Nichols appeared through the doorway.

'Josh, do be quiet,' she said. 'Of course it's not real.'

'You think the man I saw put it there, don't you?' Josh asked, still looking at Tartaglia.

'Josh,' Annie said. 'Stop badgering the poor policeman.'

Tartaglia stood up. What was the point of lying? Confirmed or unconfirmed, the story that the Guy Fawkes dummy had a real human head would be all around school by now and there would soon be coverage in the local press. Whether it had anything to do with the Sainsbury's fire was another question.

'Yes, Josh. The head's real and it's possible that the man you saw may have had something to do with it being on the bonfire. That's as much as I can tell you for now.'

'Goodness,' Annie said. 'So it's true?'

Josh jumped to his feet. 'Told you. Was the rest of his body real too?'

'It's very likely,' Tartaglia said truthfully, his thoughts already elsewhere. A human head and body parts in a burnt-out car in London. A human head and body on a bonfire in Hampshire two weeks later. Even without a positive ID of the E-FIT, what were the chances?

Outside in the street, Tartaglia turned to Ramsey. 'I'll need to speak to whoever's doing the autopsy. There are certain things they must be made aware of as soon as possible, just in case there's a link with the case we're investigating.'

His phone started to ring. Steele's name was on the screen. Turning away from Ramsey, he gave her a quick run-down of what he had learned.

'I need you here right away,' she said, as soon as he had finished. 'We've had the DNA results back from the lab and there's no familial link between Richard English's son and any of the body parts in the Sainsbury's car park fire.'

'Then maybe Richard English isn't his father either.'

'His first wife was adamant that he was. She said there was no question of it.'

'Then maybe he's still alive. Maybe he's behind all of this. Maybe he planted the wallet and keys as a double bluff. Maybe he wanted it to look as though he was definitely dead.' As he spoke, he knew it didn't really make sense. Richard English would have known that it wouldn't take them long to run the DNA tests. And anyway, why would a man like English have done such an extraordinary thing? What was there to be gained by it? They would have to investigate his background and the financial side of things a lot more thoroughly.

'There's one bit of good news,' Steele continued. 'We got a hit from the Missing Persons database. The tests confirm that the head from the Sainsbury's fire belongs to a man called John Smart. He was in his sixties and disappeared about a year ago from an address in Battersea. His daughter's listed as next of kin. Her name's Isobel Smart and Sharon's trying to contact her as we speak. I'll email you the summary of the police report, so you can look at it on the journey back, and Isobel Smart's address.'

'OK. I'll get a train from Winchester as soon as I can. Nick can stay and speak to the pathologist down here.'

Nineteen

'Please can you tell me what happened to my father?' Isobel Smart asked Tartaglia. 'The female detective I spoke to earlier didn't say much, except that he's dead and that you're treating it as a murder investigation. She said you'd fill me in.' She looked at him expectantly, her wide mouth slightly open.'

It was early evening and they were sitting at the table in the kitchen of her mansion block flat in Battersea. She had arrived home from work only half an hour earlier and was still wearing a shapeless navy blue suit and pale blue blouse. She was on the tall side and overweight, but she had a pleasant oval-shaped face, framed by neat, chin-length brown hair. Looking at Isobel Smart, the words 'functional' and 'businesslike' sprang to mind; the sort of person who usually made a reliable witness in court. She sat awkwardly in the chair, shoulders slightly hunched and her large hands resting uncomfortably in her lap, fingers tightly intertwined as though she didn't know what to do with them. Based on what he had read in the report, she had nothing to gain, financially or otherwise, from the death of her father.

He chose his words carefully. 'We've found a body, or at least a part of a body, which we believe is your father's.' He didn't know how else to describe it, not wanting to mislead her.

Her brown eyes stretched open in horror. 'A *part* of a body?'

'Yes. His remains were discovered in a burnt-out car a few weeks ago, but it's likely he's been dead more or less since he went missing.'

146

'What happened?' she asked, her voice barely audible. 'How did he die?'

'At the moment, we don't know what happened, Miss Smart, but he certainly suffered a blow to the head that would have been enough to kill him.'

'A blow? Could it have been an accident? He was often walking into things, not looking where he was going. His mind was always somewhere else.'

Tartaglia shook his head. 'I'm afraid not. And before you ask, I can't tell you anything more for now.'

She sat back heavily in her chair. Her eyes filled with tears and she was silent for a moment, turning away to look out of the window into the darkness that had already fallen outside. He followed her gaze. Battersea Park was just on the other side of the street and the distant lights along the Thames embankment sparkled through the bare branches of the trees.

'I'm sorry, Miss Smart. I wish we had more answers at this stage,' he added.

She brushed the tears away with her hands and rubbed her eyes, then looked at him. 'I guess in a way it's a relief that you've finally found him. It's been terrible not knowing where he was, wondering each day if he'd suddenly walk in through the door.'

'Do you feel up to telling me what happened the day he went missing?' The gist was in the Missing Persons report but he wanted to hear it first hand from her in case she could add any more colour.

She nodded, took a crumpled tissue from her jacket pocket and blew her nose. 'I left the flat as usual about seven-thirty to go to work. He was having his breakfast. When I came home that evening he wasn't here. His hat and coat were gone, along with his backpack. There was no sign that he'd changed his clothes, so I assumed he just hadn't come home yet. I made supper and waited, but he never appeared. It wasn't like him not to let me know where he was, and I was getting worried. I tried his phone but he didn't pick up, so I called the police but they told me to wait twenty-four hours.'

'His phone was still switched on?' There had been no mention of this in the report.

'Yes. It rang a few times and then went through to voicemail. I left several messages but he never called back. Do you think he was being held somewhere?'

'We don't know at this stage. Please go on.'

She sighed. 'I tried calling again the next day and it still kept ringing. It was a really basic model and it held its charge, unlike mine. But by the evening it was either switched off or had run out of juice. I was worried sick by then, so I called the police again.'

'What sort of phone was it?'

'Just an old Nokia. It used to be mine. He didn't want anything too complicated. He just used it to make the odd call.'

According to the summary that had been emailed to Tartaglia, the full missing person's report listed both telephone records and voicemail transcripts for the two weeks leading up to Smart's disappearance. However, he was sure he had seen no mention of phone location analysis. Even if Smart's phone were too old or basic to be equipped with GPS technology, as long as it was switched on, it would still have been sending out a signal that would give them a rough idea of his movements. He made a mental note to check the file again when he got back to the office, but if it hadn't been done, he would make sure it was prioritised.

'Can you tell me a bit about your father?' he asked. 'I under-stand he lived here with you.'

'Yes. I'm divorced and I've got no kids. When Mum died six years ago, he sold their house and I told him he could move in with me. We were always very close. I guess I was a real daddy's girl. I miss him terribly, you know.' Her mouth puckered as she tried to stop herself from crying.

'Is that him?' He gestured towards a large, framed black and white photograph on a shelf above the counter, next to a handful of cookbooks.

She gave a wan smile. 'Yes. When he was a bit younger.'

'His face looks familiar.'

'Dad was an actor. His stage name was John Sharp. He used to do loads of telly and commercials in the eighties and nineties.'

'I'm sure I've seen him. I spent my life watching the box as a teenager.' He saw tears in her eyes again and decided to change tack. 'Your father was in his sixties when he went missing?'

She nodded, looking down at her hands. 'He was going to be sixty-five the next day. My brother and his family were coming over and we were going to have a celebration.'

'It says in the missing persons report that your father was a little forgetful.'

'I suppose so, but it was nothing serious. They tried to make out that he had Alzheimer's . . .'

'They?'

'The police. I guess they were trying to find reasons to explain why he might have gone off and not come back.'

'But there was no truth in it?'

'Well, he did have some problems remembering his lines on one particular job. His agent made him go and see his doctor about it, but the doctor just told Dad not to worry, that it was all part of getting older and he just needed to get a bit more rest.'

'You told the police this?'

'Yes, but it made no difference. They wouldn't listen.'

Tartaglia had quickly skimmed the doctor's report, which had been attached to the summary of the Missing Person's report. The investigation had considered all the usual angles; all the shops and places John Smart visited on a regular basis had been checked, but nobody had seen him the day he disappeared and the police had failed to find any evidence whatsoever to trigger the launch of a full-scale murder inquiry. As with Richard English's disappearance, there were no suspicious circumstances or any known threats to Smart. Even though the report had touched on the possible issue of dementia, he wasn't viewed as being vulnerable in any way. However unreasonable it sounded to his family and close friends, the conclusion was that he had, for some reason, decided to go off of his own free will. There was nothing illegal about that.

'Did he have any close friends?'

'You'll want to speak with Jim and Tony. They were his best buddies. He'd known them both for well over thirty years.' Tartaglia made a quick note of their details. 'They're usually to be found in the Sun Inn,' she added. 'That's where Dad used to hang out even after he'd moved to Battersea.'

'You mean in Barnes?'

She nodded. 'I grew up in Bellevue Road, around the corner.'

'I know the Sun Inn well, our office is just up the road. What about girlfriends? Was your father seeing anybody?'

'No.' She replied a little too quickly and emphatically and he realised it was a sensitive subject. For the first time in their conversation, he wondered if she was hiding something.

'You're sure?' he asked, looking at her closely, noting the way she suddenly avoided eye contact.

'Of course I'm sure. After Mum died, he had quite a few women chasing after him. He was a terrible flirt but he didn't mean anything by it, he just liked the attention. Said it made him feel alive. I gave his organiser to the police so they could check up on where he'd been and who he'd been seeing. I'd quite like to have it back at some point.'

'So, there was nothing going on in his personal life? Nobody—'

'No. He was a family man, Inspector. He also valued his close friends, people he'd known for years. He didn't need anybody else.'

He still wasn't convinced, sure that there was something behind her almost prudish reaction. John Smart's sex life probably wasn't relevant and Isobel was not a suspect. But he needed the full picture of Smart's day-to-day life, however uncomfortable it might be for his daughter. If she wouldn't discuss it, he was sure Smart's friends would have no such issue. 'I'll make sure you get all of his things back when we're finished with them,' he said. 'So what would a normal day look like, for your father?'

'It depends if he was working, or not. If he wasn't, he'd be off on his bicycle after breakfast, usually to his allotment. He was very into his gardening.'

'This was where?'

'At the back of one of those big houses on Castelnau. The woman who owns it joined the local allotment scheme.'

'Sorry, you'll have to explain. I know nothing about allotments.'

'Dad really missed his garden after Mum died. He tried to get an allotment from the council, but it was impossible. It seems you have to wait for at least twenty years. Then he saw an ad in the local paper about the garden scheme. Basically, residents who have a spare plot of garden and no time to look after it themselves, let other people use it to grow veg and flowers. In return, they get half the produce. It seems to work quite well. Dad was always growing all sorts of wonderful things. I think the lady who lived there must have really loved him.'

'Do you remember her name?'

'I think it was Jane, or June, but I'm not a hundred per cent sure. I never met her but he pointed the house out to me several times. It's one of the big detached ones, a little way down Castelnau on the right if you're heading towards the bridge. You can't miss it. It's got a bright-pink front door. All very sixties, he said.'

'Apart from gardening, did he have any other hobbies or interests?'

'He was a keen photographer. He'd often disappear off for the whole day on his bike with his camera. He took it with him everywhere. He loved the river, and all the wonderful old parts of London.'

'Do you still have his photos somewhere? They might give us an idea of where he went during the few weeks before he disappeared.'

'They're backed up on an external drive, with his laptop. I put them in a storage box under his bed when I had a friend to stay.'

'I'll take them away and have them copied. I'll also need any cameras he was using, just in case he hadn't downloaded all the files.'

'He just had a little Pentax. My brother brought it back from a trip to Hong Kong for Dad's sixtieth. We were trying to persuade him to embrace modern technology and go digital. I've looked for it everywhere, but I can't find it. I guess he must've had it with him the day he disappeared.'

There had been no mention of the missing camera in the report, as far as Tartaglia could remember, and he wondered how many other little, seemingly unimportant details had been overlooked. 'Did he use the camera on his phone at all?'

'No. He said the camera was crap. He usually had the Pentax in his pocket or his backpack.'

'You said his backpack's missing?'

'Yes. I guess that's why the police thought he'd gone off on a trip somewhere, as if he'd do that sort of thing without telling me.'

'OK, thanks. Do the names Richard English or Jake Finnigan mean anything to you?'

She shook her head, no flicker of recognition in her eyes. 'Should they?'

'Possibly not. Would you mind taking a look at a couple of photos and telling me if either of these two men looks familiar?' He held up photographs of English and Finnigan for her to see, but again there was no reaction and she quickly shook her head. 'What about this image?' He showed her the E-FIT of the man who had approached Tatyana Kuznetsova.

'No. Sorry.'

'Before I go, can you think of anybody who might have borne your father a grudge, however stupid or trivial it seems? We need to follow up on absolutely everything.'

Isobel said nothing for a moment, glancing away again towards the window. 'Of course the police asked me that, when they interviewed me. I can honestly say, hand on heart, that although Dad could be really irritating at times, there was no malice in him. If somebody wanted to rip him off, he'd just shrug and walk away. Life's too short, was his motto. I keep asking myself why anybody would want to kill him.' She leaned forwards across the table. 'I've got absolutely nothing to substantiate this, but I've obviously been thinking about things a lot since he disappeared...' She looked at him a little anxiously. 'You may think I'm being silly...'

'You have a theory?' he asked, trying to make it easier for her. She seemed a sensible, down-to-earth woman and it was clear she very much wanted to get to the bottom of what had happened to her father. 'Whatever you say, I won't think you're silly at all. I promise.'

She shifted in her chair, put her elbows on the table and laced her fingers together. 'Well, it all boils down to the sort of person Dad was. By that, I mean his character. He was a real people watcher. Other people's lives and business and psychological motivation fascinated him. He said it was all part of being an actor. It used to drive my mother nuts but he just couldn't switch off. I've got a friend who's a writer and she's exactly the same. Anyway, I'd be out with Dad somewhere, on the bus or the Tube, or in a restaurant or on holiday, and he'd be listening in on people's conversations and making up names and backgrounds and whole life stories for them. They were often really funny and sometimes frighteningly accurate.'

'You think this might have had something to do with his disappearance?'

She spread her hands. 'Look, I don't know, but Dad really was very nosy, Inspector. He was like a terrier; a real dab hand at rootling out a secret.'

'You're not talking about blackmail?'

She looked shocked. 'Of course not. He never did anything malicious with it. He just liked to get to the bottom of things for his own sense of satisfaction, a bit like solving the crossword, which he also loved to do. I'm just saying that maybe, in the course of his day-to-day stuff, he saw something he shouldn't, or found out something bad that somebody wanted to keep quiet...'

'Or saw somebody somewhere where they shouldn't have been?'

'Exactly.'

'But he never mentioned anything like that to you?'

She looked a little deflated by the question. 'No. I've been over everything I remember him saying to me in the week or so before he died, but there was nothing like that.'

'Maybe he just didn't get the chance.'

Twenty

Just after eight-thirty that evening, Tartaglia decided to call it a day. He put on his jacket, shouldered his rucksack and walked out of his office into the corridor. Hannah Bird was just coming out of the ladies room. She looked different. Looking closer, he noticed that she was wearing her hair loose for a change, and had put on make-up. It suited her.

'You off out somewhere?' he asked, picking up the scent of some sort of fresh, flowery perfume.

'Just meeting a friend for a quick drink, Sir.'

'You look nice. Have fun.'

'Thanks.' She gave a self-conscious smile.

'See you in the morning.'

A drink was just what he needed, he decided, as he turned towards the main stairs. Thinking of his conversation earlier with Isobel Smart, he decided to head for the Sun Inn, which was just up the road. It seemed silly going there when he could drink at home, but Donovan would be at the flat and he wanted to be on his own for a while longer, undisturbed. Also, the general buzz of background noise in the pub somehow made it easy to switch off.

'You going home?' Chang asked, jogging up the stairs towards him with what looked like a takeaway dinner in his hands.

'Drink first,' he said, hoping Chang wouldn't try and join him. 'Thought I'd try the Sun Inn. Haven't been there in ages.'

Outside, he paused on the steps and lit a cigarette. The atmosphere at the briefing meeting that evening had been electric, with almost the entire team packed into the small room. Minderedes had just got back from Winchester, where he'd attended the first hour or so of the post-mortem on the Guy Fawkes remains. Based on a cursory examination, the pathologist had confirmed that the Guy had indeed been assembled from multiple body parts belonging to what appeared to be two adult males and a female. Luckily, the local fire brigade had been on hand at the Guy Fawkes event and had managed to put out the fire relatively quickly. The body parts salvaged from the bonfire were in a better condition than those retrieved from the Sainsbury's car park fire. Neat, regular stitches were still visible in certain places where the flesh had been laced together with what looked like twine. As with the Sainsbury's fire, the bones had been sawn through at the joint with a serrated blade. Samples of the twine had been sent off for analysis, and the DNA results from the body parts would come through the following day. They would then be compared with those from the burnt-out car, as well as with the DNA of Richard English's son. The key question was whether these remains were from the same bodies as before, or whether they were looking at a new set of victims. In the meantime, they had a few hours of peace before the media frenzy would begin.

The news that the Guy Fawkes bonfire appeared to be linked to the Sainsbury's fire changed everything, as well as complicating the picture. What looked like two multiple killings with a similar MO, in different police jurisdictions, was an operational nightmare for all those involved. Steele had gone to see her superiors at Homicide West Command at the Peel Centre in Hendon, and high-level discussions were now underway between the Metropolitan Police and the Hampshire Constabulary to determine how a joint operation would be run, with a formal press briefing scheduled for first thing the next morning. There was no standard procedure for such circumstances, and Tartaglia wondered what the outcome would be and how it would affect him and his team. In the meantime, it was business as usual, except that there was now an additional fly in the ointment: Melinda Knight, a reporter he knew who worked on the crime desk of one of the tabloids, had been trying to get hold of him urgently and had left several messages. She hadn't left any details, but it was clear she knew more than she should. Although curious, he had so far resisted the urge to call her back – the less he said to anyone, the better – and she could obtain her information at the briefing the next morning, along with everyone else.

As he crossed the nearly empty car park, he checked his watch. The post-mortem would be over by now and he wondered if there was any further news. He called Ramsey's mobile and found him at home, sounding a little shell-shocked from the events of the day.

'It's definitely a series, then,' Ramsey said gloomily. The Winchester area was hardly a hotbed of violent crime and at most he probably saw a handful of suspicious deaths in the course of a year. Serial killings, with the attendant media circus, were clearly a new experience for him and it sounded as though he didn't relish what lay ahead.

'Looks that way,' Tartaglia replied. 'Parts of the London body belong to two men who were reported missing in the last year. So far, it's the only common link. I've emailed you over the E-FIT I showed you this morning. It's quite possible your man's beard is a disguise and someone might recognise him without it. We'll also try re-jigging the E-FIT to see if adding a beard makes any difference. You might want to try both versions. Once we get them over to you, flood the place. Shops, cafés, pubs, B&Bs . . . Somebody somewhere will have seen him, plus he must have local knowledge, to do what he did with that Guy and get away with it.'

Tartaglia heard the clatter of plates in the background and a woman shouting Ramsey's Christian name. He ended the call and went out through the main gate into the street.

An old white TR6 was parked on a double line just beyond the entrance. As he walked past the vehicle, he was aware of somebody getting out. He heard the clunk of the door, followed by the click of heels on wet pavement just behind him.

'Hey, Mark. What kept you so long?'

He recognised the husky voice and turned to face Melinda Knight. 'How'd you know I was here?'

'You're not at home, so . . .'

'Are you spying on me?'

She tapped her small nose. 'Just an informed guess. Can I have a quick word?'

Short and pretty, with a deceptively girlish face and a mane of crimson-red hair, she was dressed in an ancient-looking fur coat thrown over skin-tight black leather leggings, and ridiculously high-heeled ankle boots. It wasn't a look that suited most people, but she wore it well.

'It's never quick with you and I'm busy.' He turned and started walking towards the green.

'Come on, Mark,' she called out behind him. 'Give me a break. I've been trying to reach you all afternoon.'

He finished his cigarette, tossed the butt into the gutter and turned around again. 'I'm not exactly keen to talk to you, Melinda. Last time we spoke – off the record, you said – you got me into hot water.'

'That wasn't me, Mark,' she said, catching up. 'You know

what it's like. My editor insisted on putting that stupid quote in. I don't burn my contacts. It's one of my golden rules.'

'But it came from you. I guess you must have told him in your sleep.'

She waved the remark away, saying, 'That was over ages ago. I'm single again, if it's of any interest.' She gave him a meaningful look, but he knew not to read anything into it or to react.

'It's not,' he said firmly. They had almost gone to bed together on a couple of occasions, but something had got in the way each time. It was unfinished business that would probably remain that way, if he were at all sensible. 'I'm only interested in going home. Alone.'

'Oh come on, a few moments'll do. I won't spill any beans you don't want me to spill.'

'There are no beans to spill and I've got nothing to say.'

He turned away and started heading towards the Sun Inn, although he knew that wouldn't be the end of it.

'Please, Mark. I think you'll find it's *important.*'

He kept walking. She clearly knew something; more than she should, no doubt. But how much more and about what aspect of his case, was the question. No doubt he would soon find out.

'I know you were in Aldford today, Mark,' she called out. He heard the swift tap-tap of her heels behind him. 'Don't you want to talk to me about it?

Not wanting to react and too tired to feel really surprised by anything, he hunched his shoulders against the non-existent wind and kept walking, wondering how she knew. If someone had talked, was there more? He needed to find out, but Melinda usually played her cards close to her chest and was a master at reading body language. Rumour had it that she had played poker professionally in her twenties and had once won a huge sum of money, which she'd used to buy her house. Whether it was true or not, he'd learned not to trust her, nor to trust himself with her. The trick would be to find out what she knew without giving anything in return. In his current state, he didn't rate his odds.

'I know all about Mr Fawkes and his remarkable face,' she shouted. 'Poor little boy must have got quite a shock. Must have been just like Halloween.'

It was worse than he'd anticipated. He swung around to face her, hoping his expression didn't betray his confusion. Where the leak had come from wasn't clear, but that didn't matter for the moment – it wouldn't be the first time that things had leaked during an investigation. Press briefing aside, if she knew about it, it would be all over the papers by the morning.

'Who else did you have to screw to find that out?' he shouted back.

She laughed. 'Nobody. Look, I've just got a few little questions,' she said breathlessly, trotting towards him. 'It won't take a minute. Honest. Then I'll leave you in peace.'

'I don't want to talk to you, Melinda.'

'Yes you do, Mark. You always do. Come on, let's go and get a drink and we can have a nice little chat. Off the record. And I mean it this time. Promise.'

He could smell her perfume. It was strong and spicy and he couldn't decide if he liked it or not. Her heavy silver bracelets jangled as she swept a lock of hair off her face. Her black-lined eyes sparkled. He hadn't the energy to fight. Also he needed to find out what she knew.

'Just a very quick word, then.'

She was still smiling. 'Guide's honour.'

'As if you were ever in the Guides. You've changed your hair colour again, I see.'

'I got bored of being a blonde.'

'I preferred it black.'

'Yeah, but I kept getting mistaken for Amy Lee, which got really annoying. Every time I went out for a pack of fags, I'd get pestered for my autograph. Who'd be a celebrity, eh?' She looped her arm into his and they crossed Barnes High Street and walked into the small front garden of the Sun Inn. In summer it was a suntrap and always packed, whatever the hour. But on this damp, late-autumn evening it was deserted, apart from a young couple having a smoke and what sounded like a row under one of the patio heaters. They went inside and up to the bar.

'What do you want?' he asked.

'It's on me.'

He shook his head. 'Can't let a hack like you buy me a drink.'

'Post-Leveson paranoia getting to you?'

'I don't want to be in your debt, however small.'

'Alright, I'll pretend we're on a date. Vodka and Slimline please. Make it a double. I'll go and get us a quiet corner.'

'No. We can stay at the bar. I want this to be open and above board, plus this is not going to be a long session.'

She made a face. 'OK. But let's sit outside. Please? I'm dying for a fag.'

He watched her go, noticing the easy sway of her hips, the flash of her heels, and feeling annoyed with himself that he had allowed things to get this far. He ordered her drink and a single malt for himself. While he was waiting for them, he glanced around the room. He could understand why it was popular with the locals. It was a nice, cosy place to sit and enjoy a drink, with its old wooden floors, comfy leather sofas and low lighting. The food wasn't bad either. He wondered if any of the people dotted around at various tables were Jim Adams and

Tony Boyle, John Smart's old drinking buddies. There was no point approaching any of them with Melinda at his heels. In any event, before they were interviewed the next morning, he wanted to spend more time reading through the Missing Persons report on Smart's disappearance, as well as Smart's diary, both of which were now in his bag. Just one quick drink and then he'd go home.

The barman slid the two glasses towards him and handed him his change. He carried the drinks outside and found Melinda sitting on a bench against the wall, under a heater. She took a cigarette out of her bag and put it to her lips. He lit it for her and sat down opposite.

'Cheers,' she said, holding up her glass.

'This is not a celebration, nor is it a date. Let's get down to business.'

She smiled sweetly. 'It's really nice to see you too, Mark.'

'What do you want, Melinda?'

'OK. I know about the Guy Fawkes body, or bodies, should I say? There's no point asking me how I know.'

'I didn't for a minute think there was.'

'Do you have IDs for them yet?'

'No comment.'

She was watching him closely. 'I'll take that as a "no", then, but we're talking about a serial killing, of course, and you know how everyone loves a serial killer. Now, the fire in the Sainsbury's car park, that has many similarities, doesn't it? There's this ex-con, plus two others. The killer assembles them a bit like a jigsaw puzzle—'

Tartaglia slammed down his glass and stood up. 'How the fuck, Melinda! You've gone too far. Where did you get this from?'

'Why is it too far? I just know what you know, more or less. It's only what you'll be feeding everyone else at the briefing in the morning, isn't it? What's wrong with my knowing a few hours early?'

'It's not yet decided how much will come out at the briefing. How did you get that information? Who did you have to pay?'

'Stop being so high and mighty and sit down. I didn't pay, and you know full well that as a journalist, I can't and won't reveal my sources.' She reached over and grabbed his hand. 'Anyway' she went on, 'why the hell should we have stuff dribbled out to us as and when it suits you? The public have a right to know.'

'But somebody on the inside sold you that info.'

'Not true. As I said, I didn't have to pay. Please will you sit down? Pretty please? There's more.' She opened her blue eyes wide.

How *much* more, he wondered, pulling his hand away. He needed to find out. Then he would call Steele. Reluctantly, he sank down in his chair. Why, if she seemed to hold all the cards, was she there? What did she really want from him?

'Who's been talking? Is it a member of my team, someone I work with?'

'It doesn't matter, but no, it's not, if that makes you feel better. What matters is that people are going missing. They leave home one day and don't come back. Loved ones are left waiting, hoping... Hoping that the ring of a phone or the sound of a key in the lock is the person they're desperately missing. But they're not coming back, are they? There's a nutter on the loose and he needs to be stopped. How many more victims do you think are going to be taken off the streets, killed and set on fire? How many?'

He took a mouthful of whisky. 'Save the purple prose for your rag. This isn't getting us anywhere.'

'But it's all true.'

'When is this tripe hitting the front page?'

'Tomorrow. We're calling him the Jigsaw Killer. Do you like that?'

'Jesus. Can't you give the hard-bitten journo act a break for once? You're in danger of becoming a cliché.'

'It's what our readers want, Mark. I'm just doing an honest day's work, same as you.'

He shook his head wearily. 'Honest doesn't come into it.'

There was a softer side to her, a side that he really liked, but those moments were fleeting and seemed far away. He'd often wondered what she would have been like in a more caring profession, but in the end he couldn't imagine her doing anything else. Like so many hacks he had met in the course of his work, she lived on the adrenalin buzz of making a discovery. In some ways, she was no different to him.

'Why are you telling me all this? What's the point?' he asked.

'Because I want your input. What do you think of it all? Surely even you must find it weird?'

'Murder is weird.'

'Are the killings random, do you think?'

He said nothing, just shook his head again and stared down into the dark yellow depths of his drink.

'OK. At least you can tell me who's going to run the operation. I'm assuming it's the Met. I mean, the Hampshire Constabulary have no real expertise in serial killings.'

He held up his hand. 'Just stop right there. Nice though it is to see you, Melinda, and it is nice, or it would be in other circumstances, you know I can't tell you anything. You'll find out all the answers you need at the press briefing tomorrow.'

'Let's talk in general terms, then. I'm fascinated by the

psychology of it. I mean, what point is the killer trying to make?'

'Your guess is as good as mine.'

'What about fire? Is it symbolic, do you think? Are we talking the eternal flames of punishment or purification?' She frowned. 'Problem is, I don't get it. I just don't get the point of it. Why . . .'

'You've been doing this long enough to know that things don't often make sense.'

'Well, it bugs me.' She took a drag on her cigarette and leaned back in her seat, narrowing her eyes as she blew out a series of perfect rings. 'Will you get a profiler involved?'

He shook his head. 'Come on, Melinda . . .'

'OK. I know profiling's not the flavour of the month these days. Too many bloody cock-ups, I suppose.'

He gazed at her for a moment, wondering why she was talking such a load of drivel. She was never one to waste her breath and it struck him that she was trying to hide what she really wanted in a cloud of less important things. There was definitely something else and he decided to make her work for it. 'Right. I think we've covered everything. I'm tired and I need an early night.' He knocked back the remainder of the whisky and made a move to stand up.

She put her hand on his sleeve. 'Wait, Mark, please. Just one more little thing.'

'Sorry. Gotta go.'

'This is the last thing, I promise.'

'What is it?'

'Say I'm the killer, murdering people, cutting them up, reassembling the bits . . .'

'You're making him sound like Dr Frankenstein.'

'He is a bit like Frankenstein, you're right. I didn't think of that. But if he's Frankenstein making a monster, why set fire to the poor monster, and why stop at two fires?'

He sighed. 'Why do you expect any of this to be logical? You know better than that.'

'But think about it. Even if I only kill a few people, I've got enough spare parts to—'

'Get to the point.'

'OK. Do you think there's been another fire somewhere?'

He stared at her for a moment, but it was useless trying to gauge anything from her expression. Her face was blank, as though she were asking a simple, unloaded question. But it was far from that. The same question had been popping up in his mind like a nagging Jack-in-the-Box ever since seeing Dr Moran. The basic screens had yielded nothing so far, but maybe they needed to dig a little deeper. He wondered if in fact she knew more than he did. Maybe she had uncovered some-thing – it wouldn't be the first time. Or was she just fishing?

'Another fire?' he asked guardedly.

'Another body – another collection of body parts – on a fire. You know what I mean.'

'Been, or will be?' He tried to sound uninterested, forcing his spiralling thoughts away.

She was looking at him just as intently. 'Either, I guess. I mean, somebody like this doesn't just stop, do they?'

She was right and he felt the inexorable pressure of her words. It was the race against time beloved by the media. Cold-blooded serial killers like the one they were hunting kept on killing until either they were caught or they died. The night-marish fear of every detective was failure to find them in time to save another life, but he couldn't let his worry show. 'You said "been". Past tense. The future is hypothetical. We can all theorise endlessly about that.'

'Don't be such a bloody tease. Is there a third fire? Come on, you must have had the same thought, surely? Yes? Or have you . . .' Her eyes flicked up to a point over his shoulder and she stopped speaking, mouth slightly open.

He looked around. DCI Steele was standing immediately behind him.

'Hope I'm not interrupting anything,' she said to Tartaglia, with a glance at Melinda.

'Not at all.' He stifled a sigh of frustration. Her timing couldn't have been worse.

'Justin said he'd seen you heading this way for a drink and then I spotted you two sitting out here.'

Melinda stood up. 'I'm just going.' She stubbed out her cigarette and knocked back the rest of her vodka in one. 'Thanks for the drink, Mark.' As she picked up her bag and turned to go, she made a phone sign and mouthed the words 'call me' to Tartaglia. She then blew him a kiss.

'You two looked rather cosy,' Steele said, as Melinda Knight exited through the garden gate.

'Hardly.'

'What's it about then? Or is that a stupid question?'

'Work. And it's bad news, I'm afraid. Can I get you a drink? I certainly need another.'

'Diet coke. I'm driving.'

They went inside and up to the bar. 'A diet coke and a Lagavulin,' he said to the barman. 'Actually, make that a double. On the rocks.'

'Not driving?' Steele asked.

'No.'

'Where's the Ducati?'

'In the garage for a service. I haven't had time to pick it up.'

'How were you getting home?'

'Unless it starts raining again, I thought I might walk. I need to clear my head.'

'I'll go and find us another table,' she said. 'If it's all the same to you, I'd rather sit inside.'

Twenty-One

'Same again?' Adam asked, indicating her empty glass.

Hannah Bird smiled and shifted awkwardly in her seat. 'Yes, please.'

It would be her third and this time he would slip in a double. He was dying to ask her all sorts of questions about the investigation, but he didn't want to rouse any suspicions. First he needed to get some more drink down her. They were in a pub on the Hammersmith side of Hammersmith Bridge. The walls were plastered with memorabilia and photos of the Oxford and Cambridge annual boat race and it was a touristy spot, with a terrace overlooking the river at the back. It was easy to blend in amongst the transient crowd and it was also far enough away from her office, he hoped, not to bump into any of her work colleagues. Although, even if fucking Mark Tartaglia walked in, he doubted the detective would recognise him. A lot had happened in a year and he looked nothing like his former self. At the moment he could easily pass for the old photo of Kit in Kit's battered passport.

He went up to the bar and ordered their drinks, casting a quick glance behind him at Hannah. Legs crossed, handbag tight to her side as though she was scared somebody might nick it, she stared blankly ahead of her. He wondered what she was thinking. She probably couldn't believe her luck. She was wearing a short, patterned velvet skirt and clumpy heels, which emphasised her thick legs and ankles. Piano legs, as his grandmother would have called them. Thank God her top half was relatively well covered up, but her make-up was crude, as though she was unaccustomed to wearing it, the heavy foundation only highlighting her bad skin. He assumed she had changed at work – he couldn't imagine her going about her day job looking like such a tart. She also reeked of some disgusting perfume. But the thought of her making such an effort for him made him smile. The plain ones were always the easiest; they were always so grateful for the attention. It was going to be a doddle.

He had met her only two weeks before, after trawling the handful of pubs close to the murder squads' offices in Barnes, posing as somebody on his own, new to the west London area, with a paperback and a pub guidebook to keep him company. He could spot the police contingent a mile off amongst the locals and after only a couple of false starts he had got talking to her. That she worked directly for Tartaglia – what were the odds of there being more than one detective inspector with an Italian name working out of Barnes? – and was new to the team had been a massive bonus. Lady Luck had smiled on him again. He was careful to play it cool, not probing her with any direct questions, and eventually he had asked her out. Two days later, she had phoned him to say she couldn't make it. 'They were on call.' When she had explained what this meant, he could barely contain his elation. It was then simply a matter of timing, getting all the cards to fall nicely into place.

'You know, you don't look at all like a policewoman,' he said, sitting down a few moments later with their drinks.

She smiled awkwardly. 'What do you mean?'

He almost choked at the obviousness of it all before answering, 'Well, if I knew you better, I'd pay you a compliment here, but I don't want you to think I'm cheap.' Noticing the colour rise to her cheeks, he grinned. 'I think I'd better shut up. Here's to you and good detecting.'

Twenty-two

Tartaglia ordered Steele's coke and brought it over with his whisky to where she was sitting, tucked away in a far corner of the room. He sat down and reported what Melinda Knight had just said to him.

When he finished, she sighed. 'God, that's all we need – although with the press briefing tomorrow first thing, she's only a few hours ahead of the rest of them. I'll see if I can get someone to lean on her editor and find out exactly how much she knows. We may have to persuade them to hold back some of the details. You think she may be onto something with this third fire theory?'

'I don't know. I really couldn't tell if she actually knew something and wanted to know if we were on the same track, or if she was just trying to find out if we had anything. Obviously, we searched for anything similar after the Sainsbury's fire, but post today's events, maybe we should look again at the search criteria and also widen the area. I'll get Justin onto it tomorrow. What's the news from Hendon?'

'The usual horse-trading. Discussions are still going on and I've got to go back to the office for a conference call in half an hour. But last I heard we're likely to run the two investigations in tandem, with Alan Marshall taking an overall supervisory role.'

'That sounds good,' Tartaglia said, relieved that for the time being he could concentrate on the London end and let Ramsey and his team get on with their part of the investigation.

Marshall was Steele's direct superior and a man known for cutting through red tape and bureaucracy. With him in overall charge, it would make for clearer reporting lines, with the ultimate decision-making kept in London, just in case of a problem. It was by far the best option. He quickly outlined what Ramsey had just told him.

'I also spoke to Chapman earlier,' he added. 'He confirmed that Finnigan definitely had a thing about Russian women and that he had apparently talked quite freely about getting a Russian bride off the Internet when he got out. According to Chapman, some bloke Finnigan had met in jail had done just that, although the woman had then taken him to the cleaners and run off with somebody else while he was inside.'

She nodded thoughtfully. 'So it was widely known.'

'Yes, although Chapman said he thought it was all a bit of a joke, that Finnigan was just trying to big himself up. He didn't think Finnigan would actually do anything about it.'

'But he didn't have to, did he? Somebody else fixed it all up for him, made it nice and easy, handed it to him on a plate. Somebody who knew exactly what appealed to his fantasies.'

Tartaglia took a mouthful of whisky and nodded agreement.

'Whoever's doing this is certainly clever,' Steele said. 'He knows how to pull people's strings, yet he had to use Tatyana to get to Finnigan. He couldn't do it himself, for some reason.'

'Finnigan was six-foot-four and a real bruiser. Maybe he didn't fancy getting too close.

It may be as simple as that,' Tartaglia replied. 'Although why go to so much trouble? Perhaps he enjoyed the game as much as the killing. Whatever it is, he's known to Finnigan in some capacity and is somebody Finnigan wouldn't normally trust, otherwise he could have lured the man to his death himself.

Sharon's following up on Finnigan, starting with his contacts in jail. Given the sort of man he was, he must have had quite a few enemies.'

'But surely they'd be more likely to slit his throat in a dark alley than do something so subtle and convoluted?' asked Steele.

'Maybe. We need to find somebody who had the motive, the nous and the patience to see it through. Somebody must really have hated him.'

'What about John Smart?'

'No connection so far between him and Finnigan and no sign he was lured anywhere. The Missing Person investigation looked at his phone and email records and there was nothing to suggest any form of a meeting. He just goes out one morning on his bicycle, to the shops or his allotment, or whatever, and disappears off the face of the earth. Like Richard English. If English is behind all of this, why bother to plant his wallet at the scene of the fire? So far, there's nothing to link any of the other victims to him. He could have stayed quietly out of the picture and nobody would ever have thought of him.'

'Perhaps it's a double bluff and that's what he wants us to think,' Steele offered.

That seemed implausible to Tartaglia, but he'd long ago learned that it was a mistake to look at things too logically where murder was concerned. 'As of this evening, we've got access to his accounts, both business and private. A forensic accountant will be starting in the morning.' He finished his whisky. Pub measures, even doubles, didn't go far. 'It still doesn't make sense to me,' he said, after a moment.

'You mean Richard English being alive?'

'Yes. I'm trying to see a pattern in all of this, but so far I can't find one. Richard English disappeared two years ago and is never heard of again until his wallet turns up at the scene of the first fire. A year later, John Smart disappears. Part of his body turns up in said fire. As for the other victims, there's Jake Finnigan, who went missing six months ago, plus an elderly woman and a youngish man, both so far unidentified. The lab confirmed that the body parts from the Sainsbury's fire had been frozen, so whoever's doing this is collecting them for a purpose.'

'Finnigan was in jail two years ago and only got out a few weeks before he went missing, so maybe that's why he wasn't killed earlier.'

'Yes, but was this planned from the beginning, or did the killer improvise as he went along?'

They were silent for a few moments, pondering the situation, then Steele asked, 'What about the tramp who used to hang around Sainsbury's?'

'We've tried all the usual places, but no sign of him. The timing of his disappearance is odd. I spoke to the manager of Sainsbury's, who told me the man had been kipping down outside the bakery most nights for about a month once the weather turned cold. Then, around the time of the fire, he disappears.'

'He *could* be Richard English . . .'

'Yes, or possibly the killer, or maybe they're one and the same. But if so, why bother to hang around Sainsbury's, in character as it were, for a whole month. It's one of many things that don't add up.'

Donovan emerged from Hammersmith Tube station into the fresh night air and started to walk along Shepherd's Bush Road. She had gone to meet Sally, a close friend of Claire's, for a drink and had ended up having supper at her flat. It had been difficult talking about Claire and she had learned nothing of any interest in terms of the investigation. Sally had been as kind and considerate as anybody could be, but it was all a bit awkward. The last thing Donovan wanted was her pity, but there was worse to come. Sally's flatmate had come home towards the end of the evening. It was clear from her reaction on entering the flat that she had assumed Donovan had already gone, her cheery 'Hello, I'm back' cut short on seeing her. Mouth still half open, she stared at Donovan, then quickly looked away, muttered an embarrassed 'sorry' and rushed out of the room. Not everybody was so socially inept, but Donovan had seen what had happened to the families of murder victims, and now Claire's murder had marked her out too. The tragedy hung over her like an invisible cloud. Going forward, for heaven knew how long, she could expect hushed tones, averted eyes and the pity of strangers, along with the inevitable, prurient curiosity. She was no longer plain Sam Donovan. She was the woman whose sister had been killed. The one in the papers. At that new hotel. With it came a bizarre and distasteful form of celebrity. But short of changing her name and moving to a new town, what could she do?

Shepherd's Bush Road was still relatively busy, cars and the odd bus spraying freezing muddy water onto the pavement and anybody walking along it. She decided to cut through the backstreets to Tartaglia's flat and turned off the main road into Brook Green. It was a relatively peaceful residential area of low-built late Victorian houses. She had been to Tartaglia's flat more times than she could count and had often walked back afterwards to her house near the river. It was strange to be going the other way. Her rubber-soled boots made no noise as she walked and all she could hear was water dripping from the trees and the buzz of traffic from the main road. She turned the corner into Tartaglia's street and was about to cross the road when she caught a slight movement just ahead of her. She stopped. A man was standing in the shadows under a tree. He appeared to be looking at his watch; the swing of his arm was what had caught her eye. He looked back at Tartaglia's house opposite and, as though he sensed her presence, glanced around towards her. She caught the pale flicker of a face under his dark hoodie. All she could tell was that he was tall. He turned and walked quickly away, his feet making no sound. There was something not right about his reaction and she decided to follow him. It was difficult to keep track of him in the low light. He turned into a street on the right and a moment later she rounded the corner, running now, but there was no sign of him. She heard a car start up further along and the roar of the accelerator as it sped down the road, too far away to make out either the make or model of car or the licence number. It turned into Shepherd's Bush Road and was gone.

Tartaglia walked up the path to his front door and let himself in. He collected the few bits of post from the hall table and went into his flat. The lights were on, and Sam Donovan sat on the sofa facing him, arms folded, a cup of something in front of her on the table. He could tell from her expression that something was wrong.

'There was somebody outside, Mark. About half an hour ago, when I came home. I'm sure he was watching this house.'

'Outside? Where?'

'In the street. I came around the corner and I saw him. He was standing under the tree opposite, looking up at this house.'

'I'll go and take a look.'

'No point. He's gone now.'

'You're sure it was this house?'

'Yes.'

'Did you ask him what he was doing?'

'No. The minute he saw me, he disappeared off. It was all I could do to keep up. Then he drove away in a car. He'd left it parked several streets away, which is pretty odd, unless he was trying to cover his tracks.'

'What did he look like?'

'Tall, Caucasian. Dark clothing and a hoodie. That's as much as I could tell.'

He unzipped his jacket and sank down on the sofa opposite. 'I'm pretty sure it was a journalist.' A look of horror crossed her face. 'Nothing to do with Claire, don't worry. Melinda Knight was hanging around my office when I left. She probably sent somebody to watch my home too, which explains something she said. The case I'm on is about to break big-time and she's ahead of the pack. I don't know how she found out, but there's a link between our case and one that's just happened down near Winchester. I was there this morning and either somebody spotted me, or more likely there's been a leak. I'm afraid it means no peace for a while.'

'Oh . . . OK.'

She looked a little relieved, he thought, although he was surprised she didn't instantly ask him about the case. He wondered if he should tell her about it. Maybe it would be good to involve her, keep her mind off things to do with Claire. When they worked together, she had always had something interesting to say or a new and unexpected angle. As he thought about sharing things with her, it suddenly dawned on him how much he missed her company and her companionship. 'Do you want to hear about it? It might interest you. It will be all over the papers tomorrow morning.'

'I'll head off to bed, then,' she said, getting to her feet, her face blank, as if she hadn't heard him. 'Is there any news? About Claire, I mean?'

'I'm afraid not. I've just had a drink and a quick bite to eat with Steele. I asked her about progress but there's nothing new to report, no breakthrough yet on the horizon.'

She gave him a hard look. 'The trail is cold, you mean.'

'Sam, you know what it's like. Unless you get a break in the first twenty-four hours, it's usually a long, hard slog. We're doing our best, I can assure you.'

She said nothing. Her face was white and pinched-looking and she had a glazed look in her eyes. Maybe she was just tired. She turned away and walked out of the sitting room. A moment later, he heard the bedroom door close behind her.

Twenty-three

Adam lay in bed, drifting towards sleep. He had shut the curtains tightly across the window and there was barely a glimmer of light from outside. His thoughts turned momentarily to stupid little Hannah Bird. The short drink had been a success and he had left her wanting more – a dinner date arranged for later that week. He was a good listener and she seemed to want to talk. He had learned more than enough about her, the basics of her family background and schooling in Reading, that she had read geography at university and that she shared a flat in north Finchley with someone she knew from uni who was training to be a doctor and working all hours of the day and night. She was new to London and he had also eventually established that she was new to the Barnes murder squad. He sensed that underneath her excited chatter about working for a murder squad, she felt out of her depth and was struggling to cope. He could also smell her loneliness a mile away. For a policewoman, she seemed naive, but then even the best had been taken in by him in the past. It was a surprise to learn that she was no longer involved in the Dillon case, but as a result she was less wary. Eventually, she confirmed that Sam Donovan was staying temporarily in Shepherd's Bush with 'the boss'. She had also let slip that Sam would probably be allowed back to her own house in the next day or so.

He blocked out Hannah's face from his mind and allowed the darkness to envelop him, imagining a hot summer's night, somewhere far away. He was lying on a pile of cushions in a boat, floating along a canal, little bridges passing by intermittently above him. Stars filled the sky, moonlight shimmered on the water, and he felt the gentle lulling movement of the boat as Pink Floyd's 'Us and Them' played in his head. He imagined Sam lying beside him, eyes closed, arms at her sides, still and cold to the touch. All his. He tried to picture her as he remembered her, but still she evaded him. Her pale heart-shaped face became interchangeable with others. Nameless others he didn't want to see. Others who kept forcing themselves into his thoughts and dreams . . .

He heard a noise, a light tapping sound on the window, and opened his eyes. Someone, or something, was trying to get in. The curtains billowed as though in a breeze. Was the window open? He was sure he had shut and locked it. As though by an invisible hand, the curtains peeled back and he saw the window silhouetted against the sky, suddenly glowing bright in the darkness. Through the clouds, the shifting faces swam into view, the evil old hag followed by the younger ones, pressing their damp, mouldy flesh against the glass, covering it with a foul mist until he couldn't see out. Like smoke, the edges of the faces blurred as they started to squeeze through the cracks; white vapour curled into the room, re-forming in front of him. He knew what was coming and he felt the usual dread. He closed his eyes, waiting, every muscle tensed until eventually he could smell the stinking, icy breath, felt the bony fingers first stroke his throat then grasp it, tightening their grip little by little like a vice. He choked. The fingers loosened for a second or two then tightened again. He screamed, or tried to, but no sound came out. Teasing him, the fingers gave a little. He screamed again and again. It sounded like someone else's death rattle . . .

'What the fuck's up with you?' a deep man's voice said.

Adam screamed. This time he heard his own voice deafeningly loud. The overhead light snapped on.

'Are you on something?' the man asked.

Panting, it took him a moment to focus in the dazzling light. He was in his bedroom. The narrow little guest bedroom on the ground floor of Kit's house. The chair he had put against the door to secure it had been knocked over and swept to one side. Gunner stood a few feet away at the foot of the bed, dressed in nothing but a pair of boxers. His face, neck and forearms were tanned, but the rest of him was white as snow. An enormous tattoo of a crow pecking a skull decorated his broad chest, with something written beneath it, which Adam couldn't make out. How long had he been there? How much had he heard? Was Gunner spying on him? Then another thought occurred. Did he want a shag? Was that what it was all about? If so, he was barking up the wrong tree. Not for Kit, not for anyone, and certainly not a ten-foot tall Norseman who looked like a baddie from a *Die Hard* film.

The room was oppressively dry and hot. Adam's heart flapped inside him like a wounded bird and he was bathed in sweat. He badly needed a pee. 'I was dreaming, that's all,' he said, shuffling up in bed, his head pressing back against the wall. 'I'm fine now.'

'Bloody funny dream, if you ask me. You were screaming the house down like a bloody whore. I don't give a fuck what you get up to in here by yourself, but if you don't keep the volume down, we'll have the fuzz knocking on the door. They'll think someone was trying to bloody murder you.'

Someone was, Adam thought, looking at Gunner's large hands. He was sure it hadn't been a dream. His throat felt dry as dust, his neck sore, the skin already starting to bruise where fingers had pressed and squeezed. The window was shut, the curtains drawn. The only way into the room was through the door, and the only other person in the room was Gunner. Being semi-asphyxiated was no joke. Unlike some poor, pathetic idiots, wretched Kit included, he didn't find that sort of stuff remotely a turn on. Was Gunner just another fucking pervert? His gun was locked in a rucksack under the bed, but there was no way he'd be able to get to it with this man looming large above him, studying him as though he were a specimen.

Suddenly aware of his own nakedness, Adam clutched the sheet to his body. 'Get out,' he shouted. 'Get the fuck out and leave me alone.' Gunner continued to stare at him for a moment, ice-blue eyes like mirrors. 'I said, *get out.*'

Gunner raised one eyebrow as if it was all a joke, then turned and padded out of the room, leaving the door wide open, the light still blazing. The pattern of creaking floorboards indicated that he had gone downstairs to the kitchen. Adam jumped out of bed, closed the door and moved the small chest of drawers up against it. It wasn't strong enough to hold it, but if Gunner tried to come in again, at least he would have some warning. It was one thing fighting Kit off on the rare occasions that things had ever gone that far – a quick few shots of alcohol and a sedative all that was needed to cool his pathetic lust – but Gunner looked a different kettle of fish, probably not the type to care if something was consensual or not. Leaving the light on, he got back into bed and closed his eyes. In the morning he would call a locksmith and get a lock put on the door. Then he would work out how to get rid of Gunner.

Twenty-four

Rain spattered the dirty glass of the window. It was nine in the morning and just getting light. Tartaglia lobbed the newspaper into the bin, the headline 'Jigsaw Killer' still dancing in front of his eyes. The phones were ringing ceaselessly in the main office next door, but there were not enough hands to answer them. He had taken his off the hook temporarily so that he could concentrate, but it was impossible.

'How are you doing with John Smart's photos?' he asked Dave Wightman, who had just come into the room. Short, stocky and blond, Wightman's earnest, boyish face belied a cynical mind and sharp brain. He was the youngest member of the team and the in-house technology expert.

'I've downloaded all the stuff on the hard drive and sorted it into files week by week, going back six months from when he disappeared. I've set it up in the meeting room, if you want to take a look?'

'Give me a minute.' Tartaglia reached for the half-drunk cappuccino on his desk. It was lukewarm but he needed the caffeine. He drained it and threw the empty carton in the bin, then gathered up the papers he had been reading and put them back in the file. He had found the tracking analysis for John Smart's phone for the day of his disappearance and the following day. It was an old model that used GSM technology, which gave them only a rough location to within three quarters of a square mile. According to the analysis, the phone had started off in the Battersea area first thing in the morning and by

184

mid-morning had moved to Barnes, where it stayed until either it had been switched off or the battery had run out, the following day. The fact that Smart had lived in Barnes for the best part of forty years had given weight to the view held at the time that he had probably gone back there and stayed of his own free will, possibly being put up in secret, either by a friend or a lover. Based on what Tartaglia knew of Smart, it seemed unlikely. His family and friends mattered very much to him and he would not have gone off without telling anybody.

He had spent the remainder of the previous evening going through Smart's diary and address book, trying to get a feel for the rhythm of his life, the day-to-day patterns. They were contained in an old-style Filofax binder, the entries made in a neat hand with a blue fountain pen. There were only eight months' worth of diary entries to look at, but it didn't matter. Eight months was more than enough, if what Isobel had said about her father was correct. If he had accidentally stumbled upon somebody's secret, it would have been in the recent past before his disappearance.

The week before had followed a predictable pattern. He had met up with his friends Jim and Tony on the Saturday, and gone for lunch at his son's house on the Sunday. On the Monday, the only entry was a dentist's appointment. He had been working Tuesday, Wednesday and Thursday at the BBC. On Friday, he had disappeared. There was a note in the Missing Person file to the effect that a number of people had been spoken to at the broadcasting studio but nobody remembered anything having been amiss with the actor.

The entry for the previous Friday read *4.00pm. The Bourne Legacy. R.* The Missing Person report made no mention of this having been followed up. Looking at Smart's address section, there were a large number of people whose name started with the letter 'R'. He had called Isobel that morning and asked her who 'R' might be, but she said she hadn't a clue and had no memory of her father having been to see the film. She said emphatically that when he went to the cinema, it was always with her. Something about her tone told him she was lying. He was sure now that Smart had got himself a girlfriend and Isobel was jealous. Whether or not it mattered was another question. He was due to see Jim and Tony later and would get to the bottom of it then. In the meantime, Hannah Bird had been tasked with going through the address book and speaking to everybody whose name – first name or surname – began with an 'R'.

He was about to go when Sharon Fuller put her head around the door. 'Do you have a minute, Sir?'

'Any news on Finnigan?'

'I'm going over to the Scrubs in half an hour to interview one of the warders and a couple of inmates who knew Finnigan when he was inside, but I wanted a quick word about Sam.'

'Have you seen her today?'

'Yes. I stopped by on my way in. The good news is her dad's out of danger, although he won't be well enough to travel for a while.'

'Thank God. What about her?'

Fuller made a face and pushed her glasses up her long nose. 'She keeps asking me all sorts of things about the case, wanting to know a whole load of stuff that I don't think she should know. Or at least I don't think I should be the one to tell her.'

'Like what, exactly?'

'She wants the nitty-gritty, of course. I gave her a few little bits and pieces to keep her quiet, but it wasn't enough. She wants to know exactly what we know, every little detail. I think she'd even like a copy of the pathologist's report, if she could get it. To be honest, I'd want the same in her shoes, but I don't think she's ready for it, I really don't.'

He nodded, picking up something else in her tone. 'It's way too soon. What else are you thinking?'

'I know she's on all sorts of pills so maybe it's just me being a bit silly, but—'

'What's the matter?'

'I've been in to see her every day since it happened, just keeping an eye on her, like you asked me. I get the impression she can't wait to see the back of me, which is OK, I don't want to force myself on her. I know everybody deals with this sort of thing differently and some people need more space than others. But she doesn't seem right to me.'

'In what way?'

She sighed. 'I can't put my finger on it, Sir. She's barely eating, which doesn't help, But she's a bit . . . well . . . weird, if you ask me. If only her mum was here. I think she should be watched.'

'Watched? What do you think she'll try and do?'

'I don't think she's suicidal, if that's what you're thinking. She's just a bit odd. Not acting and reacting normally, if you know what I mean.'

He nodded. 'Thanks for telling me, Sharon.' Based on the little he'd seen of Donovan, particularly the previous night, he had to agree with Fuller. She had seemed so distant and preoccupied, not at all her normal self, but he'd just accepted it as par for the course and thought no more about it. Maybe he'd been too wrapped up with everything else to take proper note, but it wasn't good enough. 'The drugs don't help,' he said, feeling a little guilty.

'Maybe that's it. She does seem a bit fuzzy. I'd be more worried that she'd step out in front of a car or a bus by accident. It's like she's not all there, like her mind, her thoughts are somewhere else.'

'In the circumstances, that's perfectly normal.'

'Yes, I know, but she *is* going out places. Yesterday when I went over to see her she was just coming back from somewhere.'

'You mean during the day?'

'Yes. She said she'd been for a walk, but she looked a bit frazzled. I don't think she should be out on her own, that's all.'

'If we didn't already have our hands full, I'd suggest you do a bit of unofficial surveillance, but I can't spare you – or anyone else – at the moment.'

'I'm happy to do it in my own time, Sir. If necessary, we can organise some sort of a rota. I know Justin, for one, will want to help. But that still leaves the daytime. She was up and about when I dropped by this morning, with the whole day ahead of her.' She looked at him as though she expected him to know these things.

He had left the flat very early that morning and hadn't seen or heard anything from Donovan since the previous night. Given everything that was going on, he couldn't possibly keep an eye on her, but Fuller had a good feel for people and knew Donovan well. She was married, with three children, so for her to offer to give up her precious family time meant it must be serious.

'OK. I'll talk to Steele and see what she thinks.'

'Thank you. It would be terrible if something happened to her.'

Tartaglia picked up a black coffee from the machine in the corridor and took it into the meeting room where Wightman was waiting. A monitor sat on the table, linked to Wightman's laptop. Tartaglia sat down beside him.

'Where do you want to start?' Wightman asked.

'The day of his disappearance, or as close as.'

'There's nothing that day. The nearest was the weekend before.'

'He had a busy week,' Tartaglia said, thinking back to the entries in Smart's diary. 'Maybe he didn't get the time. So what have you found?'

'Endless shots of some sort of family gathering with lots of kids,' Wightman said, clicking on a folder. A slideshow of a family lunch party flicked past the screen.

'OK, next.'

'This is the day before. Saturday seventeenth. Lots of photos of Barnes. I recognise most of the places. He's particularly keen on the river, and boats.'

'So his daughter said.'

'There were loads of the boat race earlier in the year. You'd have thought a handful would be enough.'

'You're not a photographer,' Tartaglia said, with a smile. 'Show me what he took in the two weeks before he disappeared.'

He sipped his coffee as he watched. Like Wightman, he recognised many of the places Smart had photographed in and around Barnes. There was a short series of pictures of a large Victorian house and garden, including a well-kept vegetable patch, presumably the one where Smart had worked; shots of the embankment, and the river with the sun setting; views of the common and its duck pond, and general shots of people walking along the high street. Nothing stood out as sinister, or even odd.

'Are there any other pictures of people?'

'I haven't gone back very far yet, but there are some of a woman taken a few weeks before he died.'

'You'd better show me.'

189

Wightman consulted a list of entries and opened a file for the twenty-eighth September. The photos showed a young woman with shoulder-length dark hair, sitting in the sunshine outside a pub or a café. She was laughing, and holding up a glass as though toasting the man behind the camera.

'That looks like the Sun Inn,' Tartaglia said, peering at the screen.

'She's pretty.'

'Yes, and a good thirty years younger than Smart. Maybe this is the girlfriend Isobel Smart didn't want me to know about. I'm seeing one of Smart's friends shortly. Do me a print-out and I'll see if he recognises her.'

As he spoke, Minderedes put his head around the door. 'Ready to go when you are, Sir.'

Twenty-five

They were twenty minutes early for the meeting with Smart's friend Tony Boyle, and Tartaglia decided to make a quick detour via the house in Castelnau where John Smart had gardened in his spare time. Minderedes pulled up opposite on a double yellow line to let him out.

'I'll park around the corner,' he said. 'Shall I come and find you?'

'No. Go and talk to the neighbours on either side and call me when you're done. I'll see if the owner is in. What's the woman's name?'

'Jane Waterman, according to the file. I called around last night but there was nobody in.'

The house was set back from the road behind a high wall, screened by two huge conifers as tall as the roof. Tartaglia recognised it from the pictures Smart had taken. He pushed open the gate and walked up the small semi-circle of drive. There was a garage to one side, with a door beside it leading to the back. Fallen leaves had been raked into two large piles on the grass, so it looked as though somebody was around. He went up the steps to the front door and rang the bell. After a moment he tried again, but there was no answer. He stepped back and looked up at the house. It was double-fronted, built in heavy, late Victorian style, with bay windows, gables and a small turret at either end; comfortable rather than aesthetically pleasing. All the windows were dark and dirty looking, as though they hadn't been cleaned in years. There was no sign of life inside. He caught the smell of burning leaves on the wind. The smoke seemed to be coming from the back, over the roof of the garage. Stepping into a flowerbed, he peered through the grime into a sitting room. A huge vase of brown dried flowers stood on a table in the window, half blocking the view, but he could see a mug and newspaper sitting on a coffee table beyond. The room on the other side was furnished as a dining room and equally empty. He was about to leave when a youngish man appeared through the side gate from the back, pushing a wheelbarrow. He was dressed in overalls, with a beanie pulled down over his hair.

'I'm looking for Jane Waterman,' Tartaglia said. 'Is she here?'

'Sorry, what was that?' The man pulled out an earphone from under his hat.

'I want to speak to Jane Waterman. Is she in?'

'She's away at the moment.'

'Where's she gone?'

'Staying with family, I think. She hasn't been well. She went off with her nephew a few weeks ago.'

'Do you have a contact number for her?'

'Sorry.'

'When will she be back?'

'Search me. She never says. Comes and goes as she pleases.'

'It's police business,' Tartaglia said, showing his warrant card. 'If she comes home, can you ask her to give me a call?' He handed the man his card. 'Who looks after the house while she's away?'

'I do.'

'And what's your name?'

'Jason. Jason Williamson. I do the gardening and a bit of maintenance. Why?'

'Have you come across a man called John Smart?'

Williamson looked blank. 'Doesn't ring a bell.'

'This would have been about a year ago. He apparently used to do the garden here.'

'Before my time, I'm afraid. The bloke before me was Polish, but he didn't stay long.'

'Why was that?'

'He nicked some of her silver. She had the police after him, she told me, but they never caught him.'

'OK, thanks. As I said, if you see her, make sure she gives me a call.'

Tartaglia found Minderedes at the next-door house, standing on the doorstep chatting to a woman holding a toddler in her arms. The house was similar in style to Jane Waterman's but recently refurbished, with clean brickwork, gleaming paint and a new-looking Porsche Cayenne in the drive. Iron gates blocked the entrance and he was forced to call out to attract Minderedes's attention.

'Woman's name is Gregson,' Minderedes said, coming back. 'The family only moved in a few months ago, so they never knew John Smart.'

'What about Jane Waterman?'

'She doesn't know her, but said she saw an old lady in a wheelchair being pushed out of the house and helped into a car a few weeks ago.'

'That tallies with what the gardener said. Apparently, she's gone off to stay with relatives. When you get back to the office, check to see if she reported the theft of some silver within the last couple of years. Apparently, a Polish gardener may have been involved.'

Minderedes made a note.

Have you tried the house on the other side?'

'Nobody in. I'll go back again later.'

Tartaglia checked his watch. 'Let's walk over to Tony Boyle's house. I could do with stretching my legs.'

Fifteen minutes later, they were sitting in the comfortable front room of Boyle's small terraced house close to Barnes Bridge, overlooking the river. A fire was burning in the grate and Boyle's wife had provided them with a large tray of coffee and biscuits, which Minderedes was making the most of. Jim Adams, Smart's other close friend, was there too.

'In spite of what the police said, it didn't make sense his disappearing,' Tony Boyle said. 'He wouldn't just go off somewhere, so I knew something must have happened to him.'

'You saw him the night before he disappeared?' Minderedes asked.

Tony nodded. 'He'd been working on that BBC thing... what's it called?' He looked over at Jim.

'It was a play for Radio 4, one of the Sherlock Holmes stories.'

'That's right. He came into the Sun afterwards for a pint on his way home.'

'He seemed perfectly normal,' added Jim. 'Other than some gripe about how little he was getting paid, not a care in the world.'

'What did you talk about?' Tartaglia asked.

'Nothing particularly interesting, as far as I can recall. I remember they'd finished the recording and he wasn't working the next day.'

'He didn't mention being worried about anything, however small?'

Tony grimaced. 'He certainly talked about the plans for his birthday at the weekend. He was really looking forward to it, although Isobel had insisted on organising it, which was tricky.'

'Tricky in what way?' Tartaglia asked.

'Well, he couldn't exactly ask Rose, could he? But I could tell, even though he didn't want to criticise Isobel, he really wanted her to be there too and I think he and Isobel had had a bit of a row about it. They were barely speaking the week before he disappeared.'

'Is Rose his girlfriend?'

Jim laughed. 'Good lord, no. She's his other daughter.'

'I didn't know he had another daughter,' Tartaglia said.

'Nor did he, until a couple of years ago,' Jim said. 'Then this woman writes to him out of the blue, saying she's his daughter. It was quite a shock.'

'Is this Rose?' Tartaglia asked, taking out the photo of the young, dark-haired woman from his bag.

'That's her,' Tony said. 'She's a lovely girl. He often used to bring her to the pub for a drink or a bite to eat. He couldn't take her home, of course, what with Isobel being so tricky.'

Jim nodded. 'Rose got in touch with him via his agent. At first he thought it was a try-on, someone after some money, or something. But then he met her and she was the spitting image of him, only pretty. There wasn't any point doing any of that DNA testing business. It was clear as crystal she was his.'

'Who's the mother?' Tartaglia asked.

'Some actress he had a fling with when he was in rep, back in the early eighties,' Tony said. 'She only told her daughter who her real father was recently.'

Jim nodded. 'John said the woman was also married so I suppose that's why.'

'And Isobel knows about all of this?' Tartaglia asked, thinking back to their conversation. It explained why she had wanted to shut out all questions about her father's private life. She had then lied about not knowing who 'R' was.

195

'Most definitely. Eaten up with jealousy, I think, poor thing. Didn't want to share her father with anyone.'

'I suppose she was just defending her mother, or her mother's memory,' Tony said. 'But Isobel refused to meet Rose and it really hurt John. His son, Ian, was OK with it in the end, luckily. He's got a family of his own and I guess he could afford to be more grown up. But Isobel was a right bitch about it, if you'll excuse my French. She said if Rose came to his birthday, she'd leave.'

'Do you know how we can get in touch with Rose?' Tartaglia asked, deciding he would speak to Isobel immediately the interview was over.

Tony shook his head. 'I haven't seen her since John disappeared.'

'She lives out of London, somewhere,' Jim said. 'I remember she was worried about missing her train home. I think it went from Paddington.'

'Isn't she an actress?' Tony asked.

'A set designer, I think,' Jim said. 'Freelance. Or at least something to do with the theatre. It's obviously in the blood, although Isobel hasn't inherited any of it. She's much more like her mother. Not at all artistic.'

'Why didn't you tell me about Rose?' Tartaglia asked, practically shouting. He didn't care who heard.

'Because it isn't important.' Isobel Smart clamped her thin lips shut as if that was the end of the matter.

They were standing in a small meeting room at the office in Marylebone where she worked as an accountant. He had hauled her out of an internal meeting, threatening to take her down to the local station if she didn't cooperate.

'This is a murder investigation. Everything's important. What else have you lied about?'

196

'Nothing. I swear. I didn't tell you about *her* because there was no point. She couldn't help you anyway.'

'I'll be the judge of that. She seems to have seen your father quite often, and he certainly seems to have cared about her. Maybe he told her something he didn't tell you.'

Isobel looked as though she had been slapped but made no reply.

'I need her phone number. Right now.'

'I don't have it.'

'I don't believe you.'

'I tell you, I don't have it. Why would I want it? I didn't want to speak to her.'

'If I find you're lying again . . .'

She glared at him, arms folded tightly across her ample chest. 'I don't have it. When Dad disappeared, she kept calling me at the office; he must have told her where I work. Anyway, she drove me nuts. She wanted to come over to the flat and look through his stuff. She probably wanted to take something . . .'

'Maybe she was genuinely worried. Maybe she wanted to find out what had happened to her father.'

'Well, she had no right. He wasn't her father. That was a story to try and get money out of him.' Tears were streaming down her face now. In a way he sympathised. The bubble of a perfect family life had been burst by a secret from the past. She had clearly idolised her father and her reaction was no different to that of a jealous lover – and equally irrational.

'What did you say to her?'

'I said the police were handling it and that I'd get a solicitor onto her if she didn't stop harassing me.'

'When was the last time you spoke to her?'

'About a year ago. She called me again and I told her the police had found nothing. I haven't heard from her since.'

'Did she contact the police?' There had been no mention of another daughter in the Missing Person report.

'How the hell do I know? And I don't bloody well care. Now can I get on with my work?'

Twenty-six

The front door slammed shut and he heard Gunner's footsteps pound down the path towards the street. He grabbed his jacket and followed him outside. It was cold, the sky a deep iron grey, rain threatening. He put on his jacket and peered around the hedge. Gunner was nearly at the end of the road, walking fast. From a distance, it looked as though he was wearing a suit. Adam followed, ready to dip into a gateway if his quarry looked around. At the corner of Kensington Church Street, Gunner stopped, scanned both ends of the road, and a moment later stuck his hand in the air to hail a cab.

As he climbed in and drove off, Adam ran to the end of the street and did the same.

'Follow the cab in front,' he said, jumping in and slamming the door. It was such a cliché but he didn't know what else to say. 'I'll give you double money if you don't lose it, but I don't want them to know. OK?'

'No problem,' the cabbie said flatly, as though used to such instructions.

The drive took them along the Bayswater Road and into Hyde Park. It looked as though Gunner was heading into town. Adam hadn't seen him in a suit before and wondered if he was going to an interview. In the few days Gunner had been staying at the house, he appeared to have no regular routine, going out and coming back at unpredictable times. He also appeared to be an insomniac, habitually making noisy forays down to the kitchen in the middle of the night. He certainly didn't seem to have a regular job.

The traffic slowed considerably as they negotiated Park Lane and turned off into Mount Street and then into South Audley Street, Adam's taxi now two cars behind. At the bottom, they turned right and, just before Grosvenor Square, Gunner's taxi pulled up on the left-hand side.

'What do you want me to do?' The cabbie asked in a bored tone.

'Drive past. Stop over there, behind that red car.'

Through the back window of the taxi Adam saw Gunner disappear into one of the houses. He paid the cabbie, waited a minute to make sure Gunner wasn't coming straight out again, then walked back along the street to where he had last seen him. Behind the eighteenth-century façade was an office building, like the majority of the others in the street and surrounding area. He took a quick look through the window at the front, but all he could see was a dark, empty meeting room. A fish-eye security camera stared out above the brass entry plate, which was engraved with the initials *G.R.M.A.* He took a photo of the plate with his phone. Wondering what to do next, he spotted a café on the corner, just a block and a half away, with tables and chairs outside on the pavement. He made his way there and sat down, tucking himself away in a corner that was well screened from the road by some large tubs of laurel. Through a gap he had a clear view of the building Gunner had entered. He turned on the patio heater and ordered a latte. As the waitress went inside, she shouted out instructions in Polish to the man behind the bar, along with a rude remark about customers who were stupid enough to sit outside in the cold. Since joining the EU, Poles had taken over London and you couldn't move without hearing their foul language being spoken. He understood the gist, having been brought up in London by his Polish grandparents who had insisted he speak Polish at home.

Using his phone, he googled the company acronym, along with the office address. It stood for Global Risk Management Associates, whatever that was. Keeping one eye on the street, he tabbed through the website menu. The company seemed to be mainly active in Africa and the Middle East, 'protecting companies' risks abroad', according to the blurb, with particular focus on the oil industry. The phrases 'security consulting', 'security solutions' and 'experts in multiple security disciplines' appeared many times, as well as the strapline 'G.R.M.A. helps its clients to make security an integral part of their business model.' Along with sections on personal and business protection, the other main tab was headed 'Kidnap, Ransom and Extortion,' with a paragraph that referred to personnel having 'backgrounds in the military and special forces'. He thought of Gunner's physique, his tanned face and forearms, the tattoo of the crow and skull on his chest. It all made sense and it filled him with foreboding. What was he doing in Kit's house? Was he really Kit's lover? Or had he been sent there by somebody else?

Twenty-seven

'So, where are we with the fires?' Tartaglia asked, looking over at Justin Chang.

It was early evening and Tartaglia had called an impromptu meeting for those members of his team who weren't still out on the road. The small room was stuffy, the heating having decided to work overtime for a change.

'I've been in touch with the Coroners' Association and asked for details of all fires in the various jurisdictions involving human fatalities over the last two years,' Chang said. 'It's roughly eight hundred incidents. The majority were fires in the home caused by poor wiring, cigarettes, chip pans catching alight. That sort of thing. There were less than a hundred cases where deliberate ignition was suspected.'

'Anything interesting?'

Chang looked unenthusiastic. 'It's difficult to tell. There's a heck of a lot of stuff to get through and it's not straightforward. So far, I've found three incidents worth checking into further, but I'm waiting for more info.'

'What about you, Sharon?'

Fuller yawned. 'Nothing new to report from the Scrubs, although both inmates I saw remembered Finnigan talking about having some hot Russian babe come to see him. Sounds like he wasn't discreet with the photos of her either. Finnigan wasn't a popular guy, by all accounts, but neither of them could think of anybody with a specific grudge. According to the warder, Finnigan mixed with a pretty heavy crowd inside, but he didn't cause any actual trouble and kept himself to himself for the most part. He'd been transferred there from Pentonville because of some sort of incident. I'm waiting for the details.'

'Any news on finding Smart's daughter Rose, Hannah?' he asked, turning to Hannah Bird who was leaning against the door, arms folded. Everything about her face and body language spoke of tiredness. He couldn't remember what her previous role had been before she joined the murder squad, but he guessed she was unused to the pace and the hours. He had seen it before, and wondered if she would learn to cope. It was either sink or swim and his bet was on the former.

'There's only one Rose, or Rosie, in John Smart's contacts,' she said, trying not to yawn. 'I've left messages on her home number and mobile but she hasn't called me back yet. Do you want to send someone over to her address? She lives in Frome, in Somerset.'

'Keep trying, but if you don't get a reply by tomorrow morning, get somebody over from the local station. It's important we find her. Smart may have told her something.'

As he spoke, the door behind Bird was pushed open and she moved aside to let Minderedes in.

'Sorry I'm late,' he said. 'I've been over at the house next door to Jane Waterman's. The woman who lives there had just got back from work. She and her husband haven't been there that long and didn't know John Smart, but she did remember the Polish gardener, Marek Nowak, because he did a few hours of gardening and DIY for them as well. She described him as always cheerful and hardworking and said she was very surprised to hear he'd run off with some of Jane Waterman's things. I've also dug out the crime report for the burglary. Waterman's nephew alleged that various items of silver and jewellery had been stolen from the house by Nowak.'

'This was when?'

'About three months after Smart disappeared. According to the report, Nowak hadn't been staying at the house long, but he had worked for Jane Waterman on and off before, so he may have crossed over with Smart at some point.'

'Did they check to see if he had a criminal record back home?'

'I don't think so. Nowak apparently did a runner, so charges were never brought. But there is mention of a girlfriend being interviewed, although she wasn't very helpful.'

'You'd better go and talk to her in the morning. She might be more cooperative if she knows it's a murder investigation.'

As he finished speaking, Carolyn Steele put her head around the door. 'Sorry to interrupt, Mark, but I've had Ian Armstrong on the phone. Someone has tipped him off that Richard English may be a victim of the Jigsaw Killer, as the press are now calling the perpetrator. I told Armstrong there was no DNA match with the London fire, but that didn't satisfy him. Is there any news from Hampshire?'

He shook his head. 'We should get the results this evening, or tomorrow morning at the latest. I spoke to Ramsey earlier and he's chasing his end too.'

'Has anyone managed to trace the tramp?'

'Still no luck.'

'OK. Let me know as soon as you hear from Ramsey. I said I'd call Armstrong back. I didn't, of course, tell him we're treating English as a possible suspect.'

When the meeting was over, Tartaglia headed back to his office just in time to see Chang bounding down the main stairs two at a time towards the exit. He found Fuller standing by the coffee machine further along the corridor, punching buttons.

'Where's Justin off to so fast?' he asked.

'Keeping an eye on Sam. It's his turn tonight.'

Twenty-eight

Adam closed the front door quietly behind him and took off his coat. He had waited at the café for well over an hour for Gunner to come out, but in the end he had given up and spent the rest of the afternoon walking aimlessly around the streets north of Oxford Street, wondering what to do. Gunner's presence in the house threatened everything, but getting rid of him wasn't a simple matter. The sheer practicalities of killing him and disposing of his body might be overcome – he had thought about several ways he might manage it, even given the man's strength and size. He could spike a bottle of his favourite drink, which appeared to be either whisky or Red Bull – and sometimes a mixture of both – with an elephant-sized dose of Rohypnol. When mixed with alcohol, it could paralyse even somebody with Gunner's physique quite quickly. And there were also other drugs he had used that had a similar effect. Once Gunner was out of it, killing him would be child's play, although he would have to think carefully about how to deal with the body. But would killing Gunner be enough? He somehow doubted it would end there. The questions kept gnawing away at him: Who else knew Gunner was there? *Why* was he there? Was it to do with Kit or something else?

The hall was dark and he paused just inside and listened. Was Gunner home? After a moment, he picked up the sound of the TV coming from the basement sitting room. He had been planning on watching a film. They were showing *The Runaway Jury*, followed by *The Fifth Element* on Film4. His mind was churning and he needed the distraction. Fucking Gunner. It was the only television, and more importantly the only comfortable place to sit, in the whole house. But he had no desire to be in there with him.

He decided to go and make a cup of tea. On the way downstairs, he stopped outside his bedroom and put the key in the lock. It wouldn't turn: the door was already unlocked. He had rushed out of the house in such a hurry earlier; had he forgotten to lock it? He didn't think so. He opened the door, went inside and scanned the room. Superficially, it looked undisturbed. The top two drawers of the small chest were exactly as he had left them, a couple of millimetres open, and the bottom drawer fully pushed in. He checked inside. Nothing seemed out of place. Using his phone torch, he knelt down and checked under the bed where he had stowed his rucksack. He could see the padlock, still intact, the numbers scrambled in the order he had left them. Then he noticed a faint line in the dust, only visible because of the angle of the light. It looked as though it might have been made when a loose strap brushed along the floor as somebody carefully lifted out the rucksack from under the bed. It hadn't been there that morning. The rucksack contained his most important possessions: his gun, his grandfather's hunting knife, sharp as ever, which the old man had used to scalp more than one Nazi in the war, and the rest of his basic kit – the disposable gloves, the plastic ties, the handcuffs and the Rohypnol. There was also five thousand pounds in cash, in fifty-pound notes. He undid the padlock and took out the two fat wads of money. He counted them out three times before he was satisfied that not a single note was missing. But maybe Gunner wasn't after his money . . .

Adam sat back on his heels. Even if Gunner had somehow picked the lock, got into his room and been through his things, and also had the skill to pick the padlock too, did it matter? It was against the law to keep a gun under the bed, but that was about it. It wasn't a hanging offence. There were no papers or other forms of ID in the rucksack. He kept what he needed on him at all times, and the rest in a lock-up elsewhere, in case he needed to leave suddenly. There was nothing in the room, or amongst his things, that could identify him. But if Gunner had gone to all that trouble to snoop, why had he made the mistake of leaving the door unlocked? Was he just careless, or was it deliberate? Did he want Adam to know that he'd been in there, that nothing was out of bounds and that he could get access whenever he liked?

Rage filled him and he dug his nails deep into his palms. Something had to be done. He would make a plan that night. In the meantime, he needed a drink; something stronger than tea. He went downstairs to the kitchen, deaf to the sound of the TV blaring from the room at the front. Ignoring the pile of dirty dishes that Gunner had left in the sink, he grabbed a glass, hand trembling, and filled it with water. He knocked it back and started looking in the drawers for the key to Kit's small wine cellar, where he also kept some bottles of half-decent brandy. As he hunted around, he noticed a business card sitting on the counter and picked it up. His heart skipped a beat. The name *Detective Sergeant Kevin Moore* was printed underneath the Met Police logo. It didn't say which section he worked for but the card was crisp and pristine. Fresh out of the wallet. He felt the blood rush to his head and stood still for a moment, trying to calm himself. It might not mean anything, he told himself. No point jumping to conclusions. He went into the sitting room, where Gunner was stretched out on the sofa in a pair of Calvin Klein briefs and socks, watching some sort of war movie.

'What's this?' Adam asked, holding up the card. The sound was so loud, he had to repeat himself.

'Copper came by today while you were out,' Gunner shouted without looking up.

'And?'

'You need to call him.'

Again he felt the rush of heat to his face, sweat breaking out across his back. 'Me? Why?'

'Because he wants to speak to you.'

'I don't understand. Why does he want to speak to me?'

'He was asking about Kit. I said you could help.'

'Why the fuck did you say that?'

Gunner looked around and gave him a dead-eyed stare. 'Because you've seen him more recently than I have,' he bellowed. He went back to watching the screen, as a helicopter exploded in mid-air.

'Why the hell's he asking after Kit? What's Kit done?'

Gunner turned to look at him again, this time giving him a curious look. 'Kit hasn't done anything. Apparently, Kit's disappeared.'

Twenty-nine

Back in his office, Tartaglia stood for a moment looking out of the window at the houses opposite. Lights were on here and there, curtains still open, revealing people going about their evening routines. For a moment, he wished that he, too, could go home, open a bottle of wine, maybe listen to some music. But he was too wired to relax, there was too much to do. Yet he felt in limbo. A lot appeared to be happening with the case, with a myriad leads being followed and potential connections being turned up, but he felt they were barely inching forwards at best. They still hadn't found the key to it all, the one detail that, however small, brings everything suddenly into focus and makes sense of the rest. Had there been another fire that they hadn't yet found? They were already stretched to the limit with the existing workload and, by the sound of things, it might take Chang days to go through the all the records. Perhaps there was a shortcut.

He took out his phone and dialled Melinda Knight's number. She picked up in a heartbeat, as though she had the phone in her hand.

'Hi, Mark. I was wondering when you'd call,' she said.

He heard the buzz of voices in the background. It sounded as though she was in a bar or pub. 'Are you busy?' he asked.

'Nothing that can't be put on hold. For you, at least.'

Half an hour later, Tartaglia joined Melinda in a wine bar just off Kensington High Street, near her office.

'Before we start, this is off the record,' he said, handing her the large glass of chablis she had requested and sitting down on the stool beside her at the bar.

'That's fine. But if anything comes of it, I want an exclusive. OK?' She fixed him with hard blue eyes.

'You mean you can't rely on your deep throat to tell you what we're up to?'

She smiled. 'Don't be cheap. Anyway, I'd rather it came from you. Do we have a deal?'

He nodded. If she helped to find the killer, she could have all the exclusives she liked. 'Now, tell me what you know about old fires.'

Melinda shifted in her seat, took a large sip of wine, then put down the glass. She folded her arms on the counter, clearly enjoying the moment. 'Where shall I begin?'

'Just get on with it.'

She smiled. 'I think this bloke, our beloved Jigsaw Killer, has done this sort of thing before. Why?' She held her finger up in the air, like a teacher asking a question. 'Because he's damn good at it, he's fluent. I can't believe the fire in that supermarket car park was his first. It was all so well researched, even down to the car he stole. Don't you think?'

'Maybe.' He couldn't disagree, although nothing surprised him any longer where murder was concerned. Sometimes a killer got it right first time, either through careful, methodical planning or just sheer luck. There was no point reading too much into things at this stage.

She gave him a sideways look. 'Have you found the tramp, by the way?'

He sighed. Was there nothing she didn't know? 'No. We're still looking.'

'Who do you think he is?'

He shook his head. 'That's not why I'm here. Now either get on with it, or I'm off.'

She grinned. 'OK. We've pulled all of the coroners' records for the last three years, which I think is enough for now. I've had two people working on it night and day and it's taken sodding ages . . .'

His phone was ringing. 'I need to take this,' he said, seeing Dr Moran's name flash on the screen. 'I'll be back in two ticks.' He answered the call and went outside to the street as he listened to Dr Moran rattle through the results of the DNA comparison.

'The samples sent over from Winchester match with victims A, B and C from the Sainsbury's fire. There's no other DNA present.'

'You mean, no match with Richard English's son?'

'That's right.'

He thanked Moran and hung up. He called Steele but she wasn't answering. He left a message, telling her what Moran had said, and went back into the bar.

'What's up, Doc?' Melinda asked, swinging around to face him, eyes alight with curiosity.

'Nothing that concerns you,' he said, sitting down again.

'Everything to do with you concerns me,' she said, prodding him gently with the pointed toe of her boot. 'Anybody ever tell you that you look like Robert Downey Jr?'

'Just you.'

'Only taller, of course . . .'

'Get to the point. You were telling me about your search.'

She rolled her eyes. 'OK. We've been through every fire involving human fatalities in the UK, looking for something out of the ordinary or unexplained. I'm assuming there's nothing flagged up on your system as suspicious, otherwise you'd know about it. Right?' She looked at him for confirmation and he nodded. 'So, if there's another body fire, it's slipped below the radar. The only way that would happen is if it looks like an accident, the victim is unknown or unidentifiable, and there are no suspicious circs so nobody bothers to delve a bit deeper. Am I making sense?'

'Perfectly. Go on.'

'Of course, that makes it all a heck of a lot more difficult to find, but I think we've got two possibles so far. Both look a little different from the norm. One's in Peckham and one down on the south coast, not a million miles from Winchester. The weird thing is that neither autopsy picked up anything suspicious about the bodies.' She sat back on her stool and folded her arms, chewing her bottom lip in a playful manner.

'So they don't conform to the pattern?'

'You mean they weren't a mixture of body parts? As I said, open verdicts were recorded on both, so of course there's nothing exciting. Maybe the pathologist was just sloppy.'

He made no comment, wanting to dampen her enthusiasm. The pathologist didn't need to be sloppy to miss a body assembled from multiple parts. In the normal course of events, without anything else to arouse suspicion, only a single DNA sample would have been taken, usually from a long bone or a tooth.

'Whatever, I still think the circs of both are a bit odd,' she said, still looking at him, trying to gauge his reaction. 'And everything's worth looking at, isn't it? I mean, you don't even have a suspect, do you?'

'Are you going to tell me anything else?' he asked, refusing to be needled. He wasn't prepared to justify their lack of success to her, although if there was no further progress soon, Steele and the review team would be on his back.

212

'Maybe. I'm not sure I trust you.'

'You'd better trust me or I'll make you hand over what you have.'

'That'll cost you quite a bit of time and you're not the sort of bloke who likes to wait, are you?' She smiled. 'It's also amazing how files can disappear.'

'Melinda—'

'There's no need, *if* you play fair. You can have it all. Do I have your word?'

'As a gentleman?'

She waved him away. 'You're no gentleman, which is what I like about you, Mark. But yes, let's do it the old-fashioned way. Let's shake on it. If I give you what we have and you turn something up from it, you promise to give me an exclusive. Will you pick up the phone and call me straight away? And I mean *only* me?' There was a determined gleam in her eye as she held out her small hand.

He hesitated. It wasn't the first time a clever journalist had turned up something interesting ahead of the police, whether from sheer fluke or hard work, and there was no point beating himself up about it. He didn't entirely trust her, but he decided he wasn't ashamed of taking any help offered. All that mattered was moving the investigation forwards. He forced a weary smile, reached over and took her hand.

Sam Donovan walked through the entrance of the Dillon Hotel into the white, panelled lobby. According to Sharon and others she had spoken to, CCTV footage had shown Claire arriving just before eight-thirty in the evening. The entry in her diary said: *Rob – Dillon – 8.30pm.* She had been a few minutes early, for one of the few times in her life. She had texted him to say that she was downstairs and he had texted back, saying he was on a call and asking her to come straight up to the room. The cameras had captured her walking through the hotel to the back lifts and going straight up to the second floor. She had clearly felt she could trust him, a man she barely knew. With the benefit of hindsight, it had been an incredibly stupid thing to do. But she didn't blame Claire, spurred on by some sort of romantic notion that had blinded her to common sense. Not that long ago, she too had been just as foolish, unknowingly putting herself in the hands of a vicious, sociopathic serial killer, a man she barely knew, who had charmed her, whom she had blindly trusted. She had nearly died, and it had almost cost Tartaglia his life too. All for the sake of a bit of romance. The killer was long gone but his shadow still hung over her, the stuff of nightmares.

She walked along the corridor, following the sound of voices and music. The bar was full of after-work drinkers. The large seating area beyond was equally full. It looked out onto an inner courtyard, which was decorated with clipped trees in pots and illuminated by strings of fairy lights. She found the lift outside the restaurant and pressed the button to go up. While she waited, she wondered what Claire had been thinking that night, when she had done the same. Had she had any doubts? Had she thought about anything other than the man she was meeting on the second floor?

Donovan got out of the lift. Room 212 was just across the corridor, the door sealed. A bunch of white flowers sat propped up against it. As she picked up the flowers, tears filled her eyes. No message. She wondered if they were from one of her former colleagues, or a friend of Claire's, or just a guest in the hotel, moved by what had happened. Maybe they were from the hotel management, although they had a personal, rather than corporate, feel.

214

The lift pinged behind her and she heard the doors open.

'Sam?' A man's voice.

She turned and saw Justin Chang walking towards her.

'What are you doing here?' she asked, clasping the flowers tightly to her chest.

'I was having a drink downstairs. I saw you come in.'

She hadn't seen him in the bar, but there were so many people he could easily have been tucked away among them. 'So you followed me?'

'I thought you'd come up here. I wanted to see you.'

'Now you've seen me, you can go.' She saw the concern in his eyes as he studied her for a moment. It was the same irritating look Tartaglia gave her whenever they spoke. If only people would leave her alone.

'It's not good for you to be here on your own, Sam,' Chang said. 'Come downstairs. Come and have a drink.'

'I don't want to see anyone.'

'My friend's gone. It would be good to talk and I can see you home, if you like.'

'Home? Where's that?' Was the house she had shared with Claire still her home? She didn't think she could ever go back there again. There were too many memories.

'I meant Mark's flat. Come on. Staying here won't do any good.'

A door along the corridor opened and a couple came out. They started walking towards the lift.

'Come on, Sam, let's go downstairs. You can't do anything here.'

Short of breaking into the room to see exactly where Claire had died, Sam knew there was nothing else to be done. She probably had seen enough and she felt like a drink. But if she went down to the bar with Chang, would he take her to task for not having returned his calls? She didn't think he was that insensitive and maybe she could persuade him to give her some more information. She carefully placed the flowers back against the door and followed him to the lift.

They found a table in a smaller bar off the main corridor. It was much quieter than the other rooms and the air was full of the heady smell of lilies coming from a tall vase on the counter. While Chang was ordering their drinks, Donovan gazed out of the French doors into the courtyard. A few lights were on in the various rooms that overlooked it. She wondered which of the windows belonged to room 212. She imagined Claire looking out, or drawing the curtains or the blinds, tried to picture the room, and the faceless man known as Rob.

'Here you go,' Chang said passing her a margarita and sitting down with his. He raised his glass, then hesitated as though not sure what to say. 'I wanted to tell you how sorry I am. I . . .'

'Thanks,' she said quickly, holding up her hand before he could say anything else. Avoiding his gaze, tears in her eyes, she took a sip of her drink, enjoying the sharp, salty taste. 'Why were you having a drink in this hotel?' she asked, after a moment.

'I was curious, I guess. Didn't get much chance to look around the day we were here . . .' He stopped and looked embarrassed, as though he'd said something wrong.

'It's OK. You don't have to walk on eggshells. I just want everybody to treat me as normal. It would make it a lot easier for me too. You said you were here with a friend?'

He nodded. 'She works around the corner.'

'Well, I hope I didn't interrupt things.'

'We were about to go, when I saw you.'

It sounded genuine. 'Is there any news?' she asked, after a moment.

'Isn't Mark telling you what's going on?'

'I barely see him. I think he's avoiding me.'

He looked surprised. 'Why?'

Maybe, like everyone else in the office, Chang imagined that if she and Tartaglia were cooped up alone together for a few days in Tartaglia's flat, it would mean only one thing. It was so far from the truth, it made her want to laugh. Although perhaps it explained why Tartaglia was giving her a wide berth. Maybe he, too, had heard the rumours and felt awkward. There had been a time when there might have been good grounds for such speculation, when she would have given a lot for something to happen between them. But it was amazing what the distance of a little time could do.

She put down her glass and looked at Chang. 'Why? Because like everybody else, you included, he's tip-toeing around me like I'm the bloody elephant in the room. Yes, I feel terrible inside. Yes, I can't stop thinking about Claire and what happened to her and it makes me sick and I don't want to eat. I can't sleep either, unless I take pills, which make me groggy so I'm in a bit of a fog. But underneath it all, I'm still me. I think the same, feel the same, function the same, yet everybody's treating me like I'm some sort of lunatic who needs to be wrapped in cotton wool so I don't damage myself or others. It's driving me mad.'

He looked shocked, maybe from the violence of her tone. 'People just care about you, that's all.'

'I'm alright. Really I am. I just wish they'd stop fussing over me and leave me alone.'

He looked relieved and smiled. 'I understand. If there's anything I can do . . .'

She could see the emotion in his eyes and realised that she had missed him. If only life were that simple. 'Justin, there is something you can do for me. If you value me as a friend—'

'Of course I do.'

'Then trust me. I'm really OK. I need you to tell me everything you know. I'm ready.'

Thirty

Back in his flat, Tartaglia sat down on the sofa and opened the two manila folders Melinda had given him. The first contained a series of papers relating to a fire in a squat in Peckham, South London, which had claimed the life of one of the occupants two years before. It had started sometime in the late evening in the back basement of the property, in a room normally occupied by a young man known as Spike. The forensic investigation concluded that the likely cause of the fire was a kerosene stove used to heat the room, which had somehow fallen or been knocked over. Localised traces of the kerosene had been found as well as the remains of a stove. Neighbours also mentioned hearing a couple of small explosions, and by the time the fire brigade arrived, the heat was too intense for anyone to enter the building. Remains of a large copper still and LPG bottles were found in the basement wreckage. Three people were treated in hospital for burns and the effects of smoke inhalation, one with a broken leg after jumping from an upstairs window. They said that as far as they knew, they were the only people inside the building at the time, but when the site was examined over the next couple of days, the remains of an adult male were found in the basement.

The man was lying on his back on what was left of a mattress. It was first assumed that it was Spike who had died. The body was too badly burnt to be identified in the normal way, but according to the post mortem examination report, the body belonged to a middle-aged man. According to one of the other squatters, Spike was in his late twenties or early thirties. Two of the three squatters who had been treated in hospital had been interviewed; neither knew who the dead man was and said they had never seen anybody other than Spike going down to the basement. They said that Spike kept himself to himself and didn't appear to have had visitors. A copy of the coroner's report recorded death by misadventure. What seemed to have sparked Melinda's interest was the fact that the identity of the dead man was unknown and nobody had been able to locate, let alone interview, Spike after the fire. It certainly didn't fit into the usual domestic fire scenario, and she had written and underlined the words 'foul play' in red, along with a large question mark. What caught Tartaglia's attention was that the long list of items retrieved from the basement included the remains of a small leather suitcase containing assorted male clothing. It had been found outside in the corridor, next to the front door. There was no description of the bag and there had clearly been no identifiable name tag or address, which might have helped to identify the unknown victim. He made a note to get somebody to find out more details as soon as possible.

One of Melinda's assistants had been to the site but it had been boarded up and any previous occupants were long gone. Photos of the house were attached to the file, as well as photos of the street. The houses on either side had suffered smoke damage and been cleared for reasons of safety, their inhabitants relocated elsewhere. But the reporter had managed to interview two women who lived on the opposite side of the street. Both had given witness statements at the inquest. Barbara Tier was seventy-two, according to the cub reporter's notes. Mrs Tier, as she apparently liked to be called, remembered the squatters and the fire very clearly. She said that she had been watching television when she had smelled smoke, but didn't know where it was coming from. She then heard a loud explosion, or possibly two explosions, and went to her front window to take a look. She saw smoke and flames coming from the house opposite. It was mayhem in the street, people screaming and somebody trying to get out of one of the second-floor windows. She thought that they jumped. She was about to dial 999 when she heard the sirens and, moments later, the fire brigade arrived.

Mrs Tier said that there were about ten people or so living in the house at any one time, although they kept odd hours and it wasn't always the same crew. They called themselves anarchists and eco-warriors; 'a load of alkies and druggies, more like,' she was quoted as saying, along with 'load of bloody scroungers'. She said that they had left rubbish lying around in the front garden and that it had attracted rats. She said that she was happy when the house had burned down, although she was sorry that somebody had lost their life She didn't remember seeing a middle-aged man in the group, but there were various people coming and going at the house at all times of the day and night and it was difficult to keep track. She remembered Spike and said that he seemed a bit more together than the rest of them and that he was actually polite. He had helped her bring in her shopping a few times. The description she gave of him was 'tall, and skinny as a broom handle, with straggly brown hair in a pony tail'. He probably didn't get enough to eat, she added. She said he usually had a roll-up in his mouth, or cigarette papers in his hands, and that he wore dark glasses all the time. She never saw his eye colour.

Leonora Mitchell, a Filipina aged forty-seven, lived two doors along. 'Likes to be called Leonie' the note said. Leonie described the squatters as a mixed bunch, some nice, some not so nice. She was an ex-nurse and said that she thought a couple of them might have had mental or alcohol-related problems. One of her sons had made friends with a squatter called Jack, who lived on the first floor and had a dog. He had moved down to London from Birmingham and had taken somebody else's place in the squat when they left. Her son had been inside the house a few times with Jack and said that the place was a bit of a tip and that everybody had heavy-duty locks on their rooms, supposedly for security, although she didn't know what they had that was worth taking. She knew who Spike was but hadn't spoken to him. She said that she'd seen him on several occasions with a young woman, although she wasn't sure if she was his girlfriend. She didn't remember a middle-aged man at the address, but said that he may not have been staying there long enough for her to notice him. The description she gave of Spike was similar to that given by Barbara Tier. She, too, said that he was always wearing dark glasses. Her description of the fire itself tallied almost exactly with Mrs Tier's, although Leonie had gone out into the street to see if there was anything she could do. She had seen Jack and his dog standing outside with a group of people watching the blaze. She asked him if there was anybody still inside but he had said that he didn't think so, unless they were on the upper floors. He said that he thought Spike had gone away for a couple of days and that the two people who lived on the ground floor, at the back, were also out in the street.

The second folder contained papers relating to a body discovered in June of the previous year on a beach on the south coast, near the Isle of Wight. It looked as though the body had been set alight on some sort of makeshift funeral pyre, and flowers and petals were found scattered around it on the sand. Clippings from the local paper speculated about it being some sort of New Age funeral, or possibly having a Hindu or Sikh connection, and a local Hindu campaigner for legalising open-air cremations in the UK was interviewed. But there were no witnesses to say what had happened. The fire had taken place at the time of the Isle of Wight music festival, on a stretch of beach often used for parties by students from nearby Southampton University. The weather was good and although the fire had been noticed by a number of people, nobody had paid much attention to it. Somebody remembered hearing loud music coming from the vicinity and the pilot of a helicopter, ferrying festival-goers across the Solent, said that he had seen a man standing by a fire on the beach, poking it with a stick.

Early the following morning, a man walking his dog along the beach had found the body. Examination of the partially burnt remains showed that the body had been laid out on its back, hands folded on its chest. The pyre had been constructed from a mixture of logs and kindling, both on sale even in June at local petrol stations. No traces of accelerant had been found at the scene. Appeals in the local media produced nothing. The post-mortem examination revealed that the body belonged to a young woman and that it was impossible to tell exactly how she had died, although no signs of foul play had been found.

Tartaglia lit a cigarette, deciding that both reports warranted further investigation. He would concentrate on the first case and pass on the second to Ramsey to follow up in the morning.

He was just putting the papers back in their respective folders when he heard the front door of the house slam shut. A moment later, the key turned in the lock of his own door, and Donovan walked into the room. He was surprised to see her. The bedroom door was closed and he had assumed she was asleep inside. He wondered where she had been and if Chang had managed to follow her.

'I need to talk to you, Mark,' she said breathlessly, before he had a chance to say anything. Her cheeks were pink from the cold and her short blonde hair stood in spikes. There was an almost feverish brightness in her eyes, which was new.

'Are you OK?'

'No. I'm not.'

'Come and sit down. Can I get you a drink?'

'I've had two margaritas. It's enough, otherwise I won't be able to think straight. I need to talk to you about Claire.'

She pulled off her jacket, threw it over a chair and sat down opposite him. 'I bumped into Justin – it doesn't matter where – and I managed to persuade him to tell me some things about what happened, things that nobody else had the guts to tell me.'

'It's not a question of guts, Sam.'

'Yes it is, but I'm not going to argue. Look, before we talk, I want to make sure you won't give him a hard time about it, OK?'

He gazed at her for a moment, wondering what exactly had gone on between her and Chang and how she had managed to persuade him to talk, if indeed she had. He would decide what to do once he found out what exactly Chang had said, but there was no point arguing about it now with her. 'OK. Go on.'

'I now know the details of what happened that night. I know about the champagne, the room service food, the Latin words that were written on her legs. I want you to talk to me about it, tell me what you really think.'

'This really isn't a good idea,' he said, shocked and angry that Chang had told her so much, although she could be incredibly persistent when she wanted something and he would have been putty in her hands.

'He's told me everything, Mark. Everything.' She looked at him meaningfully. 'I need to know what *you* think. I value your opinion more than anyone's. Let's just pretend for a moment that we're still working together and this is just a normal case we're sitting here discussing. Like old times.'

He hesitated. He didn't know what to say. They had sat in that room on so many occasions late into the night, talking about this case or that, bantering through all the possible scenarios until sometimes there was a glimmer of light. They knew each other so well he never needed to explain things in detail, she just understood, and vice versa. It was that easy shorthand he missed, along with her intelligence and sensitivity.

'Forget that it's Claire for a minute,' she said, her eyes locked on his. 'That's what I'm trying to do. Just think of it as a case and tell me what's in your head.'

He stretched back in his seat, pressing his head back into the cushions, arms reaching behind him and closed his eyes for a moment, wondering what to do. He felt suddenly tired, as well as strangely touched that it still mattered to Donovan what he thought, that she hadn't got what she needed from Chang, or anybody else, and that she wanted to talk to him. Was he stupid to care? More importantly, could she cope with it?

She leaned forward, elbows on her knees, chin cupped in her hands. 'I can deal with it, I promise,' she said, as though reading his thoughts. 'Like old times, Mark. Just you and me.'

He rubbed his face wearily and gazed at her. Like Chang, he realised he had no choice but to give in to her. 'What is it you want to know?'

'Just tell me what you really think went on.'

He took a deep breath. 'OK. I'm not running the case any more, so I don't know all the details. But from what I saw, and what I've heard since, this is what I think happened. Claire meets this man accidentally outside her office—'

'Accidentally?'

'There's nothing to suggest otherwise. She certainly thought it was accidental, based on things she said. Claire was smart. If it had been a ploy, if he'd been watching her, and he bumped into her deliberately, I think she'd have twigged, don't you?'

'That depends how smart he is. How good an actor.'

'I suppose so. You think he targeted her specifically?'

She nodded.

'As I said, we've found nothing at all to suggest it. But let's leave it to one side and just say they met—'

'But it all matters. If you get that bit wrong, you're then starting at the wrong place and the rest doesn't add up.'

He sighed, wondering if she was going to pick holes in everything. 'Look, we have to go on the facts as we know them. He spills coffee over her and sends her flowers to apologise. One thing leads to another and he takes her out for lunch. Then dinner. This goes on over a few weeks. He tells her he lives in Manchester, so he sees her when he's in town. We know that's not true; he lives in London. We assume he hides the fact because he's probably married and can't have a normal, open relationship. What he wants is a bit of fun on the side.' He stopped and looked at her, trying to gauge the impact of what he was saying. He felt uncomfortable talking to her about Claire in such a way. 'Forgive me if it sounds impersonal . . .'

'It's OK. As I said, just forget for a moment it's Claire. Say it like it is.'

'So, he wants to move things to the next level, but he's worried his wife will find out. He gets Claire to book the room at the hotel, using her credit card. She arrives as planned, but something goes wrong. Maybe Claire decided she didn't want to have sex with him after all. There's an almighty struggle and he kills her.'

'But he drugged her. Traces of Rohypnol were found in the blood samples.'

'You know how common date rape is. Maybe before it took effect, she realised what he was trying to do and tried to get away. The room was a mess . . .' He omitted the word 'bed'.

'Go on.'

'Well, so he kills her. Then he tidies up the room as best he can and legs it, taking some of her things with him. Maybe in his panic, he thinks she won't be identified if her handbag is gone.'

'But she booked the room with her credit card.'

'I agree he's not thinking straight. He hasn't done this before.'

She looked at him sceptically. 'You really think that this is a one-off? That it's a date gone wrong?'

He frowned. 'Yes. There's nothing to suggest otherwise. There are no similar, unsolved killings, if that's what you're thinking.' As he spoke, he felt like a dog that had been pulled off a trail too soon, already out of touch with the real feel and smell of the case. He was only repeating what others had said to him and it all sounded a little hollow.

'What about the words on her legs? "What I am, you will be." That would have taken thought, and time. It's hardly the reaction of a man in a panic, who's accidentally killed somebody he barely knew.'

'I agree, but people get all sorts of weird ideas from the TV and the Internet. Maybe he was trying to dress it up as a serial killer thing in order to hide what really happened.' He could see from her expression that she didn't agree.

'So, you think the Latin quote just randomly pops up in his head when he's in panic mode?'

'What you're asking is, did he plan it all carefully right from the beginning? Did he set out meaning to kill her? If so, then maybe it wasn't a chance meeting outside her office, maybe he deliberately targeted her for some reason.'

'Don't you think it's possible he *chose* her, Mark? That right from the beginning, he knew what he was doing and why?'

'That's what you really think?' He shrugged. 'Maybe he saw her in the street, or coming out of her office. Maybe he likes tall, willowy brunettes, with blue eyes.'

'I mean he intended to kill her right from the start.'

'OK. But why? Maybe he didn't want sex with her at all, maybe he just wanted to know what it's like to kill a woman. But that's a lot less credible as a theory. You know what the studies say . . .'

She shook her head. Tears stood in her eyes and he realised he had gone too far. 'You're wrong,' she said. 'He chose Claire because of who she was, not what she looked like. And killing her isn't the end game. It's just part of his plan. Everything was carefully planned, down to the very last detail . . .'

He looked at her shocked. Grief was making her paranoid. 'Hang on. There are no grounds to say that.'

'Yes there are. You remember what she had to eat?'

He shook his head. 'Not precisely. He ordered room service. The room service trolley was sitting by the door, food untouched.'

'It would be untouched. She was already dead by then. Ask yourself this: you're in a hotel room with a woman you've just murdered. Why bother to order room service? What's the point?'

He shrugged. 'To get somebody up to the room. He wanted her found.'

'He could have ordered a cup of coffee, if that's all he wanted, and it would have come a hell of a lot quicker.' She sat back in her chair and shook her head angrily. 'What he ordered was important, in its own right.'

He frowned, trying to picture what he had seen on the trolley, not understanding at all what she was getting at.

'Because it's a message,' she continued. 'Just like the words he wrote on her leg.'

'A message to who?'

'Ah. That's the key question.' She looked at him strangely and bit her lip before saying, 'It's all about the details, Mark. Every single tiny detail is significant. Isn't that what you used to say? It's why you're usually so bloody good at what you do. But this time, you're missing an important piece of the puzzle.'

'What are you talking about?'

She sighed impatiently. 'The message wasn't meant for you, but from where I am, it's all suddenly pretty clear. The champagne – Justin said it was Krug – the oysters, the turbot, with hollandaise. Don't you remember?'

He gazed at her blankly. It meant nothing to him. Her eyes were rimmed with red and she looked almost unhinged. He realised it was a mistake to have allowed the conversation to go so far. 'I'm sorry, I don't. Anyway . . .'

'Never mind,' she muttered, shaking her head. 'Maybe I never mentioned it. Doesn't matter. Do you believe in justice, Mark?'

'What do you mean by justice?'

'What do you think should happen to a man like this? A man who viciously and deliberately takes away someone's life, as though it were just a game, depriving them of a future and destroying the lives of those around them?'

'You know what I think, Sam. The system isn't perfect but—'

'No. It's *far* from perfect. In fact, it stinks. He's done this before, Mark, and he's got away with it.' Tears ran down her face as she held his gaze. 'You're just not looking at things straight.'

He spread his hand in desperation. 'Then tell me your theory. Explain what it is I'm missing. I want to help.'

She shook her head again. 'There's no point. You won't do what's needed. And to be fair to you, you can't.'

She stood up, picked up her jacket and handbag and walked out of the room towards the bedroom. He heard the door close.

He sat for a moment, stunned. However unreasonable she was being, he knew he had failed her, yet he had no idea how to put it right. He lit a cigarette and sat waiting for her to return, but she didn't. Grief affected people in many different ways and the anger she was feeling was only normal, although the paranoia was more worrying. None of what she had said made sense. There was no point in blaming poor Chang for revealing the details. If it hadn't been him, she would have found somebody else to tell her.

Wanting to try and understand her reaction better, he picked up his phone and dialled Chang's mobile. When Chang eventually answered, he sounded sleepy, as though he'd already long since gone to bed. Tartaglia gave him the gist of the conversation with Donovan.

'I just want to understand what's going on with her,' Tartaglia said. 'Somehow she seems to have got it into her head that Claire was specifically targeted and that the man meant from the start to kill her. Do you have any idea why, and what this is all about?'

'No. She asked me a whole load of questions. I just answered as best I could. I didn't know half the time what she was getting at.'

'She talked as though it's all part of a game, with some other end in mind. Where did that come from?'

'Honestly, I don't know.'

'You must have said something that triggered it. What was it?'

Chang sighed. 'I think the turning point was when I told her about the room service trolley and the food. She seemed pretty normal before that. I actually thought she was coping quite well, all things considered.'

'You said what?'

'She asked me to talk her through the crime scene, to describe blow by blow what we saw on the video.'

'Did she explain what was so important about the trolley?'

'No. But it wasn't just the timing of it all, it was what was on the trolley. It really seemed to shake her. She also got very excited about the air con being on low. It meant something to her, but she wouldn't tell me what it was. She said she needed to speak to you.'

'Thanks,' he said, imagining that Chang hadn't been pleased about that, although his tone gave nothing away. 'She didn't say anything about the air conditioning, but she wasn't making a lot of sense. I'll see you in the morning.' He hung up. He took a pull on his cigarette. Something niggled. Why hadn't she mentioned the air con to him, if it was something significant? He stubbed out his cigarette, went into the hall and knocked on the bedroom door.

'Sam, can I have a quick word.'

'What is it?' she called out.

'What do you make of the air conditioning in the room being on low? Why is that important?'

There was a small pause before she said, 'Because he doesn't want sex.'

'So?'

After a moment, the door opened a crack and he saw her shadow behind it. 'Because he gets excited in other ways,' she said. 'Because he knows he does. He's a real pro. If I'm right, I'm telling you, this was all very carefully planned.'

'Go on.'

'You got no DNA hits from the room.'

'No. But as I said, *we* think he's a first-timer.'

The door opened wider and her small, pale face peered out at him. 'Or he's already on the system, which is why he's so careful not to leave any. Killing's a contact sport, or at least it is for him. He likes to get real close. He's probably clothed head to toe in something to stop himself shedding, but he can't cover himself up completely or it will spoil the fun. He's got to see what he's doing, talk to her as he's doing it. That's all really important. That's what turns him on.'

'What you're describing is a serial killer. Somebody who's done this sort of thing before.'

'I'm telling you he has. Imagine him on the bed with Claire . . .' She paused, still holding his gaze. He said nothing, trying not to think about it. They shouldn't be talking about it. 'She's lying there drugged, totally out of it, thank God. He's on top of her, straddling her, hands around her neck, looking down at her as he strangles the life out of her. He's hot and the more excited he gets, the more he's going to sweat. The air con being on as low as it will go when it's practically freezing outside means he knows the score, he's been through it all before, and he really cares that you might find something.'

'But we found nothing.'

'Maybe he was so damned careful there's nothing to find.

But maybe, just maybe, you weren't looking in the right places. You need to check if he sweated on her. Particularly check her face, her eyes, her mouth . . .'

'Her face and mouth were tested for semen and saliva but nothing was found. And the grip areas were negative for DNA. The only profile that came back was hers.'

She said nothing for a moment, then shrugged. 'So you haven't actually profiled the tapes from her face?'

'I don't know. Look, it's not my case any longer, Sam.' Even as he spoke he realised how empty it sounded and he saw her expression harden. He couldn't be expected to follow the detailed ins and outs of the investigation, particularly given the fact he was working flat out on another case. But even if he had been stretched in fifty different directions, it still would have been a lame excuse. He owed her more than that. He also had failed to fully understand how desperate she must feel being stuck on the side-lines, even if it was the best and safest place for her to be. It was stupid to expect her to wait around passively, doing nothing. She would not rest until Claire's killer was found and, in her shoes, he would have been no different.

Her description of what might have happened seemed just about plausible, even if the look in her eyes made him question her sanity. But she had a point. It was easily possible that after everything else had tested negative, the tapes used to take samples from Claire's face and neck hadn't been prioritised for DNA profiling. They might not even have been sent off yet. It was a detail that should be followed up as soon as possible, if nothing else to tick the box and reassure her. 'I'll talk to Steele first thing in the morning,' he said, hoping to placate her. 'I'll make sure it's done.'

'Good.'

Before he could say anything else, she closed the door.

Thirty-one

Adam parked Kit's battered old VW Golf in the little street in Hammersmith by the river. It was one in the morning and he had been on a round trip, via Ealing, to see his grandparents' old house. He had set it on fire before leaving the UK a year before and it was boarded up, standing like a blackened, rotten tooth in an otherwise perfect mouth. He was still technically the legal owner but there was no chance of his ever being able to reclaim it. No doubt the council would eventually take possession. Sitting outside in the road, looking up at it and remembering the events that had led up to his escape abroad, he had felt extraordinarily detached. The thirty-plus years he had endured there, both with his grandparents and then after their deaths on his own, along with the final, absurdly dramatic denouement, meant nothing. He was dead to it all and everything it represented. It was as though the house embodied somebody else's foul history rather than his own.

Checking that there was nobody around, he got out of the car and locked it. It had been raining and as he walked along the street, his footsteps echoed on the wet pavement. A cat scuttled away under a car, the only sign of life. The houses were small and low-built, traditional two up, two down. What estate agents referred to picturesquely as 'cottages', trying to turn their mean proportions into a virtue. He had never been to the house before but he had memorised the address and he remembered what she had told him a while back about the layout when he had asked her to describe it. Sitting room and study on the ground floor, with a kitchen at the back. Two bedrooms and a bathroom on the first floor. It had been a pleasant enough dinner, until she had later spoiled it.

He stopped in front of the house, on the opposite side of the street, and looked up. It was dark inside, the curtains on both floors still open. She slept at the front, he remembered her saying. So she wasn't back home yet. He had the keys in his pocket and for a moment he fancied letting himself in and having a snoop around. But he wasn't ready yet. He wasn't quite there. Fucking Gunner was putting him off his stride, making him feel unusually nervous. No point in doing something spur of the moment and risk ruining things. He would come back again when he was better prepared.

Thirty-two

At ten o'clock the following morning, Tartaglia and Minderedes stood in Choumert Road, Peckham, outside the boarded-up house where the unknown man had died.

'You take Leonie,' Tartaglia said. 'I'll speak to Mrs Tier.'

She lived on the ground floor of a small housing trust block, just across the street. Her front windows were set back only a few feet from the pavement and she would have had a good view of the comings and goings opposite. As he approached the door to her flat, he heard the deep bark of a large dog inside. He rang the bell. More barking. Wondering if he had drawn the short straw, he heard the sound of several locks being unclicked. The door opened a fraction, on the chain, and a pale, elderly face, framed by artificially red hair, peered out. He heard snuffling behind her, followed by a deep bass growl.

'Back, Max,' she bellowed in a surprisingly loud voice, he assumed to the dog. 'Get back.'

He held up his warrant card. 'I'm Detective Inspector Mark Tartaglia, from the Met Police. May I have a few words with you about the fire across the road?'

'Will this take long? I'm not dressed.'

'Just a few questions, that's all. I've already read the statement you gave at the inquest.'

'I'll just go and put Max in the kitchen.' She closed the door behind her and locked it again, returning a couple of minutes later. This time, she opened the door a few inches, without the chain. She had put on a dressing gown and slippers, as well as a slick of red lipstick.

'Poor man,' she said, through the gap. 'They never found out who he was, did they?'

'That's what we're trying to do.'

'A journalist came by the other day asking questions about what happened.'

'I know,' he said, wanting to short cut the process. 'I just need to ask you a few more things. The dead man was in the room normally occupied by a man called Spike. From what we can tell, he was quite a bit older than Spike. Did you ever see anyone like that going down to the basement flat?'

'I wasn't out spying on them, if that's what you think. I've got better things to do with my time.'

'Of course. But was anyone else living down in the basement with Spike? There must have been at least two rooms.'

'I can't really say. Leastways, he was the only one I saw coming and going through the basement door.'

'Do you have any idea who the dead man was?'

'I'd have told the inquest if I had. My husband was a policeman, Inspector. I know how important these things are. They said he was middle-aged, but I never saw nobody like that go in the house, unless it was people from the landlord trying to talk to them squatters.'

'But you knew Spike?'

'Oh, yes. He was a decent enough sort, compared to the rest of them.'

'How would you describe him?' Although he had the journalist's notes, he wanted to hear it for himself.

'Thin as a rake. No meat on him, to speak of. Mid-brown hair in a ponytail. He always had a ponytail. And he was always in those dark glasses. Couldn't see his eyes.'

'What about his clothes?'

'Nothing special.'

'Did you notice if he had any scars or tattoos or any other distinguishing marks?' he asked, thinking about what Tatyana had said about the man who had called himself Chris.

'Not that I noticed. Sorry.'

'Was there anyone else in the house he was particular friends with?'

She shook her head. 'He was a loner. He'd speak to the others but he didn't have much to do with them. Can't say I blame him, neither.'

'Could you take a look at this image and tell me if the face is at all familiar?' He passed a copy of the E-FIT Tatyana had helped them put together through the gap. He saw her hold it out in front of her, squinting. She turned it to one side, then the other, as though unsure.

She sucked in her breath, then looked up at him. 'Is this supposed to be Spike?'

'I'm asking you if you recognise the person in the image.'

There was silence for a moment as she peered at it. 'It's not a great likeness. The hair's different and a bit darker. He wasn't a ginger. And I told you, I never saw his eyes. His face was thinner and longer. But it *might* just be him.' He could see the doubt in her eyes as she handed him back the paper.

People often said things just to try and be helpful. But 'might' was nowhere near good enough. Computer-generated images, like the old-fashioned artists' impressions, were only as good as the input and the intermediary. It had been late evening when Tatyana had helped to put together the E-FIT. Tiredness aside, memory was a tricky thing and having to describe some-body – even somebody you knew quite well – didn't always translate fluently onto the screen. Maybe Tatyana hadn't remembered Chris clearly enough for the image to be a good representation and he started to have doubts about using it. They should get her back in for a second attempt.

'Tell me about Spike. When was the last time you saw him?'

'A couple of days before the fire.'

'What was he doing?'

'He was off on his bicycle. Don't know where.'

'Did he have any other form of transport?'

'I saw him in a white van a couple of times, but I don't know if it was his.'

'Did you ever see him after the fire?'

'I saw him in the street on his bicycle one day,' she said thoughtfully. 'It was getting dark and I was dusting the windowsill in the front room. He comes along and stops right in the middle of the street outside his old house, just looking at it. It was all boarded up by then. I knocked on the glass and called out his name, but he didn't look round and a minute later he's off again.'

'This was when?'

'A few days after the inquest. I was surprised he left it so long after the fire to come back. I mean, he must've heard what happened. But maybe he didn't want to risk being spotted and having to give a statement and all of that business. I suppose he must've felt a bit guilty. After all, it was his room and his stove that caught alight and burnt that poor bugger. It might've been him on that mattress, but for the grace of God.' She peered up at Tartaglia with pale, watery eyes.

'He was just looking at the property, then? He didn't try to get in?'

'Perhaps I put him off. He didn't even get off his bike. Don't know what he was doing. He must've known all his stuff'd gone up in smoke. Maybe he was feeling sentimental. But you know, maybe he did come back again later.'

'What do you mean?'

'Well, someone broke the lock on the fence a couple of days after. They had to send somebody out to repair it, to stop the bloody kids getting in and playing in there.'

He thanked Mrs Tier and caught up with Minderedes in the street.

'I showed Leonie the E-FIT,' Minderedes said. 'She *thinks* it could be Spike.'

'Thinks?'

'Well, more or less.'

He sighed. 'I suppose it will have to do for now. When we're done here, I want you to go and find Tatyana and bring her back in. Get her to do the whole thing again.'

Minderedes checked his watch. 'I'm supposed to see Marek Nowak's girlfriend in an hour.'

'This is more important. Get somebody else to speak to her, maybe Hannah. Tell her it doesn't have to be today, if she can't fit it in. Mrs Tier said she saw Spike in the street after the inquest and that the property was broken into a few days later. I wonder why he bothered to come back. If he'd left something behind, it wouldn't still be in the house. I'll speak to Steele and see if she thinks it's worth searching the garden, although my guess is he probably found whatever it was he was looking for. In the mean-time, get hold of a copy of the autopsy report and find out what happened to the body. Also find out what was done with the stuff recovered from the basement. There was apparently a suit-case with men's clothing in it by the front door.'

As he turned away, his phone started ringing. He saw Melinda's name on the screen and let it go to voicemail. Deal or no deal, he was nowhere near ready to talk to her yet.

Thirty-three

Gunner had been up and about relatively late that morning, thundering down the stairs past Adam's room to the kitchen, the smell of bacon cooking and coffee wafting upwards about twenty minutes later. Just after ten, Adam heard him galloping back upstairs. Five minutes later the old pipes, which ran down the back of the house, started shuddering and clunking away as Gunner took a bath and, no doubt, emptied the entire contents of the small hot-water tank. He would have to wait to have his shower later. Every so often, he heard the sound of water being run again, as though the bath was being topped up. He imagined Gunner wallowing in the water, no doubt smoking one of his foul cigarettes as he listened to Kit's radio. It wasn't until nearly an hour later that he heard the sound of the bath being emptied. He got dressed quickly and waited. Eventually he heard Gunner come back down the stairs, thud along the hall, then bang the front door shut. Careful to make sure that he locked the bedroom door behind him, Adam put on his jacket, shouldered the small rucksack he carried everywhere with him during the day, and followed Gunner out into the street.

Dressed casually in a leather jacket and jeans, Gunner marched towards Kensington Church Street, then turned left towards Notting Hill Gate. At that time of day there were enough people around to make it easy to blend in, but there was no need to worry; Gunner didn't look back once. He walked with the easy, purposeful stride of somebody who knew where he was going and wasn't particularly bothered by his surroundings. He seemed oblivious to the fact he was being followed.

He crossed over Notting Hill Gate and headed north along Pembridge Villas, then turned down the Portobello Road. It was market day and the street was thronged with tourists milling around the antiques and bric-a-brac stalls. It was difficult to walk through the crowd, but Adam had no problem keeping track of Gunner. He was a head taller than most of those around him. He headed downhill, pausing at a food stall to buy a cup of coffee, then at another to buy a pastry, as though he had no plan. Adam was beginning to feel he was wasting his time and he felt hungry. Unlike Gunner, he had had no breakfast, let alone anything extra. The smell of coffee wafted from one of the stands, followed by the fresh, doughy smell of pancakes. Someone else was selling roasted chestnuts, something that reminded him of his childhood, when his witch of a grandmother used to cook them on a shovel over the fire. He could see Gunner a little way in front, stopped again in front of a second-hand bookstall. He was deep in conversation with the owner and looked as though he would be there for a while. Unable to resist any longer, he dug his wallet out of his rucksack and bought a bag of chestnuts. When he looked up again, Gunner had gone.

He stood eating the chestnuts, watching the road in front, but Gunner was nowhere to be seen. The chestnuts had barely made a dent in his hunger and he decided he needed a proper breakfast. He went into one of the antique markets, followed the signs up the stairs to a little café on the first floor, and sat down and ordered a full English breakfast. It was only when he came to pay that he realised his wallet, with two hundred pounds in cash and a couple of Kit's credit cards, was gone.

Thirty-four

Tartaglia walked into Steele's office. She had been out all morning but was now back behind her desk and on the phone. It sounded as though she was talking to somebody in the Press Office. She motioned Tartaglia to take one of the chairs on the other side of her desk and he sat down, half listening to what she was saying as he watched the rain spatter and streak down the grimy window behind her.

The autopsy report on the unknown man in Peckham had proved an interesting read. Sufficient tissue had survived to show that the victim had been drinking heavily before he died. The blood alcohol concentration level was 0.26 per cent, roughly three times the legal drink/drive limit, not that he had been driving anywhere. On its own, it was probably sufficient to render him unconscious eventually, but the results also showed traces of the sedative Temazepam. It was a lethal combination. The pathologist had removed samples of lung tissue to check for evidence of smoke inhalation. In the process of opening up his trachea, he had found scar tissue, indicating some form of surgery to the man's neck, the details of which he had fully documented. He also noted a tibial shaft fracture to the left leg, with a metal rod inserted into the bone. Results from the lung tissue samples showed that the man had been alive when the fire started, and the conclusion was that in his drunken, uncoordinated state, he must have knocked over the stove before passing out on the mattress.

Steele put down the phone and swivelled around in her chair to face him. 'Any news?'

'It looks like it's Richard English,' he said.

'What, a part of him?'

'Possibly his entire body, although until we exhume him we won't know for sure. But Ian Armstrong confirms that English broke his neck ten years ago in a skiing accident and had major surgery. I've managed to speak to the consultant who performed the operation and he said that what the pathologist found at the autopsy tallies with the procedure he'd done. Armstrong also remembered that English had once broken his leg – he thinks it was the left. Apparently, the pins used to set off metal detectors at the airport.'

She sat back in her chair and exhaled. 'So it looks as though the MO changed. Nothing new in that, I guess.'

He nodded. It would keep the press busy with endless speculation, once they found out. He could already picture the interviews with various profilers trying to make sense of the killer's actions. But from their point of view, with so little to go on, there was no point wasting precious time thinking about it. Often it was best just to stick to the facts. 'We're trying to track down the lung tissue samples that were taken, so that we can confirm the DNA.'

'Where's the body?'

'In a pauper's grave in Camberwell New Cemetery. I'll hold off on an exhumation order until we see if we can find the samples.'

'What about the body on the south coast?'

'I spoke to Ramsey and he's looking into it.'

'OK, assuming it's Richard English in the Peckham fire two years ago, why plant his wallet and keys at the Sainsbury's fire?'

'My guess is the killer wanted to draw attention to what he'd done. He wanted it known that Richard English was dead and that he'd killed him. Maybe he was disappointed that the fire had been dismissed as an accident. He must've really hated English to do what he did to him, to know that English was alive, even if he was drugged, when he started the fire. So maybe by putting the wallet and keys where we'd find them, he's saying, "I nailed him."'

'What's the connection between English and the others?'

'Still unclear.'

'Then this needs to be kept out of the press domain for now, certainly as far as any connection with the Jigsaw murders is concerned. I'll call Ian Armstrong and explain.'

He nodded. 'I need to borrow Nick's car, then I'm off in a minute to see a man called Colin Price who may be able to help. He used to be the manager of one of English's hotels until he was sacked. When he threatened legal action, he was paid off. It sounds as though English may have wanted to hush it up, for some reason. Since then, Price has been running a hotel near Oxford.'

'Tell me about Richard English,' Tartaglia asked.

Colin Price folded his hands primly in front of him on his leather-topped desk. 'You want the honest truth?'

'Yes. Warts and all, please.'

'He was a hateful man. He may have been a successful businessman, but I haven't got a good word to say about him as a person, even knowing now that he's dead. There was no kindness, no humanity.'

They were sitting in Price's tidy, spacious office in the basement of Bletchingdon Manor Hotel, a neo classical mansion surrounded by parkland, close to Blenheim Palace, just over an hour's drive from Barnes. Price was dressed in a dark suit and tie and looked to be in his early forties. Slim and of medium height, with thinning fair hair, he sat upright behind the desk, as though at an interview, his soft-featured face tense with emotion, small beads of sweat peppering his high forehead.

'You clearly feel strongly about him. What exactly did he do?'

'On the surface, it was all very businesslike. He wasn't violent and he rarely shouted. It was all far subtler than that. If he took against you for some reason, he'd find your weak spot and hound you.'

'He was a bully?'

Price nodded. 'Luckily he wasn't around all the time, but I used to dread his visits. It's why there was a high turnover of staff. I suspect he was homophobic, although of course he tried to appear the opposite.'

'What did you do wrong, in his eyes?'

'He found out I was in a relationship with somebody else who worked at the hotel, one of the sommeliers.'

'Which hotel was this?'

'Stoneleigh Park, near Dartmoor. It's the flagship hotel in the group.'

Tartaglia nodded. He remembered the brochure in Armstrong's office.

'The restaurant's got a star, or at least it did when I was there,' Price continued. 'We managed to keep things quiet – it was nobody's business and I don't like staff gossiping about my private life. We were always careful to meet outside the hotel but someone spotted us in a pub on our night off. Anyway, it was all around the hotel by the next morning. From then on, things between Richard and me changed. He never mentioned that he knew, but it was obvious. He made things very unpleasant. Luckily, I started to keep a note of things he said and did, and when it got worse, I bought myself a little hidden recorder. I knew he was trying to get rid of me and I didn't want it to ruin my chances of getting another job. They followed the correct dismissal procedure, of course, but it was all a tissue of lies. When the final warning came, I had already contacted a solicitor. To cut a long story short, I threatened to publicise the notes and recordings I had, as well as publicise some other things I'd seen Richard do. His partner, Ian, sorted things out in the end.'

'He offered you money to keep quiet?'

'Yes. Quite a large sum. He also provided me with a reference saying I'd resigned. At least I left with my reputation intact.'

Tartaglia nodded. It explained why Ian Armstrong had been keen to stop McCann from speaking to Colin Price. The incident had been an embarrassment for the company and was not the sort of thing they would like widely known. But perhaps McCann had read a little too much into it. As far as Tartaglia was concerned, Price looked nothing like the description of Chris aka Spike – the name they were now calling him – and wasn't a likely suspect.

'Do you have any idea who might want to kill him?'

Price smiled. 'When I heard he'd disappeared, well . . . But there's a big difference between wishing someone dead and actually doing something about it. Has he been found?'

'Possibly. Do you know who this man is?' Tartaglia pulled out the E-FIT of the man called Spike.

Price studied it for a moment, then shook his head. 'Wish I did. If he had anything to do with getting rid of Richard English, I'd like to buy him a drink.'

Thirty-five

Adam had found it impossible to leave the café without paying. No amount of explaining that his wallet had been stolen and that he would come back later with the money had made any difference. A large man wearing a ponytail and a sweat-stained denim shirt, who claimed to be a security guard for the antique arcade, had appeared from nowhere and blocked the doorway. Clearly burned by previous experience, the middle-aged female owner had threatened to call the police until he handed over his watch. Nothing else he had offered had been acceptable. The watch was a black-faced Rolex Submariner, which had belonged to Kit and was worth several thousand pounds, even in its battered state. It irked him to have to leave it behind, even for half an hour until he came back with some cash, but what else could he do? He certainly didn't want the police called. All for a measly fucking twelve quid fifty. The food hadn't even been that good. He made the woman sign a full receipt with her name, address and phone number. He wished he could make her write it in her own blood.

As he marched back up the hill towards Notting Hill Gate, he tried to think back. The last time he had the wallet was when he bought the chestnuts. After paying for them, he remembered holding the burningly hot bag in one hand as he struggled to push the wallet into the zip pocket of his jacket with the other. People were milling around him all the time, but he wasn't aware of anybody bumping into him or trying to distract him, while somebody else dipped his pocket. Maybe the wallet had just fallen out somehow, but instinct told him otherwise. It was annoying about the cash, but he could afford to lose the two hundred pounds. There was the cash in the rucksack under his bed, and more still in the lockup. It was also annoying to lose Kit's credit card, although it was near its limit, as anybody trying to use it would soon find out. He had others to fall back on, safely stowed away from Kit's house and Gunner.

Five minutes later, he was in Bedford Gardens. He opened the front door and found a letter for Kit inside on the floor. It looked like some sort of boring circular and he tossed it onto the hall table on top of the small pile of Kit's accumulated post. He would go through it all later, once he had sorted out Gunner. As he shut the door, he noticed a brown padded envelope lying behind it on the mat. Turning the package over, he saw with surprise that it appeared to be for him, the name Tom printed on the front in black felt tip. There was no address or postmark. It had been hand delivered. It felt like a book and he tore open the package. Inside was a hardback copy of *The Talented Mr Ripley* by Patricia Highsmith. The red dust jacket was dog-eared and foxed, and it smelt musty as though it had been kept somewhere damp. The drawing on the cover showed a pair of spectacle frames and the outline of a dead man.

He felt the blood rush to his face as he stood staring at the picture, wondering what to do. He hadn't read the stupid book, but he had seen the film and remembered the plot clearly enough to know that somebody was trying to make a point. Somebody was pulling his chain. Was it Gunner? Had he bought the book at the market stall? If so, he must have raced back to Kit's house to put it there, although why go to the trouble of putting it in an envelope and shoving it through the door? The only other person who knew him as Tom was Hannah Bird, but she didn't know where he lived.

There was a parallel of sorts between Ripley's situation and his, and between Dickie's death and Kit's, although that little godforsaken pocket of Thailand where he had holed up for a few weeks with Kit was nothing like San Remo. There the similarities ended. Ripley was a low-life conman and Dickie's killing was amateurish. By contrast, he had planned Kit's final moments down to the last detail. Nor had he scuttled the boat. It would have been a waste and what would have been the point? He had made sure nobody saw them go off in it. There was nobody waiting for their return who would notice, let alone care, that only one person came back; there was nobody to miss Kit. And even if one of the locals did remember him, he was just another in a long line of drinking buddies and hangers-on that lonely Kit had picked up at one of the many nearby tourist bars. Adam had allowed himself to be picked up. His money was running out after many months of travelling and he needed somewhere to stay while he worked out what to do next. Some drunken Aussie in another bar had told him about the Englishman with more money than sense and it hadn't been hard to find Kit and get his attention. Kit must have thought he'd struck it lucky that night with Adam, but the boot was on the other foot. The reality had probably only dawned in Kit's pickled brain weeks later, on the afternoon he died.

Each moment of that day was still sharp in his mind. It had been Kit's forty-second birthday. Adam could still feel the shimmering heat, taste the salt in the air. Kit didn't get up until almost midday, which was normal. When he eventually struggled out of bed, he was in a funny mood and couldn't make up his mind what he wanted to do. Adam remembered getting increasingly angry as time passed. The plan they had made the night before had been to go snorkelling on the reef, then have a light snack on the beach with cocktails, and watch the sun go down. It had a romantic appeal, even for cynical old Kit. The reef was one of the best in the area, but being small and remote, it was rarely visited. The drop-off where the reef met the ocean was steep and the water around it incredibly deep, going from a bright turquoise to an inky blue-black in about thirty metres. Few people ever bothered to venture far down the outer wall and whatever was at the bottom remained hidden in darkness. It was the perfect place to dispose of a body.

Even Kit, who hated most forms of physical exertion, liked snorkelling and had agreed to the idea with uncharacteristic enthusiasm. Adam had the picnic basket packed and ready for loading by the little jetty, along with the snorkelling equipment. He had also prepared a bag with some other necessary items. But it had all been too easy. As if Kit had suddenly developed a sixth sense about what lay in store, he tried to back out at the last minute. It was his birthday, after all. He could bloody well do what he wanted. Adam had been a little too forceful trying to make him cooperate and Kit had got quite nasty, calling him all sorts of unpleasant things and threatening to throw him out on his ear if he didn't shut up about the bloody snorkelling. In the end, an apology and the sight of Adam stripped down to his tight white trunks, his body oiled and brown, had grudgingly calmed him down. With the hint of something more to come in the physical line ('at long, bloody last') once the snorkelling was over, Adam finally managed to get him on board.

But the trouble didn't end there. All the way out, Kit had whinged about having 'a bit of a headache', about it being 'too bloody bright' and about Adam having brought the wrong cocktail ingredients. Adam could still hear Kit's lisping, nasal tones. He wanted Manhattans, not Daiquiris, even though Adam had twice explained that, thanks to Kit having finished the bottle the previous night, they were out of bourbon. Kit was keen to skip the snorkelling part altogether and get straight to the beach, but Adam had stood firm, deaf to Kit's whining as he steered the little boat as fast as possible towards the edge of the reef. Thank God he wouldn't have to put up with it for much longer.

He wished he could have strung it out a bit more and taken his time, but he had had enough of Kit's moaning and Kit was right: it was way too hot. Even with his tan, he was getting burnt. So there was no delicious build-up. No foreplay. He anchored the boat and before he knew it, his hands were around Kit's damp, scrawny neck and he was throttling the last desperate, gasping breath out of him just to shut him up. Like bad sex, it was all over in a matter of minutes and instead of the usual elation, he felt flat afterwards. He secured the weight belts tightly around Kit's middle and carefully eased him, feet first, over the side. As Kit slid into the water, there was barely a splash. God, how he hated him for depriving him of his pleasure. The sight of his face, eyes still open, disappearing swiftly downwards into the deep blue, was no consolation. He couldn't remember how Ripley had felt after murdering Dickie, but unlike Ripley, he had no desire to punch a hole in the boat, watch it sink, then swim back all the way from the reef to the shore. He was far too exhausted.

He stared down at the book in his hand. For a moment, Kit's face morphed onto the cover. He had had a puerile taste for practical jokes and he was laughing. Had Kit sent him the book? Had he somehow come back from the dead? Had he crawled out of the sea and been following Adam ever since, all the way back to the UK and to the house in Notting Hill? At times he felt as though someone was looking over his shoulder. But he dismissed the idea as paranoid. There could be no return from that deep, dark watery grave. The book had to be from Gunner. But if so, the Ripley idea could only be a lucky guess. Gunner couldn't possibly have any idea what had happened to Kit. He was just fishing, trying to see how Adam would react. Perhaps Gunner saw himself as Freddie Miles, Dickie's smart-ass, suspicious friend who wanted to expose Ripley. If so, there was only one ending to that particular little strand of story and Gunner certainly had it coming.

He went into the small sitting room on the ground floor next to Kit's library and started to make a fire in the grate. He used several firelighters and a huge mound of kindling and it was soon blazing away. He added a couple of broken panels of wood from one of Kit's empty wine crates and when it looked good and hot, sparks spitting noisily out onto the rug, he tossed the book into the heart of it. The paper cover curled and disappeared in seconds and soon the cloth-covered board below blistered and turned black. As he watched the pages disintegrate, he saw Kit's face in the flames. He was still smiling, mocking him. Would he always be there? Again he told himself that there was no way Kit could still be alive, but would he be his nemesis? Getting rid of the book had changed nothing and he felt suddenly feverish. He had never before felt so out of control. Somebody was slowly and viciously pulling at the vital thread that held his life together and his world was unravelling.

He heard a footstep behind him and swung around. Gunner was standing in the doorway watching him.

'What do you want?'

'Thought I smelled smoke,' Gunner said, eyebrows raised. 'You burning something?'

Thirty-six

The drive back into London on the M40 was slow, as Tartaglia hit the tail end of the rush hour. Pool cars were usually impossible to get hold of at short notice and Minderedes had offered the loan of the BMW. It was much nicer than anything available, with a decent sound system, but he missed the Ducati. He would somehow have to make time to pick it up in the next day or so. He was due at his sister Nicoletta's that evening and had arranged with Minderedes to return the car the next morning. She had called and apologised for what she had said the other evening and eventually he had agreed to go to her house for dinner. He had managed to speak to Ramsey. There were no new developments with the Aldford fire, although they had received a report that a bearded man, matching the description of the man seen hanging around at the fire, had checked in to a nearby B&B for a few days leading up to Guy Fawkes night. He had paid cash up front and had left on the night of the bonfire. According to the woman who ran the B&B, he had been driving a white van and she'd seen very little of him. She didn't know the make of the van and hadn't made a note of the licence number. Ramsey had also looked into the beach fire in some detail and had spoken to the team that had dealt with it. The results from the autopsy had been inconclusive, although it was assumed that the woman was already dead when placed on the fire and set alight. Without witnesses, let alone possible suspects, it remained unsolved and there was nothing to suggest a link with any of the other fires they were investigating.

An hour later, Tartaglia pulled up outside Nicoletta's terraced house in Islington and as he walked up the front steps, her husband John opened the door.

'Got rid of the Ducati?' he asked, welcoming Tartaglia inside.

'It's in the garage for a service.'

Inside, the house was warm and filled with delicious cooking smells. He took off his jacket and followed John down the corridor into the large kitchen at the back, where Nicoletta was taking something out of the oven.

'You're late,' she said, kissing him quickly on the cheek.

'Traffic on the M40 . . .'

'Never mind. Go and sit down.' She turned back to the stove.

'What can I get you to drink?' John asked.

'Something soft, please. I'm still on call.'

'San Pellegrino and lime?'

'Thanks.'

Nicoletta lifted the lid off a large, shallow pan on the stove and sniffed the air before turning off the gas under it. Her long black hair was loosely clipped up on top of her head. Dressed in skinny jeans and a large T-shirt, she was barefoot, as though it were still summer. Unlike him, she rarely felt the cold.

'Is it just us?' he asked a little warily. Nicoletta often tried to set him up with one of her single friends when he went for dinner. She would give her eye teeth to have him settled and married, preferably to someone she knew, as though she couldn't picture happiness in any other form. He often wondered how things would have been if he had been born first and she was his little sister.

'Yes. Just us. I thought we needed a catch-up. It's been ages.'

'About six weeks, you mean.'

She waved him away with her hand as though the details were unimportant. John handed him his drink and he sat down with it at the table.

'Where are Carlo and Anna?' he asked, seeing that she had only set three places.

'Anna's on a sleepover and Carlo's upstairs doing his homework. He had an early supper. So, tell me about Gianni. How is he? Feeling any remorse?'

The ringing of his phone saved him from having to reply.

'Hang on a sec,' Tartaglia said to his sister, seeing Mineredes's name on the screen. He got up from the table and took the phone into the hall. 'What's up, Nick?'

'Dave has found the lab samples from the Peckham fire,' Minderedes replied. 'They were lurking at the back of one of the hospital freezers. It's real lucky they hadn't cleared them out yet. They're about to do a full refurb.'

'Get them over to the lab immediately. Tell them it's urgent. I don't mind what it costs. What about the suitcase?'

'No record of what happened to it. Most of the stuff recovered from the basement was skipped by the council. I've been over to Tatyana's flat but her roommate says she's scooted back to Russia all of a sudden. I've just been to the restaurant where she worked and the manager said the same. Apparently, a man came in last night and asked for her. The manager was pretty vague, but the basic description sort of tallies with the way she described Chris, although his hair was brown, not red. The manager also said he'd seen her with him a couple of times before, that he'd come into the restaurant for a bite to eat and she'd been all over him.'

'So, what happened?'

'Well, she goes outside to talk to him and when she comes back, she tells the manager she's off. She says her mother's sick and she's got to go home right away. The manager didn't believe her. He said she didn't even bother to look sad. She just takes off her apron, grabs her coat and bag and she's out the door. He's mighty pissed off, as you can imagine. She told her flatmate later that night that a friend had given her a ticket and some money to fly home. I've checked with the airports and she was on a Lufthansa flight to Moscow, via Frankfurt, this morning.'

Tartaglia sighed. Had everything she said been a lie? Was the identikit picture deliberately designed to mislead? He thought back to the interview. She had been genuinely shaken, he was sure. His instincts were generally good and he had found her convincing enough. There must have been a vein of truth, he reassured himself. It was a lot easier when put on the spot, and usually more believable too, to distort the truth than make up something totally from scratch. Maybe she had given them a mixture of just enough reality to make it fit with other people's descriptions, coupled with a large dose of imagination to put them off the scent. All, no doubt, in return for a nice fat payoff.

'Go back and talk to the roommate,' he said. 'See if she knows anything at all about Chris or Spike, or whatever his name is. It sounds as though Tatyana must have gotten in touch with him somehow after we saw her. Either that or he knew we would come looking for her.'

'What about her phone?'

'Check all calls to and from her number. But he's clever. I'll bet he either gave her another phone to call him or she got in touch with him some other way.'

He hung up and went back into the room.

'Sorry about that,' he said, returning to the table. John was already seated and Nicoletta came over to join them, carrying a large platter of *saltimbocca alla romana*. The aroma of cooked meat, sage and Marsala filled the air. He sat down and unfolded his napkin.

'What are you working on?' she asked, helping him to a couple of escalopes wrapped in prosciutto and passing him his plate.

'Something major. You've probably seen it in the papers . . .'

'You mean the Jigsaw murders?' John asked, passing him a dish of grilled polenta.

'Yes.' He added a couple of slices, along with some mounds of steaming, garlicky spinach from a large painted bowl.

John was a criminal barrister and took a great deal of interest in Tartaglia's work. Two sides of the same coin, he always said. 'How are you getting on?'

'Snakes and ladders as usual. The phone call I just took: another largish snake.'

John smiled. 'Where've you just come from? You said you were out of London.'

'I've just been to interview somebody who used to work at Stoneleigh Park. Am I right in thinking you stayed there a few years back?'

'That's right. It was near Dartmoor. Beautiful place, although I can't remember why we were there.'

'It was our tenth wedding anniversary,' Nicoletta said, passing John his *saltimbocca*. 'You must remember.'

'Not really, apart from you spending the whole time in the spa.'

'You were working all weekend, what else was there to do?'

John nodded vaguely and helped himself to polenta. 'Well, it was certainly very comfortable. But it rained all weekend. I don't think we went out once.'

'And there was that terrible row with the chef,' Nicoletta continued. John gave her a blank look. 'There was a lot of screaming and shouting and smashing of crockery. Then there were sirens. It was all very dramatic. I think it was our first night there.'

'That's right. I'd completely forgotten.'

'What was it about?' Tartaglia asked, wondering if Richard English was involved.

'I've no idea. But the cook – the head chef – came storming out of the kitchen while we were having dinner.' She turned to John. 'He was crying, don't you remember? He told everybody to go home. I've never seen anything like it. He said some things, all pretty garbled.'

'He was drunk, that's all.'

'Maybe, but he had blood all over him. Then he took off his hat and jacket and threw them on the floor. It was all very *Fawlty Towers*.'

'It wasn't funny.'

'You're right. It wasn't. It was a bit sad. Then he walked out. I remember seeing his clothes sitting there in a little pile on the carpet, wondering whether I should go and pick them up. Then someone in a suit appeared and apologised to everyone in the room and offered us all champagne on the house. He said the chef had had some sort of family crisis.'

'That's a new euphemism for having too much to drink.'

'And that he'd been working too hard, or something like that. But I don't think he came back. The food wasn't half as good the next day. Hadn't they just won a Michelin star? Then there was a thing in the Sunday papers a few weeks later about the pressures of being a successful chef and how they often crash and burn. They mentioned him. I think I cut the piece out for you, don't you remember, John?'

'No.'

'When was this?' Tartaglia asked.

259

'Our tenth anniversary. I told you,' Nicoletta said.

'Four years ago last September,' John added.

'I still enjoyed it. I'd quite like to go back . . .'

Tartaglia let the conversation between John and Nicoletta wash over him, gazing at the huge, laden dresser that stood floor to ceiling up against the opposite wall. It had once belonged to his grandmother and, before that, had been removed from his family's first grocery shop in Edinburgh when the business expanded to bigger premises. Like many Italian immigrants coming to the UK in the late nineteenth century, they had done very well. Richard English was another self-made man, who had come from nowhere. He was the first victim, as far as they knew, followed by John Smart, then Jake Finnigan. He wondered if the order was important, if English was the lynchpin. Or if it was just the way the cards fell. As Colin Price had said, there must have been a queue of people wishing English dead. But where to start? He kept coming back to the fact that the two people who stood most to gain from English's death were his wife Lisa, and business partner Ian Armstrong. Either of them could have hired somebody to take care of English. But the way he had been killed – lured to a basement squat, drugged and probably force-fed alcohol and pills – it wasn't a professional job. Far too high risk. It also felt personal. Maybe it wasn't about money after all . . .

'Penny for them?' Nicoletta said, waving her hand in front of his face.

He looked up at her. 'Sorry. I'm a bit distracted, that's all. I need to make a call. I'll be back in a minute.'

He got up from the table, went out into the hall again and dialled Colin Price's number. He got through to the reception desk and left a message for Price to call him back. As he walked back into the kitchen, his phone rang. He heard Chang's voice at the other end.

'We've found the tramp. His name's Roger Massey and he's in hospital. He was admitted on the day of the fire.'

'Where is he?'

'St Thomas's. He had a fall and broke his leg. Apparently he's also got TB.'

'OK, I'll be there as soon as I can,' Tartaglia replied. He was sorry to leave the dinner table so soon. John would understand, but Nicoletta would not be pleased.

Half an hour later, he stood with Chang beside Massey's bed. He had been given a room of his own and lay propped up on pillows, watching *Top Gear* on the wall-mounted TV.

'You know why I'm here, Mr Massey?' Tartaglia asked, as Massey removed his headphones.

Massey nodded. 'It's about the fire. They told me you was coming.'

He spoke with a northern twang. Although a tall man, judging by the length of him stretched out in the bed, he looked frail, his face bony and hollow-cheeked, the skin leathery and deeply lined. His greyish beard was thick and trimmed short, and he looked older than Tartaglia had been expecting, maybe in his early sixties, although illness and years on the street had a rapid aging effect.

'That's right. Someone set fire to a car on the waste ground next to Sainsbury's car park. I understand you used to go there quite a lot.'

'Yeah. It were warm outside the bakery. They'd bring me out bread and stuff to eat.' He spoke quietly, as though it were an effort.

'The fire happened at night, the same day you were brought in here.'

'I'm not a suspect, then?'

'No. I just need your help. There was a body in the car.'

'I read about it in the papers.'

'OK. Do you remember anything at all odd in the days before?'

'What do you mean by odd?'

'Someone hanging around, perhaps? Someone who wasn't normally there?'

Massey yawned, showing a mouth of tobacco-stained teeth. 'There was a bloke nosing around a few nights before, having a really good scout about. He came over to talk to me. Asked me for a light. I gave him one and he gave me a couple of fags.'

'What sort of time would this be?' Tartaglia asked.

'I don't carry a watch no more.'

'Sainsbury's shuts at midnight,' Chang said. 'Was it long after that?'

'Maybe a couple of hours.'

'What else did he say?' Tartaglia asked.

'He asked if it was always this quiet. It varies, I told him.'

'How did he arrive? Was he on foot?'

'Must've been. They lock the barrier when they close for the night.'

'Do you remember any cars left overnight, either in the Sainsbury's lot or on the waste ground next to it?'

Massey paused for a moment. 'There was a Fiat Panda, dark-coloured, parked up on the waste ground by the fence.'

'When did you first see it?'

'Couple of days before I come in here, maybe. No more than that.'

'You didn't see anybody drive it in?'

'No. Must've been during opening hours.'

'Going back to this man. Can you describe him?'

'My memory's not what it was.'

'But you spoke to him . . .'

Massey sighed. 'Tallish, though he stooped a bit, like he wanted to seem smaller. Thin, early thirties at the most, I'd say. He was wearing a woolly hat. His face was real dirty, but he wasn't dark skinned. He had a bit of a beard on 'im.'

'How was he dressed?'

Massey shrugged. 'Trainers, jeans, and a socking great big overcoat. It was way too big for 'im and he looked pretty rough.'

'Was he homeless, do you think?'

'Maybe he wants people to think he is. But he was smoking Marlboro Lights, a brand new pack. He had to take off the cellophane.'

'Someone might have given it to him.'

'There was something not right about him, that's all I can say.'

'Anything else you remember?'

Massey shook his head.

'Would you recognise him again if you saw him?'

'Most definitely.'

'For someone who says his memory's not what it was, you seem to have pretty good recall.'

Massey gave a weak smile. 'I was in the military police, once upon a time.'

'I heard you were a soldier.'

'I dropped the "police" bit. Lost me too many friends.'

Thirty-seven

'What do you think, Sir?' Chang asked Tartaglia, as they left the hospital and walked towards the car park.

'I wish all witnesses were like that. Get somebody over to him first thing tomorrow with a laptop to do the E-FIT.' His phone rang and – adding to Chang, 'We'll get a decent image out of him' – he answered it to find Colin Price at the other end.

'Thanks for calling me back,' Tartaglia said. 'Were you working at Stoneleigh Park about four years ago?'

'Yes. Why?'

'I was told something about a chef who was sacked or walked out. It all sounded pretty dramatic and the police may have been called.'

'If it was four years ago, you'd be talking about Dave Simpson. He was the head chef. Very talented lad and very young to get a star, but he screwed everything up big time.'

'Can you tell me a bit more?'

'I hadn't worked with him long when it happened and I can't say I knew him well, but I think it was the usual problem of stupid hours and pressure . . . and a tricky personal life, along with booze and other substances. He just burnt out younger than most.'

'Was this anything to do with Richard English?'

Price laughed. 'It was all to do with Richard English.'

'Where can I find Dave Simpson?'

'You can't. He's missing.'

264

'Missing? Since when?' Tartaglia heard voices in the background at the other end of the phone.

'Hang on a sec,' Price said. A muffled conversation followed, then Price came back on the line.

'You said Simpson's missing,' Tartaglia said.

'That's right. According to what I heard, he walked out on his wife and kid one day and never came back.'

'Is there anyone I can talk to about him? Any friends or relatives?'

'I don't know about his family, but he was quite close to one of the sommeliers. A young woman called Chantal Blomet. She was a bit star-struck and used to follow him around like a little lamb. Simpson lapped it up but his wife wasn't best pleased, as you can imagine.'

'Do you know where Chantal is now?' Again he heard voices in the background at Price's end.

'Sorry. We've got a bit of a problem brewing here,' Price said. 'I'm going to have to go. You could try Richard's partner, Ian Armstrong. If she's still working in the company, he'd know. And if she's moved on, they'll have probably given her a reference.'

It was nearly midnight by the time Tartaglia got home. The flat was in darkness and he switched on a lamp in the sitting room and drew the shutters. He pulled the seat cushions off the sofa and picked up the pillows, sheet and duvet he had left piled on the coffee table. He threw them onto the sofa unenthusiastically, another night of fragmented sleep ahead of him.

He had eventually managed to get hold of Ian Armstrong, rousing him out of bed at his house in Belgravia. Armstrong remembered who Dave Simpson was, but the last he'd heard of him was when his wife had contacted the office to say the chef had gone missing and she'd hoped they might know where he was. Armstrong had no recollection of Chantal Blomet, but had given Tartaglia the details of the company's personnel director to contact first thing in the morning.

He was heading to the kitchen to get a glass of water when he noticed that the bedroom door was wide open and one of the bedside lights was on. He peered inside. There was no sign of Donovan or, looking around more closely, any of her things. The bed had been stripped, the linen roughly folded in a pile on top of the duvet. He checked the bathroom. Again, no sign of any of the bits and pieces she had brought with her. She had gone. He searched around for a note but there was no sign of one.

He closed the shutters and stared at the empty room with an awkward mixture of relief and concern. What had made her go? Was it the conversation they had had the previous night? He had been thinking about it on and off all day. Donovan was keeping something from him, he was sure. Whether it was something totally outlandish that she was ashamed to mention, or whether it actually had some basis in reality, he couldn't tell. He had no idea what to make of her. He could understand her obsession with trying to find Claire's killer. The issue of justice when it came to murder was one they had discussed on many occasions, but she must know that even if the killer were caught, no form of retribution could bring Claire back.

Thinking through it all again, he was convinced that something particular had sparked her off the previous night. He would speak to Chang again in the morning about what had happened at the Dillon. He needed more details of what exactly had been said and exactly how she had reacted. Donovan's theory that Claire had been deliberately targeted, that her murder was part of a grander plan, had not been easy to explain to Steele. As he spoke, he realised how odd it must sound, although Donovan's instincts in the past had been generally good. To give Steele her due, she hadn't dismissed the idea straight off. She listened patiently while he gave her a blow-by-blow account of what Donovan had said, and appeared relatively sympathetic, even though in the end she dismissed it as a flight of paranoid fancy. There were no hard facts to support Donovan's theory, and it was the facts that mattered. Even so, Steele had agreed to get the taped samples taken from Claire's face and neck tested for DNA as a priority. At least he could have told Donovan that, if only she hadn't run off somewhere.

He tidied away the dirty linen into the laundry basket and made the bed with fresh sheets. He was looking forward to getting into it and having space to spread out. He was about to get undressed and have a shower when he noticed Donovan's black laptop bag leaning against the side of a chair in the corner of the room. She must have forgotten it. It was the excuse he had been looking for. He fished his phone out of his pocket and dialled her number, but it went straight through to voice-mail. He then tried Sharon Fuller's mobile.

'Sorry to wake you,' he said, when she answered after several rings, her voice thick with sleep. 'But I've just got home. Sam's left and she's taken all her stuff, apart from her laptop. Do you have any idea where she is?'

'Her house, I imagine. Forensics finished with it a few hours ago. Hannah called her to let her know.'

'You haven't spoken to her?'

'Not since this morning,' she said, mid-yawn. 'Would you like me to go round there?'

'No. It's fine.'

267

'I can get dressed and drive over there, if you want. If you're worried about her . . .'

He sighed. 'No. I'm sure she'll be fine. Like everything else, it can wait until morning.'

Thirty-eight

'I'm pretty sure Dave Simpson's dead,' Chantal Blomet said, meeting Tartaglia's gaze.

'Why do you say that?'

'I don't know. I just have a feeling.'

She sat quietly, stiff and upright, hands tightly clasped in her lap as though uncomfortable with being interviewed. It had taken a while to track her down and it was now almost noon. She had just started her lunchtime shift at the hotel where she worked and had looked visibly startled at the mention of Simpson's name. Small and slight, her androgynous black sommelier's uniform looked slightly too big for her, although she was nice enough looking in a girl-next-door sort of way. He put her age somewhere in her late twenties to early thirties.

'A feeling? Any other reason?' he asked, wondering if she was serious.

She gave a slight shrug. 'Because he's gone, disappeared into thin air. Nobody's seen him, not even his wife, apparently. There's stuff about him on the Missing Person website, and on Facebook and a couple of the chef websites. If Dave was still alive, somebody somewhere would know.'

It wasn't that simple, he wanted to say. Sometimes people didn't want to be found, but maybe it wasn't an option she wanted to consider. Her English was fluent and without accent. He had commented on it and she explained that her mother was English and that she had spent most of her school holidays in the UK.

269

'Do you think somebody killed him?' he asked, just as his phone started to ring. He checked the screen and saw Melinda's name. He had texted her to say that he had no news yet but she still kept calling. No doubt she knew what he'd said was a lie. He had no desire to renege on their deal, but he had no time to talk, let alone work out how much to tell her, and she would have to wait until he was ready. He switched the phone to silent and looked back at Chantal.

She looked perplexed. 'No. I don't mean anything like that. More likely he killed himself, or had some sort of an accident. He wasn't a happy man. But you should probably speak to someone who knows him better than me. I haven't seen him for ages.'

He sensed there was more that she wasn't saying, but was it relevant? Simpson was only of interest because he had been treated badly by Richard English and was now missing, along with the fact that the so far unidentified male victim fitted Simpson's age profile. 'But I understood you were close to him?'

'In a way.'

'You had a relationship with him?'

A flicker of irritation crossed her face. 'No. I don't know who told you that, but we were just friends. Unfortunately, people like to gossip. I was fond of Dave, he was *incredibly* talented of course, but he was all over the place emotionally. Besides, he was married, he had a kid.' She spoke almost primly, but he didn't entirely believe her. He remembered Colin Price saying that she had been star-struck and the look in her eyes as she spoke about Simpson gave her away. Had Simpson rebuffed her, he wondered.

'I understand he was sacked,' he said.

She nodded. 'It was his fault, but it should never have ended that way. After what he did to Richard . . . well, there was no going back.'

'Did to Richard? You mean Richard English?'

The colour rose to her face and she looked confused. 'I assumed you knew . . .'

'No,' he said studying her closely, wondering at her reaction. Perhaps she thought she was speaking out of turn. 'You'd better tell me what happened.'

She looked away, her fingers pulling at the hem of her jacket. 'This was four years ago. Why does it matter?'

'Just tell me what happened, Miss Blomet.'

She shrugged and folded her arms. 'Things weren't going well between them. There was a history. I won't bore you with the details but that particular night Dave had been drinking in the kitchen and Richard caught him. There was an almighty row. He called Dave a "loser" and said he wasn't getting a single share in the business until he sorted himself out. Dave just lost it and he hit Richard. Everything in the kitchen went flying. Richard said some stuff, then Dave picked up a knife and went for Richard. If it hadn't been for the other kitchen staff, I think he might have killed him.'

'You were there?' he asked.

She looked up at him. 'Yes. I was working that night. Even though I wasn't in the kitchen, I could hear what was going on, as could most of the guests. They called an ambulance and Richard was taken to hospital. He had to have a few stitches and he had a broken nose and a black eye. Of course he made a huge song and dance about it, saying it was all unprovoked and that he was just defending himself.'

'Was that true?'

She shook her head. 'Richard knew how to needle people. He had it down to a fine art. He probably didn't think Dave would finally retaliate.'

'So Dave Simpson was sacked,' he said, remembering

Nicoletta's description of the drunken, emotional chef in the restaurant. 'What did you think of Richard English?'

'Me?' She looked taken aback by the question. 'He was a hateful man. Ask anyone. I tried to stay out of his way as much as I could.'

'What happened to Dave Simpson?'

'Richard brought charges. We all tried to persuade him not to, but he was a vindictive shit and he wouldn't listen. Dave had publicly humiliated him and he wanted revenge. So poor Dave ended up in jail.'

Again it was his turn to be surprised. 'Jail? Where?'

She hesitated. 'Dartmoor.'

He made a mental note to check as soon as he was done. If Simpson had been inside, his DNA would be stored on the National Database. They would soon be able to tell if there was a match with the unidentified male body parts from the two fires. 'Do you believe Dave Simpson meant to kill Richard English?'

She shook her head. 'Of course not. He wasn't thinking straight.'

'But you think he's capable of killing someone?'

She looked at him strangely. 'You think Dave's killed someone?'

'Just answer the question.'

'He's capable, yes. Isn't everyone, in the heat of the moment, if they're pushed too far? He certainly saw red that night, but he was already teetering on the edge. Richard just helped him over. I blame Richard a hundred per cent for what happened and I wasn't the only one.' She spoke forcefully and what she said tallied with what Colin Price had told him.

'Do you know where Simpson's wife and child are?'

'No idea, I'm afraid.'

'Does he have any other immediate family?'

'He never talked about his family, at least not with me.'

'When did you last see him?'

'I went to visit him in jail a couple of times before I left Stoneleigh Park. But it was really awkward. I think he felt embarrassed and he made it clear he didn't really want to see me. I didn't bother going back after that.'

'So, you haven't seen him since?'

She shook her head.

'Do you have any idea where he was staying when he came out?'

'No. Sorry.'

'When did you find out he was missing?'

'A while ago, I guess. Someone told me, although I can't remember who. Is he dead? Is that why you're here?'

'It's possible,' he said, getting to his feet. She looked at him curiously, but he couldn't fathom what was behind it. London had more than its fair share of disappearances and suspicious deaths in any one year and there was no reason for her to make any connection with the Jigsaw killings. It was too early to say if Simpson was linked to the killings, although like Richard English, John Smart and Jake Finnigan, he too had gone missing. Was he the unidentified male victim, or would parts of his body turn up on another fire at a later date? Or could he be the bearded man they were looking for? He needed to get hold of a visual of Simpson right away.

Transferring her shopping bags into her left hand, Donovan unlocked the front door of her house. It was warm inside, almost uncomfortably so after the fifteen minute walk from the Tube. The narrow hall smelt musty and unused. It had been barely a week since Claire had died and yet it already felt like somebody else's house. It had taken the best part of the night to tidy up and, as far as she could, she put everything back the way it had been before the police had searched the place and stripped it of various items belonging to Claire. It had always been Claire's house. She had bought it ten years before and even though Donovan had subsequently bought a half share in it and contributed equally to the mortgage, without Claire it no longer felt like home. Everything reminded her of Claire: the blue flowery curtains in the sitting room, the beige patterned carpet upstairs, the endless china ornaments dotted around the house, the clothes that overfilled her wardrobe and chest of drawers so that they barely closed, the smell of her perfume that still lingered in the air. There was little that Donovan could claim as her own, apart from what was in her bedroom. She hadn't minded before, but all Claire's things suddenly seemed lost and purposeless without their owner. When her mother and father eventually came home from Australia – her father was now conscious and his condition improving by the day – they would know what to do with it all. She carried the bags into the kitchen and started to unpack. The house would be sold, but she felt no regrets. Nothing really mattered any longer, now she knew who had killed Claire and why.

She laid the various boxes and packets out on the counter, making sure that she hadn't forgotten anything, then switched on the kettle. She hadn't eaten since the day before, but she felt so pumped up and high that a cup of tea was all she could stomach. Just as the kettle pinged, the phone rang. It had been happening every few hours since she had moved back into the house. After five rings, the answer machine kicked in and she heard Claire's voice, followed by the sound of the dial tone as whoever it was hung up. She didn't bother to dial 1471. The number would be withheld. He was checking to see if she was there. She would answer later, when she was ready, and let him know that she had finally come home.

'What have you got?' Tartaglia asked, looking up at Sharon Fuller, as she came striding into his office, grinning from ear to ear.

'I think I've found the connection, Sir, or at least one of them. Finnigan and Simpson were both in Pentonville at the same time and in the same wing. And there's more. Simpson was transferred there from Dartmoor so he could see his wife and child.'

'I thought Finnigan was in the Scrubs?'

'He was. But he was only sent there following an incident.'

'Go on.'

'Well, Finnigan and a few of his mates assaulted a couple of the other prisoners in the showers. One of the men was so badly beaten he had to be hospitalised. He was also raped by Finnigan. That man was David Simpson.'

He felt the adrenalin rush, his heart pumping. Fingers steepled against his lips, he leaned back in his chair and exhaled. At last things were starting to fall into place. 'Well done,' he said, jumping out of his chair and starting to pace around the small room as he thought it all through. The report on David Paul Simpson lay open on his desk. The tissue samples found in the hospital fridge, which had been taken from the Peckham fire victim, had been confirmed as belonging to Richard English, and the body in the pauper's grave was due to be exhumed that night. Steele was busy breaking the news to Lisa English and Ian Armstrong, although for the time being no details would be released to the press connecting English's death with the Jigsaw killings. Melinda would have to wait a little while longer for her scoop.

Was Simpson the Jigsaw Killer? He had been eliminated as being one of the other victims. They had checked his DNA profile stored on the system against the DNA profiles of the body parts from the two fires, but there was no match. He had a motive for killing Richard English, who had put him in jail, and also one for killing Finnigan, for what had happened to him once he was there. However, it wasn't completely clear cut. There was no connection so far with John Smart and, although Simpson was nearly six feet tall, the photographs on file showed a Billy Idol lookalike, with a plump, boyish face, a thick neck and short, gelled, bottle-blond hair. He was certainly overweight at the time of his arrest and he could have easily have changed his physique in a gym, but he wasn't an instant fit for the man known as Spike. More importantly, even though the MO for the English and Finnigan murders was different, both killings had required a significant degree of organisation and forward planning. He struggled to see how somebody with Simpson's volatile personality and problems could have executed the murders, in particular Finnigan's.

He turned to Fuller. 'Who were the other prisoners involved?'

'Finnigan's two mates are both still safely under lock and key, as is the other victim. None of them have been out since the attack.'

'Get back on the phone to the prison. I want to know who Simpson was close to when he was inside, if he had any other enemies, and who visited him. Every single person. Don't forget we still have two unidentified bodies to account for, one of which is a youngish male. While you're at it, speak to

Simpson's probation officer. See if they have a record of where he was living when he came out of prison and get contact details for whoever he gave as his next of kin. I have a feeling he's the key to unlocking all of this.'

Thirty-nine

Tartaglia followed Fuller out of the room into the corridor and automatically stopped at the coffee machine. He pressed the button for black, still pondering the connection between Finnigan, Simpson and English and the two still unidentified bodies. As he waited, his phone rang. Checking the screen, he saw it was Hannah Bird.

'I've just been to see Marek Nowak's ex-girlfriend,' she said. He heard the noise of traffic in the background and gathered she was driving. 'She doesn't have any idea where he went. She didn't see him for several days before he disappeared as they'd had a row. Apparently she'd told him she was seeing somebody else and he was very upset. She assumed he'd taken off because of that, although she said she didn't believe he'd stolen anything. It's more or less what she said to CID when the theft was reported. What else do you want me to do?'

'That's enough for now, I think.'

'I've also managed to get hold of Rosie, John Smart's daughter. She's in London for the day and I've arranged to meet her in twenty minutes in the high street. I'm on my way there now, if I can only just get over the bridge. The traffic's murder.'

'I'd like to see her. Where are you taking her?'

'I thought we'd go to the food gallery.'

One of the many disadvantages of their office in Barnes was a lack of interview rooms. It wasn't set up like a normal police station, with areas for public access, and if they wanted to make it formal they had to go to a station somewhere else and borrow a room. However sometimes a more relaxed atmosphere was better, and at least there were several good cafés and pubs nearby. 'I've just got a few things to do, then I'll meet you there,' he said, tipping the foul black liquid away. He could do with a decent cup of coffee to keep him going.

'I've explained about the two fires,' Bird said to Tartaglia as he slid into the seat next to her half an hour later. Rosie sat opposite, her hands tightly cupped around her cup of coffee as though she needed the warmth. He recognised her immediately from the photos Smart had taken of her.

'Good. So you understand why we're here?'

Rosie nodded. 'It's about Dad. I know he's dead. And I now know he's part of these Jigsaw killings that have been in the papers.' Her voice was soft and a little breathless and she winced as she spoke, clearly finding the subject painful. Dressed in a big, baggy, colourful jumper and gypsy skirt, with a lot of silver jewellery, she looked nothing like Isobel, Smart's other daughter.

'Then you'll know that he wasn't the only victim. We're trying to find out what was going on in his life in the few weeks leading up to his murder. There's nothing in his diary that raises alarm bells, but somewhere, somehow, he came across the person who killed him. Based on what we know, it's likely to have been shortly before he disappeared.'

Rosie brushed a wisp of dark hair from her face. 'I can't really tell you very much,' she said, putting the cup carefully back in the saucer. 'And I didn't know for weeks that he was missing. Nobody thought to tell me.' She started to ramble on about how horrible Isobel Smart had been to her.

'But you know now when it was he went missing?' Tartaglia interrupted.

'Yes. The last time I saw him was about a week before he disappeared. We went to see a film, then we had a quick bite to eat before I had to catch my train. He seemed completely normal, nothing at all wrong. We were talking about his coming down to my cottage to stay for a weekend, if only he could square it with Isobel. He didn't want to have to lie to her, but he hadn't quite plucked up the courage to tell her. I wanted to spend some time with him, get to know him a bit better. And my mother also wanted to see him. She's widowed now and I thought maybe . . . Well, he certainly appeared quite keen on the idea of meeting her again, even after so many years. I'm not sure how I'm going to break all this to her.' She started to describe how her parents had met and about their affair and how she had discovered who her real father was.

'Is there anything else you remember?' Tartaglia asked, wanting to keep her on track.

Rosie sighed. 'We talked about his work. He was doing a play on the radio the following week. There was somebody in the cast he couldn't stand and he told me some pretty funny anecdotes about them. I'm pretty sure it was a woman, not a man. And he wasn't that keen on the producer either, but Dad was a bit like that. He could be tricky sometimes.'

'You don't remember their names?' Bird asked.

'Sorry.'

'It's OK,' Tartaglia said. 'We can easily find out. Is there anything else?'

She sighed again and hugged herself. 'It's so difficult trying to think back. Half the time I can barely remember what happened yesterday, let alone two years ago.'

'Just tell us what you can. It all helps.'

He didn't want to push her, make her feel guilty for not being able to remember anything significant. It was quite possible John Smart wasn't aware of any potential danger to himself or, if he was, that he hadn't told her about it. But maybe there was something, buried under the sea of little memories.

'Well, I was just so happy to see him. We didn't get to spend much time with each other, what with my living out of London and Isobel trying to keep him on a tight rein. She was so bloody jealous.'

'But he seemed fine to you? He didn't say he was worried about anything? Even something small?'

She looked at him blankly, then shook her head. 'He looked well, I thought. He'd lost a bit of weight and seemed on really good form.'

He saw tears in her eyes. 'Do the names Richard English, Jake Finnigan, or Dave – possibly David – Simpson mean anything to you? Do you remember your father mentioning any of them at some point?'

She frowned, then shook her head. 'Sorry. I'm pretty hopeless, aren't I?'

'There's no reason why you should have heard of them. I just needed to check. If you think of anything else, however trivial, please call me.' He handed her his card and stood up. 'DC Bird will drop you back to the Tube if you want.'

'It's OK,' Rosie said. 'I'm going to pop over to the Sun Inn now, before I leave London. It's where I used to go with Dad and his mates. I think I'll raise a glass to him, wherever he is now, God bless him.'

Forty

'Is Peter there?' barked the deep voice at the other end of the phone.

'Peter?' Adam replied.

'Don't be a plonker. You know who I mean.'

'Who wants him?'

'Stop dicking around and go get him. I haven't got all day.'

Adam slammed the kitchen phone back in its cradle. It was the third fucking call for Gunner he'd had to answer that morning. The previous time, when the caller had asked for Peter, he'd replied 'Peter who?' and the caller had said 'Don't be so fucking stupid. I know he's there.' The voices were different, but they were similar in tone and rudeness. They all sounded like clones of Gunner, aka Peter. He couldn't think of him as Peter. Gunner suited him much better.

There had been no phone calls at all until that morning. He'd assumed Gunner had a mobile, although he'd never heard it ring or noticed him using a phone. It was odd that people had suddenly started calling him now on the landline. Was he feeling more secure, more master of the house? Was he intending on staying for a while? The thought made Adam seethe. He was also surprised that Gunner hadn't rushed to answer the phone, seeing as how he'd been giving out the number so freely and must know the calls were for him. Maybe he'd gone out again. And maybe, for once, he'd forgotten to lock the bedroom door . . .

Adam finished tidying away his lunch things in the dishwasher and went upstairs. The door to the sitting room on the

282

first floor was wide open and the room was empty. On the landing above, he paused and listened. All he could hear was the distant drone of traffic and the clatter of the Tube as it passed under the street further along. Maybe Gunner was asleep. He took off his shoes and crept up to the second floor, treading carefully on the old stairs, hoping that the creaks weren't too audible. The door to Kit's bedroom was ajar, daylight coming from within. He put his head around the door and peered inside.

The curtains were open and the bed was a mess, sheets and duvet half on the floor, as though Gunner had had a bad night. But there was no sign of him. He paused again and listened, just in case Gunner was in the bathroom, but there was no sound coming from inside. Apart from the bed, the room looked tidy, Kit's pictures and bits and pieces from his travels displayed exactly where they were before. But although he scouted around, there was no sign of Gunner's clothes, his shoes or large rucksack. He checked the wardrobe and the chest of drawers, which were still full of Kit's winter things, then went into the bathroom. The towels had been thrown in a pile in the middle of the floor. He picked them up and felt them. They were still damp. Otherwise there were no clothes or other personal items belonging to Gunner, only the few things of Kit's that Adam hadn't chucked away. A small puddle of water on the floor by the bath, and a smear of toothpaste in the sink, were the only other signs of recent occupation. It seemed that Gunner had gone.

He sat down on the bed and gazed around the room, not sure whether he dared celebrate. Gunner's departure had been as sudden and unannounced as his arrival. Did it mean anything? Or was he reading too much into things as usual? From his point of view, the timing of Gunner's leaving was perfect. Perhaps he should just accept it as a stroke of luck, although he knew not to trust in such things. Luck had a way of biting you back if you got too complacent. The visit from the policeman, coupled with the mysterious Mr Ripley book, had unnerved him. Even with Gunner gone, he couldn't relax back into the house, much that he'd like to. It was risky staying there any longer, but all he needed was one more night.

Forty-one

'I can't believe anyone's that vague,' Hannah Bird said with feeling, as she and Tartaglia started to walk back to the office after leaving Rosie. 'She doesn't even have her mobile switched on half the time. She said she lost it, which is why it took me so long to get hold of her. Then she found it in the fridge. Can you believe it?'

He smiled. 'She does seem a bit daffy and some people just have better recall than others.' He paused for a moment, taking refuge in a doorway to light a cigarette. Bird's broad face was etched with tiredness and he sensed her frustration. They were all working flat out, sifting through whatever came in, however nonsensical, spurred on by the desperate hope of turning up the one thing that would prove to be pivotal. He knew from experience it was out there somewhere; it was just a matter of time. They were making good progress, he reminded himself. But Bird, being new to the roller coaster ride of a murder investigation, didn't yet have that conviction.

He took a deep drag on his cigarette and started walking again, skirting around a group of shoppers who were gathered outside Barnes Bookshop, admiring the window display.

'Look,' he said after a minute, as they approached the pond. 'If there was something material Smart was worried about, and he told Rosie, she'd have gone straight to whoever was running the Missing Person investigation. And the other daughter, Isobel, would've done the same. It could easily be just some little thing that he spotted somewhere when he was out and about and he poked his nose into the wrong place. Maybe he didn't even realise something was wrong until it was too late.'

His breath plumed out on the air as he spoke. It was just beginning to get dark and the temperature had dropped. He turned up his collar and jammed his free hand into his pocket. As they passed the pond, he heard a loud quacking and flapping of wings. A group of small children and adults stood by the edge of the water feeding bread to the ducks.

'But where, then?' Bird asked.

'Where what?'

'Where do we start looking for whatever was troubling him? It wasn't like he had an action-packed life.'

'It could be something small and it could be anywhere. His photography certainly took him all around town. Maybe he was taking photos at the wrong time and somebody saw him. It could be something as simple as that.'

They walked on in silence along Station Road and had nearly reached the entrance to the office car park when he turned to her. 'I know it feels like we're going nowhere, at least as far as John Smart's concerned, but we just have to keep plugging away. Something will come up. It always does.'

She gave him a wan smile, but said nothing. She clearly didn't buy into the glass half full theory.

'Look, once you've finished the paperwork, why don't you go home and get an early night? You'll feel much fresher in the morning.'

She was saying she might just do that when his phone rang. He dug it out of his pocket and saw it was Sharon Fuller.

'What have you got?' he asked, following Bird through the gates into the yard at the back.

'I spoke to Dave Simpson's parole officer,' Fuller said. 'He told me Simpson had some sort of a nervous breakdown in prison. When he came out, the address he gave for next of kin was his ex-wife's.'

'Was she the one who reported him missing?'

'Yes. She's no longer living at that address but Nick's trying to trace her.'

'OK. While he's doing that, I want a full background report on Dave Simpson.'

He was sitting at his desk half an hour later, scanning his backlog of emails, when his desk phone buzzed. It was Hannah Bird's extension.

'I've got Rosie Smart on the phone, Sir,' she said, as he picked up. 'She wants to talk to you. She wouldn't say what it was about.'

He sighed. 'OK. You'd better put her through.'

A few seconds later he heard Rosie's voice. 'I'm at the Sun Inn and I've just thought of something Dad said. You told me to call, even if it's something small . . .'

She sounded as though she'd had a few glasses of wine in the interim. 'What is it you remember?'

She gave a long, heavy sigh. 'It was what you were saying about Dad's daily routine and his hobbies.'

'His photography,' he prompted.

'That's right. And his gardening. He used to help out at a house near here. It belonged to an old lady and he grew veg and stuff for her. He was really into it. I often used to meet him in here after he'd been working there. It's only a few blocks away.'

'Yes. We know where it is.'

'That evening, after the film, he was telling me all about what he'd been doing that day and he said he was worried about the woman who owned the house and that he might not be able to go there for much longer.'

'Worried? In what way?'

287

'I think he said she was ill, or something had happened to her.'

'But she was old.'

'Yes, but she was still quite together, mentally I mean. She couldn't do her garden any longer as she had really bad arthritis, but she used to bring him out coffee and homemade biscuits every time he went over. Then one day she wasn't there any more, or if she was, she didn't come and see him. The next day too, and the next.'

'She may have gone to hospital,' he said, thinking of the woman in the wheelchair that the neighbour had seen.

'Maybe. All I know is he was worried about her. He said she always used to let him know if she was going away somewhere, so he could keep an eye on things. When she didn't reappear, he didn't know what to do.' He could hear from her tone that she was disappointed. 'You asked me to tell you if there was anything, however small,' she added.

He thanked her and hung up. He pushed back in his chair, one foot up on his desk, staring at the computer screen for a moment. Maybe it was worth taking another look at the house. He called Minderedes but he wasn't answering. He left a message saying where he would be and, grabbing his jacket, headed back out of the office.

Five minutes later he was standing in Castelnau, outside the house. It looked much the same as before, although the piles of leaves had been cleared away, an old, red VW Polo was now parked in the drive. He went up to the front door and rang the bell. He waited a minute before ringing again, but there was still no answer. As he stepped back onto the gravel and looked up, he thought he saw a shadow pass across one of the first floor windows. It might have been a trick of the fading light but he had the feeling somebody was at home. He rang again, this time pressing the bell for a good thirty seconds, but nobody came to the door. He looked through the ground floor window into the large sitting room. The newspaper and the mug had gone, but there was nothing much else to see.

He went over to the car and felt the bonnet. It was still warm. The car was nine years old but looked in good condition, the paintwork clean and shiny. Stickers for the RHS and the National Trust were fixed to the back window, along with the slogan 'Save a Cow, Eat a Vegetarian'. He rang the office and got through to Dave Wightman. 'I want to run a check on a vehicle.' He gave the make and registration number and waited while Wightman called it through on another line. Inside, the car was equally clean and tidy. Apart from a few CDs in the driver's seat pocket, the only visible contents were a couple of empty plastic shopping bags, neatly folded into squares, and a box of tissues on the back seat.

Wightman came back on the line. 'The car's registered to a Mrs Jane Waterman.' He gave the Castelnau address, adding that the insurance was current. 'Anything else you need, Sir?'

'No. That's all for now.' He tucked his phone away in his pocket. It wasn't a crime not to answer the door and there were certainly no grounds for a search warrant, but something niggled. And instinct told him that whoever was in the house was watching him. He went over to the garage and tried the door but it was locked, as was the side gate leading to the garden. It was about two metres high, with a row of trellis above, running between the wall of the garage and the boundary. Without a ladder, it was impossible to see over the top.

Something made him look up at the house again. This time he saw someone at one of the windows, looking down at him, then the face disappeared behind a curtain. In the evening gloom, it was impossible to tell if it was a man or a woman. He was wondering whether to call on one of the neighbours to see if he could look into the back garden from their house, when his phone rang again. It was Minderedes.

'I've found Ellie Simpson. What do you want me to do?'

'Keep her there. I'll be over as quickly as I can.'

'I don't know where Dave is, or how he is, and I don't bloody care,' Ellie Simpson said with a toss of her curly brown hair.

Tartaglia studied her for a moment, wondering if she was so emphatic because she was hiding something or if it was just a defence mechanism. 'But he came here straight after he got out of jail, didn't he?' he asked.

'I took him back for Daisy's sake. He said things would be different. More fool me.'

She compressed her lips into a line of disapproval. Yet he sensed there was more than simple bitterness running below the surface. They were sitting at the small kitchen table in her flat in Clapham. Her daughter Daisy was with a friend in the next room, watching one of the Harry Potter films, the sounds of which reverberated loudly through the thin wall. He'd had a quick nose around the flat when she went out for a minute to speak to a neighbour who'd rung the bell, but he couldn't see any sign of a man's things anywhere.

'You reported him missing a couple of months later. What happened?'

'He went out to the supermarket to get some stuff for dinner but he never came home.'

'Had anything happened to make him go off?'

She shrugged. 'We'd had yet another row that morning before I went to work.'

'What was it about?'

She sighed. 'He'd got this idea in his head about opening a restaurant on his own, that one of his old clients was going to back him. But nothing seemed to be coming of it. I thought it was all pie in the sky and he needed to give it up and get a job.'

'You mean as a chef?'

'Yes. I wanted him to go to Richard English, to ask for a second chance.'

'Really?' He looked at her sceptically. She had a pleasant, open face, the most striking feature being her eyes, which were an unusual greyish green. She didn't look a fool, but sometimes emotion blinded people to the obvious. 'After everything that had happened, you really thought that would've worked?'

'I know it sounds daft, but someone told me they'd lost a chef at one of the hotels so there was a good job going begging. Chefs with Dave's talent don't grow on trees. Richard knew that what happened at Stoneleigh Park that night was as much his fault as Dave's. He'd had his pound of flesh and Dave had more than paid for what he'd done, so . . .'

'English doesn't strike me as a man with much of a conscience, and I understand your husband had problems.'

'Dave used to be an alcoholic, but he kicked the booze when he was inside. He was sober all the time he was living with us.' She stared at him almost defiantly for a moment, then shrugged. 'I thought it was worth a try, at any rate. *Anything* was worth a try from where I was standing, with the rent to pay and three of us to feed and Dave sitting on his arse all day while I went out to work.'

'But your husband didn't see it that way?'

'No. He got really angry. He said he'd rather walk under a bus than go grovelling back to Richard. He said Richard was to blame for everything that'd gone wrong in his life. He was still seething about it all when I came home that night.'

291

'Were you worried when he didn't reappear?'

She looked him straight in the eye and shook her head. 'Not to start with. I thought maybe he was trying to teach me a lesson, or maybe he'd gone out and got pissed, like old times. Once an alcoholic, always an alcoholic, and they say it just takes one drink to tip you over the edge again. I thought if he'd fallen off the wagon, he'd be feeling too ashamed of himself to come home. Even so, I was sure he'd toddle back eventually, tail between his legs. But then a couple of days went by and I did start to get worried. I thought something must've happened, that maybe he'd had an accident, so I called the police. They weren't much help, particularly when they found out he'd come out of prison only a few months back. They said he'd probably turn up again.'

She was still looking at him and he saw the emotion in her eyes. He decided she was telling the truth and that she did care what had happened to her husband. 'So you have no idea what happened to him?'

'No.'

'His parole officer told us he'd had some sort of a breakdown in jail,' he said.

'He should never have been put inside in the first place. He needed help, not punishment. And something really horrible happened to him while he was in there.'

'I know. I've seen the report.'

'It sent him over the edge for a while. When he came out, he was a different person.'

'How would you describe his character?' Motive was one thing, but it didn't sound as though Simpson was capable of the cold bloodedness and calculation required for the killings.

She sighed wearily. 'What can I say? He was a bit of a loner. Although he liked to go out drinking with the other kitchen staff after they finished their shift, he didn't have any really close mates. He was quite shy, quite inside himself, if you know what I mean. I never really knew what was going on with him, most of the time.'

'He must have been pretty organised and disciplined to run a big kitchen and earn a Michelin star. Yet he sounds as though he was all over the place, even before he went to jail?'

'When I first met Dave, he was full of energy and dreams. He wanted to be this great chef. He'd left school at sixteen and worked his way up from the bottom. He was so hungry for it. I've never seen anybody work so bloody hard . . .'

'So what went wrong?'

'Success, I suppose, and all the stuff that goes with it. If you've got one star, you then need to go for the second. What made it worse was that Richard had promised him shares in the business, but he kept delaying and delaying, stringing Dave along. It was almost sadistic. Dave couldn't cope with the pressure.'

'You said he was a different person when he came out of prison.'

She nodded. 'He was very bitter, very angry. It was eating him up. Maybe being sober made him think about things, about his life and what he'd done, how he'd screwed up his chances. Seeing it all in the cold light of day, there was no escape I guess. I couldn't blame him, but all the fun had gone out of him. When he was drinking he wasn't great to be with, but I didn't much like the new, sober, Dave either.' She folded her small, plump hands on the table in front of her and looked down at them. 'All I know is that something'd changed in him and then he disappeared.'

'You said you didn't care where he is or how he is, but you do think he's still alive?'

Biting her lip, she looked up at him and wiped away a tear with the back of her hand. 'A few months after he went missing, a friend of mine saw him at a petrol station. He blanked her, but she was sure it was Dave. I realised then that he'd just walked out on us. Couldn't even be bothered to let me know he was OK.'

'Does he have any family who might be putting him up?'

'His parents split up when he was young. His dad died a few years back and he didn't get on with his mum. He spent a couple of years in care and he said the people were really kind, but that's as much as I know. He never talked about anyone else. What is it you want with him?'

'What about mates?'

She shook her head, staring hard at him, then asked softly. 'What's Dave done, Inspector?'

'Maybe nothing.'

Tears began running down her cheeks. 'Please tell me. If he's been involved in something, I need to know. I'm still his wife. Daisy's his daughter.'

'We need to find your husband. To talk to him. Hopefully, that will be all. Do you have *any* idea where he is?'

She took a tissue from her sleeve, blew her nose loudly, then slowly nodded. 'There's one place I'd try. When my friend saw him at the petrol station, he was with this woman. From the way my friend described her, I'm pretty sure she's someone who used to work at the hotel. She used to hang around Dave like he was some sort of god. She caused no end of trouble.'

'You mean Chantal Blomet?' He failed to hide his surprise. Wondering why he hadn't picked up on it, he tried to remember precisely what Chantal had said. It had been a brief interview, and what with learning that Simpson had beaten up

Richard English and been sent to jail, his mind had been on other things.

'You think he's with her now?'

She looked up at him, curious. 'You know her, then? If he's spinning her stories about a new restaurant and all that stuff, she'll probably still be hanging around. She's like an effing limpet. He couldn't get rid of her even if he wanted to.'

He thought again of how Price had described Chantal, and her words rang true. 'Do you have any photos of your husband?'

'I've got a few put away somewhere for Daisy. Give me a moment and I'll take a look.'

She was gone a couple of minutes, finally returning with an A4 envelope. 'Here you go,' she said, sitting down and handing it to him.

He spread the small collection of photographs on the table. The majority were formal pictures from their wedding, and there were pictures of Simpson with his daughter as a baby. Simpson looked more or less the same as in his arrest photograph, an overweight, latter-day Billy Idol.

'Do you have anything more recent?' he asked, handing them back to her.

'There'll be something on my phone. I've got hundreds. I haven't had time to go through them all and delete the ones of Dave.'

She went out of the room again, returning a moment later with her mobile. She stood beside him, tabbing through, until finally she said: 'Here. This is him. It was at a friend's house-warming, just a few days before he disappeared.' She turned the screen towards him.

Ellie Simpson was in the middle of the image, wearing a silver spangled jumper, flanked by two much taller men.

Neither of the men looked like the Dave Simpson from the file.

'Which one is your husband?' he asked.

'The one on the left.'

'He had blond hair in the other photos. May I take a closer look?'

'He used to bleach his hair,' she said, handing him the phone. 'Getting beaten up in prison didn't help either. He looks completely different, doesn't he?'

He enlarged the image. The resolution wasn't great but it was as though he was looking at a different man. The post-jail Dave Simpson was several stone thinner and much more wiry. The softness had gone and his face looked haggard, as though he'd aged twenty years.

'I hated him with long hair like that,' she said. 'It suited him better when it was short.'

She said something else but he wasn't listening any more. He realised where he had seen Simpson before and sat back in the chair, still staring at the screen. He suddenly felt awake for the first time that day, as though somebody had poured a bucket of ice-cold water over him. Automatically he handed her back the phone, put his hands flat on the table and pushed himself to his feet.

'Can you email it to me at this address?' He handed her his business card. 'Can you do it right now?'

Outside in the street, as he ran towards where Minderedes was waiting in the BMW, he called Steele and explained.

Forty-two

Tartaglia tucked the torch away in his pocket and sprang upwards, grasping the large overhanging branch of the tree close to its base. He used the trunk for purchase and slowly hauled himself up into the wide crook, swinging his leg over so that he was sitting astride the branch. In the distance, he saw the bobbing lights of the torches belonging to Minderedes and two uniformed police officers coming towards him from the car park. They were in a stretch of grassland belonging to the London Wetlands nature reserve, which lay at the back of a large section of Castelnau to the east, bordered on the other side by the river. The centre had already closed for the day when they got there and it had taken a while to find somebody to open the gates for them.

The tree overlooked the back of Jane Waterman's house and gave him a good temporary vantage point. The house stood about a hundred feet away beyond a high wall, the roof and turrets silhouetted against the night sky. The garden was impressively large, with a lawn and flowerbeds and what looked like a gazebo in one corner. A quick recce had shown that the surrounding walls were too tall to climb, so they had sent for ladders and lights. In the dark, it was unlikely that anybody looking out of a window would see him; not that anybody appeared to be home. The curtains were open, with no lights on anywhere. He might be waiting there for a while, he thought, shifting his position to make himself more comfortable.

The Polo had gone from the drive when he walked past the front of the house twenty minutes earlier, and there were no lights on at the front. Having asked permission of the neighbours on either side, Wightman, Chang and another couple of uniformed policemen were lying in wait in their front gardens, well hidden from the street and from the house where Tartaglia had last seen Dave Simpson. Simpson was linked to Richard English, Jake Finnigan and, now, via Jane Waterman's house, to John Smart, but everything else was speculation. They intended to arrest Simpson and had a warrant to search the premises, but they also needed confirmation that Simpson and the man known as 'Spike' were one and the same. Hannah Bird wasn't answering her phone, so he had eventually had to track down Sharon Fuller at home, where she had just started cooking dinner for her family, and send her off to Peckham to see Mrs Tier with a printout of the photo that Ellie Simpson had emailed him.

He had been up in the tree for a good twenty minutes when he received a text from Wightman:

Red VW Polo just pulled up on drive

Is it Simpson? Tartaglia texted back.

No. Single young female occupant. Now going inside house.

Tartaglia told him to wait and do nothing. Simpson was the priority. He had borrowed a pair of binoculars from the Wetlands office and as he scanned the rear of the house, a light came on at the back and Chantal Blomet entered the kitchen. They had been trying to track her down via the hotel where she worked, without success. At least now they would be saved further trouble. He watched as she took off her coat and scarf, hung them over a chair, then started to unpack the contents of a couple of shopping bags. Moving quickly backwards and forwards between the fridge and the cupboard, she seemed very at home. When she was finished, she switched on the kettle and sat down at the table. She took a mobile phone out of her handbag, stared at the screen for a moment, then put the phone back in her bag, made her coffee and carried it out of the kitchen. A few seconds later a series of lights came on and he watched her go upstairs to what looked like a bathroom on the first floor. She pulled down the blind.

'Find out what's happened to the ladders,' he whispered to one of the uniformed officers standing below. 'Go back to the wildlife centre and call from there. I don't want any noise out here.'

About ten minutes later, he felt his phone vibrate again; another text:

Man on foot. Looks like Simpson. Going in through front door. What shall we do?

Wait. I'll come round to you

He watched the windows for a moment, but no more lights came on inside and there was no sign of Simpson. He had probably gone straight upstairs to see Chantal. Tartaglia slid over onto his front and dropped down to the thick, soggy turf below.

'Simpson's back,' he told Minderedes, who was standing below, stamping his feet up and down on the ground trying to keep warm. 'You stay here and cover the back. When the ladders arrive, climb over and come in from the rear. Text me if you see anybody come out.'

Tartaglia ran back through the meadow and out of the entrance onto Castlenau. The road was still busy with traffic from the tail end of the rush hour. It all looked perfectly normal. Hopefully, Simpson hadn't spotted anything amiss. He joined Wightman, Chang and the other two officers at the front.

'He's definitely inside?' he asked.

Wightman nodded. 'He was in the front room a minute ago.'

'OK. Let's go.'

They followed him into the garden of Jane Waterman's house. Lights were blazing in the room to the right of the front door and the TV was on, but there was nobody inside. He turned to Chang.

'Wait here in case he tries to come out the front. The rest of you come with me.'

It took a single blow from a sledgehammer to force open the front door. Wherever Simpson was, he must have heard the noise. Tartaglia paused in the hall and held up his hand, listening. He thought he heard the distant sound of running footsteps, although it was difficult to tell over the noise coming from the TV. 'Stay here,' he said to one of the officers, 'and you check in there,' he said to the other, pointing towards the kitchen. 'Dave, you'd better go and make sure Chantal doesn't escape. She's upstairs – on the first floor, I think.'

He went into the large, threadbare sitting room. It was empty. There was no other door to the room and the windows were closed. He returned to the hall and tried the door opposite.

'David Simpson,' he called out from the bottom of the stairs. 'This is the police. We have a warrant for your arrest. Come out now.' He waited for a moment. Still nothing. He called out again but there was no answer and no sound of movement anywhere in the house. He went into the kitchen.

'Nobody came this way,' the officer said. 'The outside doors are locked. I've checked them all.'

'Did you see anyone in the garden?'

'It's too dark.'

'There must be some lights for the garden somewhere.' He hunted around but couldn't find any switches for external lights. Hopefully the floodlights and ladders would be there soon. As he turned to go, he heard the sound of a whistle from the front: the alarm signal. He rushed outside.

'There's smoke coming from down there,' Chang shouted, pointing to a ventilation grill set into the brickwork of the house, just above ground level. There must be some sort of basement or cellar, Tartaglia realised, although he'd seen no sign of a door.

'Call for backup. We'll also need the fire brigade and an ambulance.'

He ran back inside. He could smell burning now. 'Fire!' he shouted, visions of the Peckham house and the explosions springing to mind. Was it a diversion, or was Simpson trying to destroy evidence? 'Fire!' he shouted again. 'Everyone out of the building.' He heard a woman scream, followed by the thud of footsteps above, then Wightman shouted. Chantal Blomet flew down the stairs towards him, Wightman just behind. She was wearing a dressing gown and little else.

Tartaglia was blocking the bottom of the stairs and grabbed hold of her as she tried to push past him. 'Where's Dave Simpson?'

'I don't know.'

'Is there anyone else in the house, apart from you and Dave?'

'Let go. You're hurting.'

'I said, is there anyone—'

'There's no one.'

'What about upstairs?'

'No,' she shouted.

'Are you sure? Where's Jane Waterman?'

'Nobody's here. Just me.'

'Where's the door to the cellar?' he shouted.

'I don't know. Let go of me.'

He increased the pressure on her wrist until she screamed. 'Where is it?'

'It's in the garage.'

'How do I get to the garage?'

'Over there.' She jerked her head towards the corridor.

He pushed her forwards. 'Show me.'

Tartaglia and Wightman followed Chantal through the kitchen into a small utility room that ran along the side of the house.

'It's behind there.' She indicated a curtain at the back of the room.

'This leads to the garage? And the door to the cellar is through there?'

'Yes,' she screamed.

'Is there any other way to get in there?'

Crying, she shook her head, but he wasn't sure if he believed her.

'Once she's dressed, take her outside and caution her,' he said to Wightman. 'A car's on its way.'

He tried the handle, but it appeared to be locked from the inside. The smell of burning was stronger than ever and smoke was curling through the gap at the bottom of the door. He turned to one of the officers standing behind him. 'Get the sledgehammer. Let's try and get in around the front, through the garage.'

Outside, he heard the distant sound of sirens from the direction of Hammersmith Bridge. The garage doors opened outwards, but the wood was dry and rotten in places and it took only a single blow to break the lock. With two more attempts, they managed to smash the doors completely off their hinges. Smoke billowed out and Tartaglia stepped back. As he wondered whether Dave Simpson had some sort of escape route, he heard shouting, followed by whistles from the back. 'Get the side gate open,' he shouted to the officer with the battering ram. Within thirty seconds they were through into the garden. As he looked around, a floodlight came on from the top of the back wall and for a moment he could see nothing in the glare.

He heard Minderedes shout, 'Over there, Sir. Behind that bush.'

As Tartaglia turned, the ground beneath him shuddered, the air exploded with a deafening bang and he fell hard onto the grass. For a moment, he lay there unable to move. At least he was still alive, he told himself, feeling and testing each limb in turn to make sure everything still worked. He felt bruised but there was no real pain. Gradually, head spinning, a strange ringing in his ears, he pushed himself up into a sitting position. The sirens were getting louder and he heard the screech of tyres outside in the road. He gazed up at the house. Flames were rising up through the windows on the ground floor and smoke was billowing out into the night air. He looked around the garden and saw Dave Simpson stretched out motionless on the grass amidst broken glass and debris, only a few metres away. Was he unconscious or just faking? Tartaglia staggered to his feet, heard somebody call out behind him and, as he turned towards the dazzling light, saw Minderedes and a uniformed officer running towards him from the back of the garden.

Forty-three

Sam Donovan got out of the bath and dried herself quickly. A bath was normally something she found relaxing, particularly at the end of a long day. She would often take a cup of tea or a glass of wine in with her and spend a good half-hour or so soaking in the water, reading a book or a magazine, or just letting her mind go blank. But tonight she couldn't switch off. She put on her dressing gown and went into her bedroom. It was dark outside and she had drawn the curtains. Before turning on the light, she pulled back the edge of the curtain a fraction and glanced out at the street below. A car had just turned into the road and she watched it pull up almost outside. With relief she recognised her neighbour's car and a couple of minutes later saw her climb out, carrying a load of heavy-looking shopping bags. She tottered along the pavement to her front door, fumbled with her keys for a good minute, then disappeared inside. Donovan continued to gaze out for a few minutes. The street was quiet, most people happily at home, watching TV or on their way to bed. It struck her again how lonely she felt.

She put on a pair of tracksuit bottoms, trainers and a pullover and went downstairs to the kitchen. She didn't feel like eating anything. She longed for a drink, a brandy maybe, or a whisky, but she needed her wits about her. She checked the room again, making sure that the back doors and windows were securely locked and that everything was ready. Then she went into the sitting room and turned on the television. She flipped through the channels until she found a film that had just started, a rom-com she'd never heard of, with Cameron Diaz. It wasn't her cup of tea, but it didn't matter. It would keep her mind off things for a couple of hours and make the time pass more quickly.

Hannah Bird sagged heavily against Adam's shoulder, mumbling something unintelligible as he tried to manoeuvre her, half lifting, half pushing her through the narrow entrance of the wine bar into the street. He had to get her out of there quickly before somebody twigged.

'Sure you don't want me to ring for an ambulance?' the manager called out after him.

'It's fine. She's had a rough day, and she's had too much to drink, that's all. I'll see her home and she can sleep it off.'

'If you're sure . . .'

'I'm sure. Thanks. It's not the first time.' He raised his eyebrows meaningfully and the manager gave him a sympathetic nod, then turned back towards the busy bar.

He had been in two minds about what to do with her. Part of him couldn't be arsed to deal with her as he knew he ought to. He felt strangely weary and there would be no real pleasure in it this time – his thoughts and dreams were elsewhere. He could have easily let her go home to her lonely bed and stew. There was no risk in it from his point of view. But she had been in a funny mood, far less amenable than before, and downing a couple of drinks in quick succession, had started to ask some pointed questions about his background, where he lived and what he had been doing abroad. She had caught him out in a couple of inconsistencies with the little he had told her before. They were nothing material and he soon recovered himself, but he saw an irritating, questioning look in her eyes that hadn't been there before. Maybe she had been lied to in the past and was particularly sensitive. He didn't really care about her history and how she felt, but she had clammed up and he had failed to get any new, useful information from her. He had eventually decided that she was a loose end that shouldn't be left lying around.

Mixed with the cosmopolitans she'd been drinking, the GHB had taken effect far more quickly than he'd anticipated. One minute she was droning on about a stupid film she wanted to see, the next she could barely sit up straight, let alone string a sentence together. She looked baffled by what was happening to her. So much for her detective abilities. Kit's car was parked only a short block away, down a quiet side street next to a row of lock-up garages, but each step was taking an age and he hoped they would make it to the car before she passed out. He looped his arm tighter around her waist, lifting her up and propelling her forwards along the pavement. He would carry her if he had to, but he didn't relish the thought.

As they turned the corner, the cold air seemed to intensify the effect of the drug and alcohol mixture in her system. She was moaning now, eyes half closed, head lolling forwards like a broken doll. They almost reached the car, but as he felt in his pocket for the blipper, her legs gave way and she collapsed forwards onto the pavement. He *had* to get her into the car before anybody saw. He popped the locks and opened the rear passenger door as wide as it would go. Locking his arms around her under her armpits, he dragged her the last few feet, her heels bumping and scraping along the tarmac. He was sweating heavily, cursing her as he struggled to heave her inert body onto the back seat of the car. Her feet were sticking out and he noticed she had lost a shoe somewhere along the way, but there was no time to retrace their steps to look for it.

He went around to the other side, opened the door and pulled her across the seat onto her back, until her head was level with the door. Then he slammed it shut and went back to the driver's side. He checked his watch. The plan had been to drive her to a quiet spot and deal with her there, where he could enjoy her final moments in full, but she would soon lose consciousness and he was running out of time: he had other more important things to do that night. But he had to go back to Kit's house first. He quickly scanned the road, but there was nobody in sight. It was as good a place as any. Bending her knees, he pushed her legs apart, climbed into the car on top of her and closed the door behind him. If anyone ventured down the street in the next few minutes, they would think they were just a couple having sex.

'Where is Jane Waterman?' Minderedes shouted at Chantal Blomet. 'Is she dead?'

Her cheeks were wet with tears and she mumbled: 'I don't know. I never met her.'

'Speak up, please,' Wightman said. 'For the recording.'

'I never met her. I swear.' She sat hunched in her chair, eyes huge, like a rabbit caught in headlights. She had changed out of her work clothes and was dressed in jeans and a T-shirt, with what looked like a man's navy blue cardigan. He noticed a small gold crucifix on a chain around her neck, which must have been hidden underneath her uniform earlier.

They were in an interview room at Hammersmith police station, on the north side of the bridge from Castelnau. Tartaglia and Steele were in an adjacent room, watching the interview through a one-way glass wall. The process had been delayed by the late arrival of Chantal's brief, Keith Whitely, a balding, middle-aged man in a crumpled work shirt and suit trousers, who looked as though he'd been woken up in the middle of the night, even though it was only just past ten o'clock.

Wightman shook his head. 'But you were staying at her house.'

'I never saw her, I tell you. Dave said she was in a nursing home, that she had dementia.'

Minderedes leaned forwards towards her, his palms flat on the table. 'That's a load of rubbish and you know it. If she was still alive, why would she give Dave Simpson free run of her house? He wasn't family.'

Chantal pulled her cardigan tightly around herself and wiped her eyes with the back of her hand. 'He was like family to her. She met him when she was staying at the hotel. She used to go there a lot. She was one of the backers for the restaurant Dave was going to open and he looked after the house for her when she went away. That's what he told me.'

She practically shouted the last sentence and, as she did so, there was something about her expression and body language that rang true. Was it possible she was actually telling the truth, Tartaglia wondered?

Simpson was in hospital, alive but unconscious. As well as some minor cuts and bruises from flying glass and masonry, when the explosion had thrown him to the ground he had hit his head hard on some paving and was being treated for head trauma. It was potentially serious and he was being closely monitored. The consultant could give no estimate of when he was likely to come around or what state he would be in. In the meantime, Chantal Blomet was their only source of information as to what had happened to Jane Waterman, and to what lay behind the so-called Jigsaw killings. Over and over again, she insisted that she knew nothing about Richard English's death, let alone about the other murders or what had happened to Jane Waterman. She said she had never heard of Jake Finnigan or John Smart, nor did she have any idea who the other two unidentified bodies were, belonging to an elderly woman and a young man. In the meantime, they were trying to trace Jane Waterman's immediate family to see if they could get a familial DNA match with the female body. The supposed nephew had been identified by the next-door neighbour in Castelnau as being Dave Simpson. Whether it had been Jane Waterman in the wheelchair, or a dummy, was something only Simpson could answer.

'What do you think?' Steele asked, turning to Tartaglia as a uniformed PC brought a tray of coffee into the interview room on the other side of the glass. 'Is she another Myra Hindley, or is she a Rose West?'

'Neither, probably,' he said, his eyes still on Chantal. Depravity and wickedness came in all shapes and sizes, but he didn't see Chantal belonging in either category. 'Whether Simpson manipulated her, or she was a willing partner, she'd have known about Jane Waterman too. I have to say I believed her when she said she didn't.'

'I agree, she did seem convincing. So you think he kept it all from her?'

'I don't know. She's definitely holding something back. Why else would she lie to me earlier about not knowing if Simpson was alive or dead? She said she hadn't seen him since he was in Dartmoor. Unless she knew he'd done something seriously wrong, why not just tell me where he was?'

Steele nodded slowly in agreement.

'As far as we know,' he continued, 'Richard English's murder kicked this whole thing off. Mrs Tier identified Chantal as the woman she saw with "Spike" when he was living in the Peckham

309

squat, so she's been with him right from when he left his wife. She must know something. Just how much, is the question.'

'Well, we can charge her with being an accessory, but if she keeps up her version of things, without Simpson to testify otherwise, we'll have difficulty making it stick. Basically, we have nothing to link her to what happened, other than the fact that she stayed at the house with him on a fairly regular basis. If her useless brief gets his act together, she'll be out of here in no time.'

He folded his arms, still staring at Chantal's tearstained face through the glass. Colin Price and Ellie Simpson had described her as some sort of groupie or hanger-on, which he decided was a bit unfair. Although she had an innocent, self-contained quality, she certainly wasn't a desperate, flaky teenager. She may have been star-struck when Simpson was an up-and-coming young chef with the world at his feet, but he doubted she would have stuck with him once she knew the horrors of what he had done.

'We'll just have to keep the pressure on, then,' he said, with the feeling that it was going to be a long night. 'My guess is that if she hears the full details of what he's done, it's likely she'll give up what she knows. I think we should tell her about the victims, show her some photos. Make it graphic and real. Any normal person would be horrified to find they've been sleeping with somebody who could do that sort of thing.'

'And what if you're wrong and she was a willing part of it all?'

'Then we'll just have to play her off against Simpson.'

'Simpson's still out cold.'

'She doesn't know that.'

Forty-four

'He says you knew all about it,' Minderedes said. 'That makes you an accessory to murder. You're going inside for years, Chantal, unless you tell us what you know.'

Chantal Blomet stared at him bleary eyed, her hair sticking to her wet cheeks. 'I don't believe you. You're lying.' Her voice cracked, but the look of shock on her face seemed genuine. 'Why would he say that, when it's not true?'

They were nearly there, Tartaglia thought, her resistance gradually ebbing. They had shown her photographs, first of Finnigan and then Smart, taken when they were still alive, and explained their connection with Dave Simpson. Given that she'd known Richard English and clearly hated him, they hadn't bothered to show her any of him. They talked about Smart's background and family in particular, and how he had disappeared without a trace just before his birthday. They had then given her the details of the Sainsbury's car park fire in south London and the Guy Fawkes fire in Aldford, mentioning the other two unknown victims – one assumed to be Jane Waterman – and shown her photographs from the post-mortems. Again, they left the fire in Peckham to one side for the moment. Tartaglia didn't want Blomet's feelings about English to cloud the situation. At first she refused to listen, saying they were making it all up, that it was just fiction. But gradually the full horror of what they described sank in.

They had deliberately not allowed her a break, except once to visit the ladies'. She returned having washed her face, but rather than looking refreshed she appeared even more deflated, as though she had perhaps caught sight of herself in the mirror and reflected on what the future might hold; that the reality of her predicament had finally dawned on her. It was often the way with people who were not used to being questioned, particularly when the possible charges were so serious. Would she have stuck with a man like Simpson if she had known about the murders? From the little he'd seen of her, it didn't stack up. Also, if she had been involved, why would Simpson have taken the risk of using Tatyana to get to Finnigan? It seemed that, after all, Chantal really had no inkling as to what he was doing. Yet instinct told him she was still holding something back.

Minderedes leaned forwards across the table. 'Why did you lie to Detective Inspector Tartaglia and tell him you thought Dave Simpson was dead, unless you knew what he'd done and you were trying to protect him?'

'I don't know. I don't remember.'

'But it was just this morning,' Wightman said. 'How can you forget? You told him you hadn't seen Dave Simpson since he went to jail. You also said that you didn't have a relationship with him. Yet we find you living with him under the same roof, sharing his bed. Basically, everything you've told us is a lie and there's only one way to interpret that. It's not looking good for you.'

She bowed her head and was silent for some moments. Then, 'I shouldn't have lied. I'm sorry,' she said. 'I just didn't want Dave getting into any trouble.'

'What trouble would that be? You said he hasn't done anything wrong.'

'Dave Simpson's as guilty as hell and you knew all about what he did,' Minderedes said. 'You helped him.'

She shook her head wearily. 'No . . .'

'What did you say?'

She sighed. 'It's not true. Whatever he's done, I knew nothing about it.'

'You ditched him when he went to jail, then picked up with him again when he came out. You were the one in control.'

'I *didn't* ditch him, I *wanted* to see him. I wanted to help him, but he said he didn't want to see me. He told me not to come. *He* didn't want *me*.'

Wightman shook his head in disbelief. 'If you want to save yourself, you're going the wrong way about it. Do you think a jury will buy your story? Do you think they'll believe that you knew nothing about what Dave Simpson was doing?'

Minderedes leaned forwards to catch her eye. 'Well? You're a clever girl, Chantal. He was your lover and you stole him away from his wife and child. Think about it. Man like that, he'd tell you everything, wouldn't he? He'd have no secrets from you. Maybe you were the one pulling his strings.'

She made no reply, just stared down at her hands as though her thoughts were far away.

Wightman then described what they thought had happened to Richard English, how he was drugged and left senseless in the basement while Simpson set the house on fire, knowing that the still in the back room would explode. He read out the paragraph from the post-mortem that detailed the evidence of smoke inhalation. 'He burned alive, Chantal. Think of that. You knew Richard English and you hated him. Did you lure him to the house in Peckham so Simpson could kill him?'

'Even if you didn't light the match, you're as guilty as he is,' Minderedes said.

She had begun to shake at the mention of English and the fire, and hid her face in her hands, mumbling something that Tartaglia couldn't hear. Her reaction spoke volumes. This was what she had been hiding all along. She knew something about what had happened to Richard English. Just how much, was the question.

'Speak up,' Minderedes said. 'You helped Simpson kill Richard English, didn't you?'

'What are you saying?' Wightman asked.

She looked up. 'It wasn't like that . . .' She turned imploringly towards her lawyer, Keith Whitely.

'Well, what *was* it like? Tell us.'

Whitely intervened. 'Hang on a minute,' he said. 'Before we go any further, I need to speak to my client. In private.'

As he spoke, Tartaglia's phone started ringing. It was Chang. He answered, to be told that Chang was calling from the hospital. Simpson had regained consciousness.

Shouldering his small rucksack, Adam walked down the street towards Sam Donovan's house. He had been back to Bedford Gardens first, showered quickly and changed, then packed up his few belongings and locked them in the boot of Kit's car, along with Hannah Bird's body. He had parked only a block away from where Sam lived. When it was over, his plan was to drive to Dover and get on a catamaran to Ostend first thing the next day. He had looked at the times and been through it all very carefully. The sea journey took only forty-five minutes, but he reckoned there was little rush. It was unlikely that Sam would be found until the next day at the very earliest, and Hannah even later, by which time he would be safely on a long-haul flight out of Europe to somewhere hot. He missed the warmth of the sun, the scented breeze from the sea at night. He had enough cash to last him a good while, particularly in some cheap backpacker destination. There would be another Kit somewhere along the way, female or male, it didn't matter.

Maybe he would never return to the UK again. But first, he had some unfinished business to attend to.

He stopped by a hedge opposite Sam's house and looked across the road. There were no lights on and the curtains were pulled tightly across the windows on both the ground and first floors. She had been there most of the day, only going out for a while mid-morning, and he wondered what she'd been doing all that time on her own. Probably sorting through her sister's things. He looked forward to telling her how pointless it all was. He was about to cross the road when he heard the thud of muffled footsteps coming up fast behind him. A jogger, wearing a dark tracksuit with a hood pulled low over his face, emerged from the shadows and ran, head bowed, in Adam's direction. Adam ducked into the garden behind, pressing himself against the hedge, listening to the rhythmic pace of the man's feet as they passed by in front of him. Cautiously, he stepped out of the shadows, watching until the jogger disappeared around the bend at the end of the road. He waited a moment, then felt for the keys in his pocket and crossed over to the Donovan house.

He tried all three of Claire's keys but none of them worked. Sam Donovan had fucking well changed the locks. He threw the useless keys on the ground and kicked them under a bush. As he wondered what to do next, he noticed that one of the windows in the bay to the right of the front door was open a fraction. Maybe he wouldn't have to break the glass after all. He tried pushing it up from the glass, then levering it up with his fingertips, but it wouldn't budge. It was either too stiff or she had locked it from the inside. He took a heavy-duty screwdriver out of his bag and, after several attempts, managed to prise it open a couple of centimetres. The stupid bitch had forgotten to lock it. She wasn't so clever after all. Careful not to make any sound, he pushed it up bit-by-bit with his fingers and climbed in. The window was screened from the road by a tall hedge and he decided to leave it open, in case he needed a quick escape route later. He drew back the curtains and glanced around the small sitting room, which was illuminated by the orange glare from the street. He had never been there before but it was just as dull as he had pictured it.

He switched on a small torch and went out into the hall. Her bedroom was at the front, directly above the sitting room, he remembered her once telling him. He paused at the bottom of the stairs, attempting to calm his beating heart. As he tried to visualise her lying upstairs in her bed, asleep, other faces started bubbling up in his mind, voices from the past whispering like sirens in his ear. *Adam . . . Adam . . .* He shook his head and blinked over and over again, until all he could see was Sam Donovan's pale face. Had she changed? Or was she the same stupid woman he remembered sitting beside him on his grandmother's best sofa, drinking iced vodka and wanting him to kiss her. He was so close he could smell her perfume, feel the warmth of her body and her breath on his check as he leaned towards her. She had wanted him so much . . .

This time there was no thug of a detective to save her. This time it was just the two of them. Butterflies fluttered in his stomach like dying things, and he smiled as he put his foot on the first stair.

He took his time, fearful of making any noise that might wake her. Halfway up the flight of stairs he felt one of the old boards give beneath his foot and there was a horrible creak. He froze, not daring to move for well over a minute, but there was no sound from above. She was fast asleep, no doubt dreaming of Prince Charming. The door at the top of the stairs was open and he stopped on the threshold, dipped the torch beam low and gazed inside. The bed stood in the middle of the room, headboard up against the chimneybreast. He could just make out her shape in the centre, huddled beneath the duvet. He closed his eyes for a moment. He was so close he could almost hear her breathing. He had waited for this for so long, rehearsing it over and over in his mind. Finally he was there. This time, he wanted her fully awake. He wanted to look into her eyes as he told her what he had done to Claire and what he was going to do to her. He wanted her to know everything.

He tiptoed over to the bed and slowly and carefully climbed onto it. Ready to grab her if she moved, he bent down and whispered:

'Sam. Wake up. It's Adam.'

Forty-five

Tartaglia and Steele stood together at the back of Dave Simpson's hospital room, watching while Chang and Fuller asked the questions. Simpson lay stretched out flat under the cover, arms limp at his sides, his skin still grimy with smoke and dirt. There had been talk of handcuffing him, but it was decided that in his current state he would be unlikely to run away and a couple of uniformed constables outside the door were considered to be sufficient security for the moment. Simpson was linked up to some sort of monitor and his head was heavily bandaged. He was suffering from concussion, as well as smoke inhalation, but a CT scan had revealed nothing too alarming. Physically, he was well enough to be interviewed, according to the attendant physician. He had been cautioned and a solicitor summoned but Simpson was saying nothing, either to his brief or the police. He stared into space as though they weren't there, the only response to their questions an occasional blink of his eyes.

Looking at him, Tartaglia felt numb. He recognised Simpson as the man he'd seen at the house in Castelnau, but he appeared different, somehow shrunken and less significant, as though his injuries rendered him more human than the cold-blooded murderer they had been searching for. The so-called Jigsaw Killer. The stuff of nightmares. There was no evidence on his surprisingly sensitive-looking hands of the cross-like scar Tatyana had described. Like so much else she had told them, it had been a lie. Was it his intention to plead insanity? Was he

318

actually insane? Tartaglia doubted it. To have carried out the murders as he had done, he had to have been in full control of his faculties. Simpson had also seemed perfectly normal when Tartaglia had first come across him in the front garden of Jane Waterman's house. He had certainly been able to function normally, and maintain some sort of a relationship with Chantal Blomet, although according to her she had only seen him a couple of times a week, on and off, and they hadn't been living together. She said that she always felt Simpson wanted to keep her at a distance.

She had eventually broken down and agreed to tell them what she knew about the murder of Richard English. She said that Simpson had come to her flat that night, saying he had nowhere to stay. He had been in a strange, wired state, unable to keep still, like a wild animal pacing up and down in a cage. Eventually, he told her what had happened. He blamed English for ruining his life. He had needed to confront English, tell him what he'd done to him, before he could find peace and move on. Simpson told her he had used some sort of anaesthetic or tranquilliser to subdue English and had transported him in the back of a van he had borrowed to the house in Peckham. A couple of people had seen him half-carry, half-walk a groggy middle-aged man down the stairs to the basement, but had probably assumed that English was just another drunk. In that neighbourhood, nobody paid much attention to such comings and goings. Simpson said how easy it had all been, until English started to come out of it and tried to attack him, knocking over the stove by accident. The flames had taken hold so quickly, it was all Dave could do to escape. Minderedes and Wightman had probed and pressed Chantal mercilessly, but she insisted that that was what Simpson had told her and she had believed him. She said it had been a horrible accident. Nothing the detectives said could change her mind. Perhaps it was the only version she found bearable.

Chantal had also continued to insist that she knew nothing about what had happened to Jake Finnigan or John Smart, and in the end Tartaglia believed her. She said that Simpson used to visit Jane Waterman quite often and that eventually she had given him a key to her house and he became her lodger. Like Simpson, she had no close family; she was lonely and liked having people around. They would talk about all sorts of things, including the restaurant he was going to set up with her help, once the sale of an overseas property finally came through. He used to cook for her and do various chores around the house. In return, she would give him money. He would also take her out in her car occasionally to do some shopping, or to the library up the road. Tartaglia imagined how frustrated somebody as talented as Simpson must have felt, reduced to such a menial role, his bitterness directed at Richard English and then Jake Finnigan. In his eyes, they were the architects of his downfall. As for Jane Waterman, Simpson had told Chantal that Jane had complained of feeling unwell and that he'd gone up to her room one morning with her breakfast and found her lying in her bed, dead. Simpson said that she looked very peaceful, as though she were just asleep. With her had died his immediate hopes of resurrecting his career.

Although Tartaglia remained convinced Simpson had started the fire deliberately, he had initially wondered if Simpson had been at least partially truthful when he told Chantal that all he wanted was just to confront English. But why then go to the trouble of taking him all the way to Peckham to kill him? A quick knife in the back, or blow to the head in a dark alley, would have done just as well. Maybe, as Simpson had described it, things had got out of hand in the basement bedroom. Maybe English had found Simpson's weak spot yet again – there were so many – and goaded him and, after everything that had happened, in the heat of the moment Simpson had killed him – or at least left him for dead.

But when Tartaglia thought about Finnigan's murder, calculated and cold-blooded in every detail, only one thing made sense. From the start, Simpson had intended to kill English. The reason for taking English all the way to Peckham was to string it out, to make him pay for what he'd done. Perhaps Simpson was also a man who liked to make things complicated. Perhaps that was what gave him satisfaction. Simpson had kept a great deal from Chantal, it seemed. Tartaglia remembered how Ellie Simpson had described her husband as a loner who kept things bottled up inside. It was easier for somebody like him to compartmentalise things and act completely alone.

Simpson was still saying nothing and had closed his eyes, either asleep now or pretending to be so. They were all tired, they were getting nowhere and, listening to the occasional interjection from Simpson's brief, Tartaglia could see the insanity plea looming large on the horizon.

Steele got to her feet. 'Let's take a comfort break, everybody. I need to make some calls, and we could all use some refreshments.' She looked meaningfully in Simpson's direction. 'We could be here all night, and tomorrow if need be. Hopefully, Mr Simpson will be fit enough by then to accompany us to the nearest station. Lying in bed doesn't really help focus the mind.'

There was no sign that Simpson had registered any of it. Wightman switched off the recorder and Tartaglia watched them all file out of the room into the corridor. He hung back.

'You coming?' Steele asked, from the doorway.

'I'll catch you up in a minute.'

Once she had gone, he turned to the bed, bent down and whispered in Simpson's ear:

'This is Detective Inspector Mark Tartaglia, Dave. You're not being recorded and there's nobody in the room except you and me. You don't need to open your eyes. Just listen.' Simpson's eyes remained closed, his breathing steady. There was nothing to suggest that Simpson had heard him but he didn't wait for a response. 'I can understand why you killed Richard English. I imagine you thought about it all the time you were in jail. It must have been eating away at you. I know you meant to kill him right from the get-go and what you told Chantal was a pack of lies, but it doesn't matter. There are those who'd say English got what he deserved. Same goes for Jake Finnigan. They both ruined your life. I guess John Smart was just collateral damage. He poked his nose in where it wasn't wanted and threatened the new life you'd made for yourself in Barnes. We don't yet know who the fourth victim is, but I have my suspicions. I think he's the Polish gardener, Marek Nowak, and you killed him – same as with John Smart – to silence him, to stop anybody finding out what you'd done. All of this I understand, even if I can't sympathise with you.' He paused, studying Simpson's thin, boyish face for a reaction. But there was none. In a way, he didn't care. 'What I don't get is why you killed Jane Waterman. You didn't have to. She offered you a home. She was kind and you meant something to her. She wanted to help put you back on your feet and rebuild your life.'

He paused again, but there was still no indication that Simpson was listening. 'We're waiting for DNA confirmation,' he continued, 'but when it comes through, you'll be charged with her murder too. Is that really what you want? Doesn't the truth mean anything to you?'

There was still no sign of life from Simpson. Tartaglia straightened himself, flexed his tired shoulders and made as if to go.

As he turned, Simpson opened his eyes and grabbed hold of Tartaglia's wrist.

'I didn't kill Jane.' His voice was hoarse and strangely high-pitched. 'I killed the others, but not Jane.'

Donovan watched Adam from behind the door, saw him creep into the room and slowly climb onto the bed, straddling the inert human shape she had created in the middle. He bent down over the mound and she heard him whisper her name. Hate filled her and she rushed forwards, a low growl erupting from her throat. He turned and, as she swung the baseball bat, he tried to duck. The blow glanced off the side of his head. He stared at her for a moment then made as if to get off the bed, lurching forwards like somebody drunk. He stretched out a hand to the wall and tried to steady himself, putting his other hand to his head and touching the place where she had hit him. He stared for a moment at the blood left on his fingers, as though he couldn't believe what he was seeing. Was it enough? Had she struck him hard enough? She held the bat ready to do it again.

'Sam?' He sagged forwards, then fell onto the floor in a heap. She switched on the overhead light. He lay there motionless, eyes closed. It looked as though he had passed out, but she didn't trust him. A small, black rucksack sat on the floor beside him. Careful not to get too close, the bat in her hand in case he should try anything, she grabbed the rucksack by one of its straps and pulled it towards her. Quickly unzipping it, she tipped the contents out onto the bed. Along with a bottle of small white tablets, handcuffs and a gag, there was a pistol, which she recognised as a Glock. She put down the bat and

323

picked up the gun. It had no safety catch, she remembered from her firearms training. Not knowing if the trigger pull had been lightened, she would have to be extra careful not to touch it until she was ready. With the gun in one hand, she clipped the handcuffs around his wrists. He didn't stir.

'Get up,' she shouted, kicking him as hard as she could between the shoulders. No reaction. She kicked him again, this time in the small of his back where his kidneys were, and he moved slightly and groaned. 'Get the fuck up.' Still he didn't stir. Had she overdone it or was he faking? She was sweating, shaking from head to foot. Careful not to get too close, she bent down and pressed the muzzle of the Glock hard against his temple. 'Can you hear me, Adam? This is *your* gun pointing at your head. Can you feel it?' She shoved it harder into his skin and slowly he opened his eyes. 'I found it in your ruck-sack, along with all the other disgusting stuff you like to use. If you don't get up, I will kill you.' Even though his hands were secured behind him, she still didn't trust him not to try some-thing. She watched every movement as he struggled to roll over onto his back.

'Take off the cuffs,' he said softly. 'They're hurting. I can't move like this. I won't do anything, I promise.'

She stared at him. He looked different from how she remem-bered him. His face was tanned, his hair streaked by the sun. She wondered where he had been living all this time, how he had managed to hide himself away. The last time she had seen him was in Ealing, a year earlier. He had taken her out for dinner and they had gone back to his home afterwards for a drink. He had then tried to kill her. It was strange to think she had once found him so attractive, but there was no shame in that. He was skilful and infinitely manipulative. He knew exactly how to prey on weakness and to seduce, and it wasn't her fault or Claire's that they had both succumbed to him. She hated him now more than she had ever thought it possible to hate anyone.

'Unless you get up *right now*, I will kill you,' she said. 'I mean it. I don't care any longer what happens to me.'

Gradually, with difficulty, using his elbows and legs, he pushed himself up into a sitting position and leaned back against the wall. He seemed disorientated, but he was probably faking. She didn't care either way. Suddenly he gasped, bent over and vomited.

'Go on. Get up.' She kicked him again.

Coughing, he slowly tried to get to his feet but, as he did so, he lost his balance and sank down onto the edge of the bed. 'Christ, I feel sick. You really whacked me hard, you know.' He sat there, shoulders hunched, looking strangely pale and pathetic. Then, after a moment, he frowned and said, 'You were waiting for me.'

'Yes.'

'How did you know?'

'You wanted me to know. You couldn't help bragging, could you? Which is why you left those clues.'

'Clever little Sam.'

'They were things only I would pick up on, so it was clear you were speaking to me. What you wrote on her legs . . . *Eris quod sum*. What I am, you will be. It was meant for me. It was a warning of what was to come.'

Coughing again, he nodded. 'You're right. I was thinking of you all the time and I did sort of want you to know. I wanted you to think of me too, to know that I was coming for you. What other clue in particular did you pick up on?'

'The food on the room service trolley. It was exactly what I had for dinner when you took me out that night.'

'It was a good dinner,' he said, with a faint smile. 'I'm glad you remember. The Krug was fucking expensive, but it was worth it. *You* were worth it. We could do it again sometime.'

She shook her head, amazed. It was as if what he had done meant nothing, as though the horror of it was locked away in some parallel universe and their relationship was perfectly normal, like one-time lovers who had met up again by chance.

Slowly he eased himself off the bed and got to his feet.

She raised her arm and pointed the gun. 'Stay right there or I'll shoot.'

'Come on. You wouldn't shoot me, would you Sam?' He took an unsteady step towards her. 'Why would you want to do that?'

'Don't move. I *will* shoot you.'

'But then you'd be no better than me, would you?'

'I don't care what I am any longer. And there's no point sending you to jail.'

'But you do care, Sam. There's a part of you that still remembers that dinner, sitting on the sofa together . . .'

'Shut up. If you come any closer, I will kill you.'

He shook his head. 'I don't think you've got the guts.'

She felt the trigger with her finger. She was so close to pressing it. Maybe he was trying to provoke her. Perhaps he wanted her to kill him. Did it matter? What mattered was what he had done to Claire and the others. The sad young girls and women he had groomed and seduced and lured to their deaths. She could still remember some of their names, their faces, the details of what he had done to them, the families left broken in his wake. She had never killed anyone before. Never even been close to it. But it was the only way. The gun felt light in her hand. All she had to do was press the trigger, then it would all be over.

He was staring at her, smiling broadly in a lop-sided way, showing his perfect white teeth. 'You haven't got the fucking guts, have you Sam? Stop being a silly tart and put the gun down.'

As he moved towards her, she closed her eyes and squeezed the trigger. Nothing happened, no pop, no recoil. She opened her eyes and saw the surprise in his. She relaxed her forefinger, then squeezed the trigger again. Nothing. The slide was locked, the magazine empty. He rushed at her, hitting her with his head and the full force of his body weight, and together they fell to the floor.

Tartaglia punched the button for a large black coffee and waited while the machine buzzed into action. He was in a corridor, not far from Simpson's room, Steele still on her phone elsewhere, updating her superiors on the current state of play. As he watched the cup slowly fill, he kept thinking about what Simpson had said. *I killed the others, but not Jane.* It was all he had said, closing his eyes firmly afterwards and letting go of Tartaglia's arm. But it was enough. The way Tartaglia saw things, it hadn't made sense for Simpson to have murdered Jane Waterman and he was pleased with the confirmation. Revenge had been Simpson's main motivation, followed by self-protection, and her death didn't fit in with either. He was just wondering how he was going to explain to Steele that he'd extracted an unofficial and unrecorded confession out of Simpson with no witnesses present, let alone Simpson's solicitor, when he saw her practically running along the corridor towards him. She wasn't a woman ever to hurry and he wondered what was wrong.

'Mark, there you are,' she called out. 'I've just had a call from the lab. They've processed the tapes from Claire Donovan's face and they found DNA. You're not going to believe this. It's Adam Zaleski's.'

He stared at her for a moment as he took in the information, reached automatically for the cup, which was now full. Adam Zaleski, the serial killer known as The Bridegroom, the man who had tried and failed to kill Sam Donovan a year ago, who had disappeared afterwards without trace. He remembered her pinched, tired face the other night, the strange look in her eyes as she tried to talk to him and her tears of anger and frustration as he failed to understand. Her words rattled through his head in a discontinuous fashion, something along the lines of *he's done this before, Mark . . . you're just not looking at things straight . . .* She had said that the food on the room service trolley was some sort of message – a message not meant for him, but presumably for her. Of course, she was talking about Zaleski. He'd been incredibly stupid not to understand. Then there was all that stuff she'd said about justice and it all being crystal clear from where she was standing. She had tried to tell him that night. She had wanted him to know, maybe wanted his help. He had just been too wrapped up in his own thoughts to listen and he had dismissed it all as a flight of fancy resulting from her mental state. He felt sick, his heart heavy. He had failed her so badly.

'She knew all along,' he said.

'Who knew? What are you talking about?'

'Sam knew it was Zaleski all along,' he mumbled, staring at the coffee cup that was burning his fingers as he tried to block out Steele. He replayed again in his head what Donovan had said about justice, or the lack of it: *Do you believe in justice, Mark? . . . What do you think should happen to a man like this?*

When he had asked her to explain her theory of what had

happened to Claire, she had dismissed him. 'There's no point. You won't do what's needed.' Jesus!

He looked up at Steele. 'She's going to do something stupid.'

Donovan pushed Zaleski off her and sat up. He lay on his back, staring unfocussed at the ceiling, lips moving as he mumbled something unintelligible, blood and saliva bubbling from his mouth. The black, knurled grip of the knife stuck out of his chest at right angles, blood still flowing freely from under the hilt. It was a Fairbairn-Sykes combat knife, the stiletto blade seven inches long, designed for slipping easily between the ribs and penetrating deep into the flesh of a human being. A former boyfriend who had been into martial arts had given it to her. Up until tonight she had always kept it in the desk drawer in her bedroom, using it for mundane tasks such as opening letters or packages. Tonight, as a precaution, she had strapped it – in its sheath – to her calf. The knife had certainly done its job well and, with his hands tied behind him, even if Zaleski had had the energy to try, there was no danger of his pulling it out. She could smell his vomit and his blood; her hands were slippery with it. Blood had also soaked her T-shirt, which felt cold and wet against her skin. It wouldn't be long, she thought. Then it would all be over.

She heard a footstep behind her and looked around. A very tall man stood in the doorway. He was dressed head to toe in a black tracksuit, the hood pulled down low over his face so she couldn't see his eyes.

'Who the hell are you?' she asked faintly, too tired to move, let alone try and make a run for it.

He pulled back the hood, revealing very short fair hair and a deeply tanned face. 'Sorry. I didn't mean to give you a fright. My name's Peter. Peter Ward. Are you OK?' The tone of his voice was reassuring. As he spoke, his eyes turned to Zaleski on the floor.

She nodded. She felt suddenly sick, brought her knees up to her chest and rested her head on them. She started to shake.

Peter crouched down beside her and put a muscular arm around her. 'Don't worry. Take a deep breath. You're safe now.'

She breathed in and out, at first in shallow gasps, then slower and deeper. After a minute or so, she started to feel calmer and leaned back against the wall.

'You're not hurt?' he asked.

She shook her head. 'It's his blood, not mine.'

'Did you stab him with the knife?'

She nodded.

'Bloody hell. You've done my job for me.'

He knelt down over Zaleski, felt his pulse, then peered at his face, pushing up each eyelid in turn with his thumb. 'There's no way he'll be coming back to trouble us again.' He picked up the Glock from the floor and tucked it into his belt.

'It's his gun,' she said, finding it difficult to speak.

'I know. It was me who emptied the magazine.'

She looked up at the gaunt face and met a pair of strange, ice-blue eyes. They were like the eyes of one of those sleek, grey dogs, she thought, although the expression was kinder. 'You know him?'

'I don't know who he is, but I've been sharing a house with him for a few days and keeping tabs on him in my spare time, with the help of some mates. I followed him here tonight. I think he killed my uncle.' He held out a huge hand and gently lifted her to her feet.

She unstrapped the knife's sheath from her calf and kicked off her trainers. At least there would be no more deaths.

'Did you know he'd be coming?' he asked, looking at the sheath.

'I wasn't sure if it'd be tonight, or tomorrow, or the next day. But I knew it wouldn't be long.'

'You'd better give me that, then. Just say you had the knife lying around in your room. It's self-defence, of course, and you and I know he had it coming in spades, but I wouldn't want the police getting any silly ideas about premeditation, if you get my drift. The law's a funny thing sometimes. Next thing you know, instead of you being the victim, they'll be banging *you* to rights for his murder and his bloody family will be suing for damages.'

She nodded and handed him the sheath, which he tucked away in his pocket. Although grateful for his words of support, she was too exhausted to explain that she probably knew the law better than he did. She had set a trap for Zaleski, using herself as bait, leaving the ground floor window unlocked, knowing that he would find it. She had armed herself with the knife and secreted other weapons about the house in case she needed them and had waited for him to come. She could hardly argue spur of the moment self-defence. She hadn't really thought about the consequences before, let alone cared what happened to her. All that had mattered was to avenge Claire's murder in whatever way she could and to make sure that Zaleski wouldn't escape to kill again. She had also somehow wanted to make him feel fear and suffer for all the evil he had done, but there had been no specific plan. In the end, it hadn't happened the way she had imagined it. It was all over so quickly. The only consolation was the look of surprise, followed by horror, in his eyes as she shoved the knife deep into his flesh. It would have to do. Now that he was dead, she must pull herself together, think things through carefully and get her story straight. As far as she was concerned, justice had been done. There was no point ending up in jail for his murder.

'Are you going to be OK?' Peter asked.

'Yes, I think so. What happened to your uncle?'

'It's a long story, but he suddenly disappears off the radar out in Thailand, where he's been living on and off. There were some odd emails, which we're sure didn't come from him. Then a few weeks later this random bloke pops up in Uncle Kit's house in London, behaving as if he owns it. As I said, I've been following him, trying to find out who he was and what he was up to. He seemed to be interested in a house in Brook Green . . .'

She frowned, things slowly clicking into place. 'Was this a couple of nights ago?' She gave Tartaglia's address.

'That's right. He'd been watching the house.'

'So it was you. I saw you in the street when I was coming home. You ran off.'

'Yeah. Sorry.'

'We thought you were a journalist.' She felt dizzy and sat down on the edge of the bed for a moment, as things started to slot into place in her mind. So Zaleski had known all along that she was staying with Tartaglia. No doubt he had followed her there from her own house the day after Claire's murder. It would have been easy, nobody paying particular attention. Perhaps he didn't want to risk attacking her at Tartaglia's. Or maybe, for reasons she couldn't fathom, he wanted to wait until she was back at home to kill her. He was a sharp judge of character and he knew her well enough. He rightly anticipated that she would eventually return. The anonymous calls to the house had been made by him, as she had suspected, checking to see if she was there.

'Who is he?' Peter said, jerking his head in Zaleski's direction.

'His name's Adam Zaleski and he's killed several people. If you thought he'd killed your uncle, why didn't you go to the police?'

'We didn't have any proof. We couldn't get access to my uncle's bank accounts or anything, which is why I decided I had to find out more on my own. He called himself Tom, but it was pretty clear it wasn't his real name. I kept an eye on him for a few days and I searched his things, but there was nothing I could go to the police with. He was equally suspicious of me and he did a rather amateurish job of following me on a couple of occasions. I wanted to find out who he was, so I got a mate of mine to nick his wallet. There was nothing in it apart from some cash and a couple of my uncle's credit cards. Uncle Kit was pretty tight with his money. He'd never have given his cards to anyone, so I knew then that something definitely must've happened to him, but it was all still pretty circumstantial. Without Uncle Kit's body, or anything else, I didn't think the police would take me seriously. I tried to scare him into doing something to give himself away. I thought maybe if I kept up the pressure he'd crack, but then I realised he had other plans. When he came back to the house earlier this evening, he looked as though he was packing up his things to make a run for it, so I followed him here.'

Too exhausted to reply, barely able to keep track of what he was saying, she stood up. As she did so, she caught sight of herself in the mirror. Zaleski's blood was smeared and spattered over her face like war paint. She had told herself repeatedly that somehow she would get through it and now, seeing her reflection, she realised that finally she had. She was still alive and the nightmare was over.

'Will you call the police?' she asked Ward, with a final glance at Zaleski. 'Before I do anything else, I need to get out of these disgusting clothes and take a shower.'

'Of course. I'll wait for you downstairs.'

As he turned to leave, she heard the screech of tyres outside, followed by car doors slamming and the sound of sirens coming at speed towards them down the street. Peter crossed the room and peered out through the curtains.

'Looks like the cavalry's already here.'

'Can you go and let them in, please? I don't want them breaking down the front door.'

Forty-six

'Drop me here,' Tartaglia said to Minderedes, as they turned
the corner of Shepherd's Bush Road into Brook Green. It was
just past seven in the morning. The sky was dark and heavy
with cloud, a light drizzle falling. He had been cooped up in
overheated, airless rooms all night and he wanted to walk the
last few blocks to his flat in order to clear his head. He was
looking forward to a shower and maybe a quick nap before the
questioning of Simpson resumed later that morning. He hated
all-night sessions but it had been worth it.

He had arrived at Sam Donovan's house to find her alive
and Zaleski dead. Donovan had been taken to Hammersmith
Police station, along with a man called Peter Ward who had
also been at the house, and who claimed that Zaleski had
murdered his uncle out in Thailand. Ward was an officer in
the Parachute Regiment, lately returned from Afghanistan.
He had an unblemished military record, according to his
direct superior, who had been woken up in the middle of the
night to confirm his story. Ward described how his mother,
his uncle's much older half-sister, had become worried when
she had failed to speak to her brother on his birthday, something which she had done every year. When she tried to
contact him via email, the replies had been uncharacteristic
and had set off alarm bells, but the local Thai police had said
there was nothing amiss. They had sent somebody over to
Kit's house and been told that Kit had gone away. They didn't
seem to want to inquire further. Next thing Ward and his

mother heard, the shutters in the house in Bedford Gardens were open and lights were on in the house, as confirmed by one of the next-door neighbours who used to keep an eye on the place when Kit was away. When they had tried ringing the house, a strange man had answered, saying that Kit was still out in Thailand. Ward had then watched the house on and off for a couple of days and had seen a man coming and going, and sleeping in his Uncle Kit's bedroom at the front, but there was no sign of his uncle. Deciding to find out more, he had moved in and shared Kit's house with Zaleski for a few days, while keeping him under surveillance with the help of some friends. He had given the police a log of some of Adam Zaleski's movements over that time, which included a visit to his former home in Ealing. There, just a year before, he had attempted to murder Sam Donovan, before setting fire to the house and disappearing abroad, his last recorded whereabouts being on a plane out of Paris' Charles de Gaulle airport bound for Indonesia. Tartaglia had also nearly died in that fire at Zaleski's house and he wondered what Zaleski had felt as he sat, apparently for nearly three quarters of an hour, in Kit's car outside the burnt and boarded-up shell of the home where he had lived for almost all his life.

The little they had managed to piece together previously of Adam Zaleski's background revealed that he was the child of a young woman of Polish descent who had committed suicide shortly after he had been born. He had been taken in by elderly grandparents and there was anecdotal evidence of Zaleski having suffered physical abuse, both at home and at the Catholic school where he had been sent. By all accounts he had hated his grandparents, and it seemed likely that he had murdered at least one, if not both, of them in that house, as well as others too. Tartaglia couldn't begin to imagine what memories the house must have conjured up for Zaleski, as he sat in the fading light gazing at what was left of it. But he had no interest in whether it was nurture or nature that had shaped Zaleski into a predatory and cold-blooded killer. Endless analysis of a killer's background and childhood often missed the point: some people simply enjoyed killing.

What exactly had happened at the Donovans' house was still unclear, but he had managed to speak briefly to Sam before she was taken away to be interviewed formally by others elsewhere in the building. He was struck by how normal she appeared, all things considered, and he felt deeply relieved. Rather than scar her, the horrifying events leading up to Zaleski's death seemed to have had a cathartic effect. The dark cloud that had hung over her had lifted. Although exhausted, she seemed more positive than he had seen her in a long while, much more like her old self. She had actually smiled at him and allowed him to put his arms around her. Speaking to Steele later, the general view was that in the circumstances, Donovan had used reasonable force to defend herself and was unlikely to be charged.

Rounding the corner into his street, he saw the familiar white TR6 parked half up on the pavement immediately outside his house. His first instinct was to turn away, but it would just be putting off the inevitable. He jogged up to the car and peered in. The windows were misted with condensation but he could just make out the shape of Melinda fully reclined in the driver's seat, apparently asleep. He rapped on the glass and saw her start. Peering dazedly up at him, she cranked down the window.

'What are you doing here?' he asked.

Melinda yawned. 'You woke me.'

'Why are you here?'

'You know why. We need to talk.' She stretched her eyes open wide, blinked a couple of times, then rolled the window up again. Gathering her things together, she climbed stiffly out of the car and he held out his hand to steady her. She wasn't dressed for the cold and she shivered, pulling her short leather jacket tightly around herself as she locked the car.

'I've been here for bloody hours,' she said plaintively, licking her finger and rubbing away smudges of mascara from under her eyes.

'You should get yourself a transit.'

'Ha, ha. Why wouldn't you return my calls?'

'I've been a bit busy.'

'I thought we had a deal. What's been going on?'

How much should he tell her, he wondered, as he turned and walked away towards the front door.

She followed him inside, into his flat.

'Sit there,' he said, pointing to the sofa. 'I'll make us some coffee and then we can talk.'

Melinda sank down in the middle of it, proceeding to unzip her ankle boots and rub her feet. He went over to the player and selected some music, then walked down the corridor to the kitchen. He packed some coffee into a pot, filled it with water, and put it on the stove, replaying in his mind the events of the night as he worked out which parts he should tell her and which to edit out. There would be an official briefing later, but he had no problem giving her a lead. If it hadn't been for her, they might still be scrabbling around in the dark.

The fire at the house in Castelnau had been put out quite quickly. The main structure of the building appeared relatively undamaged by the explosion, which had been set off in a dustbin just outside the back door, more as a diversion than anything else. A thorough search revealed a maze of passages and small, windowless coal cellars leading from the garage to the basement of the house. An old-fashioned wooden workbench was pushed up against a wall in one of the cellars and although it had been scrubbed clean, the surface tested positive for blood, which they assumed was human. Beside it, stowed in a small tool chest, were a series of very sharp knives, an electric saw, a hacksaw with a serrated blade, and a couple of pairs of meat shears, along with several long upholstery-style needles and butcher's twine. In a small fridge they found an opened bag of Transglutaminase – known as TG, or meat glue, in the catering trade – used to bond flesh together. There were more bags in the two freezer chests alongside, which also contained a selection of human body parts, all neatly dated, vacuum packed and labelled: Jane. Jake. John. Marek. The body parts would be subject to a series of post-mortems which, in the absence of a full and detailed confession from Simpson, might at least offer some idea of how they had died. DNA testing was also expected to confirm that they matched the body parts found in the Sainsbury's and Aldford fires. They would try to trace Nowak's family in Poland for DNA confirmation. According to Chantal, she had only started coming to the house a few months before and claimed not to know anything about what Simpson had kept locked up in the garage. She looked so genuinely horrified when Minderedes told her, that Tartaglia decided to believe her.

He generally avoided speculating about why a killer behaved in a particular way. Sometimes their actions were designed to play games with the police and media and also to shock. It was often just a smokescreen. But he didn't feel this was true of Simpson. His behaviour shed some genuine light on his personality. In the absence of any insight yet from Simpson himself, it was all they had. If he had been asked to characterise Simpson, he would have described him as angry, vengeful and damaged, yet his actions spoke of an orderly, practical mind. In spite of everything that had happened to him, Simpson had sobered up and reinvented himself after coming out of jail. Maybe the regeneration wouldn't have been complete without getting even with English. One thing then led to another. Perhaps killing English had failed to satisfy him. Or maybe the opposite was true: perhaps it had given him a taste for revenge, a desire to put his chaotic world back into some sort of order. However much emotion had played a part in the murder of Richard English, the planning and execution of Jake Finnigan's murder showed all the cold, calculating traits of a psychopath.

Why Simpson had dismembered Jane Waterman's body when she had been so kind to him, Tartaglia couldn't fathom. But maybe as far as Simpson was concerned, the answer was purely practical. She was dead, and there was nothing he could do about it. He was used to butchering the carcases of dead animals during his daily working routine and it was just a way of dealing with the awkward question of what to do with her body so that he could remain undisturbed in the security of the house. That had been his overwhelming priority. It then made sense to do the same with the bodies of John Smart, Marek Nowak and Jake Finnigan. Why Simpson had chosen to sew the body parts together and set fire to them in a public way could only be guessed at. Was he seeking some sort of recognition for what he had done? Why else leave Richard English's wallet at the scene of the Sainsbury's fire? English's murder would never have been discovered without it. Perhaps Simpson was just thumbing his nose at the authorities. Or, in mixing the parts up together, he was trying to depersonalise the victims and render them anonymous. In any event, it was about power and taking control, something that had been badly lacking in Simpson's own life. He thought of what Melinda had said. Like Frankenstein, the composite bodies that Simpson set on fire had become his creations. God-like, he could give and he could take away. Remembering the way the boy had described him at the Aldford fire, he had probably taken pleasure watching them go up so publically in smoke.

They would be running a full background check on him in the morning, but Tartaglia was sure that Simpson must have been in care at some point in the Aldford area and had attended the annual Guy Fawkes Night celebrations. Only somebody with local knowledge could have done what he did. However, the choice of the Sainsbury's car park location had probably been one of practicality rather than anything else. The size of the car park was the important factor, as well as the relative lack of security. It was a good twenty minutes from Choumert Road, as well as from the flat that Simpson had shared with his family when he first came out of prison. The Internet would have given him more than enough information to make his choice, followed by a quick recce in person. He wondered, as Melinda had suggested, whether Simpson had planned another two fires, which would have used up the remaining body parts in the freezers. Would he have stopped at that point? Would it have been enough? Somehow, he doubted it.

Tartaglia smelt coffee burning and saw that it had boiled over. He grabbed a cloth, took the pot off the stove and poured out two small espresso cups. There was no milk in the fridge, so Melinda would have to have it black. Back in the sitting room, the Bob Dylan/Johnny Cash version of 'Girl from the North Country' was playing. Melinda had taken off her jacket and was sitting cross-legged in the middle of the sofa in a half-lotus position. 'I love this song,' she said, looking a little more alert than before.

'Me too.' He handed her a cup and sat down opposite with his.

'If you had to think of one song that sums you up, what would it be?'

'I don't know.' He was not in the mood to play games.

'I'd say it's 'Free Bird'. You know, Lynard Skynyrd.'

He said nothing, letting the music wash over him. 'Free Bird'. One of the great lead guitar solos. He didn't remember all of the lyrics but he got the gist. A man who wanted to be free, who wouldn't change. What was wrong with that? And as for her, she was hardly one to talk about a failure to commit, if that's what she was getting at. She was like a butterfly. But she didn't seem to be complaining.

She smiled contentedly. 'Nice place you've got here.'

'Thanks.'

After a moment she said, 'You know, I've decided to call you the Jigsaw Man.'

'What?'

'Think about it. It's what you do for a living, piecing together stuff. Don't you like it? I was thinking of doing a nice little profile on you.'

He sipped his coffee, too tired to respond. In her world everything, however complex or subtle or extraordinary, had to be reduced to a song or a tag. Like 'The Jigsaw Killer'. It sensationalised Dave Simpson but it didn't do him justice, let alone capture the abuse and harm that had driven him to cold-blooded murder. He drained his cup. Maybe a detective was nothing better than a robotic Jigsaw Man, a puzzle solver, but he begged to differ. When he was feeling more awake, he might take it up with her.

'We make a good team, you and I,' she said, raising her cup.

He shook his head. 'We are not a team. Don't go getting any ideas.'

'Why not? I like to aim high. It always gets me places. Now give me the damn scoop.'

Tartaglia couldn't help laughing. 'Of course, that's all you're really interested in.'

She raised an eyebrow. 'What else is there?'

He was just wondering if he should take her at her word when the doorbell rang.

'I hope that's not another journalist,' she said sharply.

'Unlikely.'

'Well, tell them to go away. You're busy with me.'

Having no idea who it could be at that hour, but half grateful for the interruption, he got up and went outside to the front door. He opened it to find Sam Donovan looking up at him from the path.

'Sam . . .' He fought back a yawn, generated as much by confusion as tiredness. She hadn't been far from his thoughts all night and delighted though he was to see her again so soon, words failed him. His first instinct was to go to her, put his arms around her and hold her close, as he had done a few hours earlier in the small, dingy interview room in Hammersmith Police station. Not caring who might see them, he had hugged her tight to his chest and closed his eyes, feeling the warmth of her, thinking how much she meant to him and how much he had missed her. He had so nearly lost her. The awkwardness between them had melted away momentarily and he had thought back again to the time, not so long ago, when Zaleski had tried, and nearly succeeded, to kill them both. Their relationship had been simpler and easier then. If only . . . But there was no point dwelling on the past, the missed opportunities, the mistakes, or longing for that land of lost content. Aware again of the gulf that separated them, he stayed where he was.

'I know it's early,' she said. 'But I hoped you might be awake.'
'I've just got in.' He scanned her pale face with concern. 'Are you OK?'
'I'm fine. Better than I've been for a long while, in fact.

She was still dressed in the same clothes she had been wearing several hours before in the police station and it dawned on him that she, too, hadn't been to bed yet.

'Come in. You must be shattered. I'll make you some coffee, although I'm afraid there's no milk.' What she would think of Melinda being in the flat was neither here nor there, he decided. He was past feeling embarrassed about such things and he had never held himself out to be a saint. As for Melinda, things with her would just have to wait until later.

'That would be nice, but there's something I need to say first.' Leaning against the porch, she looked up at him intently. 'I owe you an apology, Mark.'

'An apology? What for?'

'Before Claire died, when we last saw each other back in the summer . . . I said some things. I just wanted to tell you I didn't really mean them.'

He remembered their conversation in the bar that night and the bitterness of her words. They had hurt him more than he cared to admit, but with the benefit of hindsight he knew they had also been fair. 'Well, thank you, but it's OK. Really. I deserved it all.'

She shook her head. 'No. I was just angry and I was being stupid. There was a lot going on and I wasn't myself. I've had time to think and I just wanted to say I'm sorry. That's all.'

He shrugged. 'You don't need to, but thanks.'

'And thank you also for putting up with me, having me to stay . . .'

'It's what friends are for,' he interrupted, feeling awkward. He wished he could articulate it better. If only he didn't feel so tired. There was a lot he, too, wanted to say, but where to start? He hadn't been a particularly good friend. There was so much more he could have done. She had trusted him, she had tried to tell him what she knew about Zaleski. If only he had listened to her and taken her seriously, things might have been different . . . At least she was safe.

'Are you coming in?' he asked, sensing there was more she wanted to say and wondering what other of his inadequacies would be touched on.

'Yes. I'd like to. The thing is, I've got a favour to ask. And please feel free to say no, if it's not convenient. As you know, my house is a crime scene now and I've been kicked out again. I could go to a hotel, but . . .'

Relief flooded him and he smiled. 'Of course you can stay. As long as you like. But let's go inside, it's freezing out here.' He put his arm around her.

'Mark, are you coming?' Melinda called out in the background. 'What's going on out there?'

Donovan hesitated. 'Sorry. Didn't know you had company. I'll come back later.'

He shook his head. 'It's fine. Melinda's an old friend. I only got home ten minutes ago and I'm happy to welcome all sorts of waifs and strays at this hour. It's great to have you back and I really mean that. Although this time, you can take the sofa.'

She laughed as he ushered her inside and the sound warmed his heart. 'No problem,' she said. 'That's the least I can do.'

Acknowledgements

A number of people have helped me in the writing of this book. Particular thanks are due to my editor, Jane Wood, and to Katie Gordon at Quercus; to my agent, Sarah Lutyens, and the team at Lutyens and Rubinstein; to Dave Niccol and Tracy Alexander, both so generous with their time and tireless in answering my many questions; to Ollie Moore of the Black Rat in Winchester, for giving me an insight into the world of a successful chef; to Henry Worsley once again, this time for his input on the firing of semi-automatic pistols; and to Lisanne Radice – as always, the voice of reason. Lastly, I couldn't have written this book without the support of my friends and family, in particular my husband George and children Clio and Louis.

ELENA FORBES is the author of the Mark Tartaglia mystery series. The first novel in the series, *Die with Me*, was a finalist for the Crime Writers' Association John Creasey New Blood Dagger; and the second novel, *Our Lady of Pain*, was a *Globe and Mail* Top 10 Crime Book and a *National Post* pick for Best Crime Fiction. She lives in London, England, with her husband and children.

ALSO AVAILABLE
IN THE MARK TARTAGLIA SERIES

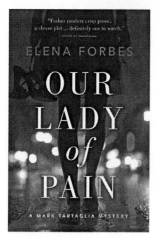

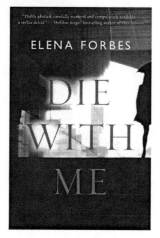

CPSIA information can be obtained at www.ICGtesting.com
Printed in the USA
LVOW06s2126281115

464373LV00005B/17/P